CHEERLEADER HOTTIE FIRED!

I0684283

CALLIE LAMBERT AND EVAN MARQUARDT

Hollywood's HOTTEST NEW COUPLE?

UPERMODEL LUCIANA:
Au revoir aris, hello ollywood!

MANX MURDER MADNESS:

Stunning **NEW** details on Gabby's last night!

Beyond Hollywood Strip

SHAMRON MOORE

This is a work of fiction. All of the characters, organizations, and events portrayed in this novel are either products of the author's imagination or are used fictitiously.

BEYOND HOLLYWOOD STRIP

Copyright © 2014 by Shamron Moore
Cover Design by Anthony Foley
Tabloid Design by Marija **Vilotijevic**

Published by Vigliano Books
1020 Park Ave
New York, NY 10022

All rights reserved. No part of this publication may be reproduced, stored in or introduced into a retrieval system, or transmitted, in any form, or by any means (electronic, mechanical, photocopying, recording or otherwise) without the prior written permission of the copyright owners. Any person who does any unauthorized act in relation to this publication may be liable to criminal prosecution and civil claims for damages.

For my Munchkin

Beyond Hollywood Strip

1

"Mademoiselle, may I offer you something to read?"

Callie woke to a big-boned woman standing in front of her, holding a basket of periodicals. What the...? Who was this creature? And why were her bedroom windows round like those on an airplane? It dawned on her. Air France. Paris-bound and L.A.-free for the next three weeks. She smiled at the flight attendant and reached for a copy of the New York Post. She scanned the headlines: *Man Bludgeoned to Death by Hairbrush. Americans and the Fat Epidemic. Raccoon Saves Woman From Burning Home.* Blah, blah. She flipped to Page Six and did a double-take: *Cheerleader Star Axed.* Feverish, she read the article.

Callie Lambert, lead actress of The Cheerleader Chronicles, will not be returning next season to the hit TV show. An insider reports the beauty's contract was not renewed, in large part, because of her chronic tardiness. "Everyone was fed up with Callie's unprofessional attitude," says the unnamed source. "She often showed up late and the producers decided to cut their losses. Stephanie is

*the new star of the show and everyone is thrilled at how
down-to-earth she is."*

Stephanie must have planted that; the wording was typical
of someone shady like her. The nerve! The lies! Well, the
half-lie. Sure, Callie realized she often lacked a sense of
time, but certainly that wasn't the reason she was let go.
Money. It all boiled down to money, and the simple fact
was Stephanie was cheaper. *Down-to-earth my foot*, Callie
thought. What a crock! A publicity still of *The Cheerleader
Chronicles* glared fro m the page; Callie and Stephanie
posed side-by-side, both wide-eyed and pouty, with wind-
blown hair and legs for miles. No one could guess from the
photo just how annoying Stephanie was. And tacky. And
desperate. Humph! She wondered how long it would take
the Wilders to realize they made a massive mistake in hiring the blonde.

"It is what it is," Callie said out loud, and tossed the paper
on her tray.

"Did you say something?" said the male passenger next
to her.

"I was just talking to myself," she said. "Nothing important."

Crrr, crrrr. The man stirred the ice in his Remy Martin.
"Don't I know you from somewhere?" he said.

"I don't think so."

He examined her face and squinted behind jumbo spec-
tacles. The lenses were so thick his eyeballs jumped out in
3-D. "You sure about that? I could swear we've met."

Callie gave him the once-over. He was seventy, easily, with a full head of snow white hair. His red cashmere sweater stretched tightly over his beach ball stomach and matched the frames of his glasses to a T. There was no way she'd forget such a character.

"Nope. Wrong girl."

"Hmmmm..." Crrrr, crrrr, crrrr. An ice cube flew out of the glass from the force of his stirring. "I'm going with my gut on this one. I say we've met. But allow me to introduce myself just the same." He extended his right hand and extracted a business card from his shirt pocket with his left. "Earl Barletta. And you are...?"

"Callie. Nice to meet you."

"Cal-lie," he said thoughtfully, pondering each syllable. "You got a last name or are you a one-name only kind of gal?"

"Lambert. Callie Lambert."

"Cal-lie Lam-bert." He twisted his face. "Doesn't ring a bell. But with a face like yours, a name doesn't much matter." Earl sipped his cocktail. "What's your line of work, Callie?"

"Acting," she said. "And yours?"

"Law. I'm semi-retired, but I still practice. I'm off to my daughter's wedding. She can't get hitched close to home, like a normal person. She and her husband-to-be have to travel all the way to another country, for complication's sake." Earl whisked the Remy with his swizzle stick.

Callie wondered when he'd give his wrist a break. And her ears, too.

"My nephew's an actor," continued Earl. "Does fairly well. Not that he's a Connery or a Cruise or anything, but he makes decent dough. Personally, I don't see how you can stand it. Doesn't seem to be a very stable profession."

She shrugged. "It's not bad. It's not all it's cracked up to be, but I've done alright."

"Do you see yourself doing this in five years? Ten years? The lifespan of an actor can't be that long. What else have you got on your plate?"

"I don't know. I just need to clear my head for a bit and get out of town."

"Good for you," said Earl. "Ever been to beret country?"

"Never."

"Well, one of two things will happen: either A, you'll love it, or B, you'll high tail it back to Los Angeles quicker than you can say oui. No in between. Me, I don't mind the French, as long as it's only for a short period of time. They're kind of like tequila. A couple shots are fine but any more than that and you'll have a headache. It's terrific you're getting out there and seeing the world. Adventure is healthy and highly underrated. You're how old—twenty-five, twenty-six? When I was that age I was always on the loose, jumping on a plane here, a train there. I couldn't keep still. I wanted to eat life in one big bite, the whole damned world, all at once."

Maybe Earl had a point about acting and its shelf life; did she really want to stay in a business with zero stability? Branching out in another field wasn't a bad idea. But in what? More than that, though, she wondered how many more hours lay ahead of her in the sky. Tyler and his boyfriend, Timothy, had arrived a week prior and would be waiting for her at de Gaulle. She was anxious to catch up with her friend and explore the city.

"By the time I reached thirty, I had more stamps on my passport than you could shake a stick at..." Earl droned on and Callie's lids became heavy. Crrrr, crrrr, crrrr, crrrr. She nodded off to the tinkling of his ice.

2

Tyler dropped ten Euros in the street vendor's palm and handed Callie a baguette. "Merci, beaucoup. Here, skank. I'm warning you, though, these hot dogs—or whatever they're called over here—are contagious."

"I'll take my chances." She bit into her sandwich. "Mmmm. How is it possible that everything tastes better in France? The cheese, the butter, you name it."

"I'm fully convinced their dairy is rigged. Those cows are hooked on something illegal. How else can you explain me gaining ten pounds in less than two weeks? The spare tire that trainer helped me lose is back."

"No way. That's practically a pound a day."

"Believe it. This belly is back in full force. You could roll me down the Champs- Elysees. Thank God Timothy doesn't seem to mind. He says he'll take me any shape or size. My kind of man."

"Look at you," cooed Callie. "All settled down and Mr. Married. You're so cute. And completely in love. I don't re-call witnessing this Tyler before."

Tyler kicked a pebble as they strolled down the street. "Maybe the Parisian air is dry humping my brain senseless.

Or maybe it's being away from those cynical Hollywood hos. Whatever it is, it's working for me."

"You two are a great match. Very opposite, but you know what they say."

"I swear, every day I'm morphing more and more into Betty Crocker," Tyler said. "I barely want to go out anymore. When we're not working, we're cooking or watching a movie on the couch or playing with Timothy's dog. He's a big homebody, being a writer, and now he's turned me into one, too. And what's more, I love it. I absolutely love it. I feel so good about my life right now."

Callie sighed to herself. She missed the closeness, the coziness of a boyfriend.

People work better as a pair, she concluded; she desperately wanted to find her other half. More than ever. "I'm happy for you, Ty."

"Thanks, whore."

Leave it to Tyler to make "whore" sound sugary. Callie asked, "How's the job going?"

"Working me to the bone. This afternoon is the first full day I've had off since I got here. But I can't complain; I do love my work and the cards are all lining up. A group of us—all models and hair and makeup pros—are going out Saturday. You're welcome to come with Timothy and me."

"Gee, I don't know. Little ol' single me going out on a Saturday night in Paris? You'll have to twist my arm," Callie teased.

"Don't I know it. In that case, I may as well tell you about some good news, before the others break it to you..."

"Please, do tell."

Tyler cleared his throat and took a swig of Perrier. "I worked alongside Jean Girard the other day. You can't get much bigger than Jean in the cosmetics industry."

"I've heard of him," Callie said. "He makes this concealer that's to die for."

"That concealer really put him on the makeup map. I slap it on Old Bag Barbara before an event and poof! It wipes the hag right off her face. The man is a genius. Anyways, he was impressed with my technique and we got to talking and really hit it off."

"That's an amazing contact to have," said Callie.

"That's the understatement of the year. He was a lot more down-to-earth than I would have guessed. Very professional and all business. He asked me if I want to come work for his company."

"That's awesome! Did you say 'yes'?"

Tyler gave her the side eye. "Does this bitch look stupid? Of course I did. I'd be a fool not to take a position as head makeup artist for a multi-million dollar company. Tyler Bragg's freelance days are over, ladies and gentlemen, can you believe it?"

"Congratulations!" squealed Callie. "If anyone deserves it, Ty, it's you. You've worked your tail off. Not that it was difficult for Jean Girard to ignore the obvious talent right in front of his nose."

"He's not one for small talk or blowing smoke up anyone's ass, either. His no-bullshit reputation is no joke."

Callie looped her arm through Tyler's. "I didn't even know he had an L.A. office."

"He doesn't," Tyler said. "There's a branch in New York but the company is based solely in Paris."

The glint in Callie's eyes disappeared and she stopped dead in her tracks.

Tyler continued. "This is monumental for my career, Cal. Timothy is all for it, too. We've talked everything over. Says the beauty of being a writer is he can work anywhere in the world. And he loves it here. So do I."

"But, but, Ty..."

"Listen, now, I don't want you to worry your little head over my end of the rent. Our lease isn't up for several months, I know, and I'll honor my end of it. I'll give you the cash up front to cover..."

"Who cares about that?" Callie spat. "I just can't believe you're moving to Europe! When are you going?"

"As soon as I finish up an editorial assignment and the fashion shows I'm booked for. I'll be done by next week. Jean wants me here permanently as soon as possible. Timothy and I are going back to L.A. next week to pack and we'll be back in Paris by the end of the month."

"But where are you going to live?"

"Jean isn't exactly short on cash or connections, Cal. He's putting us up in an apartment over by The Ritz until we find a place of our own."

"Tyler, this is, this is so, so..."

"So what, skank?"

"So crazy!" She plopped on a bench overlooking La Seine. This couldn't be! Her best friend moving an ocean away? And all so suddenly, too! Judging by the tone of Tyler, you'd think he was musing over what silly suit he should don for an evening out on the town. What about his car and furniture back home? How nonsensical. Most perturbing, thought Callie, was how she was supposed to function without him.Her escort to parties, red carpet events, her makeup artist and stylist, her confidante, her shrink. Her main man. This was so unfair!

Tyler threw the remainder of his sandwich in the trash and crossed his tatted arms. "Well, well. Isn't this a complete one-eighty? A minute ago you were congratulating me and now you're acting like someone forgot to feed you your bottle. What gives? What's gotten into you? Aren't you proud of me? If the roles were reversed, I'd be thrilled for you."

Callie bit her lower lip. "I don't want you to move an ocean away. I don't want you to leave me," she said softly.

"But, Callie, this is an incredible career opportunity. Don't you get that?"

"I get it. Trust me, I get it, and I am proud of you. But you're my best friend. What am I going to do without you? I have no one in L.A."

Tyler sat next to her. "Sometimes, I swear, you're such a child. You're acting like I have leukemia or that I'm transferring to Antarctica. Heavens to Betsy, it's Paris we're talking about! Not exactly a rinky-dink spot. Think how exciting it will be when we catch up with each other. Every visit will be a vacation."

"I don't mean to be a big baby. Of course this is fabulous news. But it's so unexpected." She wiped a tear from her eye.

"Lord, here she goes," Tyler grumbled. "Getting all dramatic on me."

"You've thrown me for a loop. I want you with me in California. Yes, I am selfish. I want you for myself. There, I said it. Sue me."

Tyler squeezed Callie's shoulder. "It goes without saying I'll miss you lots. Not having you or my mom or any others around the corner makes me a little sad. I just don't wear my feelings on my sleeve, I guess. You know I love you. Like a cold sore, I love you."

Callie grinned; she couldn't help it. Tyler had that effect on her. She stood up and pulled Tyler to his feet. "Come on. Enough of my sulking. I'm taking my BFF out to celebrate."

Tyler's entire carriage perked up. "Now that sounds more like it," he chirped.

"I'm ordering the best champagne in the house, in the most beautiful city in the world, and this skank won't take no for an answer."

3

Timothy whistled while making his way down the suite's hallway. He often whistled whenever deep in thought, and lately, he was deep in thought most of the time. It pertained to his debut novel, a-year-in-the-writing; it remained largely unfinished. He was used to writing short pieces for magazines—not megalong books with tens of thousands of words. He smoothed the light brown hair on the top of his head before rapping on the door. "Callie, are you decent?"

Callie grinned from behind her computer. Timothy was so modest, so serious in comparison to Tyler's flamboyant personality, the contrast humored her. She tightened the knot of the bath towel on her body and sat up straight behind the desk. "Yes, Tim, come on in."

Timothy poked his head around the corner before walking in the room. "I'm off. Mac and I are going to a bistro for the day. Hopefully I'll be able to figure out the ending to my novel." He tucked his laptop under his arm and spun a Pashmina scarf around his neck.

"Have fun. Do you and Ty have dinner plans tonight?"

Timothy frowned. "No, I wish we did but he's working late, unfortunately. That boy's clocked in more hours during the past week than all of last month. What are you up to?"

She flicked a comb through her wet hair. "I was thinking of checking out a museum. After I check a pile of e-mails."

"Sounds good. I'll probably catch you back at the hotel later." He swooped out of the room and Callie slurped her coffee. Zing! Bold and black, the java packed a serious caffeine punch. Her body hummed as her fingers clicked away on the keyboard. "Let's see, what have we here," Callie muttered as she checked her inbox. Zappos, Bergdorf, and Sephora desperately missed her. Lots of fan mail, mostly from men. And something from Candice.

Hey, mama, what's shakin' with your bad ass self? I left you a message on your phone but haven't heard from you.

Callie deleted the e-mail and moved on to a note from Paul.

Hope Paris is treating you well. Ron Finkelstein's office called and wants to know if you can come in tomorrow to read for a new Mark Wahlberg thriller. He thinks you'd be perfect as his wife. I'm trying to push the reading back but he usually moves pretty fast with these things. I'll see what I can do.

Damn it! What were the odds? No sooner had she landed overseas than a big-time director wanted to see her ASAP! She cursed and returned to her inbox. Junk, junk, more junk. And something from an Emily G.

13

Beyond Hollywood Strip

Dear Callie,

First off, I hope I'm not bothering you. I'm not one of those people I've seen harassing you on the news, I promise you. I found your e-mail from your website. This is probably going to come as a shock, but you and I are related. I'm your half-sister.

Callie choked on her coffee but kept reading.

I've wanted to write you for a while but I didn't know what to say or how to say it. Well, I'm a big girl now (in my last year of college) and my mother, Annabelle, encouraged me to introduce myself. I know this is a little awkward but I hope we can meet some day in the future—or at least talk. Congratulations on all your success.

With love, Emily

Callie stared at the screen and read the letter again. And again. And then reread it a fourth time. Sister? This couldn't be real. It must be a joke. A sick, pathetic joke from some loser with a lousy sense of humor and no human decency. Callie did the math; if this girl, Emily—supposing she was even real—was in her last year of college, that would make her about twenty-two, assuming she enrolled right out of high school.

It meant she was four years younger than Callie. And just a one-year-old when their dad died...It was possible...

No! Callie gave herself a mental slap. If that was true then that meant her beloved father had cheated on her mother, and that just wasn't possible. The "sister" included her phone number—area code 618. Illinois. Callie considered calling her and giving a piece of her mind. But she wanted to be smart and cool about it, and it wasn't the right thing to do. Not yet, anyway.

The tone of the e-mail was especially grating. It was grating because it seemed genuine. An abnormal subject that was shockingly normal. She'd received dozens of lewd, malicious, and bogus correspondence from fans and haters alike, but this letter didn't fall into any of those categories. Startling, yes, but real.

Annabelle, Annabelle...Callie wracked her brain. She didn't recall her parents ever mentioning a secretary named Annabelle. There was spindly, spinster Colleen and a temp named Annie but...wait. Annie. Was that short for Annabelle? She remembered meeting Annie just once when she was in kindergarten and other than being a tall brunette, the woman was nondescript. Annie and Annabelle. Could they be one and the same?

She grabbed the phone to call her mother but hung up before it even rang. How could she address such an embarrassing subject, especially when her mother had her own issues battling cancer? Ludicrous. She considered dialing her grandmother but nixed the idea; that was the last thing Grandma Esme would want to hear—that her son was a philandering, baby-making fool. She wasn't close enough with Aunt Margaret to feel comfortable. Step-father, Tony—forget it. Tyler was busy working. Candace was a spastic narcissist, incapable of focusing on anyone but herself. That only left Dr. Freisch. She'd make an appointment when she returned home.

She groaned and banged her forehead on the desk. The Parisian getaway was off to one catastrophic start.

4

allie traced the inner rim of her eye with black kohl and took a step back from the bathroom mirror to admire the cat-like sootiness. "Perfect," she deemed her handiwork. What time was it? She glanced at her Cartier tank—9:55. She needed to hurry; Tyler and Timothy would be ready any minute.

"Skank!" Tyler called from the living room. "I realize Europeans eat late but I'd like to make it there before breakfast. How long till your pussy's ready?" Timothy admonished him for his choice language.

Callie chuckled to herself; they were fast becoming a modern day gay version of *The Odd Couple*. "Hold on to your panties, Ty. I'll be ready in one sec." She adjusted the belt on her crepe jumpsuit and took one last look at herself. Ready, Freddie. Paris, lock up your sons.

The three hopped a cab to Cabaret, where they were whisked to a large table. Tyler introduced his guests to the half-dozen people already assembled.

"Have a seat, folks," Poppy, a preppy makeup artist informed everyone. She adjusted the hipster glasses on her nose. "Marco and Luci are running late. You know how Luci is—she gets here when she gets here."

17

"As long as the wine and food are on time, no complaints here," Tyler said.

Callie took a seat next to a muscular model with a chiseled, scruffy face. He leaned towards her. "I am Eduardo," he said with a husky accent. His eyes burned with the intensity of a blowtorch.

"Nice to meet you. I'm Callie." She waited for Eduardo to shake her hand or nod or do something to acknowledge her introduction. But he only continued to stare. She folded her napkin and smiled. "You're a model, I presume?" She counted the length of time it took for his response. One second, two seconds, three—

Eduardo finally blinked. "Yes, you could say that. Just don't tell anyone."

Was he trying to be mysterious or was he just plain stupid? Being a male model, Callie guessed the latter. What a waste of good looks, she thought, and swigged her vino. The sea bass that was soon before her was much more interesting; it was just as flaky as Eduardo, only rich and buttery. Her surroundings—the patrons as well as the décor—were finely upholstered. The music was soft and slinky. Altogether, the vibe was pleasant and she enjoyed that no one seemed to recognize her. But, still, she was distracted. The small talk at the table bored her. Her mind kept jumping to the e-mail from the "sister," Emily...What did she look like? Did they have similar features? Was she kind and gentle? Was she a funny, loud person? Or stoic and sincere? Was she impatient, as Callie was? Was she creative, or did she use more of the left side of her brain? Was she bitter that she grew up without her father?...Wait, Callie told herself; stop jumping to conclusions. This girl probably did not even exist—a figment of an overly imaginative loser who had nothing better to do than to prey on innocent people's emotions. Gulp, gulp, gulp...Callie downed her Rose and the waiter refilled her glass. Only one kind of person would pull such a prank—an asshole. "Sister," please. Ha!

Tyler poked her in the rib. "How's your food?"

"Great," Callie said absently.

"You're awfully quiet. I figured you'd be chatting Eduardo up a storm. He's totally your type," Tyler whispered.

Callie speared a broccolini. "Except for one small problem—the poor thing rode the short bus."

Tyler giggled. "He's a bit dense but he sure is easy on the eyes."

"Who cares? I could find that in L.A. any day of the week."

"There are only two types of models—" he held his hand up and counted off on his fingers, "—the dumb ones and the bitchy ones. The women are bitchy and the men are bitchier. Trust me on that one. Take Luciana, for example. She'll be here soon."

"Who's Luciana?"

"Another model. We've worked together twice since I've been in Paris and she's a bit much. She's used to having all the attention in the room. Her dad is some Fortune 500 CEO. Luci didn't wear diapers as a baby, she wore hundred dollar bills. Her dad's so rich, he bought her way to the top."

"Really?"

"Yep, everybody knows it. Her dad paid people to put her on magazine covers, billboards, you name it. Miss Hoity-toity's had the world handed to her on a platinum platter. Bitch doesn't bother with silver. I doubt you'll get along with her."

Callie shrugged; she had better things to worry about than how beautiful or spoiled a complete stranger was, or whether she was likable. What she really wanted was to spill her guts to Tyler. But the chance hadn't presented itself. A piece of fabric grazed her forearm; she turned to her left and was confronted with a taut pair of thighs. Her eyes went further north; a Pucci-wrapped glamazon towered over her. Chocolate, waist-length hair, straight as a sheet cake, covered her clothes hanger shoulders.

Callie guessed this to be the woman in question.

Luciana Dickerson had always been a privileged young woman. Without so much as lifting a manicured finger, she had sailed through life with flying colors. The Canadian-born stunner spoke five languages and boasted a wall full of trophies from her childhood equestrian competitions. At sixteen, she catapulted to fashion stardom after being discovered vacationing in Turin, her mother's homeland. With a flawless complexion and a size zero body, her life looked preposterously perfect.

"Luci! Come sit by Leland and me," Poppy said. She scooted over in the booth to allow Luciana room. "Where's Marco?"

Luciana sat down and threw her clutch on the table. "Marco isn't joining us. I just broke up with him."

"Oh, no!" Leland, a Louis Vuitton-bedecked waif with immaculately coiffed eyebrows, clutched his hand over his mouth. "What happened? You two were sheer spectacularity together. The supermodel and the photographer—the ultimate fashion fantasy!"

Luciana rolled her eyes. "He was cramping my independence. I hate that."

"But, like, he's a premier talent," Leland persisted. "You can't find a catch like that every day, honey."

"You mean he can't find a catch like me every day," Luciana winked. "I deserve better. I'd rather date a garbage man than a controlling schizoid. He went mad when I brought up moving to Los Angeles again. You should have seen him! Flipped. He's known this for a while, I don't know why he decided to go berserk now of all times."

"Callie, here, lives in Los Angeles," Tyler said between mouthfuls of beef bourguignon. "She's an actress."

Luciana perked up. "What kind of work have you done, Callie?"

"I'm on a TV show," Callie said. "Series regular. Let me clarify that—I was a series regular. *The Cheerleader Chronicles*. We parted ways a few weeks ago."

"Holy smokes. I've caught that show a few times in the States. You're very good." Luciana's toffee brown eyes sparkled with approval.

"Thank you."

"A big network show...you're living my dream. That's exactly what I want to be doing. Why on earth did you quit?" Luciana had already wolfed down a slice of bread and was working on her second.

"Umm. Creative differences," Callie said. No point divulging the ins and outs of her dirty laundry.

Luciana smiled knowingly. "I understand. I'm almost ready to kick the fashion biz to the curb. How many times can I play mannequin and pretend to be brain dead?"

"As long as they're signing the checks, babe, just go with it," Leland quipped. "You're making a ton of money being young and hot."

"Leland, honey, I'm twenty-six, an octogenarian in model years. I would have quit years ago but my parents think I should stick to what I do well. What they don't understand is I'd rather be doing something I love and earning nothing than something I hate and earning bazillions."

Callie admired Luciana's spunk. "My mother wasn't supportive of me, either. But I didn't care. I stuck with it."

Luciana gasped. "Really? You didn't have the approval of your parents?"

"Nope. If you want something badly enough, ignore all the people who bring you down and concentrate on what's ahead. That's what I've always done, anyway."

"Wow. I wish I had your determination." Luciana grew quiet, lost in thought, when a distinguished-looking man approached her. She jumped up and kissed him on both cheeks. "Dominic! What are you doing here?" The man

22

whispered in her ear and she giggled. "I can always count on you for a laugh, Dom. Take me for a spin, won't you? I need to blow off some steam. Excuse me, folks." Luciana grabbed his arm and shimmied to the dance floor.

5

Callie tapped her foot, impatient for the fax to spit out the copies. For such a modern hotel, the technology was surprisingly ancient. Paul had faxed a portion of a script over a half hour ago and it was just now finishing up. Only eight pages, too. She snatched the papers. The more she read, the deeper her brow furrowed. She dialed Paul's office.

"Tell me," Paul said, "what do you think? A pretty radical departure from the usual roles you're offered, wouldn't you say?"

"It's, uh, different," Callie said evenly.

"Did the synopsis come through okay?"

"Yeah, I've read everything. I don't know, Paul..."

"If you want to go in a different direction, I can't think of anything to shake things up more," he said. "So you're in?"

"Hold on, Paul, hold on." Callie searched the page for a specific paragraph. "Let me read you something. 'Greta's face has seen better days. For being just thirty-three, her skin is remarkably wrinkled. Her chin is broken out in red blemishes and a cold sore hangs off the side of her mouth.' This is the least glamorous role I've ever read."

"You said you didn't want to play the bimbo anymore," Paul said.

"But that doesn't mean I want to play a haggard trash heap, either, Paul. Gritty, yes. Plain, yes. But a herpes-crusted gutter whore?"

"It definitely goes against type," Paul said with cheer.

"Isn't there anything in between a hag and a slut I can play?"

"There isn't. Not right now, anyway. The role Ron had in mind for you was Wahlberg's wife. He thought you would have been perfect, but you left town."

"Well, pardon me for having a life."

"Sometimes you have to strike when the iron's hot, Cal."

"What was I supposed to do, turn right back around to L.A. after landing Paris?"

"Yes. In this industry, there's no room for dilly-dallying. It's a first come, first served kind of thing. You have to be ready to move at a moment's notice. It's just the way it goes, unless you're A-list and can call the shots. And how many A-listers are there in a town with a million actors?"

Callie's cheeks burned. "When they say, 'Jump,' I say, 'How high?' Is that it? I don't do that. I'm over that bullshit. I'm no one's bitch."

"Is everything okay, Cal?" he said. "You seem a little tense."

"Just dandy," she muttered. She dropped the papers on the floor. "Actually, I got, a, uh, an e-mail from this girl. I don't—I'm not sure if she's my sister or..." She let all of the familial drama fly and wondered why she hadn't thought of confiding in Paul sooner.

"And you found all of this out when?" Paul said when she finished.

"Three days ago. I haven't done myself any favors by keeping it all bottled up."

"Sheesh. That's heavy. This must have knocked the wind out of you."

"Bowled me over," she muttered. "Do you think it's a hoax? Does she want money from me or something? I just want to know what gives."

"There's an easy way of finding out," said Paul. "I have a friend who's a PI—his daughter used to be one of my clients. Jerry is his name. He's been at it for thirty years. I don't know how he works his magic, but he always comes through. Why don't you have him do a little sniffing around for you?"

Callie yanked the hair elastic from her ponytail. "That might not be a bad idea."

"I'll give him a call. It will put all doubt to rest. Who even knows, maybe this will be a blessing in disguise. Think positive."

"Maybe. But right now, it just feels like a horrible pain in my ass."

"Listen," Paul said, "I want you to enjoy yourself. You've been under a lot of stress lately. Go have fun. As for that film—"

"I'm going to pass."

"No problem. I've said it before: don't take a role that doesn't speak to you. Hold your ground. There will be many more opportunities out there."

"It's just frustrating. I feel like I've come so far—"

"You have," Paul interjected.

"—and accomplished more than I ever thought possible but then reality smacks me in the face. At what point can I have the pick of the litter?"

"It's tough. I understand your frustration but try not to focus on what you can't change and focus on what you can change. The second you stop believing in yourself, you've lost all control. And that's when all hell breaks loose."

Callie rubbed her temples. Her head felt ready to combust. "Thank you for everything, Paul. I'm going to take a nap and see if I can kick this headache."

"Any time, young lady. Take one for me, while you're at it. The last time I found time to take a nap, Reagan was in office. Go take a load off. And do yourself a favor and don't give any more thought about that e-mail until Jerry looks into it. He'll get everything sorted straight, believe you me. One way or another."

6

The crowd buzzed and crackled. Callie peered at the hundreds of people sitting behind her, gabbing away on their phones and with their neighbors. The anticipation for Dominic Augustine's fashion show had reached a fever pitch and it was standing room only as fashionistas anxiously awaited the unveiling of his latest collection. She had never seen so many eccentric, well-dressed individuals in one room before; enviable fur coats, oversized sunglasses, and off-kilter hats filled the ballroom at the Hotel Noir. Next to her, in the front row, sat a gnarled, flame-haired woman with a fascinator so large it blocked Callie's peripheral vision. The spinster fluttered her embroidered hand fan with such vigor, Callie's hair billowed.

"Ack," Callie hacked. She plucked her brunette strands out of her sticky, lipglossed mouth and turned to Timothy. "Have you ever been to one of these before?"

"Are you kidding?" Timothy said. "I barely wear socks that match. Since meeting Tyler, I've learned more about fashion than I ever thought possible."

"I hope we get to go backstage when the show is over. Tyler said he could probably arrange it. He gave our names to security so we can—"

Prince blared through the sound system, cutting Callie off. The lights dimmed and the show opened with a spotlight on a willowy brunette. The girl's hair was pulled in a messy bun and layer upon layer of smoky shadow framed her eyes. She sashayed down the runway in a killer tuxedo jacket, all pout and attitude, a rock n' roll Power Bitch. Callie made a mental note to snag the jacket on her next shopping excursion.

Ten minutes later, the show was over and Dominic emerged to take a bow. The lights flipped on full blast and Callie rose from her front-row seat. "Come on, Tim. Let's check out the backstage madness." They zipped through the crowd and made their way to the runway's side entrance. The burly security guards checked their IDs before waving them through.

Backstage bustled with models, media, and an army of stylists. Journalists interviewed Dominic and cameramen snapped pictures of the models sheathed in his designs. In a sea of boisterous faces, it was difficult spotting Tyler. "Wherever the most photographers are, that's where we'll find him," Timothy said. Sure enough, they spotted Tyler posing with a group of models, all of whom held flutes of bubbly.

"Hey, kids!" Tyler shouted. He bounced over to hug them. "Glad to see the goons didn't give you any problems coming back here."

"It was a breeze," said Timothy. He slipped his arm around Tyler's waist. "The girls look fab, babe. Beautiful job."

"Top notch, Ty," Callie said. "The problem is, now I need a complete wardrobe overhaul."

"Thanks, guys. Though I have to admit I had a lot of help; the insane bone structure of these girls makes my job easy."

A tall African model grabbed his arm and exclaimed in a heavy accent, "So, I understand we are stealing Tyler from you Americans!"

"My boyfriend is coming with me, Arjana. There's just one person you'll have to do battle with and that's Skank, here." Tyler pointed at Callie. "She's the only one in California opposed to my French takeover."

Damn this Arjana. Why did she have to bring up that sore subject? Callie was thrilled for Tyler's career opportunity, naturally, but that didn't make her pity herself any less. What was so thrilling about losing her best friend to another country on a completely opposite time zone?

"I can't believe it," Arjana said. Her ebony arms glistened from many coats of lotions and highlighters. She snaked them around Tyler and Timothy's necks. "How could you keep him from us? California has enough makeup artists without holding on to one more. Besides, you Americans are hopeless. With all the fashion and beauty pros out there, one would imagine you people would be more put together, no? Most of you look as though you don't even run a comb through your hair." Arjana tipped her head back and howled.

Is this bitch high? Callie flashed a saccharin smile. "Yes, I suppose you do need Tyler more than we do. The French need all the help they can get to pry that stick out of their snooty asses." She excused herself and meandered down a dark corridor in search of a bathroom. A dingy, partially askew door was marked *toilette*. She guessed she was in the staff's quarters but didn't care; all the cafe au laits she had consumed were about to pose a problem. Callie wiggled the handle but it was jammed. With a little elbow grease, the door flung open and she tumbled into a cramped, musty cave. A tiny lightbulb hanging from the ceiling provided the only light. So much for glamour. A girl dressed in a black suit was parked on the toilet seat, weeping into a wad of tissue.

Callie recognized her tailored, familiar jacket from the catwalk. "I'm sorry. It wasn't locked."

"I know," the girl sniffled. "It's broke. I was just leaving." She stood up and, in her stilettos, was a full foot taller than Callie. "Wait. Callie, right? We met the other night. It's Luci."

With radical makeup and hair, Luciana was unidentifiable. What a change from the girly girl at Cabaret, Callie thought. "Nice to see you again, Luci. You were fierce out there. Amazing."

"Yeah? Tell that to my parents. They don't think I'm too amazing right now. I just called them to break the news that I just walked my last show. I've decided this is it, I'm over this business. Done. And, you know, it's exciting but kind of bittersweet, too. I wanted to share some of my feelings and they read me the Riot Act. Every kid wants to be reassured they're doing the right thing, right?"

"Yeah, of course."

"I mean, they're my parents. Couldn't they have something encouraging to say? You'd think I told them I'm becoming a nuclear terrorist. Not that they think modeling is the noblest profession—they don't. They're not the doting kind to begin with, but as long as I earn a pretty penny, they keep quiet. Everything is a dollar sign to them."

"I'm sorry to hear that."

"It's the first time my father has ever called me outright stupid and so I'm thinking, gee, maybe I really am making a mistake. Maybe I should just stick to what I do best. Maybe it's not worth going out on a limb and trying something different."

Callie shook her head. "It's always worth trying something different. If I never moved to California, I'd still be filling cavities in a sleepy Michigan town, probably married to an uptight workaholic by now and bored to death. If you play it safe, Luci, life passes you by."

Luciana smiled through her tears. "Risks are important, you're right. There's a rumor—an urban myth by now, it's been floating around so long—that my father paid companies to hire me for their campaigns."

"I've heard that, too," Callie said.

"What a crock! I don't even know how that got started. Probably by a bunch of jealous assholes. Everything I've accomplished, I've earned. Everything. And I'm proud of that." Luci peered at her reflection in the cracked mirror. "The good news is, my eye makeup hasn't budged one bit. Thanks to Tyler's work, I could go through a hurricane and come out looking perfect. But these red eyes of mine...oh boy, that's what's hard to cover up. Tell me, is there much press out there, Callie?"

"There's a bit, yes."

"How much? A dozen?"

"Two dozen, tops."

"Lucky me," grumbled Luciana. "Such wonderful timing. I wish I could bail but I have to go make nice and congratulate Dominic for the cameras and act like his collection is the greatest thing since a rock hard penis. I don't usually talk so crass, but I'm a tad bitter today."

"I know the feeling." Callie unzipped her Balenciaga. "I should have some Visine in here somewhere..."

"That would be a godsend."

"I tote my entire house with me when I travel. Here you go."

"You're an angel." Luci threw a few drops in each eye. "Anyway I could get a dab of gloss, too?"

"Of course. Sheer, creme, or shimmer?"

Luci flashed a thankful grin. "A girl after my own heart. Sheer, please. Something pink, if you have it."

"Are you kidding? I come prepared." Callie handed her a tube.

"Perfect, thank you." Luci swabbed the lacquer on her pillowy pout. "Much better. I'm a new woman. So, being an actress, you must be used to temperamental drama queens like me."

Callie swirled a powder puff across her forehead. "Are you kidding? A little crying is nothing. With the egos I deal with on a daily basis, you're nothing short of normal. And, trust me, in Hollywood, normal is a compliment." She was happy to make Luci smile again.

"You're probably right. I'm sure you've seen it all. Alright, enough of this nonsense. I have to go give some face." She grasped the door handle before spinning back to face Callie. "I'm sure you have plans, but I was thinking we should grab coffee sometime. Say, tomorrow. Any interest?"

"I'd like that. I can always use some coffee. Where are you thinking?"

"Where are your digs?"

"InterContinental Marceau."

"Hmmm." Luciana tapped her fingernails on the molding. "Are you in the mood for the Left Bank, or is that too far?"

"I've never been to the Left Bank."

"One of my favorite haunts is Cafe de la Rotonde. I'll pick you up. Let's say two o'clock."

"Two it is."

"Au revoir, Callie. Don't forget, this thing doesn't lock, so watch yourself. And thank you for everything. I really mean that." Luciana flung the door open and soldiered off.

7

uciana's skinny bangles, stacked high up one arm, clinked and clanked as she tipped her coffee mug. Judging from the way light bounced off the bracelet's pavé-set stones, Callie could tell she wasn't messing with cubic zirconia.

On anyone else, the bling would be tacky but Luci was so effortless, so refined in her ivory turtleneck and stretch wool trousers, the effect was elegant. She plucked a newspaper from her purse and dropped it next to Callie's cup. "Check out page three," she instructed.

Callie leafed through the paper and found a black-and-white photo of a beaming Luciana hugging Dominic. The size of her smile rivaled that of her teased hair. "If I didn't know any better, I'd guess it was your wedding day," said Callie. "Unfortunately, I can't read French. Can you translate it?"

She cleared her throat. "Luciana Dickerson has strutted hundreds of catwalks during her impressive ten-year career as a high fashion model. But it's Dominic Augustine that holds a special space in her heart. 'Dominic was the first designer I worked with at the very beginning of my career,' the

Paris-based Dickerson says. 'It only seems fitting that I end my career with him, too.' Miss Dickerson opened Dominic Augustine's fall collection last night to thunderous reviews. 'Noir chic,' 'impossibly tailored,' and 'sex on stilettos' are a few of the phrases critics used to describe Mr. Augustine's newest collection. Blah, blah, blah..." Luciana skipped to another part of the article. "'I hate to see her leave the fashion world, but I understand the need to spread her wings. I'm just trying to figure out who I can bring in as my new It girl. No one cuts a jacket like Luci. She's my good luck charm. She puts the sex in sexy.'"

"Nice write-up," said Callie. "You see? There was nothing to worry over."

"Thanks to you," Luci said. "If you hadn't given me a hand I would have looked like a bloodshot, miserable mess."

"Trust me, I know how brutal the press can be first hand. No need giving them free ammo," said Callie.

"I know. I Googled you this morning. You have quite the tabloid history. I had no idea."

"Last year was slightly nuts," Callie said.

"I bet. Of course, I've heard of the Manx Murder before—who hasn't, unless you live under a rock—but for some reason I hadn't attached your face to the story. That whole ordeal must have been very difficult for you."

Callie nodded and bit into a pastry.

"I actually met her once. About two, two-and-a-half years ago when I was in New York."

"Gabrielle?" Callie said.

"Yes. She was incredibly beautiful. Her features, that bone structure...Perfect, really. Had it not been for those breasts, she could have done high fashion. My booking agent, Christos, and I went to dinner with Tom Johannesburg and one of his producer friends. Gabrielle came with. Tom had me in mind for one of the leads in his new movie but the part was stupid and completely gratuitous and I wasn't interested."

Callie's ears perked. "Small world. Which film?"

"It was a thriller or horror or one of those things. Something silly."

"Was it Nympho Cheerleaders Attack!?"

Luciana was slow to answer. "Yes. I don't mean any offense—"

Callie waved her hand.

"—it just wasn't the kind of project I had in mind for my cinematic debut."

"I don't blame you, Luci. Trust me, I'm not offended. Which part were you up for? Kiki?"

"No. Kiki had already been assigned to Gabrielle."

Callie blinked and allowed her brain to absorb the info. One of the leads? That left just one other role—Layla. It made sense; both girls were lithe brunettes with small busts. But hadn't Callie been assured she was the first, last, and only choice? How many other girls had been offered the role before Tom and the Wilders settled on her?

Was she their second pick or third pick? Or something worse? She felt as though a baseball bat had whacked her in the stomach. "So you were Layla, almost."

"Almost never cuts it. Even though they told me I was their only choice, I knew they had offered the role to at least one other girl—this Croatian model I can't even pretend to stomach. That sealed the deal for me. No one wants to be leftovers. Besides, they fed me the oldest line in the book, you know?"

Callie's heart plummeted another rung. "Ain't that the truth."

"I hope this doesn't bother you, because we've all been there. Show me a model or actress who denies it and I'll show you a liar." Luciana reached across the table and dusted a crumb off Callie's blouse. "Gabrielle stood out to me because she was so sweet and polite. Tom, not so much."

"Gabby was the nicest girl I've ever met. A really kind, old soul. I sure do miss her. Tom's trial is coming up in a few months and I'm dreading what the press will dig up, rehashing all the awful details. It's a horrible situation any way you slice it. Who cares what happens to that dirt bag? Whether he gets life or fries in a chair, Gabby is gone for good and no verdict is bringing her back."

"It's sickening," agreed Luciana. "How do you plan on avoiding all the inevitable attention?"

"By jetting off to the Bahamas and camping out under a coconut tree."

"You know what I would do? I'd twist it around and turn the negativity into something positive. Start an organization under Gabby's name or write a book and donate the proceeds to a domestic violence group. Something to honor her while maintaining your dignity. You want to be able to look at yourself in the mirror every morning."

"Basically, I need to turn the lemons into lemonade."

Luciana banged her knuckles together and her bangles danced. "That's precisely what I mean. Make it your own. I was really down the day of the fashion show, that's true. That was a rare moment you witnessed. I thought, 'I'm single again and lonely, my parents think I'm nothing but a flighty nincompoop, boo-hoo.' And then I slapped myself. Yes, I did! I literally slapped myself right across the face. What have I got to feel sorry over? Come on, Dickerson, check yourself! I have so many good things going on, why pout over a few measly glitches? The victim card is so overplayed." Luciana squared her shoulders and re-crossed her legs.

Time ticked away and the minutes spun into hours. By five o'clock and several lattes later, the girls had covered everything from Sarkozy's shoe size ("They look so big in comparison with the rest of him that he looks like Ronald McDonald," Luci proclaimed) to the similarities in their mothers (both overbearing women with big hair). For having such dissimilar upbringings, they discovered they had more in common than either would have guessed.

Luci checked her cell. "Shoot. I have to run. Six o'clock meeting with Christos."

The girls dashed out the door and made their way to Luci's car.

"Did Tyler mention he's moving out of the L.A. home we both rent?" Callie buckled up in the passenger seat.

"Only about ten times, and to anyone within the vicinity of fifty kilometers."

Callie giggled. "That sounds like Ty. Listen, if you come to L.A., Luci, I want you to know you have a place to stay, if you need one. My house is pretty big—4,000 square feet—and very private. I know you're used to lavish mansions and a probably a full staff of—"

"What makes you say that?" snipped Luciana.

"Tyler inferred it."

Luciana sighed. "I'm always surprised at people's misconceptions of me. Just because I was raised with money doesn't mean I live in a castle and have a chauffeured Rolls Royce. The truth is, my Paris apartment is one-eighth the size of your house, if that, and my Fiat is seven years old. I travel so much, I guess I just don't see the point in splurging for all the bells and whistles."

Luci made a sharp turn and Callie grabbed the dashboard to steady herself. "When you're in L.A., you're welcome to stay with me," Callie said. "Come next month. It will be just me, myself, and a pool."

"You have great taste so your place must be lovely. I love a girl with panache; it's a dying art, and there isn't enough of it around anymore. Thank you, Callie, I just may have to take you up on that."

The car wove through traffic down Avenue Marceau. Dusk had fallen and the Eiffel Tower twinkled in the distance, beckoning like a lonely mistress.

8

"You had coffee with *who*?" Tyler speared his egg yolks with a crust of bread.

"Luciana. What's so awful about that?" Callie said.

"It's not awful, it's just...odd. She doesn't seem like your cup of tea."

Callie rose from her chaise to grab a croissant off the in-room dining cart. "Actually, we get along really well. She's a cool girl and smart, too. I never would have guessed she'd be so down-to-earth. Or that someone half my size and twice my height existed."

"Luci would have made Karen Carpenter look like Dom DeLuise," Tyler said with an arched brow. "I'm not denying she's all shades of fabulous, looks-wise, but I'm not a fan. Too bossy."

"Not really. I think she's just really driven and knows what she wants."

"Yeah, she's a good business bitch. One of the few successful models who doesn't burn the candle at both ends. Not that she's a saint—or so I've been told—but you won't catch Her Royal Highness with a dirty nose."

Beyond Hollywood Strip

A notion struck Callie: Tyler was jealous of her tight—or potentially tight—friendships. Possessive, even. He didn't like Candice nor Luci, and he had never even made an effort to get to know Gabby. He didn't seem to like any of her close friends. Especially the strong, opinionated ones. He disliked the competition, she theorized. What was more, his hair was a bed-head mess and product-free, a first for Tyler. Callie smelled trouble.

"Where's Timothy?" she asked.

"He left in a huff earlier this morning. We had a spat last night. Our first."

"That's too bad. What happened?"

Tyler paused to swallow a bite of egg. "He visited me on location yesterday. Aside from one female model, it was an all-male shoot. These guys are all buff and shirtless, but whatever. I see it all day long, so it's a yawn. So, Timothy arrives on set and cops a 'tude—decides I'm getting too close to one of the guys, that I'm flirting with him. He acted like we were in high school and it pissed me off."

"Were you?"

"Was I what?"

"Were you flirting with the model?"

Tyler's eyes popped out. "I may be a lot of things but a two-timer is not one of them. Contrary to what you see on TV, not all gays are a bunch of nymphomaniacal sluts. Besides, if I want to maul a slab of beef, I sure am not doing it with my boyfriend standing next to me. Please. This bitch is reformed. A saint. Have been since Timothy and I got together. I said

to him, 'God, what's gotten into you?' What was I supposed
to do, tell the guy to fuck off and apply his own bronzer? Not
like I was hired so people could gather round and watch me
wipe my ass. No, I'm here to work. I can't help it if the guy
has a body of death and I'm professionally required to touch
it. He was acting like I randomly crashed a photo shoot just
to molest Mr. Muscles—who, by the way, was barely out of
high school. I must have been quite a site standing next to
him, looking like a flabby old woman."

Callie chuckled. "We all have our moments. Timothy's
generally not a jealous person, is he?"

"I didn't think he was, but I was obviously wrong. And I'm
not amused."

"What you two need is some quality time together. You've
been working almost nonstop, Ty. You could use a break
before you're here full time."

"I know, skank, but I can't exactly starve to death. Heavens
to Betsey, it costs a week's salary just to buy a bread crumb.
I'll rest when I'm dead. I'm making dough, way more than
Timothy makes writing his column, that's for sure, and if
this move to Paris is going to work, he better get used to
long hours with pretty people." Tyler plowed through his
frites before leaning back in his chair, stuffed. "What's new
on the business front? Heard from Paul lately?"

Callie scowled. "Sort of."

"Why the glum face? No work on the horizon?"

"I had an offer to play a diseased old hag. I passed. Paul
also said that a casting director who had me in mind for a

Mark Wahlberg flick gave the part to another girl since I'm not available for a reading until the end of the week. But that's not all; a producer asked him if I was, quote, 'against increasing my bust size.'"

"Oh, snap!" shouted Tyler. "I thought Paul always stood up for you regarding your tiny titty situation?"

"He always has. He was uncomfortable bringing it up, I could tell. And he won't name names, but he told me several industry people have suggested I get some surgical help in that department. Nothing outrageous, no Ds or anything crazy, but a little oomph could help me grab leading lady roles."

Tyler wrinkled his nose. "Tell me you're not paying Dr. Coop another visit any time soon. You've always been against flotation devices."

"But I may be reconsidering. Maybe by filling out a little I'll look more grown up and be treated like a serious actress."

"More like by filling out you'll be treated like a bigger piece of ass. You're just feeding into the stereotype, Cal."

"I don't know," Callie muttered. "Like I said, I don't want a chest like—God bless her—Gabby's, but if people are commenting on my lack of boobage, it's a problem."

"It's only a problem if you allow their stupidity to get to you. Besides, big boobs are so out of vogue. These girls who get their tits blown, they think, 'Gee, I'm so hot because I have big, fake boobs.' No, princess, sorry, that doesn't mean you're hot; that only means you have big, fake boobs. And there's nothing more desperate than a bitch with mega water balloons sewn on her chest."

"Give me a break, I hardly want to be one of those girls, Ty."

"I know, but once you get an idea in your head, all bets are off. Just remember, more Charlize, less Charo. Yes, I heard you say you don't want them big big, but you're not a complete pancake, so why bother? Plastic surgery is like crack—once you start, you can't stop. Every day I meet a girl who's one surgery away from cat woman territory. Not cute."

Callie picked at her pastry. "Ty, I've been meaning to tell you something that happened the other day. It's the strangest thing..." Callie forged ahead and recounted the e-mail she received from Emily. Tyler listened with bated breath.

"I feel like I just watched the latest *All My Children*," he said when she had finished. "I'm speechless, and Lord knows that's something that doesn't happen too often. When are you going to call her?"

"I'm not," said Callie. "Not yet. Paul has a PI who's doing a little sniffing around to see if she's legit. It smells fishy to me."

"What, like she's trying to squeeze money from you? Why would she make up an elaborate lie like that?"

"I don't know why. It's a ballsy thing, if it is a lie, but you never know. You've never heard any rumors about my family, have you?"

"No, I haven't."

"People talk and gossip so much. Especially in small towns. You've never heard any juicy little tidbits? Come on, cough it up."

"You're being weird. You're paranoid."

"'Just because you're paranoid doesn't mean they're not out to get you,'" Callie quoted. "Tyler, I swear, ever since I landed in Paris, it's like I stepped into a bad episode of the Twilight Zone. I just want everything to make sense. I want things normal again."

Tyler smacked his hands several times, a human gong. "Earth to Skank! You live in Hollyweird, the nation's capital of crazy. Besides, you can't cherry pick the good from the bad; it's all a big ol' wad of crazy that makes up the game called Life. So strap on your seatbelt, girl. You'll get through this. You always land on your feet."

"You're right," she sighed. "It's not the end of the world."

"Hell-to-the-no, of course it's not. My dad left my mom, after he tired of beating her, when I was seven. Took up with some Korean who spit out three rug rats and we never heard from him again. Try that on for size. Just think, somewhere on this green earth, little Asian Tylers are running around terrorizing poor souls. You're not the first with a dysfunctional fam and you won't be the last, either. Besides, you don't know the full story. Maybe your mom and dad were swingers and had an open relationship. Or maybe she was skanking around on him and he wanted to get back at her. Who knows, but there's always more than meets the eye."

His subtlety is as mild as ever, Callie mused. "All highly unlikely scenarios, Ty, but I get your point. My poor mom. All this time I thought she was the difficult one, that she had all the issues and my dad was the saint. I guess I've never looked at either one of them as fleshed-out human beings, with needs and disappointments and failures. It's weird thinking of your parents as being, you know—flesh and blood people."

Tyler pushed the dining cart away from his long legs and stretched. "To this day, I refuse to acknowledge my mother has ever had sex. It's just a filthy visual. In this contorted head of mine, I was an immaculate conception."

"I wasn't referring to their sexuality, just their issues in general," Callie chuckled.

"I have a hard enough time trying to figure out my own issues, let alone other people's. It's a miracle I have any brain cells left. Anyhow, can we ditch this subject? I'm having a visual of my mother getting plowed and don't want to lose my breakfast."

"Actually, I have to get going," Callie said. "I'm taking a drive to the country to meet a writer-producer friend of Paul's. Could be a really great connection. Nanette Vernadeau. Ever heard of her?"

"Nope."

"Neither have I, but apparently she's a pretty big deal. I may as well squeeze a little networking out of this trip."

"Ohhhh, I see," Tyler said. "So that's why you asked to borrow my rental car. Off to meet a secret friend, hmmm?"

"Hardly. Nanette, in case you couldn't tell from the name, is a woman."

"Well, knowing you, it wouldn't surprise me if you dipped in the lady pond from time to time. You're acting different, all fidgety."

Callie zipped her motto jacket. "Not at all, I'm just anxious to hit the road. Her home is all the way in Amiens, I've got a two hour drive ahead of me."

"Why on earth don't you just take the train? You won't have to worry about getting lost."

"I'm looking forward to clearing my head, alone," Callie said.

Nanette of Amiens. It sounded like a novel in the realm of *Anne of Green Gables*. Callie pictured Nanette with a large bun pinned on top of her head and a frilly apron wrapped around her waist. Years ago, back in Michigan, she never would have dreamt of driving in a foreign country to a stranger's house. Not because she was scared but because it meant stepping out of her comfort zone. Her move to L.A. changed that; many of her inhibitions went out the door. The new and improved Callie drove to towns in Northern France, knowing little about her destination, weathered map in lap.

Tyler shooed her with his hand. "Alright, go, go. Clear your head and network. One thing, though: you'll be back in the pit of smog and silicone soon enough, so for the love of Mary, deal with the sister drama later so it doesn't spoil your trip."

"I know," Callie sighed. "I'm trying."

"Try harder, whore. If Paris can't distract you, nothing can. You only have two days left, so do your gay proud by making them fabulous."

9

here the hell is this place? Maybe I made a wrong turn.

Callie gripped the wheel tighter as she bobbed and bounced over the ill-paved road. She may not have a clue as to the whereabouts of her destination, but the scenery was straight out of a Tolstoy novel. Lush, green as a sprig of mint, and, most importantly, smog-free. Finally, some strictly solo time, a few hours where her thoughts could marinate in peace. And what better terrain for an adventure? She rolled her window further down and inhaled the air until her nostrils compressed. *I could get used to this*, she thought. The mid-morning fog squeezed and cajoled the car before giving way to a glorious patch of sunshine; a rambling brick house loomed several hundred yards in front of her. The smoke curled from the chimney in thick, inky ribbons. A slim woman in her late forties greeted Callie at the front door. Her brown bob framed her peaches-and-cream complexion.

"Hello, hello! Mademoiselle Callie, no? Nanette Vernadeau, pleasure. Please, come inside."

Nanette led the way through a corridor. Her trim hips swayed with each delicate stride and Callie wondered if she always walked with a wiggle. "You made good time. I didn't expect you for another half hour."

"I hope I didn't come at a bad time. I'm usually either super early or very late," Callie said sheepishly.

"My dear, that's the story of my life. Late or early and never anything in between. Mostly, I run late, unfortunately, but at least I make a memorable entrance." Nanette swung her sitting room door open with a hand that looked as though it had never lifted more than a porcelain teacup. Nattier blue curtains and pillows accented the snowy walls and furniture. A massive fireplace covered nearly an entire wall on one end of the room. Callie was certain she could eat lunch off of the blonde oak flooring without worrying about ingesting so much as a molecule of dirt.

"Please, help yourself." Nanette pointed to the spread on the coffee table. She settled in an antique velvet armchair and folded her hands in her lap.

Callie was still full from breakfast but didn't want to seem rude. She picked a cookie to nibble on. "Nanette, your home is absolutely beautiful. I wouldn't ever leave if I lived here."

Nanette's rosy lips parted into a smile. "Thank you, you're very kind. I enjoy Paris but I like to get out of the city as much as possible. I can hear myself think here, I can breathe easier and my creativity flourishes. Tranquillite is what I call this home."

"That's the perfect name for it. Hits the nail on the head."

"Paul visited Amiens a few years ago and he said if more people had a place like Tranquillite to escape to, no one would need Prozac. Of course, he exaggerates, but he does indeed have a point."

"How long have you known Paul?"

Nanette squinted and counted in her head. "Twenty-three—no, no, that's not right— twenty-five years now. He was my very first agent back when I was an actress."

Callie's eyes grew. "I didn't know you were an actress. Paul didn't mention that." Nanette let out a hearty laugh. "My dear, that's because there's not much of an acting career to mention. I was only in the game for five short years, maybe less. Nanette St. Cyr, I was known as back then. Little part here, small part there, usually in a bikini—or a miniskirt, at least. The last film I did was in the '80s with Pacino, but it was a big-time flop. And then I moved back to France, married, raised two children, and wrote a few screenplays. My husband and I dabble in producing when it suits us. But I hardly had the kind of career you have. Paul tells me you've done well for yourself."

"Paul is being kind," Callie smiled.

"I happened to catch the *Nympho Cheerleaders* movie last week. You were the best part. The only part, in my opinion, that was any good. You have that glorious something...a certain quality that's difficult to describe."

"Thank you very much, Nanette. But trust me, it's not much of a career at the moment. It was, but as of last month, I've been officially unemployed. For a while, I was on a roll but I ran out of steam. It's embarrassing to admit it, but it is what it is."

"Blah! Nothing to be embarrassed over. You're too hard on yourself, Callie. I'll tell you, once I was so broke as an actress—I couldn't land a single part to save my life—I dressed up as Cinderella outside of Grauman's Chinese Theatre. I posed for pictures with all the tourists and made sixty-nine dollars in tips. Not bad, eh? Ha. It wasn't a terribly common thing to do twenty years ago, not like it is nowadays. Today you have everyone from Superman to The Three Stooges standing on Hollywood Boulevard. Everything about this industry is cyclical. Everything. Just like the tide. Even when you're down, you're never out."

"Right now I can't catch a break. All the powers-that-be see me as something different than I see myself," Callie griped.

"How do you see yourself?" asked Nanette. Her voice was soothing and while her accent was thick, her English was impeccable.

"Well..." Callie paused and searched for the proper words. "I see myself as...well, as a leading lady. Both drama and comedy."

Nanette scowled. "That tells me nothing. I mean, what do you bring to the table? What do you offer besides a pretty face? Are you witty? Are you particularly adept with monologues? Even if you're a natural comedienne maybe your talents lie more in connecting with the audience through your eyes. You have very soulful eyes, exotic and sorrowful, and that's extremely enticing on a thirty by seventy foot screen. You have to know your strengths as an artist, otherwise, how can you sell someone else on your talents?"

Good point, Callie thought. "I just want a decent role, that's all. I'm not finicky, but I am particular. I don't want to play the hooker, the stripper, or the tramp."

Nanette warbled a throaty laugh. "My dear, you've just named the only top three roles Hollywood offers women! You'll stay unemployed all your life if you hold on to that way of thinking."

Callie smiled. "I guess you're right, but I'm serious. It may sound unrealistic, but if that's all they're offering, I'm not biting."

"It's okay to play the tramp or hooker—just make sure she's a charming tramp or a wise hooker," advised Nanette with a wink.

"That's the thing," Callie bemoaned. "Those roles are usually stupid or vapid or the producers require you to be stark naked. As long as there's some integrity behind the role, I'm in like Flynn. But if all they're looking for is a trashy piece of eye candy, I can think of a thousand Hollywood floozies who can fill that order."

"Callie, you remind me of someone I know. Your—what's the word...chutzpah, I think it's called—is appealing."

"My mother has always said chutzpah is a fancy word for being arrogant and stubborn. My problem is that I'm stubborn. I'm a bull, a Taurus."

Nanette showed off a dazzling Rembrandt smile. "My husband is a Taurus. They're the best. And with all due respect to your mother, chutzpah isn't something negative; it's a positive attribute, a compliment, and you have it in spades."

She stroked her chin and her aqua eyes became steely. "I just recently finished my latest screenplay, my first in five years and my directorial debut. I think it's something you should read."

"I'd love to," Callie said. "What's it about?"

"It's about a young woman who moves to a foreign land and meets the love of her life—with a twist. It's romantic, but not sappy. Dramatic and dangerous. There's no perfect little bow on it, it does not have a typical Hollywood ending. It's about love and loss. You'd be quite perfect as the lead. I first thought so when I watched *Nympho* but I didn't want to say anything when Paul called me—in case I didn't like you or you didn't have the right energy. Now that I've met you, I know positively that you are the right girl. You are Jeanette, no doubt about it. Would you like to read it?"

Callie's face lit up. "I—I'd, yes, of course. I'd love to."

"I'll fetch it." Nanette returned with script in hand. "I've been working on this little gem for twelve years. Yes, you heard that right—twelve. On and off. More off than on. I know I'm partial, but the female lead, Jeanette, is such a plum part. I've auditioned a list of actresses this long—" she displayed a three foot gap with her hands, "—but none of them suit me. Their look is right but their attitude is all wrong. And, trust me, the wrong attitude will kill the whole thing."

"Have any of the parts been cast?"

"Most, yes. Casting began last year and production begins in June. Isn't it preposterous out of all the roles, the part that remains unassigned is that of the lead actress? It's the most important part! This business really is absurd. But, somehow, it comes together at the last possible moment. I've trimmed it from 140 pages down to 115, but, of course, you won't have time to read it all here. Go ahead and take it with you."

"I leave for L.A. in two days. I probably won't be able to get it back to you by then—"

"I'm not concerned about that. Take it with you. I don't usually give out my work in its entirety to someone I barely know, but I trust you. More than that, I trust my instincts. And then there's Paul; Paul has spoken very highly of you and I trust him, too. You know, years ago, we had a little thing going on, Paul and me. It only lasted six months or so, but I've always had a soft spot for him, as a friend. He's a good man, kind and honorable. He won't steer you wrong."

Callie was so overcome with the joy of a new project she did not hear the latter part of Nanette's sentence. "I cannot wait to read your work, Nanette. I'm so grateful, I can't even tell you."

"My pleasure, my dear, my pleasure. If, after you're done with it, you can't see yourself in it, just say so. I won't be offended. Maybe disappointed, but not offended."

"I'm sure I'll adore it." Callie gripped the tightly bound pages and read the cover page—*The Foreign Affair*. She couldn't wait to devour it back at the hotel.

"I'm having another cup of tea. Would you care for any?"

"I'd love some, thank you." Callie would have, at that moment, drunk Nanette's urine, if it so pleased the Frenchwoman.

"I'll boil some more water." Nanette floated out of the room.

Callie flipped past the cover to read the first scene.

INT. ROLAND MUSSO'S BEDROOM - NIGHT

We're looking DOWN on ROLAND and JEANETTE MACVEY. They're lying on their sides, facing one another. Both are in their late twenties and dressed in 1940s street clothes. CLOSE on their faces.

ROLAND

I'll never leave you. You know that, don't you?

JEANETTE remains silent.

ROLAND

It's only going to be us, you and me. You believe me, don't you? Just the two of us.

JEANETTE nods but still says nothing.

O.C., we hear people speak in hushed tones, dream-like. Each voice overlaps the next.

WOMAN #1 (V.O.)
Didn't I tell you not to trust anyone?

WOMAN #2 (V.O.)
You'll pay for this with your life.

MAN (V.O.)
I'm your end and your beginning. Never forget that.

WOMAN #3 (V.O.)
It wasn't supposed to end like this...not like this,
not this way...

FADE TO BLACK.

The hair on Callie's arms stood up straight; she rubbed the goose bumps. Never could she have guessed the best part of her Paris excursion wouldn't be found anywhere in Paris but in a little town outside of the city. Thanks to Paul. Holy moly, she thought, Paul reached in his magician's hat and pulled Nanette out like a rabbit. All hail the mighty Angers! Come rain or shine, he always came through. Somehow, some way, when she least expected it. Always had. Paul, God love him.

10

Boom, boom. Boom, boom.

Her heart raced like a stock car. This wasn't supposed to happen. She wasn't supposed to be nervous. Callie Lambert doesn't allow any man to make her nervous.

Boom-boom-boom!

Damn it; now her heart was beating faster than ever. "Just call him back," she said to herself. But she couldn't. Her hands were as stiff as a corpse. "Okay, on the count of three, you dial the damned number. One, two..." She dialed Mitch Gracie's number but it went straight to voicemail. She abhorred leaving voicemails. But what the hell?

"Hi, Mitch, it's Callie. I just got your message after being abroad for a few weeks—" That sounds so pompous. "—I mean, I was overseas in Europe, and I just got back. Well, I didn't just get back, I actually got back a week ago—" Wait, that came out wrong..."—or close to a week. It feels like a week, I've been so jet lagged. Anyway, I'm calling you back—" Duh, idiot, of course you are. "—and I'm looking forward to catching up. I hope Buffalo treated you well and I'll talk to you later."

She dropped her phone on the nightstand like a hot potato. This was ridiculous. Even Bedroom Eyes didn't make her this nervous. What was it about Mitch Gracie that caused her to be so anxious? Not anxious, like panic attack anxious, but... unnerved, that was the word. He made her feel unnerved. She itched the back of her neck. Maybe he wouldn't call back and she wouldn't have to deal with him. That would be the easy, wussy solution. But a large part of her wanted him to call her back. Mitch was sharp, sexy, and, most importantly, different than the usual Hollywood schmucks. The no-bullshit persona she had originally found so annoying was the trait that set him apart from the pack. He was the polar opposite of any guy she had ever been attracted to before, let alone dated. A true rough-around-the-edges cowboy. A Southern simpleton. Maybe the two of them weren't such a great mix...

She grabbed her flat screen's remote and searched the channels for something brainless. The house was silent— too silent—and felt completely empty without Tyler. He had officially moved out two days ago; he had taken all of his clothes and small personal possessions but left his furniture. "I'll leave it with you for the time being, skank, if you don't mind," Tyler had said. "No use carting it all over the globe if I don't need it yet. I should probably dump some of the stuff, like that beat-up chest of drawers, but I've had it for twenty years and I can't seem to get rid of it. Like a bad case of the herp."

Even though Callie's home was fully furnished, there was an echo without Tyler. It had only been eight months since she last lived alone but she had grown accustomed to him being there and didn't particularly like that he no longer was. It was lonesome and the house felt hollow and bleak, like a deserted hotel. Oh well, she sighed, at least there was an abundance of privacy; one could never have enough.

Rrring!

She checked her caller ID. Mitch. *Here goes nothing*, she thought. "Hello?"

"Well, hello, yourself. Welcome back to the US of A, Miss Lambert," Mitch said. He sounded as mellow as ever but there was cheer in his baritone, a spring in his voice.

"Thanks, Mitch. It's good to be back."

"How was Paris?"

"It was everything I've read about and then some. I wanted to go back as soon as I landed in L.A."

"Ain't that the truth? I lived in Germany and France for a few years while my dad was in the service. Yeah, I was one of those Army brats. I love to travel but there's really no place like home."

"I agree. I'd forgotten just how fantastic my bed is. And how was your trip to Buffalo?"

"Buffalo wasn't bad. Not exactly Paris, but not bad. I pulled sixteen hour days, so when I wasn't on set I was sleepin' in my hotel—or tryin' to sleep, anyway. I don't have a whole lotta luck in the sleep department."

"Really? That's too bad…"

"When am I taking you out?" Clearly, Mitch Gracie was no fan of idle chit chat.

"Oh. Ummm...I don't know, how's your schedule?"

"Jam-packed for the next three months, but what does that matter? You find time for the important stuff. At least I do."

"I do, too." She didn't want Mitch thinking she wasn't interested. Of course, she was very interested but more than a little shy.

"I have front-row tickets to Tony Bennett this Saturday. My manager gave them to me but he can't make it. Why don't we go?"

Mitch Gracie liked Tony Bennett? Callie was thrown off.

"You don't like Tony Bennett, I see," he said when she didn't answer.

"No, no, I do. I love Tony Bennett, I just didn't expect...I didn't know you—"

"Let me guess, you wouldn't expect a country bumpkin like me to like Tony Bennett. I probably come across as more of a Toby Keith kinda guy. It's my accent, I know, I get it all the time." He chuckled and Callie felt silly.

"Being that you're from Alabama, yeah, I would have guessed you'd be into country, I guess," Callie said.

"I hate country," Mitch said. "Can't stand it, never liked it, never will."

"Good, that makes two of us."

"Then I guess it's settled. Concert is at Staples, starts at seven. I can pick you up at six, if that works."

"That sounds terrific, Mitch, I'd like that. I'll text you my address."

"Perfect. The Hick Prick will see you in a few days."

Callie's cheeks burned with embarrassment. He wasn't going to let her live that crass nickname down. "Please, can we forget I ever said that?"

"No way. Not lettin' you off the hook that easily. Besides, I get a kick out of it. One of these days, I'll have to share the moniker I came up with for you."

"Is that so? I have a moniker?"

"You're damned right you do. You think you're the only one who's crafty with words? Think again, missy. I guarantee this Hick Prick coined your name before you coined mine, believe that."

"What is it?"

"Nope, not gonna tell you yet. Make you sweat a little first." Mitch chuckled. "I gotta run, catch you later."

"Catch you later, Mitch." Callie nestled in the covers and turned to her favorite reality show, *Long Island Sugar Babies*. But she couldn't concentrate. Her mind kept jumping back to her conversation with Mitch. Tony Bennett, huh? And he had lived in Europe, too. Hmm...No one could say the Alabaman was predictable, that's for sure. She felt bad that she initially dismissed him as an unfortunate hillbilly. The more details he revealed, the more intrigued she became. The former Hick Prick was turning out to be more multi-faceted than Callie imagined. She looked forward to finding out what other surprises he had hidden up his flannel sleeve.

11

ize twelve. Size eight. Size ten...Callie surfed the racks at Barney's. Good gravy. Since when was it so difficult to find a dress in a small size? And in something other than black? A bright, flirty number was in order for her hot Saturday night concert date, not a funeral frock. She turned to another rack and dug away.

"Callie? Hey, girl! It sure has been awhile."

A punky blonde appeared from out of nowhere. It took a second, but Callie realized it was Nicole, her *NCA!* co-star. The two hadn't exactly been cozy during filming—she remembered Nicole being nothing but jealous and judgmental towards Gabrielle—but Callie gave a warm smile all the same.

"Hi, Nicole. Yeah, it sure has."

"I like your shorter hair. You look great."

"Thanks. You look nice, too."

Nicole raked her fingers through her spiky locks. "Nah, I look the same as ever. Not much has changed in that department. Or in any department, for that matter. I'm working here part time since the acting work has been a little slow. I get a sweet discount and my best friend is the manager so, you know, it's not bad. But what about you? You've been all over the place. Man, I wish I had one-tenth of your luck. What's your latest gig?"

"A period piece set in the forties, a romantic drama. Production starts in June," said Callie.

"Coolness. The lead?"

"Yes. The script is phenomenal. A complete 180 from *NCA!*"

"Wow, that's dope. Big budget?"

"About 15 million." Callie held a magenta blouse up to her torso.

"What are they paying you?"

Callie's head jerked. Nine hundred grand, you tactless twit. "My agent hasn't hammered out all the details of my contract just yet."

"Wow," Nicole repeated. "Must be nice having an agent working so hard for you. Mine doesn't do shit and I had to switch agencies again. Third time in a year, can you believe it? Soooo frustrating. Is your agent looking for any rocker types? I still have all my piercings, by the way, I'm just not allowed to wear them to work." She touched her right ear, which was adorned with ten silver studs. "I take my nose ring and Monroe piercing out. Not my ears, obviously."

"Actually, Nicole, I don't think Paul's taking on any new clients. Especially now that he's a manager." That was a half-truth; even though Paul had switched to the more hands-on title of "manager" months ago (thanks to Callie as his primary bread-winner) and trimmed his client list in half, she knew he was always open to new talent. Given the said talent was, of course, talented. As far as Callie was concerned, Nicole didn't measure up.

"I can really use all the help I can get," said Nicole with a pout. "I'm gonna be late on my rent again this month, thanks to my stupid agent dragging his tail. If you could put a word in for me, that would be awesome. You know, wave your Callie wand and work your magic."

Damn it. Callie hated being the middle man. On one hand, it was annoying when people bugged her to pull strings, but on the other, she felt sorry for Nicole; she knew first hand that being an out-of-work actress was a tough, pride-swallowing ordeal. She could fully relate to the frustration. "I'll see what I can do, Nicole. Paul has a lot of connections, maybe he can recommend someone."

Nicole bounced on her heels. "Sweet! I'll give you my contact info before you go. So, what kind of outfit are you searching for? What's the occasion?"

"I'm going on a date this weekend, to a concert. I want to find something festive but not overtly sexy."

"Gotcha. Maybe a nice punchy orange or turquoise. You checking out Wrist Slashers, by any chance? They're playing Saturday."

"Uh, no. We're seeing Tony Bennett."

Nicole's pale face went blank. "I've never heard of that group, but let's see what we can find. You have such an amazing figure with a tiny waist, you should totally show it off. What are you, a two? Follow me, I'll show you a few things that just came in." Nicole sped to the other side of the room and Callie barely kept up with her long strides. "Who's the lucky guy?"

"His name is Mitch. We met on the set of *Cheerleader Chronicles*."

"No way. Mitch Gracie?" Nicole slung several dresses over an arm.

"Yeah. What a small world. How do you know him?"

"I don't but my roommate does. Charlene. She moved to L.A. a few months ago and used to date him. I'd watch out, Callie, if I were you. Char says he's a real dog and left her at a party. Like, drove off and totally abandoned her at a stranger's house. And she was in town visiting the jackass all the way from Alabama! Can you believe that?"

Callie thought back to the party the night she met Yves Rousseau. "Actually, that's not really how it went down. See, your roommate left out a few key parts—Mitch took her to a party and then she met some Z-list actor and they were all over each other. He couldn't even find her at the end of the night so he left her there. It must have been humiliating for him, don't you think?"

"Umm, Z-list? The Z-lister is none other than Burke Hammond."

Callie arched a brow. "And he should be familiar to me because..."

Nicole's mouth fell open. "Because he's done major stuff on MTV and his parents own a football and baseball team. The Hammonds have more money than God. I can't believe you've never heard of him. Charlene would have been majorly stupid to ignore him."

"But she was there with Mitch. You know, her boyfriend. That was an awful thing to do to him."

"I know, but sometimes you gotta seize the opportunity, right? Mitchie boy should know how the game is played—everyone else sure does. It's who you know and who you blow."

"For the record, I've never had to resort to that," Callie said.

"Well, I would have done the same as Char. Think of all the doors Burke could open for her. I mean, they haven't hooked up since and he hasn't helped her out yet, but you never know, right?" Nicole hung several dresses in the dressing room.

"Right," Callie deadpanned. "You never know." She nixed helping Nicole out then and there. Morally decrepit individuals weren't at the top of her Good Samaritan list.

"I'll let you do your thing while I get back on the floor—I just saw a few customers walk in. I'm so glad I got to see you, Callie! It's so great catching up with old friends, isn't it? Don't try any of those dresses on without showing me. I want to see every last one of them on you." Nicole closed the dressing room door and zoomed off. A waft of patchouli clung in her wake.

Callie smiled at the assortment of designer duds in front of her. She hadn't been on a date in far too long and the closer she got to Saturday, the greater her excitement became.

Butterflies swirled in her stomach and her hands were clammy as she pried a dress off the hanger. She planned to make the Southerner weak in the knees and nothing less than a dazzling visage would do. She slid a jersey sheath over her head and wiggled it down over her hips. Oh, yes, Mr. Gracie, watch out. You're about to get Callie-fied.

One after the other, Callie slipped the other two ensembles on and off in record time, two minutes flat. She couldn't decide which she liked best but figured she'd better make it quick if she hoped to avoid another Nicole encounter. And if she hoped to get a mani-pedi before meeting Paul for dinner, she'd better make it snappy. Decisions, decisions... Screw it, she'd take all three. They fit her like a glove and a girl could never have too many dresses. Off to the cash register. And, thankfully, there was no sign of Nicole.

"Will this be it for you?" asked a young male associate in a shocking pink bow tie and skin-tight cords.

"Yes, thank you." Still no Nicole. Good.

"We have some fabulous gold accessories that just came in, if you'd like to see them." He popped the censors off the garments.

"No, thank you."

"There's a long, drapey chain necklace in that case over there that would look especially great with this orange dress. Halle Berry was just photographed wearing it."

Callie glared at the man. "These three and these three only. Nothing else, thanks, I have to get going."

He fired a look of bitch and bagged her items.

Beyond Hollywood Strip

It was only when Callie neared the exit when she saw a splotch of platinum spikes several yards away. Nicole was knee-deep in conversation with a customer. "This vest would be so totally killer on you. My girl, Char, wore it to a party and every guy there said how utterly major she looked..."

Callie clamped a pair of oversized shades on her face and stepped out without a peep.

12

"Paul, I'm bored." Callie speared a blue cheese crumble with her fork.

Paul Angers looked up from the rack of lamb he was attacking. "What do you mean, you're bored?"

She surveyed the dinner crowd at Ago from their private corner table. "I need another project to occupy myself with."

"Let me get this straight—you just got back from the most glamorous city on the planet; you have a writer who's so taken with you she's throwing you in her movie without so much as a screen test—as the lead, no less—and you just got nominated for a Public Choice Award. And you're still not 'occupied', as you say? You need your head examined, young lady."

"Wait, give me a chance to explain myself. What I mean is, I need a side project. I think it's healthy. Something I'm passionate about. Why put all my eggs in one basket? *The Foreign Affair* doesn't start for months and I'm trying to figure out what to do with myself."

"I wish I suffered your dilemma. Enjoy it, Callie. You're going to be working your little tail off in a few very short months, enjoy this down time. By the way, Nanette wanted me to make sure you don't change anything about yourself. She was adamant about that—no fillers, no Botox, none of that bologna. That goes for tanning and extreme haircuts and color, too." He dabbed his mouth with a cloth napkin.

"I don't do that stuff anyway, Paul. Please."

Paul gave her the side-eye. "This coming from the girl who got her schnoz tweaked just weeks before she shot a movie."

Callie's eyes bulged. "Who—"

"Yes, my dear, I know all about that. And before you ask who told me, no one told me. I'm just attune to details and notice everything. You know darned well you charge ahead full throttle once an idea comes over you. As your friend and manager, I owe it to you to let you know the dos and don'ts. It goes without saying *The Foreign Affair* is a huge deal for you—huge. I don't want anything screwing it up, especially something stupid."

"Let's go back to the part of me being bored," Callie said. "I've been giving a lot of thought about starting a charity in Gabby's name. I could give a positive spin to something awful. Maybe I can help someone out who's in a bad place. You know, lend my name to something I can be proud of. I want to give back and I'm in a position to do just that. What do you think?"

The only noise that broke up the silence was Paul's slow, steady chewing. "I like it," he finally said. "Give a silver lining to that whole debacle, is that it?"

"Exactly. It's the least I can do for her memory. As her friend, I owe her that much."

"I like it, Cal. I like it a lot. You know, I saw on CNN today that Johannesburg got life."

Callie waved her hands to shush him. "I don't want to talk about him. I don't want that asshole to have anything to do with this and I definitely don't want to give him a shred more publicity than he's gotten already. It makes me sick mentioning them both in the same sentence. That's the only stipulation I have—this charity has to be all about Gabby, not her murderer."

"Understood. Knowing you, I'm sure you researched this already, but fill me in—how does one start a charity? You have to apply to the IRS, if I'm not mistaken."

"I wrote a mission statement last night. That's step number one. I need to figure out if I should set it up as a trust or a corporation, that's step number two. It's pretty involved but I've made up my mind to see it through. I have the perfect platform, being in the public eye."

"You certainly do. This is great, Callie, very admirable. Let me know whatever way I can help. I'm on board."

"I appreciate it, Paul, thank you."

A waiter approached their table. "Signorina, are you finished?"

"I am, gracie," Callie said.

He cleared her plate but couldn't stop staring at her low-cut cami, even as he turned to walk away. His foot caught the leg of an adjacent chair where Callie's purse was situated and it tumbled to the floor. "Mi dispiace molto!"

"No harm done, it's only a purse," she assured him.

"I'm so sorry, signorina, so sorry," he repeated. He bent down to pick up her purse and gather the items that escaped.

"Thank you," Callie said as he handed her her things—a pack of gum, car keys, and a random business card:

Earl Barletta Attorney-at-Law
Who the hell is this and how did he get mixed in my stuff? She tapped the card on the table. Earl, Earl...And then it dawned on her.

"Everything good?" said Paul.

"Yeah, I was just trying to figure out how I got this guy's card. It's a lawyer I met on my flight over to Paris. He practices here in L.A."

Paul glanced at the card. "Oh, yes, Earl Barletta. A doctor friend of mine hired him years ago when she was sued for malpractice. Spoke highly of him. You're going to need an attorney to draw up the paperwork for your charity. Why don't I give him a call for you?"

"Please do. I want to get this show on the road."

"Consider it done." He pocketed the card and paid the bill. "Shall we?"

They made their way outside to the valet. An Escalade with bold, blinding rims and fresh dealer plates pulled up. A dozen paparazzi appeared seemingly out of nowhere and their flashes popped as the driver exited the vehicle. Callie strained to see who had caught their attention. Fried, flaxen hair—Callie could spot glued-in hair extensions twenty feet away—was perched high on the girl's head in a ponytail. A stretchy minidress, two sizes too small, barely concealed her painful-looking cleavage. The poster child for vulgarity, the queen of all trailer ladies, Stephanie Schueller, had arrived. Callie's mouth contorted in scorn.

"Schueller must have tipped them off," Paul whispered. "She always does. Has a deal with the paps and gives them a cut of whatever her pictures sell for."

"Figures," Callie muttered. "Mix one part plastic with equal parts Wet n Wild, add a healthy dose of dumb, wrap it in pleather, and you'll get that." She wished Paul's Navigator would arrive ASAP. There was no way she wanted the press to catch her and her former co-star together. Callie's pride still smarted over being fired. Her wounds felt even rawer upon seeing Stephanie's devil-may-care mug.

Stephanie shoved both arms on her hips in mock indignation while the paps snapped away. "How did you guys find me?" she bellowed, all teeth and meticulously applied makeup. "You're getting too good. Oh, my God! Callie! How are you, girl?" She rushed over to Callie, hovering by a plant.

"Hi, Stephanie," Callie said through clenched teeth. Her mouth tasted of vomit.

"This is too funny! Both of us chillin' at Ago. Ha ha." Stephanie wrapped her orangey-bronze arms around Callie. A plethora of flashbulbs exploded.

"Callie Lambert, where you been hiding out, sweetie?" shouted a paparazzo. "You look hot as hell!" Click!

"Is this the first you seen each other since ya got canned, Callie?"

Beyond Hollywood Strip

Click, snap, click!

"Girls, can you squeeze closer together? I wanna get a tight shot!"

Damn you, Trailer Lady! Callie loathed being an accessory to Stephanie's publicity machine. Her body stiffened as Schueller squeezed her tighter. Callie managed a weak smile before Paul yanked her away.

"Excuse me, ladies and gentlemen, we need to get going. Miss Lambert is here for dinner, not a press conference," Paul said. The Navigator pulled up and he guided her to the passenger door with a protective arm.

"Callie, come back, we love you!" the paps shouted.

Callie didn't exhale until the SUV pulled away. "Thanks, Paul. Ugh, that was foul."

"That's what I'm here for," he said.

Callie's chest felt tight and her breathing quickened. She struggled to roll down her window.

"You okay, Cal?"

"I need some air."

Paul pressed a button and her window opened.

Callie gulped the cool spring air. Great. She had only been back in L.A. for ten days and already she was panicky and craving another vacation. It had been weeks since she last popped Xanax but figured now was as good a time as any to break her streak. Pink Floyd streamed over the radio and she cranked it.

I have become comfortably numb...

Callie unscrewed the bottle and dumped several pills in her mouth. Come to me, my sweet.

"There's a case of water in the back seat. Help yourself," said Paul.

"I like to chew it. Works faster." She was annoyed at herself for allowing others to rattle her cage; she swore to get her nerves under control. I'm better than that. It was high time she took command of the reigns and the only place they belonged, she decided, was in her own two hands.

13

Sapphires or diamonds. Or sapphires and diamonds? Which to choose, which to choose...Callie ogled the merchandise piled on the velvet-lined tray. She had narrowed the potential purchases down to three but it was difficult settling on just one.

"Personally, I think this Riviera suits you," George, the salesman at Van Cleef and Arpels, cooed. He took a diamond necklace out of the case and draped it across his hand. "It makes a statement but at the same time, it's timeless. You can't possibly go wrong."

Callie fingered the price tag. $249,999. Ouch. "I don't think so," she said. Leave it to the salesman to push that one. Maybe she should have just hired a stylist for the Public Choice ceremony, that way she wouldn't have to splurge—she could simply borrow some one-of-a-kind jewels. But she wanted to actually own an investment piece. Besides, she booked a big role and deserved a pat on the back. Which to choose....The bangle, with its Mystery Setting sapphires, lured her back. The piece had first caught her eye in the pages of *Vanity Fair*, looped around the Queen of Jordan's wrist. True, $42,500 wasn't pocket change, but for months, it had induced many a wet dream.

"This is the one. She has my name on her."

"Very good," said George. "I'll go polish and box it up for you."

Her jewelry reverie was broken by her iPhone. She didn't recognize the number but answered it anyway.

"Callie? Hi, it's Luci. Luciana Dickerson. Am I catching you at a poor time?"

"Not at all, I'm just indulging in a little retail therapy," Callie chirped. "How are you, Luci? How goes Paris?"

"Everything is wonderful, thanks, but I'm not in Paris at the moment; I'm in L.A. My manager has a number of auditions and meetings set up for me this week."

"Great! Where are you staying?"

"With him in Brentwood. His house is lovely but it's under construction. It's dreadfully noisy and I haven't gotten much sleep the last two nights—"

"What on earth are you doing there? Come over to my place, Luci. I told you, any time you like, you're more than welcome to stay with me."

"I don't want to be a nuisance," Luci said. "That's very generous of you but—"

"Don't be silly, Luci, I insist. It will be fun, like we're back in a college dorm. Except I never went to college and I doubt dorms are 4,000 square feet with a view of the Hollywood sign."

An aging female customer with a caught-in-a-wind-tunnel face shot Callie a sour look. Callie ignored the woman and chatted away. "It's so quiet where I live, Luci, you can hear a pin drop. You'll get plenty of beauty sleep."

"Mmm, that sounds mighty tempting. I swear, these past few days, I haven't had bags under my eyes, I've had a ten-piece luggage set."

"Then it's not even a question, consider it a done deal."

"You're a doll," said Luci.

Fantabulous! She and Luci were bound to have fun together. The truth was, even though Callie liked the Canadian native very much, she was lonely. She hated admitting it—it made her feel needy and weak—but she didn't enjoy living alone as she once had. Maybe she just wasn't used to it anymore or maybe it was because it was a reminder that she didn't have a special someone in her life. Whatever the reason, she did not find solo living all that appealing. Funny, whenever Grandma Esme used to ask if she had managed to snag a man, Callie got frustrated—as if a man could possibly complete her life. Now that Grandma no longer asked, Callie was very much wanting a relationship...ironic. Perhaps a puppy or kitty was in order, a little munchkin she could dote on. A pet had been out of the question when she was growing up because her mother was allergic, but it would be nice to give a furry rug rat a nice home. She'd have to check out the Humane Society.

Luciana arrived at Casa de Callie hours later, along with a fleet of cargo. "I packed everything short of my Fiat," Luci said as she and Callie lugged her bags to one of the spare bedrooms. "Red carpet, boho chic, casual elegance, work-out gear—I've got something for every occasion."

"Better to be prepared," Callie chirped. "There's nothing more embarrassing than being inappropriately dressed."

"That's how I feel, too. I'm going to a premiere tonight—a last minute thing my publicist arranged—and I'm glad I thought ahead to bring a few gowns."

"Which flick?"

"*Village Idiots*. Barry, my publicist, thought it would be good to be seen. Hi, take a picture, good-bye—one of those quick things. Why don't you come? If I could score an invite, I'm sure a last-minute RSVP would be no problem for a real actress like you."

"I have a date tonight, a fellow actor named Mitch. I met him on the set of my show." Callie felt her cheeks burn and wondered if it was an obvious blush. If Luci noticed, she didn't let on. "So, what are you wearing to the premiere?"

"I was hoping you'd help me pick the winner," Luciana said as she sifted through mounds of clothing.

"Let's see the nominees." Impromptu fashion shows had been the best part of living with Candice—the only fun living with Candice—and Callie looked forward to indulging her girlie side again with her new housemate.

Luci stripped to her thong and stepped into a metallic sheath. "I hope nudity doesn't bother you. During my runway days I was in and out of clothes so much, I was naked more often than clothed."

"Um, Luci, have you seen *NCA!* all the way through? It has more skin than a gynecologist's office. And *Coquette*, too, for that matter. Ooh, I like that one."

Luciana pirouetted. "It's from Kaufman Franco's spring collection. One of my all-time favorites."

Callie had never seen anyone with a frame as sinewy as Luciana's; the model's legs alone proclaimed their own zip code. Coupled with her slender arms and mile-long hair, she appeared lengthier than ever. For once, Callie felt big-boned and stumpy, like a slovenly dwarf.

"Luci, are you going with a date tonight? Because if you are, you're going to give him a heart attack."

Luci giggled. "Well...I sort of am...." She switched into a calf-grazing leopard number. "Barry arranged for me to go with a client of his, Chad Blake-Shepard. Have you heard of him?"

"I know Chad," Callie said. "He had a guest star role on my TV show last year. He's doing lots of romantic comedies now, isn't he?"

"Mmm-hmm. We both grew up in Toronto."

"I always thought he was gay."

"He is. That's why Barry set us up. Zip me."

Callie zipped the back of Luci's dress. "I don't understand."

"Barry pairs his gay clients with straight girls all the time. You've never bearded before?"

"Never," said Callie. "It seems so..." She searched for the proper adjectives. "Complicated."

"Actually, it's just the opposite. Chad and I both benefit from the arrangement—it's better for business if he looks straight and I need to make the Hollywood rounds and be seen. A win-win. We have a six month contract that stipulates we can't romantically be seen with anyone else. So if I do find a boyfriend—which I won't because a relationship is the furthest thing from my mind right now—"

"Famous last words," Callie interjected.

"—I have to be extra careful to keep it on the down-low. And I don't mind." Callie gave a knowing look and crossed her arms. "Really, I don't. It's a small price to pay if I want to make this transition. Part of the game. Mutually beneficial. Okay, so what do you think of this one? Callie, your phone is blinking. Looks like you have a message."

"I prefer the first so far. The animal print looks like you're trying too hard." Callie grabbed her iPhone; she did indeed have a message. Must have missed the call when she was outside helping Luci.

"Hey, darlin'," said Mitch Gracie on her voicemail. "Look, I'm really sorry, but the Hick Prick is gonna have to cancel tonight. I know it's short notice and I hope you haven't gone to much trouble, like buyin' a new outfit or a fancy pair of shoes or any of those things girls do, but I just can't swing it. Let's reschedule. Something unexpected came up...I'll have to explain it to you later in person. I do apologize it's such late notice. Hope you have a nice evenin'."

14

That son-of-a-bitch. How rude! What could have happened that was so stinking important Mitch couldn't wait until the morning—and Sunday morning, at that—to straighten it out? Calming all those butterflies, the leg and bikini wax, the Van Cleef & Arpels bangle she planned on pairing with her slinky new outfit...all the effort in vain.

Callie's veins pumped overtime with boiling blood. "Fuck you," she spat.

"Pardon?"

"Sorry, Luci, I didn't mean you."

"You look like you're ready to blow a gasket. What happened?"

"Nothing except an insensitive prick just canceled our date at the eleventh hour."

"Why on earth would anyone cancel on you?"

"I don't know. I just don't know but I feel really stupid right now."

"Don't feel stupid." Luciana circled her arm around Callie. "I'm sure that's happened to everyone at one time or another."

"Has anyone ever cancelled on you, Luci?"

"Well....no, not exactly. But a date did keep me waiting, once, for a whole hour. I had just flown home after Milan Fashion Week. I was exhausted but, still, I managed to be ready on time, and what does the jackass do but show up an hour late. That counts—sort of—doesn't it?"

Callie looked doubtful. "Not really, no."

"Look, why don't I call Barry and let him know you'll be coming to the premiere with Chad and me?"

"No. Thanks, but no. You go have fun. I don't want to be a third wheel."

Luci cocked a hand on her thirty-four inch hip. "The man is gay. You'd hardly be a third wheel. It'll be a girls' night out."

"I don't—"

"Come on, now. How are you going to say no to your pour little houseguest? That would be extremely inhospitable." Luci batted her lashes with the fervor of a silent movie star.

Callie sighed. "How long would I have to get ready?"

"Red carpet starts at seven sharp. Which means we should arrive at 7:15."

Callie checked the time—4:24. Plenty of time to get herself camera ready and grab a bite to eat with room to spare. "Alright, I can handle that."

Luci took charge. "Perfect. Chad and Barry are picking us up. I'll give them directions to your place, and I'll send my hair and makeup team over, too. They'll need to set up in about—oh, half hour. They won't be here long—I don't take much work and I bet you don't, either. I'll tell them to send over an extra makeup artist to get you ready. Hey, now"— she silenced Callie's protests with a pointed finger—"I've got it covered, so hush."

"Thanks, Luci." She couldn't imagine what exactly Luci needed in the way of beauty preparation—bare-skinned, she looked better than ninety-nine point nine percent of women with full faces of cosmetics—but she was appreciative for the treat. It had been ages since Callie last posed for pictures, or so she felt, and the pressure was on to bring the media an artillery of glam. Her appearance at Ago didn't count, she figured, but the memory was fresh enough to make her cringe. A-W-K-W-A-R-D. What better way to redeem herself than on a red carpet?

Yes, indeed. A bona fide photo op was long overdue. And this time she'd be prepared to give some serious face.

15

The coiffed brunettes scooted into the limo. Two men were waiting for them inside—a muscular Ken doll of a specimen and Billy Joel. Wait—Callie did a double take—he was too fat to be Billy Joel. But with the large, bovine eyes, sparse grey hair, and a Brooklyn accent, he certainly looked and sounded an awful lot like the Piano Man. "What's goin' on," he said (it was a statement, not a question) in between chomps of chewing gum. "Barry Kraut, good to meet ya."

"Good to meet you, too. Chad, how are you? Long time no see," Callie said. She remembered the chiseled cutie as extremely polite and well-versed, with the memory of an elephant. Chad had his fellow actors' lines memorized before they did.

"Oh, my goodness, Callie Lambert!" Chad kissed both her cheeks. He looked leading man perfect in a custom navy suit. "Well, well, this is a pleasant surprise. You look stunning. Luciana, you didn't tell me you and Callie are friends."

Luci adjusted her fishnet stockings. "Callie and I met in Paris last month and hit it off."

"What a small world it is," Chad smiled. "Champagne, girls?" "I'm on a cleanse," said Luci.

"I'm not," Callie quipped. "I'd love some."

Chad handed her a flute of bubbly and poured himself another. "So, Callie, are you still repped by Paul Angers?"

"I sure am. How about you?"

"I switched management. I'm with Gary Benson now. He's meeting us at the premier."

Gary Benson. Bedroom Eyes' manager. "Ah, yes. I know Gary—"

"So this is the lowdown," Barry interjected. "Chad and Luciana, listen up. I spoke with *Stars R Us* and *Got It!* and they're definitely running your picture in next week's issue. All you gotta do is give them a little soundbite, something cute to print alongside it. Don't leave each other's side and smile, smile, smile. I got interviews with *Tinseltown TV*, *Lights, Camera, Hollywood!*, and *Rise and Shine L.A.* lined up, too. You don't need to get specific how you met—keep it short and vague—but if they ask you, mention you both went to the same school back in Canada. Say you were high school sweethearts and you've just now reconnected. The public goes nuts for that. Easy stuff. Got it so far?" Chad and Luci nodded and Barry continued. "Chad, make sure to tell 'em your new movie comes out next Friday and it's PG."

"Perfect for the entire family," Chad added cheerfully.

"Right. Perfect for the whole family—Mom, Grandma, little Timmy, the whole clan. Everyone really eats that apple pie crap up. Luciana, I'm a reporter. I wanna know why you aren't modeling anymore. Go."

Luci cleared her throat. "Modeling is great, and I had a good run, but I'm more than just a mannequin. I've always been creative, and I'm looking forward to branching into acting."

"What kind of projects you got on the horizon?" Barry barked.

"My agent and I are entertaining many different movie offers at the moment. I'm choosing my debut carefully because I want to find the perfect part."

Barry scowled. "Don't say I or me so much. Makes you sound narcissistic. We want to choose the perfect part. Make sure you phrase it that way. Got it?" Luciana nodded.

"Alright, not bad," Barry said. "Callie, I'm curious—what are you here to promote?"

"I'm not," she said.

"Huh? What do ya mean?"

"I have a movie in the pipeline, but I'm not here to officially promote anything. I just want to have a good time."

Barry scowled. "To each her own. So, Luci and Chad, you got it? Everything cool, clear, and kosher?" Barry smacked his hands and sped up his gum chomping. "Alrighty then. That's what's happenin', that's what's goin' on, let's do it."

The limo dropped them off at the Arclight in Hollywood. There was a decent smattering of camera crews—twenty or so—but nothing close to what Callie had encountered during the madness of the *NCA!* days. *I can do this*, Callie said to herself. This is cake. She worked the press line solo while Chad and Luci interviewed together.

"Yancey Love, here, with *Showbiz Style*. You're looking mighty fine tonight, Callie. Who are you wearing and how has your fashion evolved since the Manx Murder?"

"Miu Miu," said Callie, "and I would say that I tend to stay a little more covered up than I used to."

"I bet, I bet." Yancey secured her earpiece. "If you could be any fashion accessory for a day, what would you be and why?"

What is this, amateur hour? "Sunglasses. Because they're cool and help shield me from the meddlesome press."

Yancey laughed, loudly and nasally. She searched her notebook for more questions, but Callie had already moved down the press line.

"Are kitten heels a fashion do or don't?"

"Being from a small town, have you ever met a real life village idiot?"

"Nail polish on men; yay or gay?"

"Do you know what product Gabby Manx used on her hair to make it so shiny? No? What about her favorite brand of body bronzer?"

Callie had forgotten just how stupid the questions could be and tried to curb her eye-rolling. She really could have used Paul to help field the nonsense.

A short, grungy manatee shoved a microphone in her face and shouted, "Miss Lambert! Hi, J.J. Markstein from *The QT*. Some say Stephanie Schueller stole *The Cheerleader*

Chronicles right out from under you. How do you feel about that?"

Callie smiled into J.J.'s camera. "I want to focus on the future, not the past." Good job, girl. Take the high road.

"You don't think she took over the show you helped create?"

Callie hadn't thought of it that way. She grit her teeth. "I think she adds a, uh, different dimension to the show. I don't give it much thought, honestly. I start a new film in July, so obviously I've moved on."

"Back to Stephanie real quick," persisted J.J. "She said in an interview at the premiere of *The Grand Ole Osprey* last night, quote, 'Callie is yesterday's news. Out with the old, in with the Schue.' Do you think she took over because she's more talented?"

Jesus Christ! Callie's smile froze. "Stephanie did her best to look, talk, and act like Gabrielle. It wasn't a question of talent. The girl is a knock off."

J.J.'s long, drab face perked up. "'A knock off,' you say. You don't think she deserves to be on a hit show?"

"She scored a role after sleeping with the director. What does that tell you?"

"Interesting. Can you elaborate—"

"Gotta run, J.J." She had had enough with these questions. The last person she wanted to talk about was the Trailer Lady. As it stood, she probably said too much. Damn it. She should have ignored those questions altogether and switched it to something positive. Mention the charity she was starting instead of....Oh, well. Spilt milk.

"Callie! Callie, over here!"

Ugh! Who was it now? Callie whipped her head back to see Luciana waving at her. "Callie, come take a picture with Chad, and me," Luci hollered.

The three actors smiled in unison while Barry and Gary stood off to the side looking on.

Snap, snap!

Callie curbed a yawn. Another day at the office, in the Land of Make Believe.

16

Smoke hung above the partygoers' heads, a burly, toxic canopy. Between the perfume, booze, and tobacco, the patio at the Chateau Marmont was everything Callie pictured a Tijuana brothel smelling like. She took a step back and coughed.

"Hey, you got a light?" a girl slurred. Her hair was pulled so tightly in a bun, her eyes took on a feline shape. She clutched a bronze statuette and swayed in her gauzy dress.

"No, I don't smoke," Callie told her. And even if I did, I wouldn't give one to you. She recognized the girl as April Marin, and she had just beat Callie as the "Most Babelicious TV Actress" hours earlier at the Public Choice Awards. From what Callie had heard, April was a coked-up, tri-sexual floozy, a sitcom actress with little more to offer than a china doll face and a willing tongue. A dime a dozen. April had the reputation of, at just twenty-five, bedding the majority of Hollywood's movers and shakers. And it was those individuals, her partners-in-whoredom, that were most likely responsible for her award. Hell, they should just rename it the Pubic Choice and be done with it, thought Callie.

"Sure, you do, Callie, I know you got a light, don't you lie to me," April groaned. A tall man in a well-cut tux came up behind her and clutched her arm.

"April, you okay, babe?" said the man. "You look a little wobbly. Why don't you come back to our table and sit down?"

"I don't wanna sit," April piped. "I wanna smoke."

He fished a lighter out of his pocket and lit the cigarette dangling from April's mouth. April took a hearty drag. "See what a sweetie this guy is? I don't care how many people tell me to dump your ass, you're AOK in my book." She blew a kiss before sauntering off to chat up a group of admirers at the bar.

"Wow," Callie mused. "I can only imagine how she treats the help."

He laughed. "She's just joking. Tonight's a big night for her, so I'll let it slide."

"I know. I was up against her in the same category."

The man focused his heavy-lidded gaze on Callie before recognition struck his face.

"Ah-ha. That's why you look so familiar. Callie Lambert, right? Jack Kushner. I'm not only April's boyfriend, I'm also her agent."

"Lucky you," Callie sassed. She wasn't in the mood for small talk. Where was Tessa? Her hairdresser pal had tagged along to the awards show and after-party but Callie hadn't seen her since the limo dropped them off a half hour ago. The goal of the night was just to greet a few industry acquaintances, smile for the cameras, and head for the Hills—preferably in an hour or less. Bang, bam, bye. Watching a thriller in bed, outfitted in comfy PJs, was vastly more appealing than playing the game of ass and air kissing in a tortuous pair of platforms. Tracking Tessa down put a wrench in Callie's MO.

"You here with your team?" said Jack.

"My manager was here, yes," Callie said. "He just took off a few minutes ago."

"Really? That's not very professional to up and leave his client in the middle of a big shindig such as this."

"I don't mind. He's had a headache all day."

"I don't know. I never like to leave my clients alone in a room full of sharks if I can help it. Seems a little—I don't know—*off* to me." He sipped a whiskey and gave the glittery crowd a once-over.

"My friend, Tessa, came with me, too. She's floating around here somewhere. Petite, pixie hair, bright yellow dress. Maybe you've seen her?" Callie sipped her champagne.

"You're kidding, right? This place is more packed than the mall on Black Friday. And unless she's in the business, I probably wouldn't know her." "She is. She's an actress as well as a hairdresser."

"What's she been in?"

"A few indies and the new McDonald's commercial."

"Then I most certainly wouldn't know her," Jack snickered. He swirled the ice cubes around in his glass. "I only deal with B minus and above."

"Excuse me, but I need to find my friend and get going."
Enough of this blowhard.

"Whoa, whoa, missy. Just one moment, if you don't mind.
I have to congratulate you on the new Vernadeau project.
She's one tough cookie and apparently you charmed her
socks right off her. Not an easy task."

Callie's eyes widened. "You heard about that?"

"You know this town's a tiny, incestuous world. My best
friend's sister is best friends with Paul Anger's secretary,
Ursula. Bet you didn't know that." Jack revealed a set of
choppers Mr. Ed would have envied.

"I sure didn't."

"Boy, oh, boy." Jack shook his head and laughed. "It's
funny how things intertwine in this town. Forget six degrees of separation. Ha ha ha. Around here, in our neck of
the woods, it's three degrees or less. Without fail."

"That's funny...." Callie slowly inched away. Hopefully
Jack would get the hint.

"Back to *The Foreign Affair*." Jack's smile vanished. "Paul,
our common denominator, secured this role for you?"

"It's kind of unusual how it came about. I met Nanette in
France by way of Paul—she's a friend of his."

"Get out. You mean to tell me you scored it by
chance?"

"Pretty much. It was very random. She had just seen
Nympho Cheerleaders and thought I'd be perfect."

Jack shook his head. "Tsk, tsk. This concerns me. Every
actress under the age of thirty must have auditioned for

Nanette. Naturally, I figured Paul had you read for it. You would have been first on my list of clients."

"Well, the part is mine and that's what I care about. It's official and I've signed on the dotted line."

"Of course, of course. It's just a little alarming when you think he could have put this deal together sooner and didn't. You're his biggest client, after all. Right?"

"I, um...I am, I guess, yeah. That sounds a little cocky of me—"

"No it doesn't. You're stating a fact. You have to remember, you are his top priority. Or at least you should be, anyway. It would be a crime to slow your momentum down now because of a bum agent."

"Manager," Callie corrected. "And thanks for your concern, Jack, but Paul is not a bum."

Jack shrugged. "Luckily, for you, Nanette gave you her seal of approval, but imagine if you never met her. I have to confess, it makes me wonder what other career opportunities you're missing out on if Paul let something like this fall through the cracks."

Callie's mind whirled; Jack could very well have a point. What if Paul wasn't on his toes? She was in her prime and needed a solid, take-charge front man steering her. Maybe that explained why she had gone through dry spells without booking anything. Maybe Paul wasn't as competent as she thought and he was skating by on his sizable commission and not putting enough effort in. Maybe—

"Anyhow, Callie, congrats again." Jack raised his glass to hers. "I'm off to locate April. Swing by our table for a drink—we have more magnums of brut than you can shake a stick at."

She smiled feebly and Jack strode off. He darted through the crowd until he reached his drunken target. The theme song of *Jaws* pumped through Callie's head.

17

"Honey, you shouldn't have. Really, you are something else. Man alive, I'm telling you..."

Callie had never heard Grandma Esme so excited before. She had planned on purchasing a Cadillac or Mediterranean cruise or something haute-couture for her grandmother's birthday. But just days earlier, Esme made the confession: "You know, Honey, what I'm going to buy next time I'm out? A fryer. I found my mother's recipe for empanadas and it calls for one. Dr. Vaisman will be none too thrilled to hear I've been eating fried food, but I don't see anything wrong with a little moderation. I saw a real nice one on HSN the other day..." Callie ordered the fryer along with seventy-eight pink long-stemmed roses, Esme's favorite.

"And your flowers are something else, dear. They haven't opened yet and they're just the prettiest shade of pink. They came with the nicest vase with butterflies all over it, cuter than a bug's ear. Just lovely."

"I'm so happy you like it, Grandma. Maybe you can put your fryer to use next time I'm in town."

"That goes without saying. I know you were just here but it feels like it's been years already," Esme said. "I called your mother this morning. She sounded real chipper, said she's the healthiest she's been in months. Tony took her for a trip to North Carolina a few weeks ago, you know. I'm so glad; she really needed a vacation. And she sent me some lovely snapshots."

"Yeah, she sent them to me, too," Callie said. "She's looking very tanned and svelte. And very healthy."

"Isn't she? She's lost quite a bit of weight and so proud, showing off her figure on the beach, looking just as healthy as can be. Oh, and I almost forgot, along with the pictures, she included a sweet-as-can-be birthday card. Imagine, all she's going through and she remembers my birthday. Isn't that nice?"

"Very nice," agreed Callie. "When we last spoke, she said she was crawling out of her skin from the cold, damp weather and couldn't wait to soak up some sun. You know how dreary Michigan is. I swear, the sun only makes an appearance once a year."

"Oh, phooey. You know darn well it comes out twice a year, Cal, what's wrong with you." Esme giggled at her joke. "Honey, I watched those Public Choice Awards last night and I have to say, I think it was rigged. That girl who won, I've seen her show and let me tell you, it's the silliest, trashiest program. You should have won hands down— not that I'm biased. Just based on her outfit alone, she should have been disqualified. Awful, just awful. I'm sure it was expensive, but all those crystals made her look cheap."

"You should have seen her in person and up close," said Callie. "Those shows are usually fixed, Grandma, pay no attention. Did you like my outfit?"

"That goes without saying. You are always beautifully dressed, dear. And I like that young man who was with you, too. Handsome."

"Young man? Paul is the only one who came with me to the show, Grandma, and you've met him. He's in his fifties."

"No, no, of course I know who Paul is. They announced your name and then the camera moved in close and I saw a man on your left. A real looker."

"I think he was just a seat filler, Grandma."

"Oh." Esme sounded deflated. "I thought maybe he was a new boyfriend."

"No, I didn't bring a date."

"I see. I don't want to pry, dear, but are you still single?"

"Single as a dollar bill."

Esme sighed. "You know, I really liked Evan. Do you two ever talk?"

"No, Grandma."

"I really liked him."

I heard you the first time. "I really liked him, too, but he wasn't good for me."

"That's too bad, but you know best, dear. I'm happy if you're happy."

Callie took a seat at the kitchen table and started up her laptop. She surfed Saks' intimates section while Esme rattled on.

"I've decided I'm growing tomatoes this year, once spring comes," Esme said. "I can freeze them and have them all winter long."

La Perla Balconette Underwire Bra—$350. Into her cart it went. "That's great, Grandma."

"And did I tell you what the neighbor next door has been up to?" Esme said.

"No. What's her name, Georgia?" Callie followed the link to matching underwear.

"That's right, honey. Georgia. The nicest woman. Her husband used to work as a salesman for Russell Stover. He was always on the road, selling candy."

Click! Into the cart went the matching thong. "Mmm-hmm."

"She had the darndest thing happen to her peonies the other day..."

Callie racked up a $1,200 lingerie tab before cashing out. She had no one to model the skivvies for and her drawers overflowed with more bras than she could possibly wear in a year. No matter; life was more savory with a sexy foundation.

"And wouldn't you know, Georgia was at the grocery store yesterday and said they raised the price of bananas by twenty cents..."

Callie logged in to her Hotmail account. At the top of the heap was an e-mail from Jerry D'Orsay. The subject box simply read "Emily." Her pulse quickened.

Callie,

Per your request, I've done my best to inquire of the details regarding your sister, Emily, I've uncovered the following:
*   Emily is working on her masters at Illinois State. She was adopted as a baby by Chuck and Annabelle Grimes of Belleville, Illinois. The father has since died but the mother owns a small flower shop in the area. I've attached a photo I was able to locate of Emily. If you have any questions, I'll be in my office for the remainder of the day.*

She opened the attachment and gawked at the dirty blonde in the photo. She was pleasant-looking with kind, greenish-blue eyes. Despite these two dissimilar features between the girls, the rest of Emily was like looking in a mirror; the mouth, the heart- shaped face, the nose—Callie's old nose, that was—were one and the same. Still, something about the girl was throwing Callie off. She expected to see their father in Emily, one or two features similar to Dad's, but Callie was having trouble spotting a smidgeon of Lambert blood. And what of this adoption business? Callie bit her lower lip.

"Honey," Grandma Esme said, "are you listening?"

"Yes, Grandma." Callie willed herself to focus on Esme's conversation. It took everything she had to keep quiet; she had a massive desire to scream her lungs out and divulge everything to her grandmother. But she didn't. She let Grandma yak away and bit her tongue. As soon as the women said their goodbyes, she dialed up Jerry.

"Hi, there, Callie. What can I do for you?" Jerry said in a gravelly voice.

"Jerry, I just read your e-mail but I'm confused about something. Emily and I, we look alike, but she doesn't look like my dad at all."

There was a pause on Jerry's end. "Well, no, I can't imagine she would look like your dad."

"But she's my half-sister, right?"

"Correct."

"Then why doesn't she look like my dad? She doesn't have any of his features."

"That's just the thing—she doesn't look like your dad because she's not related to your dad."

"I'm not following..."

"Didn't I explain all this?"

"No, you didn't."

"Huh. Guess I must have forgotten. No, you and Emily don't share the same father. You share the same mother."

18

"Mother?" gasped Callie.

"Yes. Virginia DiPrizio, maiden name Novak?"

"Yeah, that's my mom."

"Yep, you both are related by way of your mother. She gave Emily up as a baby, three years before you were born."

"Before?" A bulldozer could have driven through Callie's gaped mouth.

"That's right, before. She's older than you, as I said."

"But—what? That can't be possible. That would mean I—I mean, she..." Callie struggled to string the proper words together. "But why would my mom do that?"

"I'll tell you this: I'm the wrong person to answer those questions. I've got no whys and wherefores. I've just got cold hard facts, plain as that."

"I understand," she sighed. "Anything else you forgot to tell me?"

"Don't think so."

"I didn't see a, um, bill attached. How much do I owe you?"

"Bill shmill. Pauly's been a good friend and I'm glad to help out."

"Thanks, Jerry. I can't think of anything else right now, I guess..."

"If you do, give me a buzz. Good luck, Callie."

Callie pulled at the neck of her tee. Ugh; she was sweltering. A breeze poured through the French doors but the house was stuffier than a British monarch. Or maybe she was just riled up and light-headed. She pulled a can of soda from the fridge and guzzled. The bubbles burned the back of her throat. Ah...

Of course, she was aware Virginia had been married once before, but the only thing her mother divulged was that the union had been brief and an awful mistake. Callie knew next to nothing about the man, including his name, but wondered if he was Emily's biological father. Callie wondered if her dad knew his wife had given away her firstborn. Was anyone in on the secret? And what a secret! A double life, really. As it stood, no further details could shock her. Emily might well be the spawn of her mother and Richard Simmons; Callie wouldn't have bat an eyelash.

The house alarm beeped. Luci was home. She walked through the foyer, her Smart Phone pressed against her ear.

"Yes, Dad, I know. I haven't decided on my next project yet. Yes, I've had plenty of offers but I don't want to settle on just anything. You know me—I'm picky. I want it to be the perfect part. I know, don't worry—I'll be making money again soon. And thanks for reminding me, but I realize I'm not getting any younger. Beggars can't be choosers, you're right. Can we talk later? Good-bye, Dad." Luci collapsed in a dining room chair and growled.

"You okay?" Callie asked.

"Never better," said Luci. "I don't know why I bother justifying myself to my family. In particular, my father. Nothing is ever good enough, he needs to constantly question my decisions, like I'm a nincompoop. 'I told you this was a bad idea, Luciana. This acting bullshit isn't putting any pennies in your piggy bank. You should be taking any and every offer that comes your way and stop being so goddamned picky. Money is money, make that dough.' And then he added, 'Beggars can't be choosers.'"

"I know that line well," Callie snickered. "My mom's used it on me many times."

Luci slammed her fist on the cherry wood table. "Isn't it infuriating? He may as well stamp 'loser' on my forehead. That's what he's calling me—a loser. As if I should be so lucky that someone would even think of giving me a job, that I should fall down on my knees and thank my lucky stars someone took pity on me." She threw her hands up in grand gestures, like a maestro. "Do you realize I've been earning my own living since I was sixteen? Sixteen! I've earned millions, all on my own. I'd say that's a pretty good sign of just how well my brain works."

Callie took a seat next to the frisky Canadian. She was thankful to focus on someone else's familial problems instead of her own. "Maybe he means well but he can't help himself."

"That's stupid," sniffed Luci. "It shouldn't be difficult to be supportive. When I have kids, I'll support them no matter what."

"My mom is opinionated like your dad. She just has to give her opinion. Doesn't matter if it's the wrong time or place or she phrases it wrong. I don't think she even knows when she's being negative, half the time. She's gotten better this last year but—"

"Consider yourself lucky, Callie. My dad hasn't gotten any better—neither one of my parents have. Only worse. It's always what they want. How about what I want for a change?"

"What exactly do you want?"

Luciana lifted her head high. "A little credit would be nice. I've accomplished quite a bit in my twenty-six years. Just on modeling assignments alone, I've been to thirty-three different countries. I've been plastered all over Times Square and in every fashion magazine from L.A. to Australia. One year, I won nine equestrian competitions—and was chastised for not winning ten. Do you know for my parents' thirtieth anniversary I treated them to an African safari? A six-hundred-dollar-a-night hotel and my mother said, 'It was cute, Luci, but it wasn't up to our usual standards.' Usual standards. Can you believe that?"

Callie puffed her cheeks and exhaled. "It sounds exhausting. I'm glad I don't have that kind of pressure."

"It's never enough. I could always make more, do more, give more, be more. More, more, more. Good God, I give up." Luci rubbed her makeup-free eyes. "I should just accept that offer."

"What offer?" Callie said.

"For a new fashion segment on *Hollywood Hotspot*. It would be a show within a show, a five minute Luciana Dickerson special every night."

"That's fantastic! The show's been around for ages and everyone watches it, Luci. Think of all the exposure you'll get."

"I'd rather have your career, Callie. Look at you—you're a real actress. Film, television, you do it all. You've got this incredible sense of freedom where you don't allow anything to hold you back, not family nor foe nor circumstance. I wish I could let it slide off my back the way you do. You know, I've never said this before—" Luci's voice dropped a decibel. "—but I envy you and admire you at the same time. And I never envy anyone. It's always the other way around; usually everyone envies me. Anyways..." She hopped to her sneakers and slung her satchel over her shoulder. "You don't need to hear all this. I'm just a chatterbox today."

"You're fine, Luci, don't worry." Callie felt awkward, as though she were a little girl who just got caught eavesdropping. "Listen, what I've learned in Hollywood so far is this: plan on nothing going as planned. You never know what kind of doors this show could open for you. Sometimes fate takes a hand."

Luci cupped the guardrail at the bottom of the staircase. "Let's just say it's not the splash I planned on making for my big debut. But, like my father says, money is money, and

Beyond Hollywood Strip

I'm not getting any younger. Guess Dad is right on that one. I'm off to shower; that spin class at Equinox really kicked my ass." She bounded up the stairs, two at a time. Her hair bounced rhythmically with each step and rippled behind her like blackened strips of taffy.

19

Earl Barletta's Pasadena law office was much like the man himself—large, seasoned, and colorful. Bookshelves lined the walls and were filled with enough literature to give a public library a run for its money. Marble sculptures, most of them nude with many of them missing arms and heads, were situated on plush, red carpet. But the crown jewel, the star of the room (excluding Earl) was the barge-of-a-desk he presided behind, an intricately carved hunk of wood.

"What do you think of my desk?" Earl said.

"It's definitely roomy," she said. "Like a boat."

"That it is. I had her custom built when I first started practicing law forty-two years ago." Earl rubbed a spot of the desk that wasn't buried in pictures and paper. "She's born witness to every kind of legal squabble known to mankind. The tales of woe would knock your socks off—put any soap opera to shame."

"I bet." Callie took a seat across from Earl.

"So, your manager, Pete—"

"Paul."

"Paul, I mean..." Earl ruffled through a folder. "He told me about you're interested in starting a foundation, a charity, for a deceased friend."

"Very much."

"Good for you. Here, take a look at some paperwork I pulled together." Callie leafed through the papers.

"Can I get the layman's version?"

"Since you don't have a single source of funding, such as a corporation—say, Chrysler—or a rich aunt, it will be a public company. It can take six, seven, eight months, sometimes more, to get all the paperwork filed—and it's a lot of paperwork. The IRS are bastards when it comes to this stuff, slower than death. The whole process takes a while, but as long as you realize it's not an overnight shebang, we'll get this show on the road. I've highlighted what I need from you to get started. Here—take my lucky pen." He handed her a monogrammed writing instrument and adjusted his glasses—tortoise frames that perfectly complemented his tawny button-down. "France treat you well?"

"Yeah, great."

"Wish I could say the same. The wedding was beautiful but everything that could go wrong did. The power went out at my hotel, my luggage got lost, our flight back home was delayed—it was incredible, just incredible how many times things got screwed up. Like one of those National Lampoon's vacation movies. How's the career going? Any movies on the horizon?"

"Yes, I start a new one in June. I'm excited to really stretch my acting chops this time."

"Good for you. You the lead?"

"I sure am."

"That's terrific. What genre?"

Callie halted her writing. "It's a period piece, a romantic drama."

Earl looked disappointed. "Sounds like something my wife would like. Me personally, I love a good suspense flick, something smart with a lot of action, like a James Cagney or Cary Grant picture. The movies nowadays are so muddled with special effects and flashy graphics, I can hardly stand it. My nephew, I think I may have mentioned, is an actor."

"Yeah, you mentioned that on the plane." Callie worried that, with all of Earl's chatting, she'd be tardy to her appointment with Dr. Freisch.

He folded his hands across his gut. "He's been on quite a roll. They've got him scooting off to Ireland for his latest, some medieval something or other that takes place in an old castle. You may meet him; he borrowed my steam cleaner and is supposed to be dropping it off sometime this afternoon, after he finishes an audition. He's a good kid with a smart head on his shoulders. When he was in grade school, he started his own lawn mowing business. He's always had some business cooking, been a hard worker his whole life. I like that. I wish my kids had the same work ethic. What did you do before you started acting, Cal-lie?"

"I was a dental assistant in Michigan, where I'm originally from, and when I moved to L.A., I waited tables. Not exactly a glamorous start."

"That's alright. We all have to start somewhere. My first job was pumping gas. I was—let me see, how old was I?...

Thirteen, fourteen-years-old. I was on my feet all day, running around filling up cars, washing their windows—a real quick son-of-a-gun. I did well in tips, too—"

Knock, knock.

"Who is it and what do you want?" shouted Earl.

"It's me, Uncle Earl," said the voice on the other side of the door. "Come on in, Me."

Callie's back was to the entrance. The latch opened and she looked over her shoulder. Mitch Gracie stood in the doorway.

20

"Well, hello, there, Miss Callie," Mitch said in his Southern drawl. "This is a surprise."

"It certainly is," Callie said. She tried to not appear excited at the site of the Hick Prick. But he looked so cute, so sexy in his ass-sculpting Levis and bicep-clinging T- shirt, it was impossible to feign disinterest.

"You two know each other, I see," Earl said. "How did this come about, Mitchell?"

"Callie and I were on a TV show together," Mitch said. "I was a guest star and she was a series regular. I had no idea she was a client of yours, Unc."

"A brand spanking-new client. We met on a plane, of all places. I was en route to France for Delilah's wedding and Callie was sitting next to me."

"I'll bet she gave you hell," Mitch smirked. "We sure butted heads at first, didn't we, Cal?"

Callie gathered her things. "Actually, I hate to run off so suddenly, but I have a doctor's appointment in Westwood. Earl, can I sign this and get it back to you later?"

"Absolutely, I just thought it would be helpful to sign it here at the office in case you had any questions for me. But go ahead, I don't want to keep you." Earl checked his Rolex. "If you leave now, you shouldn't hit traffic."

"Thank you so much. I really appreciate all your help. I'll drop the papers off in a few days. Nice to see you again, Mitch." She scurried out to her car.

"Callie! Hey, wait up, will you?" Mitch was hot on her heels. "Damn, girl, you sure walk fast. Why haven't you called me?"

"Why haven't you called me?" she spat.

"I did call you."

Callie's nostrils flared. "Yeah, you called to cancel on me. You haven't tried to get a hold of me once since then."

"What, I'm supposed to chase you down? You want me to keep callin' and pray I get lucky enough for you to answer? That's not how I play, darlin'. You don't want to talk to me, fine—I'm not gonna beg. I just figured you would have called me back or texted or gotten a hold of me by now. It goes both ways, you know."

Callie flung her car door open and threw her purse in the passenger seat. "What was I supposed to think when you canceled on me last minute? I felt so stupid, like a pile of dog dung. You've got a lot of nerve, you know that? Who the hell do you think you are, standing me up?"

Mitch laughed. "You really do have a high and mighty opinion of yourself, don't you? All those magazine articles you've read about yourself have gone to that little head."

"Don't be jealous, Mitch. Maybe if you finished elementary school, you'd be able to read, too. Reading and

116

writing isn't part of the basic curriculum in the South, I guess." No sooner had she spewed the words than regret stung her heart. She averted her eyes. "Sorry, that was mean."

"You're such a child. In the future, if someone has to cancel on you due to a life-threatening illness, it may be best to keep your holier-than-thou opinions to yourself until you know the whole story. Where I grew up, I was taught not to judge something I know bullshit about. Maybe manners aren't something Yankees know much of. Just a thought, you know—just sayin'." He turned on his heel.

"Wait, Mitch. Please, come back." Callie ran over to him and touched his arm. "I'm sorry; that was wrong of me. What do you mean, 'life-threatening' illness?"

Mitch shoved his hands in his pockets. "I called you from the hospital. And I would have called you sooner but I was hopin' I would have felt well enough to take you out. But I didn't. There was just no way I was makin' that concert. I was at Cedars for a few days."

"What happened?"

"I'm diabetic," Mitch said, "and what I thought was a common cold turned into pneumonia. I got pretty run down in Buffalo. I wasn't takin' care of myself properly. I was working so many hours that I wasn't sleepin' much or eatin' right and by the time I got home, it all caught up with me. The day after we spoke, I was sicker than a dog."

Callie's eyes melted. "Don't I feel like a horse's ass. Why didn't you say so in the beginning?"

"I didn't feel comfortable, especially leavin' it on an answering machine. I'm no cry baby and I don't wear my heart on my sleeve—not my style at all."

"So you'd rather me think you were a jerk than a wimp?"

"Unequivocally, yes. And, yes, I can also spell the word 'unequivocally'."

Callie smiled. "I wish I would have known. I guess I shouldn't have jumped to conclusions but—"

"But your ego can't stand it," he interjected and brushed a strand of hair away from her eyes. "Let's call a spade a spade. You are a brat, you know that? You know it's true."

Callie propped her hands on her hips. "Me, a brat? You're the cocky one."

"Maybe so, but you're high-maintenance and demanding, which I am not. You're not like Schueller or one of those girls, but you're definitely much more Hollywood than me. Still, I can't help myself. I don't know what it is about you, but I want to know more. There's just somethin' you've got..." Mitch leaned in close to her, until their lips almost touched, before pulling back. "I should let you get goin'."

"You tease," she said. "If you promise to take me out, I promise to never be an egotistical bitch again."

"I don't know if you should make promises you know you can't keep." Mitch's eyes glinted. "But it's worth a shot. I suppose you're booked this weekend?"

"My friend, Luci, and I have a spa day planned tomorrow, but that's it so far. Got any ideas?"

"Yeah, I do. How 'bout if I give you a call later and we'll see if we can work something out?"

"I'd like that, Mitch. A lot."

"Until we meet again, then." Mitch headed back to the office while Callie stared at his rear.

21

"Doc, I think I'm going mad, I really do," said Callie. She propped her feet on Dr. Freisch's leather ottoman. "This family I have...had... whatever tense you want to use, is so confusing. And everything seems fraudulent. I was this only child and low and behold, from out of nowhere, I have a sister. I feel like I don't even know my family anymore. Or did I ever know them? I'm not sure. The only thing I'm sure of is that for the past two days I've had diarrhea."

Dr. Freisch slowed his already slow breathing. His nasal exhale lasted a solid seven seconds. For a small-statured, one-hundred-and-eighty pound man, he sounded like someone double his size. He always had, and the deeper his concentration, the more tempered was his breathing. He flicked the ends of his salt and pepper beard and said, "Why haven't you discussed this with your mother yet? If you talk all this out, maybe you can gain some clarity."

"I don't want to talk to my mom."

"But why?"

"Because I'm pissed. I'm royally pissed. Betrayed. All my life, she's had this high-and-mighty attitude. Always critiquing me and having this Holy Roller view on nudity and morality. And come to find out, all this time, she's kept this big, dark secret. What a hypocrite. You know, I really kind of hate her right now."

"Hate is a strong word," Dr. Freisch said.

"Maybe," she snarled, "but it sums up the way I feel right now. I don't trust her and I don't want to talk to her."

"That's exactly why you need to talk to her, Callie. I realize you're upset—"

"Pissed," Callie corrected.

"Pissed, fighting mad, however you describe it—I hear that loud and clear. But it's in your best interest to sort it out with your mother. Get it all out in the open."

She squirmed in her seat. "Obviously it's not something she wanted me knowing since she did such a good job keeping it from me all these years."

"Your sister coming forward has changed all that," the Doctor said. "The time has come for your mother to address the situation she created and face the music."

"I don't know, Doc. I don't know what to say to my mom. How and why Emily found me is a mystery but as of right now, I don't want to talk to her, either. She thinks she can just show up in my life and, presto! All is honky dory. Well, it's not. It's not okay to invade my life just because she has decided she's ready. But I guess I'm the only one who got that memo."

"You may feel differently once you give it a little time. You need a chance to digest all this." Dr. Freisch crossed his khaki-trousered leg. "Given the choice, would you prefer being in the dark and not knowing about your sister? If you could choose, would you rather not know she exists?"

Callie tiled her head in thought. "I guess so, yeah."

"Mmm-kay, well..." The Doctor tugged at his beard. "Just because something isn't easy doesn't mean it has to be distasteful, you know. Look at it this way: this twist has opened a whole new world for you. Why don't you try embracing it, in all its perplexity and strangeness and randomness? You may find yourself pleasantly surprised."

Callie looked less than enthused.

"How are the panic attacks?"

She brightened, ever so slightly. "They're better. I haven't taken any Sister Xani in two weeks. I hate having others dictate how I feel. I want to learn how to get a grip on the situation and stop the panic before it even starts."

"Cognitive therapy. I've always preached cognitive therapy. You can change your body's reaction if you rewire your thinking patterns. It's all on how you frame it."

"Easier said than done. I have twenty-six-year-old wires to redo."

"That's nothing," he said. "When I started practicing cognitive therapy, I was thirty- six, so you have ten years on me." He pulled out a stack of papers from his desk. "Here, take this home. It's a list of things to remind yourself. Simple, logical ideas. The real test is applying them, and that can take some getting used to. It's not something that can happen overnight. But it is something you can work towards."

"So if I learn to practice this cognitive therapy, I'll never have any more panic attacks?" Callie asked.

"I can't promise you'll never have a panic attack but if you realize that what you're feeling is just a temporary sensation—and you're not in any grave danger where your life is being threatened—you can reframe the way your brain processes anxiety."

"It can't hurt to try. Thanks, Doc." Callie stopped by the receptionist to schedule a follow-up appointment. "Can you mail me the bill, Helen? I forgot my credit card at home." Her Visa was on her laptop, compliments of a midnight shopping spree.

Helen sorted through the mail while simultaneously plowing through an apple muffin.

"Sure, I'll get that out tomorrow. You're still at the same address, an apartment, aren't you?"

"No, I'm at a house. Have been for a while."

"Goodness, let me update your file." She hauled her doughy body over to the computer.

"It's 5367 Lookout Mountain," Callie said. "Nine, zero, zero, four, six."

"Okay. Hold on...Nine...Zero...Zero...." Helen pecked away at the keyboard. Callie was reminded of the rent due in a few days. She cringed at writing a check.

Six thousand. Egad. She never would have taken the pad had she known Tyler would be jumping ship. Maybe she should have taken up his offer of chipping in half, but she felt awkward taking her friend's money; his bank account wasn't nearly as robust as hers. The fact that he offered spoke volumes of his character. Such a sweetheart, Ty. Still, six grand every thirty days was steep for a home she barely occupied half of—if that (roughly the equivalent of six pairs of Louboutins a month, she figured.) And quite often, she wasn't even home.

Callie heaved her purse over her shoulder and opened the door bearing the off-center plaque:

THEODORE K. FREISHCH, MD.

"Thanks, Helen."

Helen resumed her muffin gobbling. "Oh, sure."

22

Evelyn, the manicurist, lacquered Midnight Cami on Callie's short, square nails. The blackish blue enamel was rocker chic perfection.

"It's too bad you can't make it tonight to the party," Luciana said from the spa chair next to Callie's.

"There's always a party in L.A.," Callie yawned. "Every night is a new party."

"But Genetic Management pulls out all the stops when they throw a party. Trust me, I've been their client for ten years. The best food at the chicest venue with lots of influential bigwigs."

"Once you've been to one Hollywood shindig, you've been to them all," Callie said. "I'd much rather be on a hot date than surrounded by caviar and pretentious Hollywood peeps."

Luci aimed her wet finger tips at the portable fan on the armrest. "I have no room in my schedule for love. It takes too much time and I don't have any to spare. *Hollywood Hotspot* has already given me my first assignment: the royal wedding in Copenhagen."

Callie's eyes lit up. "The Danish royal wedding? How exciting. It's just around the corner, isn't it?"

"Mmm-hmm, next week. I imagine the fashions will be interesting but I can't say that I have much interest in the event. I've met the Duke many times. Before he started dating his fiancée, he used to be a big fixture on the social circuit. He was at every fashion show, made sure he always had a beautiful girl on each arm and tons of models stocked on his yacht in the South of France. It didn't matter to him that most of them were hookers, he just had to be seen. Privileged people are often the tackiest."

"I've never met royalty. Did he hit on you?"

"Millions of times. But I would never go out with him. I don't go for show-offs and I'm a tough nut to crack. If a man thinks he can get in my bed just because his bank balance has multiple zeros, he's got another think coming."

Callie adjusted the massage speed on her spa chair. "I bet it will be uber glamorous. It's right up your alley, Luci."

Luci shrugged. "There should be some fabulous clothes and celebrities. I guess it's just that I don't want to be covering the news—I should be the one causing it."

"And I'm sure you will. I know you're aware of this, but you're not the kind of girl who goes unnoticed. I wish I had people throwing offers at me when I first moved to L.A. It would have been a whole different ballgame. I was slinging hash before I booked a role."

"Slinging hash?"

"Waiting tables."

"I've waited tables before," Luci said. "Right before I started modeling. I wanted to know what it felt like to earn my own money, so my father got a job for me at The Four Seasons. It was just so...dull. I lasted two weeks. Where did you work?"

"Harry's Hamlet."

"Hmmm...I've never heard of that hotel."

"It's a diner in the Valley."

"Oh." Luci turned back to her fan.

A beep sounded from Callie's cell. A text message read:

Are u in the mood tonight for something mellow or does it have to be glitzy...? I have a few ideas but let me know.;-) -Mitch

Callie was perturbed Mitch found her so superficial. She wanted to straighten out his faulty perception of her, and pronto. Careful not to smudge her polish, she texted back:

Mellow sounds great. :-)

Ten minutes later, the girls galloped out of the salon just as Callie's cell rang.

"Hey, there. Hick Prick here."

Callie grinned. "Ah-ha. I'm speaking to the official HP, am I?"

"The one and only, accept no imitations," Mitch said. "Am I catchin' you at a bad time?"

"Not at all. Luci and I were just leaving the salon."

"Okay, so about tonight..."

"Yes?"

"I hate to do this to you again." Mitch lowered his voice. "But I'm going to have to cancel."

"Excuse me?" Callie huffed. "Who do you think you are—"

"I'm kiddin', Cal, I'm just kiddin'. Sorry, I couldn't resist."

The color returned to her face and she sighed with relief. "Not funny, Alabama. My Greek temper was about to make a guest appearance."

"I bet it was. In all seriousness, I was wonderin' how you felt about goin' to Malibu. It's been so gorgeous lately, and yesterday when I was there surfin' there was the prettiest sunset, I figure why not take it in again?"

"I love sunsets. Much better than sunrises."

"I've always thought so, too. How does Moonshadows sound? We'll grab a bite on the deck and take it all in."

"That would be perfect, Mitch."

"I've taken the liberty of makin' reservations already. I can pick you up at six-thirty. Cool?"

"Cucumber cool."

"Cucumber cool," repeated Mitch appreciatively. "I like that. Well then, consider it a date, Lambert. And you may wanna wear somethin' warm, too, 'cause it's been a little chilly."

23

The ocean air, brackish and chill, caressed Callie's face and gave her cheeks a punch of color. She buttoned her cardigan.

"Here, take this. I don't need it." Mitch swung his thick scarf off his neck and held it out but she shooed him away. "Ya sure?"

Callie nodded. "I'm fine, thanks. Besides, you need it, I'm sure."

"Not at all. I'm hot-blooded by nature."

She hesitated before grabbing the scarf and tying it around her neck.

"Much better." Mitch winked. "I knew you needed it; you had cold written all over your face."

They sat across from one another at a cozy booth on the deck at Moonshadows. The sky was splashed with neon orange and pink, like a Tequila Sunrise. Callie sipped her Mojito and examined Mitch through her sprig of mint. His messy, sandy waves were perfect in an I-don't-give-a-damn kind of way and combined with his henley and medium wash jeans, he resembled a lumberjack, Callie thought—a sexy lumberjack. But it was the dimples that got her fire roaring, those adorable little clefts of skin that would pop out when he smiled or frowned. As un-L.A. as Mitch was, his surfer good looks and nonchalance gave him a decidedly L.A. vibe.

"So do I pass the test?" he said behind his menu.

"What?"

"I see you checkin' me out over there. Have I passed the test?"

"Oh." She blushed. "Yeah, you have. With flying colors."

Pop! There went the dimples. "Good. Cause I didn't bring a change of clothes with me. Usually I take a whole slew of clothing for when I surf and have auditions and all, but today's laundry day and I haven't a single stitch in the Jeep."

"You must be knocking them dead at your auditions, because your uncle mentioned you start filming in Ireland soon," she said.

"My uncle's great, isn't he? A little quirky and long-winded, but he's got a heart of gold. He's been married to my mom's sister since—God, way before I was born, and I'm twenty-seven. But, yeah, I have a small part as a knight. Headin' to Ireland and Scotland next month. I can't complain. A year in L.A. and I've been doin' pretty well."

Callie swirled the straw in her mouth. "Have you warmed up to L.A. at all?"

"I love L.A.—love it. I'm a big nature freak. It's just the people that get under my skin. People in the industry and their egos, mostly. I promise you, I'm not nearly as pricky as I came across when we first met, but I can see how I must have sounded like a self- indulgent jackass."

"You did come on a little strong, I have to say."

"You're more than welcome to start calling me the Hick Prick again, go ahead."

"Who says I ever stopped?" teased Callie.

"Keep it up, and I'll never tell you what your little nickname was, darlin'. And trust me, you'll wanna hear it, cause it's good."

Their waiter approached. "Have you two decided on an appetizer?"

Mitch spoke up. "We've been busy talkin' and haven't decided yet. I'll take another Diet Coke in the meantime."

"Very good, sir. Take your time." The waiter turned to Callie and said quietly, "I hope you don't mind me saying this, but I've been a huge fan for some time. You were the best thing about *Cheerleader Chronicles*."

Callie smiled before he turned away.

"You get that a lot, I'm guessin'," said Mitch.

"Not always. You'd be surprised how often I fly under the radar."

"You? Fly under the radar? No way."

"Why 'no way'?" Callie asked with a splash of indignation.

"Because you've courted the press for a while now. Egged 'em on. You must like it— a little bit, at least. We're both actors, so it can't be denied we like attention, right? C'mon, admit it."

"Wait, wait—go back to what you just said," Callie said. "How in the world have I courted the press? I'm the one who turns the other way when a paparazzo shoves a stupid camera in my face."

Mitch set his menu down and propped his elbows on the table. "I mean posin' for *Coquette*, takin' on flashy performances, you know, things that scream for attention. Nothin' bad about it, and don't get me wrong—I'm not sayin' you deserve to be hunted down when you run about your business. But you gotta know certain career choices are gonna bring you extra attention."

"I don't look at it that way at all. I haven't posed nude for extra attention, I haven't taken my top off on camera for extra attention. I've done all that because I wanted to. Simple as that." Callie narrowed her eyes and added, "What is it, exactly, that you mean to say?"

Mitch tore off a hunk of bread, "I mean nothin' by it except I think you're better than that."

"Oh, really?"

"Yeah, really. Pure and simple. Most girls who look like you can't act their way out of a paper bag. But you can act. Most of 'em got marbles for brains, but you're sharp as a tack. You undermine your talent when you march down Bimbo Lane with all the rest of 'em."

"Thanks—I think—but I'm not doing any bimbo-oriented roles any more. But so what if I wanted to? Who knows, maybe I'll want to do a great big nude scene again in the future. I never say never."

"And I'm sure you'll look fantastic, but what would you be proving? That you're hot and desirable? You don't have to take your clothes off for anyone to see that, Cal."

Callie felt as though she should be angry, but, then, Mitch wasn't trying to insult her—he was complimenting her. Even though the compliment felt more like a critique, it was an honest opinion. "I haven't looked at it that way before, Mitch."

He shrugged. "Just the way I see it, that's all. I don't mean to preach. So, what looks good? I was thinkin' 'bout the prawns."

They both chose crustaceans as their entree, but Callie was too busy feasting on the Hick Prick to notice her food. He was disciplined ("I may have a beer on weekends, but on school nights, I stay clean"); flirtatious (half-way through dinner, he said, "You know, you're lookin' a little lonely over there. If you wanna sit next to me, I promise not to bite." She happily obliged); and, as the night wore on, candid ("You know what I still haven't gotten used to? The mass amounts of coke in L.A. and how it's so casually passed around. I'll be out and someone always says, 'Want a line?' 'Want to do a bump?' 'Dude, got any blow?' It's bizarre to me, like it's no different from sippin' a cocktail—it's on the same level. Me, I have no tolerance for drug users. My older sister died of an overdose and it was the single worst time of my entire life.") From all she could detect, Mitch was a stand-up, all-American guy with one lone weakness: sugar. He allowed himself one spoonful of Callie's sorbet.

"You like Jimmy Durante?" Mitch said while they drove home. He turned the radio up a notch.

"I don't know much of his music," she said.

"Before we moved overseas, my Gramps used to babysit me all the time. He was always listenin' to Jimmy, Ella Fitzgerald, Vic Damone—that kinda thing. I'm fond of a lot of older music 'cause of Gramps."

"How old were you when you and your family moved?"

"Oh, let's see, I was twelve when we skipped over the pond. Kickin' and screamin', I was, too. All I wanted to do was play baseball and go fishin'. I didn't like this big change, and having to learn German and French and all that. But I guess if I never lived there, I never would have become an actor."

"Oh?"

"One of my teachers in Germany introduced me to theatre. I was hooked." Mitch laid his hand on Callie's knee. The heat from his hand made her twitch like an overactive radiator. She wished he would move his hand further up north but he kept a gentlemanly distance from her upper thigh.

"Want to come in?" Callie said. They were on her doorstep, seconds away from her bed.

"I do, but I'm not."

"Why?"

"Because I already promised to run a buddy of mine to LAX—my roommate. Housemate, actually. He's catchin' the Red Eye."

"I see." Couldn't the guy call a cab, Callie thought? Why couldn't Mitch be a thoughtless asshole?

"I'll gladly take a raincheck, though." He tipped her chin up to his mouth and kissed her in deep, lingering mouthfuls.

"Just come in," Callie murmured when he came back up for air. "You'll still have time to pick up your friend."

"Why be rushed?" he whispered before kissing her again. "We have all the time in the world. Let's do this again soon, okay?"

"Yes, let's. Sooner than later."

"You got it." He paused to give her one last peck. And then he was gone.

24

"Where the hell is my flatiron?"

Luciana wielded through clothes and toiletries, to no avail. The normally immaculately dressed supermodel had a 30% off sticker glued to her butt, a testament to her frazzled state. She flew around the room like a possessed hornet.

"I think I saw it in the powder room," Callie said.

Luciana gave a quizzical stare. "What was I doing with it in the powder room? Oh, that's right. My outlet blew and I used the one downstairs. Of course!" She raced downstairs and sprung back up them just as fast with iron in hand. "I always wait until the last moment to pack for the airport. Always. And I always drive myself crazy, every time." Her bun came loose and the chocolate waves spilled down her arms. She pinned it back up and said, "My ride is coming in a half hour and so far, I only have three suitcases ready to go."

"What are you wearing to the wedding?" Callie asked from the corner of Luci's bedroom. She was sprawled on the floor, on her stomach, nursing a glass of Pinot Grigio.

"I seriously have no idea—none. What does one wear for a big, European royal wedding?" Luci said. "Ball gown, suit, cocktail dress...I seriously haven't a clue. So I'm bringing all of the above, and then some."

"I just assumed you've been to one of these things before."

"Me? No. I hail from Canada, not nobility." Luci rifled through a shopping bag. "*Hollywood Hotspot* arranged a fitting for me last week and I chose this amazing, one-shouldered Valentino and a few strapless Marchesa numbers. But, get this—the stylist calls me today, last minute, and said she was just told the palace doesn't allow bare shoulders. So I had a few hours to shop for a whole week's worth of outfits. Insanity!"

"Still," Callie sighed. "It sounds all shades of glamorous."

"To me, it sounds like it's nothing short of a three-ring circus," Luci sniffed. "It's positively creepy the Duke has invited so much media. Not just to the parties and reception, mind you, but to the ceremony itself. Some things should be left sacred. I doubt I'll ever tie the knot, but if I do, I sure won't let the whole world snoop in. Then again, the Duke would make his cat ring bearer if it meant an extra headline."

"That sounds like a lot of people I know here. Maybe the Duke should consider a career in Hollywood," Callie chirped.

"I dare say he's already tried." Luci zipped her last suitcase. "Alright, I think that's everything. Callie, I want you to know how grateful I am for you opening up your home to me. I never forget a kindness, you know."

"No problem," Callie said. "I'm glad to be of help. When you come back—"

"That's the thing, I'm not coming back. I mean, I'll be back to collect a few things, but I found a new home."

Callie blinked. "What do you mean?"

"I've been house hunting and found a place on Benedict Canyon."

"You did? Wow, so soon."

"Yes. I signed the papers this morning. It's a lovely Tudor property, furnished, with a little garden and rose bushes. Adorable, really, makes me feel like I'm in the countryside."

"I see. That's great, Luci. Congrats." Callie scowled and slugged her wine.

"Thank you." Luci jumped as a horn sounded from outside. She rushed to the bedroom window. "The town car is here. They're early; they weren't supposed to get here until eight. I'll buzz him in. Can you help me haul these downstairs?"

Callie lugged a suitcase to the front door. She poured herself another glass of vino after taking a swig straight from the bottle.

"Take all of these, please. Load them up," she heard Luci tell the driver in the foyer. *Rats*, Callie thought; *alone again.* She had fully expected—and wanted—Luciana to keep her company longer. Tyler had been completely wrong— the girls got along just fine and enjoyed an easy rapport with one another. And if she had planned on parking her Canadian butt for an extended period, Callie was going to ask her to chip in for rent. Alas, no cigar. Greener pastures awaited Luciana in Benedict Canyon. Damn it all.

"Callie? Callie, where are you?" Luci wandered in the kitchen. "There you are. Okay, I'm off. Hugs."

Callie gave her a squeeze; she hated good-byes. Always had. She'd rather just forgo them altogether. "Safe travels, Luci. Call me when you get back?"

"Sure. Catch you later." Luci bolted out the door. Evidently, she wasn't much of a good-bye girl, either.

Callie wandered, sluggish, up the stairs. Her bare feet boomed a hollow thud that echoed through the corridor.

"With the Duke of Denmark set to marry American socialite, Frederique DeWitt, in just a few short days, the excitement swirling the nuptials has reached a feverish pitch," boomed the living room TV.

Pinot sloshed on the floor as Callie pattered down the hall and checked out the segment.

"Our own Luciana Dickerson, the most recent member to join our *Hollywood Hotspot* team, will be on hand to cover all the festivities and fashion. Luciana certainly knows a thing or two about being fashionable; she's been seen accessorizing hottie actor Chad Blake-Shepard's arm and for the past decade, she's been one of the biggest faces of high fashion." A video montage of Luci's most glamorous career moments flashed on the screen: Luci gyrating down a catwalk; Luci, soaking-wet, rolling on a Caribbean beach; Luci arriving at a New York City gala on the arm of Dominic Augustine. Callie wondered if the willowy stunner had a bad or unexceptional angle and realized that no, she did not. Her perfectly formed features were always photogenic.

"And now, we jump to Emily Ackerman as she takes *Hollywood Hotspot* on a tour of Joan Van Ark's drop-dead-gorgeous mansion."

Emily. Oh, Emily....Lonely and tipsy, Callie resolved to call her. That very minute. She located her number and dialed. Rrring. Rrring...

25

A paralyzing thought ran through Callie—what on earth was she going to say to Emily? And, East Coast time, it was eleven at night. Maybe she should hang up and try her in the morning when she was good and sober rather than—

"Hello?" said the voice on the other end.

Damn. Too late. Callie cleared her throat. "Hi. Emily?"

"Yes. Who's this?"

"It's Callie."

Pause. Then came a peppy, "Hi, there, Callie. I didn't expect to hear from you."

"Yeah, well...if this is a bad time, I can—"

"No, no. I was just wrapping up my studies for the night. So..."

"So..." Callie echoed and then blurted, "So how long have you known about me? How did you find out about me?"

Emily exhaled. "Ever since my dad's death last year, I've been interested in finding my birth parents. My mother—my adoptive mother, but my only mother, as far as I'm concerned—has been really supportive in helping with my research. So I've been doing some investigating and discovered we're related."

"Have you talked to my mom—er, your, our mom—yet?"

"Well, I, um—I don't know how much I should say..."

"All of it," Callie blurted. "I assure you, Emily, you cannot shock me any more than you already have."

"Okay. Well, yes, I have talked with her. Several times. I contacted you both around the same time—I think I wrote to her in late February and you in March—but I didn't expect to get very far. Virginia wrote back a few weeks later and we've been speaking on and off for a couple months. She's been very kind."

Huh? A couple months? Callie stood corrected—it was possible for her to be further shocked. "This is all news to me. She hasn't mentioned any of this," Callie said.

"I, uh...I don't think she wants you to know, and I didn't tell her I contacted you."

"What?" Callie said. "Why wouldn't you tell her you wrote me? Why hide something like that? This doesn't make sense."

"Geez, this is awkward," sighed Emily. "Okay, here goes: Virginia has mentioned you many times—said she has a daughter from her second marriage but she'd appreciate it if I didn't contact you, that this was something you didn't know about and she wanted to keep it private. I didn't tell her I had already e-mailed you, because, at this point, I figured you weren't interested in talking to me. So why worry her and rock the boat?"

"I sort of see your point."

"That's why I'm really surprised you called. Months have passed and I didn't expect to hear from you at all. As a matter of fact, I didn't expect to hear from either of you, let alone both of you."

"I'm chock full of surprises," Callie mumbled.

"Callie, look; I haven't meant to upset you. That's not my goal, I swear, and I don't mean to cause friction between you and your mother."

"Too late to worry about that."

"Yes, I suppose it is. You know, Virginia has really helped me out—she's answered a lot of questions I've had and I'm very grateful."

"Such as? What kind of questions?" Callie was anxious to cut through the grizzle and get straight to the meat.

"Let's see, where to start...She was a single woman, just nineteen, and didn't have the means to support a child. Said she strongly considered it, but it just wasn't feasible, especially with her in college and her boyfriend no longer in the picture. And her parents were very conservative and pressured her into giving me—"

"Whoa, Nelly," warbled Callie. "Back up a little. Boyfriend? She had back to back marriages and I was born when she was twenty-one. That much, I do know. So what do you mean, 'boyfriend'?"

"She got pregnant by a college boyfriend, before she was ever married. Someone named Casey."

"Noooo," Callie said. "My mom would never do that— she'd never have an illegitimate kid. There's just no way."

"It's true."

"No, I don't believe it. Tell me something else. Prove it."

If Emily was offended, her tone didn't reveal it. She said, "Alright, then. Her parents died in a car accident the year after I was born, she married an abusive guy named Jim—they only lasted a few months—and then she left him and married your father, Alex."

Jim. That was the bastard's name. "Jesus Christ. You know more about her than I do."

"As hard as it's been for me, it's been even more difficult for her. All of this dredging up the past—none of it has been easy for her."

"It hasn't been easy for any of us," Callie sputtered. "You think it's easy to just wake up one day and be told out of left field that your life isn't what you thought it was? I get this random e-mail, making this crazy claim, and I don't know what to think! You know, it seems awfully selfish to just crash my world because you've decided it's in your best interest. Stone-cold and selfish."

"I'm sorry," Emily said calmly, her voice soft and sincere. "I'm not here to cause trouble, but I want to know about my past and where I came from—who I am and how I got to be me. I think I've got the right."

Callie slurped her wine. "But don't you get it? The timing, the secrecy—it's all...all...shady. It's wrong, all of it. And I don't know what to make of any of it."

"We have to start somewhere, don't we? Personally, I look at it as the beginning. I have to tell you, I've been following your career a few years now—way before I knew we were related. So you can imagine the shock when I found out. I just want to congratulate you on everything you've accomplished. It's really something, what you've made of your life."

"Thanks. But it doesn't really take much brain power—not like getting a Master's does. What's your major?"

"Psychology." Emily laughed. "And yes, the irony is not lost. I've always loved psychology and began working on my masters last year. My life is pretty quiet, not half as interesting as yours, I'm sure. But I'm happy and healthy and my family has been wonderful throughout this whole ordeal. And, I have to say, you're lucky to have such a supportive mother; Virginia is really proud of you."

Callie's brows rose. "She is? In those words, she said, 'I'm proud of Callie'?"

"Yep, she's mentioned it many times. That's surprising?"

"Mom has never been the most open with her feelings. Believe me, she'll be the first to criticize something if she doesn't like it, but when it comes to divulging her innermost thoughts—that's a totally different story. We haven't had the closest relationship. More often than not, we've fought like cats and dogs."

"Oh, I see. I don't know the ins and outs of your relationship..."

"It's complicated," Callie added.

"But I do know she really loves you."

Silence. Callie broke it by saying, "Nice meeting you, Emily, but I should—um, you know—get going."

"Of course, of course. It was nice meeting you, too, Callie. Oh, and how did you want to handle the situation with Virginia? She's supposed to call me sometime this week. Should I tell her we've talked? Or should I hold off? It's up to you."

"I don't care. Say whatever you want."

"Whatever is best for you, Callie, just let me know."

"I don't care. I really do not care." Callie's patience was wearing thin, in part thanks to Emily's perkiness.

"Alright. Well, I hope we can talk again soon and maybe even meet one day—we have so much to catch up on. Wouldn't that be nice?"

Callie was in no mood to rush into sisterhood; their conversation, exacerbated by Cakebread Cellars, overwhelmed her. Forgoing a farewell, she hung up, cradled her face in her hands, and wept.

26

"How could you do this to me?" Callie cried and shifted her weight to one hip. "How could you do this to me? How could you do this to me?" No matter how she enunciated the words, she just wasn't connecting with the material. She reread the scene, the most pivotal and emotionally challenging in Nanette's entire screenplay. Nope. No use; she wasn't on her game. Last night's Emily convo distracted her, try as she did to shove it to the back of her conscience. And her noggin—her poor noggin pounded like a piston (snap to it, Aleve!).

To hell with it. Mitch would be by soon to pick her up for lunch, their second date. Although a matinee screening didn't really feel like a date—something about the afternoon wasn't romantic and sexy enough to be considered a full-blown date. Technically, though, it was, and she was more than a little excited. Only one thing puzzled her—why wasn't he tripping over himself to crawl up her skirt? Most men weren't lackadaisical when it came to pursuing sex, but Mitch's pace was decidedly low-key. His Southern nature, perhaps. Sometimes it was as though his even-keeled temperament bordered on disinterest, but it only fanned

Callie's flame. She longed to break his cool. Somewhere hidden beneath the collected exterior was a buck wild cowboy, and long ago she had set her mind to making his blood boil.

"Hey, good lookin'," said Mitch as Callie swooped into the front seat. His face hadn't seen a razor in three days and the stubble carried a subtle look of "bad boy"—a low caloric version. Diet Badass.

"What's shakin', bacon?"

"You," he grinned. "Been looking forward to seein' you."

"You have, have you?" she cooed.

"I most surely have. I would have asked you out for the evening rather than the daytime if it weren't for my acting class tonight."

"That's what I should do! I've been struggling with a scene for my new film and I need to schedule an appointment with Deirdre Coleman. Thanks for reminding me."

"If I could be of any help, I wouldn't mind lookin' it over with you. Not that I'm confusing myself for Laurence Olivier or anything."

Callie giggled at his dead-pan reference to a previous spat. "I'd love that. I'm after all the input I can get. So, what's this movie we're catching?"

"It's a screening of a pseudo Hitchcockian flick playing at Sundance Cinemas. It won a bunch of awards at Venice and I thought it would be worth checkin' out."

"Perfect, I love suspense. *Rear Window* is my second favorite movie, after *Gilda*."

"You're kiddin'. I'm usually not one for redheads, but I was always crazy about her, too. My gramps was stationed in Hollywood during the second World War and got to meet her." A bum pushing a shopping cart darted in front of traffic and Mitch laid on his horn.

"Your grandpa met Rita Hayworth? I'm jealous."

"And Orson Welles. Met them at a taping of a radio show. Said she was prettier in person but didn't think much of him." Mitch swung into the underground parking garage. He kept a respectable distance from Callie. He didn't put his arm around her, didn't try holding her hand. But his eyes held a naughty glint and she couldn't help but feel a gravitational pull. Sexual static cling.

They stood in line at the concession stand, behind a waify strawberry blonde.

"I don't want any butter on it," the girl said in a loud, Alabaman twang. "But if you can put just a teensy-weensy bit of margarine on it, whatever is low in fat, I'd be most grateful."

"We don't carry margarine, ma'am," the concession boy said. "It's just this standard, buttery topping."

"You don't? Okay, then, just put a tad bit of butter in the middle of it—like, layer it. I don't want it on top because then it's just a pile of grease and it sticks under my nails. And my friend, here, wants...wait, where did she go? She must be in the ladies' room. That's it for me, just the popcorn." She turned around and her eyes met Mitch's.

"Hi, Charlene," said Mitch.

"H-hi, Mitch. How've you been?"

"Great. And you?"

"Same. Working hard with a coach to get rid of my accent. I'm doing good, though."

"This is my friend, Callie."

"Yeah, I know who she is." Charlene looked Callie up and down before turning back to Mitch. "I shot an episode of *Pilgrim's Posse* last week."

"Oh, yeah?" Mitch said. "I guest starred on that show a few months ago. What part did you play?"

"I played a Vegas showgirl."

"Great. Guest star or co-star?"

Charlene's blue eyes darted west to east, then back to west. "Um, I didn't really have many lines. But I got to really act, know what I mean? I was able to showcase my skills without having to say much and having words get in the way."

Mitch smirked. "I get it. You were background, you mean. An extra."

"Um, well, not really. I may have had a line or two, I don't really remember, but I'm not sure if they're gonna use it or..." Charlene's voice trailed off and she strained her neck. "Where in tarnation is Kim? 'Scuse me, I have to go find my friend."

"My ex," Mitch whispered as Charlene scurried off, sans popcorn.

"I gathered. I thought you said you prefer brunettes?" She stepped up to the counter and ordered a slew of munchies.

"Love 'em. Charlene was the first non-brunette I've dated and I'm pretty certain my last, too. I'll stick to the dark side of things."

"Seems like a piece of work."

"You have no idea. Funny how sweet she seemed at first. Like night and day. I was dating Miss Apple Pie one minute and the next I wake to find a cheat, a ragin' lunatic."

"Good riddance," said Callie. "I'm sure she'll fit in L.A. just fine."

They took a seat inside the theatre, on the opposite side of the room as Charlene.

The film, with its violent twists, sent Callie's pulse into overdrive—she jumped several times and even let out a yelp. Mitch chuckled at her but she didn't mind; it gave her an excuse to scoot closer and hold onto his ripped arm. Mmmm. *This is nice*, she thought. *I could get used to this.* She rested her head on his shoulder. Maybe matinees weren't so shoddy after all.

27

"Your breasts are very nice. The shape, the proportions. For being so small-boned, you have a good amount of tissue to work with. Your left is a little smaller than your right, but that's fairly common and can be corrected. I'd use an implant about 20 ccs larger than the right. I'm thinking nothing more than a small to medium C-cup, unless you're going for the Dolly look, in which case I'm sure you know I'm not the man for the job. I always want to attain a natural look. Now, don't kid yourself, your breasts won't be entirely symmetrical, but I'll make them as similar as possible."

"Just how symmetrical can you make them?" Callie asked Dr. Coop.

"Let's put it this way: they didn't start off as identical twins and so they won't end up identical twins, but they'll be sisters—two very close sisters." Dr. Coop squeezed the base of Callie's breast. "I'd recommend a periareolar incision. You have a nice sized nipple to work with."

Callie made a face. "I was kind of hoping to go in through the armpit."

"I'm not fond of the transaxillary incision. It doesn't allow for the most accurate placement. I've had the best results with the inframammary and periareolar, but I find that this border here"—he used his marker to make a dotted line at the bottom of her nipple—"hides the scar extremely well."

She caught her reflection in the full-length mirror behind Dr. Coop. *What a sight I am.* Nothing on her upper half but a flimsy paper gown. It gaped in the center to reveal her little buds marked up and down with dark blue ink. Not her best fashion moment.

Dr. Coop reached into a cabinet and extracted two different implants. "Feel the difference. One is saline, one is silicone. I don't think I have to ask which one feels better."

"Silicone for sure," said Callie. She quashed the squishy device. "Is it durable?"

Dr. Coop took the implant from her hand and threw it against the wall. "A semi-truck could drive over one of these. The newer models have improved by leaps and bounds since I first started practicing. The wonders of technology. They're not lifetime devices, it's possible to have a faulty implant just like a tire or anything else, but chances are, these buggers aren't going anywhere. Whenabouts are you looking to do this?"

"August or September. As soon as I finish up a movie." She wasn't taking a chance pissing off Nanette and Paul. Her augmentation would have to wait until the end of the summer. She planned on keeping her decision to herself; comments from the peanut gallery were both unwanted and annoying. Who was anyone else to make a judgment about what was best for her ta-tas, anyway? Those people didn't have a clue; they should try working in an industry where Malibu Barbie perfection was not so much a plus as it was a requirement. An unspoken requirement. A poke here, a nip there, a tuck and a snip everywhere. Perfect, perfect, perfect. All the body parts in La-La Land had to be in buoyant, gleaming, taut condition, otherwise a crafty tramp would round the bend and sneak up on you, snatching that potential Oscar-winning role from underneath your Brian Atwoods. The maintenance and expectations were exhausting but what choice did she have? Callie inwardly groaned but she vowed to stay in tip-top form. Naysayers be damned.

Dr. Coop wiped the ink off her chest and inspected her face. "Your nose is looking better and better. The swelling can take years to go away fully, especially at the tip. But just looking at you right up close, you'd never know you had any swelling left or, more importantly, that you even had anything done. No one would ever know."

"Hopefully you won't say the same thing after my implants," Callie said, half-jokingly. "I want two perky mounds, not too big, not too small. That's all. Just a little more than a handful."

"Mmm-hmmm," Dr. Coop said absently as he scribbled in her chart. A framed sign next to him on the wall read: Perfection is unattainable, but striving for perfection is always within reach.

Callie wasn't so sure about that; at the rate Dr. Coop was charging, (whatever happened to a returning patient discount?) she expected diamond-threaded sutures in her incisions. She dressed and Dr. Coop's longtime secretary, Bethanny, whisked her away.

"You said you're looking for August/September? Let's see what he has open." Bethanny flipped through a ledger. "The doctor's usually very busy then, lots of sprucing up to do before school starts...He has a slot on August 29 and one on September 22."

"Nothing in between?" Callie asked.

"Unfortunately, no, everything else is booked. Oh, wait, I take that back—he also has September 18."

Callie ran her tongue along her lower lip. She better play it safe and stick with September. And even numbers, too; odds made her nervous. "Let's do September 18."

"September 18th it is. I'm going to need to hold your place with either a credit card or check. Half now and the other half is due two weeks prior to surgery, at your pre-op."

Bethanny swiped Callie's Black Card.

Callie exited through the waiting room. A pretty, petite blonde flipped through a magazine and Callie did a double-take. Was that Candice's friend, Jackie? It had been two years since they had last seen each other and she wasn't sure.

The girl looked up. "Hi, Callie."

"Hey, Jackie. How have you been?"

"Not bad. I figured it was time to upgrade my girls. I had them done a few years ago but I'm bored with them. I need something bigger. I have the va, but I need more voom. What's life without the voom?"

Callie stared at Jackie's thirty-seven inch chest. If that wasn't 'voom', what was? "I haven't had the chance to personally thank you for referring me to Dr. Coop. I'm really pleased. Great call, Jackie."

"Isn't his work insane? I'm glad I could help. What are you in for this time?"

"I'm just here for a, uh, check-up." Callie patted her nose. "He wanted to make sure all is well."

Jackie frowned. "That's no fun. If I don't tweak something at least once a year, I get antsy. Last year it was cheeks and a little lipo. It just makes me feel good, you know? Like therapy, only with a scalpel. That's so L.A., right? But I'm a native, so whatever—just how we do. Have you talked to Candice lately?"

"No. Have you?"

"Yeah. She just sent her invitations out."

"Invitations to what?"

"She didn't tell you? Wow, it really has been a while since you guys have talked. She's getting married. Yep, end of September."

"Married? Candice?" Callie couldn't control the shock in her voice.

"She sure is. I don't know much about the guy, except that he's a trust fund baby from New York. They only met a few months ago, but she seems really happy, so good for her."

"Jackie?" Bethanny stood in the doorway. "Hi, dear. Dr. Coop is ready for you."

"Awesome. Catch you later, Callie. Therapy calls." Jackie flew out of the chair so fast she stumbled in her Uggs.

28

"My dear, how are you?" Nanette grasped Callie's shoulders and kissed both cheeks. "Thank you for coming to meet me. I'm still jet lagged, I'm afraid, and hardly in the mood to battle my way through traffic. You're looking lovely, but maybe a little too tan. You've been laying out, no?"

"I only laid out at my pool for an hour yesterday," said Callie.

"Blech," Nanette spat. "Are you trying to make me pull my hair out? Stay out of that horrid sun now until the film wraps, I beseech you. It's only until August. You can handle that, can't you? Remember, I need you to be a porcelain doll and you're only making the makeup artists' job more difficult. Come, I need fresh air. My room is so stuffy."

The women exited Nanette's suite and made their way to the rooftop cabana at the L'Ermitage. Mrs. Vernadeau had arrived earlier in the week for pre-production meetings and last-minute casting changes.

Nanette inhaled deeply and surveyed the sun-splashed mountains in the distance. "Ahh, isn't this lovely? What a view. And see? You can avoid the sun and still enjoy the marvelous outdoors."

"It's gorgeous. I don't even feel like I'm in L.A.," Callie said. "And I'll be good, Nanette, I promise. On the plus side, I wear SPF every day."

"Good girl. I've always taken wonderful care of my skin, since I was a young girl. It's my one saving grace." Nanette patted her creamy cheeks. "Tell me how your fitting with Marisa went this morning."

"Just fine," Callie said. "She's very nice, too. Everyone is."

"My wardrobe team is the best, aren't they? If I want a particular dress—a chartreuse Givenchy duchess satin from 1955—Marisa will scour the ends of the earth and bring me not one, but three."

"I especially love the vintage tweed suits and felt hats."

"You have the features and figure to do them proud. I'm sorry I could not make it. I was in a production meeting for literally the entire day, otherwise I would have been there." The Frenchwoman yawned. "I need some coffee, I think. And a pastry, something to hold me over until a late dinner with my cinematographer. Would you care for anything? No? Oh, good, I see a waiter coming our way." A staff member waltzed by and she placed her order.

"Is your husband in town, too, Nanette?" asked Callie.

"No, Roger won't be here until the first week of production. He's taking care of some business in Paris. You'll love him, he's very easy-going, very light and always telling jokes. I'm much more serious. I'm the bad cop, you could say. But he's been my partner in everything for so long—in business, in life, in love—that frankly, I don't know where I'd be without him. May I ask, do you have a special someone in your life, Callie? You do, you do! Look at that smile on your face."

"I'm casually dating someone," Callie grinned. "Sort of, kind of."

Nanette laughed her signature throaty warble. "I love it. What is life without love, eh? What is the lucky gentleman's story?"

"He's an actor," Callie began sheepishly. "Mitch Gracie is his name. He's picking me up for dinner this evening. And he's a year older than me, from the South. And he's a great kisser, too. We've only gone out twice but so far, it's been really nice."

Nanette's eyes danced. "Good. Let him woo you. Women nowadays are far too eager. A man has to court you—they want a bit of a challenge, to romance you. The good ones do, anyway."

"He's different," Callie smiled. "Not your run-of-the-mill L.A. guy. I couldn't stand him at first. I found him so annoying, but we had instant chemistry."

"Sexual tension is often that way. The man finds the woman annoying and the woman finds the man even more annoying and then, voila! A love match is born."

"What's different about Mitch is his pace. He has this kick-back, I'll-see-you-when-I-see-you attitude that's intriguing.

We've taken things pretty slow, and I've never taken things slow. All my relationships have moved fast. Too fast, maybe, looking back, so this is new territory for me."

"This is good, then. This means you are maturing. And, if I may say so, it is very American to speed everything up. And why? Why rush?"

"That's exactly what Mitch told me. He said he's not in any rush."

Nanette pushed the sleeves of her gauzy blouse up over her elbows. "He sounds smart. Now a fling—okay, I understand rushing with a fling. But anything genuine, something with substance you want to last longer than a quick blink— that is worth taking your time. And it's titillating to go slow. How sexy would a striptease be if the girl took everything off in ten seconds? Same in love."

The waiter dropped her order off and Nanette dug into her Pain au Chocolat, tearing off bites in a dainty, delicate fashion. She had more grace eating with her fingers than most people armed with a knife and fork. "I cannot believe filming begins in just three weeks. Most of it will be done here, as you know, but several locations in Detroit have been added."

"Detroit? I thought we were going to New York?"

"That was the original plan, but to keep production costs down, we're switching to Detroit. It will be made to look just like New York, it's done all the time. If it were solely up to me and I had free range, we would of course be in New York, but, alas, I'm just the wee director and one of five producers. It will be fine, we'll make due. I'm so excited for you to meet your leading man, Pierre, at the read-through. He's wonderful, so talented, so handsome. Between you and me, the studio refused to hire him at first because he's had his share of addictions, but he assured me those days are far behind him. I've got a lot riding on him, but he's my Roland—the only actor I ever saw as Roland, down to the last hair on his head. How are things going with the acting coach? In your last e- mail, you mentioned you've been preparing with Deirdre Coleman."

Callie sat up straighter and puffed out her Wonderbra-ed chest. "I have, and believe you me, you'll be pleased. I'm really preparing. Deirdre's been working with me for hours at a time. Short of whipping me, she's doing everything to get me in fine Streep form. Mitch has given me some really good pointers, too—he had a chance to look over the script with me before he left."

"Careful not to overdo it. Sometimes an actor works too hard at something and it ruins the magic. One of the qualities I noticed about you is your primitiveness."

Primitive? Callie grimaced. "That doesn't sound very attractive, Nanette."

"Nonsense. I'm not calling you a primate, I'm saying you have this organic spark—it's real, it's feral, it's the essence of you. It's one of your strongest qualities as an actor.

Whatever turmoil is going on there—" Nanette pointed at Callie's heart "—translates onscreen. Please, don't spoil your magic."

Nanette explained things in a way that made Callie feel special; she couldn't help but wonder what kind of a person she would have been if she had grown up with a mother like Nanette. Her thoughts often veered on the subject whenever she met a nurturing older woman, someone she clicked with, with the commonality of mutual respect. Virginia had never given proper respect to Callie's opinions and individuality. Thank God for her grandmother; Esme made up for what Virginia lacked.

Nanette ordered another pot of coffee as the sun began its retreat. Callie excused herself and said, "I have some work to do before my date. I'm creating a charity in a friend's honor and I had no idea how much it entailed. It's incredibly detailed but I'm on a mission."

"That's wonderful," Nanette said. "I want to hear more about it. Perhaps I can help in some way. We will talk soon, I'll call."

It was a glorious seventy degrees and Callie lowered the top of her BMW for her ride home. *You just can't beat this*, she thought. Without a doubt, the weather was her favorite part of the city—better than the ocean, the shopping, the good-looking men. One ray of sun held more charm than the town's entire acting community, herself included. A rickety white Honda caught her eye as she rounded her driveway. The beater was parked close to her gate—a little too close. She tried to make out the driver in her rearview mirror but his windows were tinted. She pressed the button on her visor. The wrought iron gate parted just as a man hopped out of the Honda. He was Hobbit- like, with long, greasy hair, and bolted to her car.

"You Callie Lambert?" he said.

"Who wants to know?"

He tossed a manila envelope in her lap. "You've been served."

29

The man darted off and Callie picked her jaw off the floorboard. What the hell? She waited to open the envelope until she was safely inside her house.

Defamation. She was being sued for defamation of character. The petitioner was none other than Stephanie Ann Schueller and she was asking the court for ten million bones. A monsoon of panic flooded Callie; her lungs constricted and she became dizzy. The sensation trickled down her extremities, with the familiar prick of "pins and needles" on her fingertips. She thought of Dr. Freisch and his cognitive therapy approach. Frame it, she told herself. It's all in how you frame it. But she couldn't find a way to put a ten million dollar lawsuit into context; where was the silver lining in that?

Sister Xani to the rescue. If ever there was a time...She downed a pill and phoned Paul.

"Hey, there, young lady, I was just thinking about you. Ron Finkelstein's office called and was wondering—"

"Paul, you got a minute?"

"Sure, I do. I'm always all ears."

"No, I mean, in person. You still at the office?"

"Yes, I'll be here another hour. What's this all about, Callie?"

"I'll be right over." Callie plowed through Beverly Hills and made it to his office in fifteen minutes.

Ursula looked up from her desk as Callie breezed in. "Hi, Miss Callie, how are ya?"

"Never better." Callie whisked past Ursula and flew into Paul's room. "Schueller is suing me, Paul."

"What are you talking about?" Paul said.

She threw the papers on his desk. "This is what I'm talking about. I was just served. By the greasiest, most vile looking troll, too, I may add."

Paul studied the documents. "What's this interview you gave to *The QT*? How come I've never heard about this before?"

"Remember I mentioned attending a premiere with my friend, Luciana? A reporter there kept asking me questions, trying to rattle my cage," Callie sighed.

"That's what reporters do. The bigger question is, why did you answer them?" Paul said.

"Well, I just figured—"

"You never have to answer any questions. It's not like you're being interrogated for a crime and they're going to haul you off to prison if you don't tell them who you're wearing or what your favorite fucking color is." Paul closed the office door. "Why didn't you just get your photo taken and steer clear of the reporters?"

"I didn't think it was a big deal, and I could handle things," she said with a shrug.

Paul pressed his lips together. "Look, that's what I'm here for, to shield you from riffraff so you don't have to worry about putting your foot in your mouth. And as long as we're on the subject, a publicist would have been a good idea yesterday."

"I told you, I don't trust them," Callie spat. "PR people are scum. That idiot you introduced me to, Kat, was the worst idea ever."

"I see, so I'm somehow to blame for this mess? Just because you didn't get along with Kat Killian doesn't mean all publicists are shit, Callie. Now look at you; you've got a ten million dollar lawsuit on your hands, because you thought you could handle everything on your own."

"Gee, Paul, thanks for being so comforting."

"Callie, I'm upset because I'm frustrated—this could have been so easily avoided. If I had been there, I guarantee this wouldn't have happened. And that's my job, filtering bullshit so you can focus on your job—acting. Did you really say these things on camera? That the reason Schueller got the part is because she slept with the director and copied herself after Gabrielle?"

"Yeah, I did," Callie said defiantly.

Paul threw his hands up in the air. "Well, young lady, congratulations—you sank your own ship. I'm always on your side, but with this one..."

Callie clenched both fists. "Oh, really? Is that so?"

"Really, and yes, that is so," Paul fired back.

"Okay, then, Paul, okay—let me get this straight: you mean to tell me you were on my side when you never even got me an audition for *The Foreign Affair*? Every other actress under the sun apparently tried out, but, nope, not me—and I would have aced it! Is that what you call being on my side?"

Paul wrinkled his brows. "What are you talking about?"

"At The Chateau Marmont. After you went home, Jack Kushner approached me and we had a long conversation."

"I'm sure that was entertaining," he scoffed. "That guy's reputation is more soiled than a dirty diaper."

"He said he couldn't believe you never had me audition for Nanette back when she was first casting her movie. He thought you were slacking off and not looking out for my best interests."

Paul crossed his arms and stood straighter. "Kushner said that? Let me tell you something—Jack Kushner is a slime ball of an agent who'd sell his own grandmother for a nickel. We're talking about a guy who used to say he worked in the entertainment industry while he stocked videos at Blockbuster. You mean to say you doubt my integrity, my commitment to your career? That's what he thinks or what both of you think?"

"Jack brought it up and it got me thinking. Is it true what he said—that every girl under the age of thirty auditioned for the part?"

"A great deal of girls auditioned, yes," Paul conceded.

"Then why didn't I? Why didn't you go to bat for me? I'm not paying you to sit back and wait for something to drift along!"

Paul shook his beet-red face in disbelief. "You are something else, Callie. Something else. You've got a lot of nerve, and it's thoroughly insulting, but if you want to go there, that suits me fine. I'll tell you something—I did go to bat for you. Several times, as a matter of fact. When I first heard Nanette was casting her movie, who do you think the first person was I suggested for the lead? You. And when she said 'No, Callie seems cheap'—her words, not mine—who do you think tried to convince her she was wrong? That's right, I did. For months, I called her every week, pushing her to audition you, but she wasn't interested. Nanette is one tough broad—a lady through and through, but if her mind is dead set against something, forget it. And she had her mind dead set against giving you a chance. Didn't matter she hadn't seen any of your work—she was put off by your Manx Murder and *Coquette* associations. I just didn't have the heart to tell you. Lucky for you, she caught *NCA!* in the middle of the night and realized, lo and behold, old buddy Paul was right—Callie Lambert would be perfect as the lead. And it just so happened you two were in France at the same time and that lazy, incompetent guy, Paul, thought to arrange a meeting. So, tell me now, Cal, who has your best interests at heart—Kushner or me?"

Callie looked down at her ballet flats and Paul took a deep breath.

"I've always given my all, Callie, nothing less than one hundred and ten percent."

"Paul, I'm sorry I offended you. I didn't know any of this, otherwise I never would have said these things."

"And I'm awfully sorry about the lawsuit—better give Barletta a call as soon as you can, if you haven't already. I don't mean to come down hard on you, I just want the best for you and I've done my absolute best for you, always, but if you're not satisfied, it's probably best we part ways."

"But—"

"I apologize for cutting this short, but I'm supposed to meet a client in a half hour. It's his first red carpet and he's pretty nervous."

"Can we please talk later?" she said. "After we get a chance to cool off a little and think things through."

"I think that's wise." Paul packed his attaché and avoided eye contact.

Callie left the office calmer than when she had arrived but with a heart much heavier.

30

Of all the times for Earl Barletta to be out of town, he chose the last week of May, the single worst week of Callie's professional life. She had him on speaker phone while she drove home (for the second time that hour).

"I decided to surprise the wife for our anniversary and take her to a resort," Earl said. "The Phoenician in Scottsdale—ever been?"

"No," Callie said.

"I'll tell you, the service here is top of the line. I'm a very picky rascal but I am much impressed. We had a mud wrap earlier that was out of this world, the best my skin has ever felt. Amazing, the technique this gal used."

Earl cloaked in nothing but mud and coke bottle glasses. It was a visual Callie didn't wish to entertain. "So, Earl, about that lawsuit I just told you about..."

"Yes. Try not to give it much thought. There's not much you can do until I've looked everything over and I won't be back for another four days."

"But I'm really freaking out. I've never been sued before! And ten million? How is that even possible?"

"Relax, Cal-lie, relax," said Earl in his drawn-out mono-tone. "That number is just a guesstimate of the potential wages the plaintiff claims she lost. Proving it is another matter altogether. It's done all the time, some jerk throws a gigantic number out there to scare you. They never get the amount they ask for—that's assuming they even win the damned thing. A bunch of phony baloney."

"Well, it sounds pretty real to me and I'm freaking out."

"Listen, don't freak out. There are a billion ways the case can fall apart before it even goes to trial. Save yourself the anguish. Tell you what, swing by my office on Monday first thing and we'll sort it out."

"Okay, Earl."

"And one more thing—you said you're on tape making disparaging comments about Miss Schuster—"

"Schueller."

"—Schueller, during an interview?"

"Unfortunately," sighed Callie.

"What, like a segment on the radio?"

"No, on a TV show."

"Get a hold of that footage. I'll need to take a look at it."

"I haven't actually seen it air," Callie mumbled, "but I'll try to find it."

"Don't 'try', just do it. Stay strong and suck it up. Look at it this way: you know you've really made it when someone files a multi-million dollar lawsuit against you. That's what I tell all my clients. Welcome to success."

"Yeah, I'll be sure to give myself a pat on the back when we hang up."

Earl's laughter boomed from the speaker. "Now you're talkin'. Alright, Cal-lie, toodle-loo."

Callie tallied up all she'd spent in the last month on unnecessary things—the designer clothes, jewelry, pricey spa treatments, implants—and felt squeamish. Then there was the necessary expense that made her even sicker: Earl. No way around it, she'd have to curtail her spending in a major way. No more sapphire bangles. No more Italian handbags. Sure, she had plenty of money saved, but hardly the kind of cash to cover a potential judgment of ten million. For the time being, luxury wasn't an option.

Ten million. Fuck, fuck, fuck! She couldn't stop obsessing over that number—her brain was stuck on autopilot. What if she had to pay even an eighth of it? That was still $1,250,000! How on earth was she going to pay her bills? How was she going to survive? Callie wondered if the Trailer Lady alerted the media. Probably. Capitalizing on anything, even something as negative as a lawsuit, was right up her pleather-lined alley. How embarrassing!

Screech!

She peeled in her driveway and half-expected to see the paparazzi or the greasy Hobbit standing in her front yard. Of course, they weren't. Her place was dead calm, thank goodness. At that chaotic moment in her life, silence was music to her ears and exactly what she needed to regain her composure. She had to think. Just think things through.

Lord, she was dehydrated. She poured herself a glass of sparkling water and plopped on her couch. No music, no light. Just silence.

What if I have to start giving interviews to the rags to make some bucks? All they're going to want to talk about is Gabby and Evan. But maybe that's the only way. I could always take one of those cheesy gigs where they pay me to party at a nightclub, too. Drunken idiots that don't know their ass from a hole in the ground, but I could manage for a few hours, I bet. Wasn't there a diet company Paul mentioned who wants me to pimp their supplements? Seventy grand to stand in a bikini and hawk some bogus pills. Skinnie Minnie, wasn't that it? Hmmm...Maybe I could deal with being their spokeswhore. I'll feel like a fool, but so what? I may not have much of a choice. I may have to take any job that comes my way. Or is their offer even on the table since Paul and I are through? God, I hope we're not through. I shouldn't have come down on him like that! What was I thinking?

She reread the lawsuit a fourth time. Surely Earl could find a loophole—couldn't he? That's what lawyers were good at, skirting around an issue and reconfiguring it. The Trailer Lady's name jumped off the page in putrid, jumbo lettering. Shyster should have been her last name, Callie fumed. The fire in her belly returned. Who the hell does this lowlife think she is? No one is fucking with Callie Lambert! Stephanie wanted to tango, so be it—Callie would give her a first class lesson in how to shimmy with the big girls. That media whore wasn't going to bully or intimidate her into forking money over just to make her go away. No, siree, she'd fight this tooth and nail, even if it meant giving Earl her last dime to do so. And if defending herself drained her bank account, she'd have to build it up again—through hard work, not by pimping out low-rent companies and selling herself out to gossip sites. Stooping was for chumps, and there were plenty of Schuellers out there who had no qualms about stooping (and then some). Callie knew she had come too far to demean herself now. So she had another storm to weather—so be it. Big whoop. She'd make it work. She always had.

Callie slammed her fist in the cushion. There was no way around it; if war was the main course, she'd take a heaping helping.

31

Callie's iPhone rang and lit up the otherwise dark living room. Mitch. She had completely forgotten about their date. "Hi, Mitch."

"Howdy," he said. "I just wanted to tell you I'm running a little late. My call-back took longer than I thought and I just got home."

"I'm glad you said that. Same here. There's been a lot of drama I've been dealing with."

"You alright? You sound pretty upset."

"I'll tell you all about it when you get here."

"You know, Callie, we don't have to get together tonight if you don't feel like it. You won't offend me."

"You mean you don't want to see me?"

"No, that's not what I mean. It just sounds like you got a lot on your mind and I don't want you to feel pressured."

"But do you want to see me?" she said.

"I do. Very much."

"Good. I want to see you, too. I've got a lot on my mind right now. Let's just say I'm going to be writing a lot more checks to your uncle in the near future."

"Your charity foundation, right?"

"No, no, no. Something completely different. Try a lawsuit."

"Oh, man," he groaned. "I'm so sorry to hear that but I'm dyin' to know the story behind it."

"When you come over, I'll fill you in."

"By the way, Callie, I have no problem stayin' in. I swear, I don't mind a bit."

"Good, because honestly, I'm in no mood to go out."

"That makes two of us," he said. "We'll order in and take it easy."

"Perfect, Mitch. See you soon."

Over Kung Pao Chicken and fried rice, Callie filled Mitch in on her eventful afternoon.

He shook his head and took a slurp of Diet Coke. "Hot damn," he said. "That is one ugly mess, Cal. I feel for you. But if anyone can handle it, it's my uncle. As for your re-lationship with Paul, try not to sweat it. I bet you two will work it out. Managers and their clients get into it a lot. It goes with the territory; sometimes you butt heads. I've got-ten into drag-outs many times with Herb, my agent."

"You have?"

"Sure. One time, his secretary ran into his office, frazzled, to see what all the commotion was about. If someone isn't doin' their job and slackin' off, then you better believe I'm gonna let him know it. And I'm not including Paul in this, so don't get the wrong idea. Herb's the one workin' for me. Not sayin' I don't respect him—I do—but every once in a while things need a shakeup. It's healthy. Every time we get into it, Herb turns around and scores a big gig for me. Every time."

"Paul and I aren't like that," Callie said and dabbed her mouth with a paper napkin. "We've always gotten along and he's kind of father figure-ish. I don't want our relationship to end and if I have to grovel to get back in his graces, I guess that's what I'll have to do. It wasn't so much what I said but the way I said it. It was the wrong time, too. Everything about it was wrong, Mitch."

He reached over and rubbed her back. "It'll right itself. You two are tight and this is just a speed bump. It's good that you're humble enough to admit your mistakes, look at it that way. Take Schueller—she wouldn't know humility if it bit her on her ass. I never liked her from the moment I met her. Did I ever tell you she came on to me a couple times?"

Callie choked on a grain of rice. "No, I would have remembered."

"Once when she was visiting Brant on set—she came up behind me at the craft service table and rubbed her chest on my back—and another time at the party where I left Charlene—the night I talked to you by the valet. Schueller and I passed each other on the way to the bathroom and she pinned me to the wall and tried to stick her tongue down my throat."

"No, she didn't!" she blurted.

"Swear on my sister's grave. I was disgusted, completely grossed out. I wouldn't touch her with my enemy's hand. She's so vulgar and I despise vulgar women. Turn-off, big time."

She sighed. "I know she's a slutty moron, but this lawsuit has me feeling like a bad person. Like I'm being reprimanded for being a naughty kid."

"Darlin', I don't know much about law and I'm not gonna pretend I do, but lots of these cases never even make it to court. You hear of celebrities dropping lawsuits all the time because they don't factor in the hard part—proving their case. All bark, no bite. That, or they settle out of court."

Callie vehemently shook her head. "I am not settling. That's not an option. The thing is, though, she can prove I said unflattering things about her. It's true, I did imply she's nothing but a moronic slut."

"A girl who speaks her mind and the truth—I like that."

"I'm serious, Mitch. There's nothing I can say to defend myself."

Mitch set his chopsticks in the empty take-out carton. "That's where my uncle comes in. There's a reason he charges what he does. Just do one thing for me: stop beatin' yourself up. Sometimes we say the wrong thing and sometimes we get it right. Happens to all of us. You just happen to have a lot of sass and it slips out every now and then. And your sass is damned cute."

"I wish I would have shut my big fat mouth and stifled the sass. Especially in front of a camera. What was I thinking?"

"I have an idea—in the future, save all your sass for me. I love it. Turns me on."

Pop! went his dimples. He patted the spot next to him on the couch. "Come here."

She slinked over and propped her back against the armrest. "What do you have in mind?"

"Give me your feet. I'm makin' you relax. No more talk of these idiots." He propped her bare feet in his lap.

"Ooh, full service, I see."

Mitch plied her muscles into submission. His hands were so warm, so brawny, her tendons became liquified. She was the human equivalent of a sirloin in the process of being tenderized.

"I never would have guessed you have such a magic touch," she said.

"It's all about slow and steady pressure. Gettin' right in that arch is important. And right above the back of the ankle—that's a part a lot of people forget about." He moved up to her calf and then the hamstrings. Shivers darted across her skin and, unconsciously, she arched her back.

"Whatever you're doing, don't stop. Feels soooo good," she murmured.

He placed a palm between her thighs and marveled at how deeply she trembled; feverous and pliable, she was putty in his hands. His lips trickled up and down her neck, grazing, nibbling, taunting her. She grabbed him by the nape and pressed her lips onto his. They pawed each other's clothes off against a backdrop of heavy breathing. Panting became moaning, moaning turned to screaming, and months of sexual tension gave way to the heave of sweaty flesh.

32

"Whoa, whoa, girl, slow down a minute. You've worn me out. My batteries still aren't recharged from last night." The sun poked through the blinds and fell on Mitch's chest.

Callie climbed off him and sank in the sheets. The sun poked through the blinds and spilled across her body, illuminating her sweat beads like nacre on a pearl. "I'm a little randy, I guess."

"A little? Holy Christ. Whatever you were doin', promise you'll do it again. You're incredible. Just give me a minute." He pet her breasts and stomach.

Her body reverberated with post orgasmic tremors. Their early morning romp had followed the previous evening's acrobatics, with very little intermission. Behind Mitch's cool facade lay a volcanic, virile wild man. Oh my, oh my.... How long had it been since she had gotten laid, anyway? There had been oral with a hot extra from the *Cheerleader Chronicles* and a make out session with a jazz musician at Tessa's Christmas party, but she didn't count those occurrences. Who had she last had full-on sex with? Petru, that was it. He had been her last. Christ Almighty, Callie thought;

it had been awhile. Sex was intensified two-fold; after what felt like a century of celibacy, it felt great based on the human contact alone, but with a talented lover thrown in, it was nothing less than electric. Still, who was she kidding? A speculum would have given her cheap thrills.

Callie hoisted herself up on an elbow and asked, "So you feel satisfied?" It wasn't a question so much as an affirmation.

"You're kiddin' me, right? Look at me, I'm floating," he mumbled, eyes closed. "Come here, you. Come closer."

She laid her head on his torso. "I'm starving. Are you starving?"

"Famished. We worked up quite an appetite."

"Why don't I make us some breakfast? You want some eggs?"

"That would be spectacular. And some toast, too, if you have it."

"I do. How do you like your eggs?"

"Over hard, lots of salt."

"Coming up." She tied a robe around her waist and skipped to the kitchen, humming to herself. She grabbed the loaf of bread from the island and danced to the toaster. What a way to start the day; nothing like an orgasm to get the morning off on the right foot.

Ring! went her cell.

Must be Paul, thought Callie. He's calling to make up. I sure am glad, I hate being at odds with him. But her caller ID showed it wasn't Paul. It was her mother. Callie wrinkled her nose. Answer or not answer? Not answer. What about if it's important, though? Just answer it. A five minute chat and you're clear. "Hello?"

"There you are," Virginia huffed. "Didn't you get my message?"

"Hi, Mom. What message?"

"The message I left on your answering machine a few days ago. I was calling to check in because it's been weeks since we last spoke. I was starting to get worried."

"Oh, that message. Yeah, I've just been busy with pre-production stuff for my movie—you know, rehearsals, studying, meetings. Getting back in the swing of things."

"I realize that, but all you had to do was call me back and let me know you're alright. You know how I get, Cal; my middle name is Worry."

"Sorry, Mom. How are you feeling?"

"Good, very good. Healthy as a horse."

"Your treatments are going well?"

"Everything is more than just fine. My oncologist has cleared me. That's why Tony and I took that little trip. Just a small celebration together."

"Mom, that's the best news! Why didn't you say so earlier?"

"I didn't want to jump the gun. I was a little worried it was just a fluke, but, I have been assured, it is not."

"That is fantastic news. That just made my day. Made my year, actually."

"You and me both. I cannot even tell you how much freer I feel. Like I just got off death row. You know what else is making me happy these days? My new figure. Did you get the photos I sent you? The ones we took in North Carolina?"

"Yes. You look great in your swimsuit, super thin. As a matter of fact, it's the thinnest I've ever seen you." Callie could feel her mother beaming.

"Thank you. I found myself a real dandy of a Michael Kors swimsuit, and I'll be darned if it doesn't make me look like a million bucks. You don't realize how lucky you have it, being thin your whole life. You have a supernatural metabolism, it's just not human."

Callie flipped the eggs. She couldn't think of any small talk and what she did have to say needed to wait for another time, when they were face-to-face—not now, when a hot man was waiting in her bed. "Mom, um..."

"Yes?" said Virginia.

"I don't want to be rude but, uh...well—"

"Go ahead, I'm listening, Cal."

"It's kind of personal and I'm a little uncomfortable saying this, but—"

"I know. I know exactly what you're going to say."

"You do?"

"Yes, yes, I do. I've been waiting for it. Emily told me she spoke with you. I'm sure you're angry with me and I can only imagine the shock you felt when you first found out. I meant to tell you eventually, Callie, I did, but—look, it's hard. It was hard enough admitting to myself I got pregnant and gave up my child, let alone admitting it to anyone else.

I've carried this guilt for too many years. Why are you so quiet? What are you thinking? Please, say something."

"Actually, I was going to say a friend spent the night and I can't talk for long because I'm making him breakfast."

There was a long pause. Virginia finally said, "Oh, I see. So, who is this new boyfriend? Anyone I'd recognize?"

"No. We should save it for another time, Mom, and I'll tell you all about him."

"Whomever it is, I hope you're being careful, Callie. You need to be taking precautions."

"Don't worry, Mom, I am."

"Well, now that the cat's out of the bag, we may as well talk about it. Say whatever you want, I can handle it. Go ahead, fire away."

Really? You chose a fine time for this discussion. "I can't believe you kept this from me all these years. I'm just...I'm baffled."

"I didn't conscientiously try to deceive you, Callie. We all have secrets, things that seem, at the time, better left buried. I've never claimed to be a saint."

"But sometimes you made yourself out to be one. When I first got Emily's e-mail, I thought it was a hoax. I didn't believe it."

"I can't blame you. I wish she would have asked me before she did that. It's the kind of news that should have come from me," Virginia huffed.

"Emily said you two have talked several times. Have you met her?"

"No. We've talked on three occasions but we haven't met yet."

"'Yet'? So you're planning on getting together?"

"I don't know, Cal. Maybe, down the road. Why is that so bad?"

The spatula slipped from Callie's fingers and dropped to the floor.

"A stranger suddenly appears in your life after twenty-nine years and wants a mother-daughter relationship and that's supposed to be normal? It's not and it isn't fair, either. All my life, I've been trying to get closer to you and all of a sudden some idiot thinks she can waltz right in and be best friends with you in a few months? No, I don't think so. It doesn't work that way."

"Callie, it's not like that at all. She has a mother already; she's just looking for some closure. Why are you so judgmental?"

"I'm not. Maybe you just feel guilty."

"Maybe I do—heaven forbid. Is it really so shocking I have a conscience? I can't just shut off my emotions, you know. I may not show my soft side all the time, but I do have one. I'm hardly made of steel and bolts, the heartless witch you're making me out to be. I could really use your support, not your criticism." Virginia dissolved into tears.

"Of course I don't think you're heartless, Mom," Callie said gently. 'I'm just trying to put all the pieces together."

"Where is that tissue? I know I put one in my pocket somewhere..." Virginia blew her nose. "Put yourself in my shoes, for once. This is hard enough without having you come down on me."

"I'm sorry, Mom."

"It's not about being buddy-buddy, either. I'm just trying to help out and make things right. She sincerely seems like a nice girl and I owe her some answers. I don't see why that threatens our relationship, so there's no need to get territorial."

"You're right. Does Grandma know?"

"Certainly not. Esme wasn't keen on us marrying to begin with. Picture throwing an illegitimate child in the mix. She'd have stuffed my head in a Kalamata olive."

"What about Dad?"

"No, I never told him. I did tell Claire—we've been close for thirty years now—but most people had no clue. My parents thought it would be a good idea if I went up north to stay with Cousin Katie, so that's what I did for my last trimester. People just assumed I was vacationing there for the summer but I was petrified I'd be found out. What on earth would I tell them? What would they think of me? It's shameful and private and hardly something I'm proud of."

"Didn't you consider an abortion?"

"Jesus Christ!" Virginia gasped. "Have you lost your marbles? Of course I didn't. What a thing to say. You know how I feel about that subject. It wasn't even an option."

"It would be an option for me," Callie said.

"Callie Catherine Lambert, I'm going to pretend I didn't hear that."

"It's the truth. If I got pregnant, I'd have an abortion for sure. There are too many unwanted children growing up and the earth is overpopulated as it is."

"Really, now—are you trying to make my heart jump out of my chest? Because you're doing a fine job of it. Abortion is a sinful, heinous act. End of subject."

Callie sighed; they would always agree to disagree. "Do you regret giving her up?"

"In some ways, I do. But what I really regret is not telling you a lot sooner. I feel badly it's sprung on you this way, Cal."

"When I first found out, I was really angry with you—irate. It's still weird, but I'm better now and warming up to the weirdness, if that makes sense."

"It does. It's a start, I suppose. I just don't want you to be ashamed of me. I was so afraid you would be."

"I'm not ashamed of you, Mom. As you said, we all have secrets. Some just stay hidden."

"I was so young, Cal, so young. Just a nineteen-year-old kid. Being pregnant was the last thing my parents or I wanted. Casey, the boy I was dating—if he had married me, I would have kept Emily, I would have. But he took off like wildfire when I told him I was expecting. Never heard from him again."

The smoke alarm screeched and Callie jumped a foot. The stench of burnt toast circulated through the kitchen. "Hold on, Mom, hold on." She grabbed a towel and beat the alarm until it quieted.

"Callie, you need some help down there?" shouted Mitch.

"I've got it under control, thanks," she hollered. "Sorry about that, Mom."

"You're busy. We'll talk about all this later, when it's quiet and we have more time," said Virginia.

"Okay. We'll have plenty of time when I'm in Detroit later in the summer. Part of my new movie is being shot there. And I was just thinking, I bet I can arrange a little walk-on part for you. Maybe something with a few lines."

"You don't say! That would give me one heck of a kick. I've always wanted to be in the movies. They'll do my makeup and find something pretty for me to wear? Something that shows off my new waist."

"For sure. You'll love the fashions, Mom. It's set in the 1940s."

"Ooh, that sounds so glamorous, Cal. But here's the thing—what if the hairstylist doesn't know how to do wigs? Even though I finished my last round of chemo, my hair hasn't started growing back yet and you know how particular I am about my wig. Should I do it myself?"

"No, the stylists are all very skilled, Mom. You'll be in good hands, I promise."

"That's good to hear. As long as it doesn't involve porno. No porno of any kind."

"I assure you, Mom, it's not remotely pornographic."

"No nudity, none of that. Just because I'm not as vocal in my disapproval the way I used to be, doesn't mean I don't have an opinion. I won't be involved in anything filthy."

"I know, Mom, I know. I'll talk to the director first chance I get."

"I'll be anxiously waiting. That would be something, I will say. Claire is going to be green with envy! Okay, kiddo, call me when you can."

"I always do." Callie made a new batch of toast, taking care not to burn it again. She loaded up a tray and marched off to serve her stallion.

33

*"In today's Celeb 411, we at **Hollywood Hotspot** can exclusively report Callie Lambert is throwing the book right back at Stephanie Schueller. Lambert, currently shooting the feature film, **The Foreign Affair**, here in Los Angeles, was slapped with a ten million dollar libel suit by Schueller in May, only to turn around and countersue her onetime co-star. When asked to comment, Lambert's rep, attorney Earl Barletta, said, 'The truth will come out in the wash, and my client is not at all worried. Miss Lambert is looking forward to March, so that she can put this matter to bed.'*

Across the country in The Big Apple, the pint-sized star of the blockbuster flick—" Callie flipped the T.V. off. "Sorry, but I'm about to OD on so-called celebrity news, including stuff about myself. How many times can they repeat the same thing and act like it's breaking news? Earl filed this weeks ago."

"I don't know how you can even watch that crap. Bunch of cacklin' hens. Must be a girl thing." Mitch yanked a drawer from its chest and plopped it on his bed. "My uncle is so gonna fry her."

"I hope so—like a forgotten chimichanga left in the deep fryer. He says we have a great counter attack because of all the inflammatory things she said about me prior to anything I said about her. Schueller picked the wrong girl to piss off."

"She sure did. No one messes with my girl." Mitch stopped packing long enough to plant a kiss on Callie's lips. "What time you due on set?"

She licked her lips and smiled—his kisses left the sweetest taste on her mouth, like a caramel that mated with a pinecone. "Not until noon. So far, filming has amounted to driving down a road, driving up to a building, and pulling over on a bridge. Exciting, huh? I haven't had any interaction yet with any actors because we're filming the last scenes first, after my character's lover dies. The car is pretty sweet, though. It's a Buick Roadmaster, a barge. Oh, and as of yesterday, we are officially without a leading man. Pierre, the guy who was going to play Roland, got axed before he even started."

"Axed? When was he supposed to start filmin'?"

"Less than three weeks. I know, crazy, right? The insurance company told Nanette that he failed his drug test and she's livid. She's so nice, so soft-spoken and elegant, I had no idea she has a bad temper."

"How bad is 'bad'?" said Mitch.

"Let's just say I could hear her yelling in the production office—with the door closed, twenty feet away from me. She called Pierre and told him if he wasn't in rehab before the day was through, she'd personally put a bounty on his head. I feel bad for her—she fought for Pierre, against everyone's advice, and he swore to her he was clean."

Mitch chucked a handful of shirts in his Samsonite. "Wait, you say his name is Pierre? Real tall, dark-haired fella?"

"Yeah, that's him. Pierre Vronsky."

"I worked with him on a film last year, right before *The Cheerleader Chronicles*. Talented guy, but a total fuck-up. He's been a heroine junkie on and off for years. Every time he cleans up, he falls back off the wagon."

"Well, apparently he's a good liar because he assured Nanette his druggie days were long gone and she believed him—and Nanette's not easily snowed. Now, the producers are scrambling to find a replacement, so everything's really tense on set."

"Shit, I imagine they are. Did you tell them you found the perfect replacement in the form of a sandy-haired Southerner—'bout five foot ten, ruggedly handsome, and a Hick Prick to boot?"

Callie sandwiched her arms around him. "I did, but they're looking for someone much more wholesome, without an attitude."

"What a pity, 'cause I've got tons of attitude."

"I know you do. Are you ever going to tell me what nickname you came up with for me or do I have to pry it out of you?"

"Depends how you plan on pryin'," he smirked. "If it involves no clothing and lots of sweat, pry all you want, darlin'."

She nuzzled his neck. "I'm serious. You promised you'd tell me, and you've done nothing but keep it to yourself for months."

"Actually, I confess I didn't just keep it to myself. I shared it with some of the crew."

"What?"

Mitch's smile stretched from ear to ear. "Yeah, I admit, I did. Just a few grips. All in good fun, just as a joke. It wasn't mean-spirited."

"Well?" Callie swung her hands on her hips. "I'm waiting."

"Remember, it was back when we irritated each other. The Nympho Bimbo."

"You're kidding me. That's it? That's the name?"

"Uh, yeah, that's the name. You look disappointed."

She rolled her eyes. "I referred to myself as The Nympho Bimbo. I came up with that one years ago."

"I thought The Nympho Bimbo was original and kinda funny. No?"

She made a sour face. "Not really."

"Okay, then. Sorry, your royal highnass." Mitch scooped her little body into his. "My deepest sympathies."

"You smart ass." Callie stared deep in his eyes and became serious. "Mitch, I don't want you to go. These last few weeks have been so nice, I don't want them to end."

"Ditto, kiddo. I've enjoyed every second of you. The good news is, it's not endin' for long. Just a small interruption, then we'll pick up where we left off when I get back."

"I know, but I miss you already."

"Trust me, I miss you already, too, but you're gonna be so busy with your movie, you won't even notice I'm gone. And, honestly, babe, if you don't feel like drivin' to the airport, Paul can run me over. No obligation, I know you're busy."

She quizzically raised her brows. "Paul who?"

"My housemate."

"Oh, right, I forgot. No, don't be silly I'm happy to take you, that way I get to see my man an extra hour."

"Thanks, darlin'. Say, what's goin' on with you and your Paul? You kids make up yet?"

She shrugged. "We haven't really talked. He e-mails me important things, like my schedule, but so far we've avoided actual conversation."

"You want me to introduce you to Herb and his partners?"

"No, hun, thanks. I'm just going to give it a little more time before I make a decision. I never realized Paul is so hyper-sensitive, but it's starting to annoy me. Like I'm walking on eggshells."

"Just remember you're in the driver's seat. You have your pick of the litter and tons of quality agencies would love to have you on their roster."

"I know. But enough about that. You deserve a little parting gift, don't you think?" She ran her fingers along his groin and dropped to her knees before Mitch had a chance to respond.

"Ohhhhh, man," he groaned. "Your tongue is amazing..."

She came up for air and ordered, "Over there, on the bed. Lay on your back."

"Cal, this is awesome, babe, but we gotta go soon."

She unbuckled his belt and pushed him down on the mattress. "Don't worry, this won't take long."

"God, woman, you're gonna make me miss my flight—"

"Sssh." Callie peeled his jeans off. "No more talking. I want every square inch of you inside me—now. Ireland is just going to have to wait."

34

allie's loafers were coated in desert dust. The weather was so hot, so dry, crunchy cinders wafted on her tongue. She strode across the street, up to a Craftsman house. "Hello? Anybody home?" Another knock, and still no answer. She wiggled the handle; it was unlocked. She stuck one foot in the house, then the other foot, slowly creeping forward.

"Cut!" said Nanette. "Callie, do something for me. After you say 'Anybody home?,' give a ten count before you try the door. Remember, Jeanette is timid, she's frightened. Take your time."

Callie exited the house and went back to her mark, just off the shoulder of the road.

"Will do. More European and less American, you mean?"

"Exactly, ma cherie."

"Back to one," Jeremiah, the First AD, said. "Places, everyone, places. Okay, picture is up, quiet on set...and...background action!"

Two nicely dressed older women began walking down the sidewalk, past one of the front yards where three small children played with their mother. A black 1940 Cadillac cruised by and one of the women waved.

"Action!" Nanette shouted.

Callie repeated the door scene, this time to the director's exact standards. "Okay, moving on to Scene 35, people," Jeremiah said. He strode on set with a clipboard and an Evian. A lipstick-stained straw bobbed in the bottle. "Here you go, Callie. They'll be setting up the next scene a half-hour, easy, if you'd like to kick back." She sucked on the straw so hard it collapsed.

"Yeah, I think I will. Ugh, it's brutal today. Especially in these long-sleeve clothes."

"Hotter than a monkey's ass crack. They picked a helluva day to be in Woodland Hills." Jeremiah wiped his red, bearded face with the back of his hand.

"I'll be in my trailer, where there's air conditioning," Callie said.

With a fifty-five inch flat screen, elliptical machine, pilates equipment, and full service kitchen, her on-set digs showcased just how far she had come since her *Keep It Sexy* start. She unbuttoned the heavy tweed jacket and stood by the vent. The AC blasted her. "Ahhhh," she moaned. Much better. She scrolled through her iPhone while the cool air blasted her body. Two missed calls, both from Luciana. What had that little devil been up to, Callie wondered? It had been awhile since they had spoken. She still had some of Luci's belongings, but obviously nothing the glamazon considered valuable.

Callie called her back. "Hey, Luci Lou."

"Hey, yourself, Callie Sue. I'm back in town."

"Welcome back. You've been in Europe all this time?"

"No, I've been shuttling all over. From Denmark, I went straight to Paris, then flew to L.A., then back to Paris and now I'm back again in L.A. for a while. Busy, busy. I've been a busy bee."

"Wow, I guess. *Hollywood Hotspot* has really put you to work."

"They have, but that's not the main reason I've been traveling so much." Luciana's voice bubbled with excitement, like a flute brimming with champagne. "I met someone."

"Ooh, tell me more."

"I can't really say too much..."

"I won't blab, Luci," Callie said.

"No, I know you won't, but I still have to be careful. You see, I've been a bad girl. But it just, you know, happened. This man, he's very...God, how do I say it?"

"Endowed?" Callie offered.

"Married. And endowed, too, but he's married. Not only did I never expect to meet someone, but I never expected to meet a married someone. I'm in over my head."

"Is he at least separated?"

"Sort of. It's more of a marriage of convenience, since he and his wife are in business together. They've been living separate lives on and off for years. There's been massive holes in their marriage way before I came along."

Probably because he was cheating on her, Callie thought, but she held her tongue. "How did you two meet?"

"At the Duke's wedding. I interviewed him for my style segment. He has the most gorgeous eyes and was dressed so very dapper, in head-to-toe Armani, this really fantastic suit. We clicked, but didn't exchange numbers or anything like that—it would have been awkward, being that he was with his sister. Off we go on our merry ways and since I had a few days off, I returned to my apartment in Paris. Who should I run into at a neighborhood bistro? You guessed it. Him. Turns out he lives in Paris, too. How insane is that?"

"Criminally," Callie said. "What's his name?"

"I can't say. We have to keep everything on the down low, as much for me as for him. What a home wrecker I'd be, if the press got wind of this. I can see it now— 'DIRTY DOG DICKERSON CHEATS ON BOYFRIEND WITH MARRIED MAN.' I'd be toast."

"For the record, I would never rat you out, Luci."

"I know you wouldn't, but it's easier to keep everything secretive and not risk any slip-ups. I'll call him Mr. X. So, running into Mr. X was more than coincidental, and I wasn't going to let him get away again. Since then, we've been together as much as possible—as much as our schedules allow, anyway. Call it crazy, call it scandalous, whatever you want, I call it fate. I am so in love with him."

"I'm happy you're in love, Luci, and I don't want to be Negative Nelly, but what about his wife? Is he leaving her or—"

"Yes, he is, but the timing has to be just right. He'll do it, that I'm certain of. It's been coming down to this for years and I don't feel the least bit guilty over it. Besides, guilt is a useless emotion and serves no purpose."

"Just be careful. I don't want you to wind up hurt."

"Me? Ha! I'll be just fine. It's the guy you should worry about."

"You're probably right, there," Callie laughed.

"Of course I am. How's it going with your man?"

"Mitch and I are great. Never in my wildest dreams did I think I'd fall for someone like him, but he's so sweet and protective, I stand corrected."

"That's wonderful. Don't you just love surprises? They're so underrated. We'll have to toast our love lives, next chance we get. And your movie? Have you started it yet?"

"Yeah, I'm in my trailer as we speak."

"As in your trailer on set?"

"Yep. They're lighting a scene and I'm cooling off."

"God, look at you! You have the most enviable career, Callie."

Callie tugged at her itchy pantyhose. "It's 105 degrees and I'm in a wool suit. Trust me, Luci, if you could see me, you wouldn't be envious."

"It is stifling today. I'm driving through the Valley and my air is cranked to the max."

"Why don't you swing by the set? I'll introduce you to everyone. You can network."

"Thanks, but I have to record a bunch of voiceovers at the studio," Luci said. "Afterwards, I'm headed with Chad to a Warner Bros. party. You need to come."

"I doubt I'll be done in time, Luci. When does it start?"

"Oh, you know Californians' schedules—whenever o'clock. Just come by whenever you wrap. It won't get going until late, anyway. I don't want to be stuck playing Chad's doting girlfriend. You were right—bearding is dreadful."

"You're over it already? You've got four months left, don't you?"

"Don't remind me. I don't get on very well with men who are prettier than me, I've realized. Chad's the bigger star here and in Europe I'm used to getting all the attention. Bugs me to pieces. He'll be so busy having his ass kissed by all his colleagues, he won't give ten cents about me—except when a cameraman comes around. So, then, you'll come?"

"I'll try."

"Not good enough," said Luci. "Say, I picked up the most beautiful Balmain cocktail dress when I was in Paris. Embroidered black lace. It's yours for the night. I need to have the hem dropped, but it should fit you just fine."

The last time Callie went out with Luci, she wound up getting sued. Not that it was Luci's fault, but hanging with the supermodel could be a potential landmine.

"I can't believe I'm being bribed with Balmain," Callie laughed.

"Vintage Balmain."

That settled it; Callie had to make the party. It would have been wicked to refuse.

35

The Warner Bros. lot was aglow in red; the lighting, the buildings, and the floral arrangements were all crimson. Amsterdam's Red Light District had been recreated in honor of Chad Blake-Shepard's new film, *Sex for Sale*, complete with lingerie-swathed models standing behind glass-lined windows. A DJ spun sex-themed tunes in his own private booth and the aroma of cherries and bourbon filled the air as guests sipped the evening's signature cocktail, the Sexalicious.

Callie nodded appreciatively at the no-expense-spared soiree; it was the perfect occasion for the drapey Balmain that clung to her figure. Luci had sent her personal assistant to drop the dress off and she had been right; it fit Callie perfectly. She had wrapped by ten o'clock, and within the hour, was on the Warner lot. But where was Luci? Callie texted her again. No sooner had she pressed "Send" than a lofty brunette in a strapless red dress loomed in the distance. With the funky lighting and fog machine, it was difficult to make out the girl's face. She clung to the arm of a fair-haired man several inches shorter than her. Luci. Without a doubt. Who else stood that tall? The girl dropped her suitor's arm and pranced over to Callie.

"My, oh, my," Luci said with a whistle. "I think that dress was tailor made for you."

"Hi, Luci!" Callie hugged her.

"What do you think of the dress?"

"I'm in awe. This is the most beautiful piece I've ever worn," said Callie.

"It belonged to Wallis Simpson. Or so I was told. God, you look smashing."

Callie spun. "Thanks for loaning it to me. Speaking of smashing..." Callie scoped Luci out; what was different about her? The hair and clothes were just as gorgeous as ever, as was the makeup. But she had changed, somehow. The Luci standing before her wasn't the same girl she had said good-bye to weeks before. Her entire face had a luster no blush or highlighter could mimic. "Luci, you're absolutely glowing."

"Am I?" Luci held her hands to her cheeks and smiled. "I'm happy, I guess. Really happy, for the first time in a long time."

"Mr. X?"

Luci vigorously nodded. "I left Paris less than a week ago and I miss him already. Like crazy. But I have to focus on my career and deal with this Chad situation. I'll tell you, Callie, I'm ready to shave this beard right off. I don't know what I was thinking. My team told me it was a good idea for all of the publicity but they never warned me I'd lose my mind in the process."

"Are you two supposed to go on dates certain nights of the week or how exactly does it work?"

"Three nights every week, like clockwork. The Ivy, Madeo, whichever restaurant has the most paparazzi. And then red carpet events, of course. He throws a diva-tude if he can't find me the moment there's a camera around—but as long as we get the shot, that's all that matters. See that guy over there? The one in white?" Luci pointed to a group of people surrounding Chad. "That's his boyfriend, Trey. He's an animation artist. He positively hates me and wants Chad to come out already, but Chad is too concerned with moving up the A-list ranks to care. Last week, I was approached by Gary, Chad's manager, and he asked me if I was opposed to being artificially inseminated with Chad's sperm. Said it would really help Chad's bankability with the soccer moms of America. I told him to drop dead."

"Welcome to Hollywood," Callie smirked.

"What a crock," Luci said.

"Luci, why don't we grab a drink and drown away the political BS?"

"I can't; I took a Vicodin earlier for my cramps, so I'll have to stick to club soda. If I mix it with alcohol, Gary is liable to have a knife in his back."

"Oh, Gary's here, too?"

"Yes, unfortunately. He's gross, always coming up with low-end shenanigans for his clients so he can make a buck. And he preys on young girls, most of them underage." They walked over to the bartender and ordered.

"My ex used to be his client and I always thought Gary seemed pretty nice," Callie said.

"Sure, he's nice. But if you stand in his way, he turns into a lunatic. Gary is a control freak, if ever there was one."

"Did I just hear my name or was I dreaming? Luci, cupcake, why the sourpuss face?" Gary Benson stumbled over.

Luciana rolled her eyes. "Why, if it isn't the world's hardest-working jerk-off in showbiz. Get lost, Gary."

"Charming, as always," said Gary with a smile. "Callie, babe, how are you? Well, hello, hello. What a dress. Dior?"

"Balmain," Callie said.

"Stunning. Say, Luci, why aren't you with Chad? The photographer is making the rounds."

"I need some water," said Luci.

"I'll get your water. You go do your job and play the ever-so-loving girlfriend."

"You're forgetting one thing, Gary—I'm not your client, so please, mind your own business."

Gary sipped his bourbon and took a step towards Luci. "And you're forgetting, doll face, that my business is your quote unquote boyfriend, and that boyfriend employs me. And by employing me, that means I, in turn, manage his career and whatever personal bullshit affects it. And you, for the time being, are affecting his career, which means that Chad has made you my business. So, I'm asking you again, real sweet with a cherry on top, go over and do your fucking job. Please."

Luci grabbed her water and said to Callie, "I'm going to check on Chad, be back in a minute. Steer clear of the bottom feeders, they're really hungry tonight."

Gary watched Luci sashay off. "Her beauty is exceeded only by her bitchiness. Thinks she calls the shots in every goddamned situation she knows shit about. You two friends?"

"Yes, and I really like her," said Callie.

"Yeah? Try managing her. She's impossible." He emptied his Johnny Black. "Talk to Ev lately?"

Callie shot the side-eye. "Considering we didn't part on the best of terms, that would be a no."

"What a dynamo that guy is. Pisses money. He's filming a TV spot in Japan. A guest judge on a talent show. They're nuttier for him there even more than here, can't get enough of him. I gotta hand it to him, I don't know how he maintains such a breakneck pace. He's always busy, always has his hands in lots of different cookie jars."

"You can say that again," she sniffed.

"What's new with you?"

"I'm busy with a new movie, *The Foreign Affair*."

"*The Foreign Affair*...oh, the Vernadeau project, right? I've heard of it. Pierre Vronsky is the male lead, isn't he?"

"Was. He failed his drug test."

"Again? Goddamn it. I was really hoping he'd stay clean this time."

"He seemed fine at the read-through. He was coherent and funny and looked really healthy." She took a sip of her frothy cocktail.

"What a shame. Such a great actor. This just happen?"

"Yeah, yesterday. That's one way to put the squeeze on—"

A girl in a skintight halter dress collided into Callie's Sexalicious. The drink, glass and all, toppled to the floor. Better the floor than the dress, thought Callie.

"There you are, Gary-cakes," slurred the girl. "I've been looking all over for you. Get me another drink?"

"Jesus H. Christ," rumbled Gary. "That's all you have to say, Jessica? Look at the mess you made. How about apologizing to my friend, Callie, here. In case you don't know, this is the Callie Lambert, and she's a pretty big deal."

Jessica looked Callie up and down. "Sorry." To Gary: "So, can I have a drink now?"

"Don't you think you've had enough?" Gary said. "Please excuse her, Callie. She's had a rough day."

Jessica flipped her hair off her shoulders. "How would you feel if you didn't get a part just because the casting director is an ugly old toad? I waited a whole hour to read one fucking line."

"No, sweetheart," Gary said. "You didn't get the part because you couldn't remember your one fucking line."

"Save it already," Jessica spat. "She just wanted to give me a hard time, that cunt."

Gary looked at Callie in chagrin. "Jessica just moved here from Nebraska. Hasn't had a whole lot of luck, so I'm helping her out a little. The casting director is a friend of mine and let her audition as a favor." Lowering his voice: "Pretty kid, but not much up there."

Callie snickered. "You're kidding me."

"I know, imagine that—an L.A. broad without a brain. The third Jessica I've had this year and each one gets dumber than the last. Must be in the name or something. They don't make 'em like you anymore, cupcake. I'll go get you a new cocktail. Come on, Jess." Gary led Jessica to the front of the booze line just as Callie felt her arm being tugged. Luci had returned.

"Back already?" Callie said.

"I told you, as long as they get the picture, that's all that counts," said Luci. "You just avoided a second round of Gary and his jailbait."

"I don't like to start trouble, but I won't let some chauvinist bulldoze me. If he wants to think he can one-up me, let him, but I'll have the final say in the end. I could have that pervert blacklisted—and after this Chad charade is through, I just may."

"How are you going to do that?"

"Connections. I always follow through with whatever I say I'm going to do." Luci pulled Callie to a large, open space. "Come on, enough of these idiots. I want to dance."

36

"Okay, Cal. I can see you. Can you see me?"

"No, I can't see you at all. I've never Skyped before, maybe I'm not pressing the right thing..." Or maybe it was the alcohol. Callie sat cross-legged on her bed and scooted closer to her laptop. She could hear Mitch's voice but he wasn't yet visible on her screen. She banged away on the keys until finally his mug popped up onscreen.

They were supposed to have spoken sooner but with the time difference, poor cellular reception, and their crazy schedules, there hadn't been any time. Only a few "Thinking of you" and "Morning, sugar" texts had been exchanged—and one where he said "Ireland = beautiful but sick of the food already. Like cardboard."

"Finally, I can see you," she said.

"Great." Mitch grinned. "Look at you—that hair, those lips. You look like you just stepped foot off of a John Huston flick."

She touched her side-parted waves. "I just got home from a party with Luci and haven't had a chance to wash my face. I met her straight from the set, so I'm covered in enough highdef makeup to smother an army."

"Leave it on, you look fantastic."

"No way, I can't sleep in my makeup. I'd have to switch to doing Noxema commercials instead of movies."

Mitch guffawed. "I bet you've never had to worry about a pimple in your life."

"Trust me, Mitch, I've had my share."

"Nope, I don't buy it. So, tell me all about what's been going on with you."

"Let's see...well, everything is going well. I was—"

"Sorry, babe, hold on a minute, they're calling for me in the other room. Be right back." Mitch reappeared after several minutes. "Sorry 'bout that. The stunt coordinator needed to go over something."

"If this is a bad time, I can call you later."

"Don't be silly. I'm the one who called you, remember? So what all is goin' on?"

"Nothing, really. I just miss you, Mitch. I can't stop wondering how you're doing."

"Aw, babe, you're sweet. Ditto."

"I don't like these long breaks apart. It's not normal. It sucks."

"Come on, it's not that bad. Just the way it is in our line of work, is all. Don't you worry 'bout me. I'm takin' care of myself and workin' hard. Puttin' in sixteen hour days, but I'm havin' a blast."

Having a blast? That wasn't what Callie wanted to hear. And didn't he miss her, too? He had said so in a text, but it would be nice if the words actually came out of his mouth. "I'm glad someone's having fun. It's been pretty boring for me."

"There was this scene we filmed yesterday—you're gonna love this—where I was walkin' around in my armor, with my shield and sword, and all of a sudden I slipped and fell flat on my ass. Took down two people behind me, too, like a Stooges skit. I was—aw, shoot. They're callin' for me again, Cal. I better go. We'll talk later."

"Already? I was hoping for a little Skype nookie." She dropped the bodice of her dress and exposed her breasts.

Mitch sucked in his breath. "You have to do this to me now, don't you? Mmm, you look good enough to eat...I'm sorry, babe, I hate to say this, but I have to take a rain check. We've been trying to coordinate the stunts on this scene for days and I gotta run through a rehearsal."

Callie pouted. "Fine."

"Hey, there, no need to pout. Cal...look at me...Callie?" Mitch's soft brown eyes pierced through the screen. "I really miss you. I'm havin' fun and whatnot, don't get me wrong, but I, uh..."

She held her breath. "But you...?"

"I'm beat. I'm ready to come home and just kick back."

Not exactly the deep, passionate words she had hoped for. "I bet," she sighed.

"I'll to talk to you soon, sweet cheeks."

Callie jumped up and stomped over to the sink. She began scrubbing the layers of war paint off. Was she really asking too much of him? Extracting some emotional depth from that boy was like pulling teeth. Argh! She had no intention of pulling teeth.

211

Beyond Hollywood Strip

If she wanted that lot in life, she would have stayed in Troy working in Dr. Ryder's dental office. Since when were relationships supposed to be that difficult? Better to cut her losses early on before things became too complicated, she figured. Enough was enough. What was the point in trying to extract blood from a turnip? Furthermore, why was she dissecting everything while tipsy? Better to wade through things later when her head was clear. She grabbed a fresh towel from the cabinet and knocked a stack of washcloths on the floor. A knotted piece of fabric lodged between the hamper and the wall caught her eye; she scooped it up. She had never seen the scarf before and judging from the expensive, buttery texture it could only belong to one such person—the always fashionable Luciana Dickerson. Callie doubted the girl had ever owned anything less than silk charmeuse or Caviar leather. Vogue-worthy beauty, a burgeoning new career, and money to burn—what a life. Every facet of Luci's bio, down to her torrid affair with Mr. X, seemed ripped from a *New York Times* bestseller. Even if the liaison ended in heartache, how riveting being involved in something so exciting, so sultry and utterly decadent! Callie swooned; she would gladly take heartache over indifference any day of the week. Indifference was a deal killer, worse than death.

She splashed the remaining mascara smudges away and called it a night.

37

aliborka Birkhead—known simply as Miss D to those in the biz—was a giant in the makeup industry, in both reputation as well as sheer physicality. As the key MA, she was known in the industry as the Purveyor of Puckers, the doyenne of the perfect lip. For thirty-three years, her hands wove magic and transformed thin, wilted lips into voluptuous buds of perfection. Not that Callie needed much help in that department, but Nanette was a stickler for perfection, and on movie sets, there was no bigger cosmetics bee than Miss D. "Nanette wants the ripest shade of red for your ballroom scene. Not too blue, not too orange, not too matte, not too glossy," said D. She blurred the hard line of Callie's lip liner with her finger. "I'm giving you the Ultimate Ava."

"What's that?" Callie asked.

"A look that's bold and sexy but still ladylike, much like Ms. Gardner herself. How wonderful to be filming at the Biltmore. It's so historic, such a beautiful hotel, isn't it?"

D dabbed a Q-Tip along the edge of Callie's mouth.

Callie sat in the chair, mummy-still. Her big scene was coming up—her character, Jeanette, was about to find out that Roland, the man she had just eloped with, was a spy who had orchestrated her father's death two years ago. But Callie couldn't be more disinterested because two things were distracting her: one, she wanted to know what the deal with Mitch was and two, she had been greeted earlier in the morning with a voicemail from Emily. "Hi, Callie," Emily had said. "I hope you're doing well. I'm doing okay. I'm just enjoying my summer break. I finished up my finals and start an internship in a few weeks. It just so happens it's at UCLA. Funny, isn't it? Since I'll be so close to you, it would be great to grab a cup of coffee or lunch. I know you're really busy, but it sure would be nice, if you can spare a little time..."

Why couldn't she just stay in her own little corner in Florida and let Callie be? Or take an internship in Alaska. That would make things easier. Geographical distances equaled zero obligation. But with Emily being just around the corner, it was an entirely different story. The girl seemed sweet but Callie worried a sit down would open a can of worms.

"Everything alright, Miss Callie? You sure are quiet today."

"Yeah, I'm just tired," Callie mumbled.

"Didn't get much sleep last night?" She blotted Callie's lips with a sheet of tissue before slicking on another coat.

"Not really."

"I'll send for some strong coffee. We can't have the lead actress dozing off in front of the camera, can we?"

"Thanks, but I'm fine."

"I found the perfect elixir for insomnia in an old copy of that Martha Stewart magazine. You take a cup of decaf chamomile tea and mix it with steamed milk and add raw honey. Make sure it's whole milk, not skim, and the honey can't be processed—it's got to be raw. And then..." D rattled on in her nasally pitch for the next ten minutes. Callie had no choice but to listen; she was stuck, held hostage by a tube of Clarins.

She wondered if Miss D had always sounded so nasally and talkative—Chatty Kathy on helium. And she ended every sentence with a question. Maybe it was an Aussie thing.

"...So if ever you can't sleep, do try that remedy and let me know how you like it. Here you go, I think we're done now, aren't we?" D capped her lip brush and gave a satisfactory smile.

Finally, Callie thought. "Thanks, Miss D. If anyone looks for me, I'll be in my trailer going over my lines."

"What about your hair? Don't you want to go see Stella so she can take those rollers out?" said D.

"She's going to take them out right before we shoot so that my curls don't fall."

"Gotcha—what with this heat and all. Okay, sweetie."

Callie stepped outside in time to witness a homeless man projectile vomiting on the corner of South Grand and West 5th. *Ahhh, the beauty of downtown L.A.,* she thought as she passed the craft service table. Every time she saw craft services, she thought of Mitch and the very first time she laid eyes on him. What a cutie. So toned and tanned and—

"Hey, there, Callie. I was just looking for you." Jeremiah held up his walkie talkie. "Never mind, Darren, I found her."

"What, you guys put a man hunt out for me?" she said.

"Nanette asked me to find you. She needs to talk to you."

"What about?"

Jeremiah squinted from the direct sunlight. "I know nothing. I'm just the messenger. She's in her trailer."

Callie knocked on her door.

"Come in," Nanette said. She looked up from her stack of papers and peered behind tiny reading glasses. "Just the girl I want to see. Oh la la, that color! Miss D, she is magnificent."

Callie smacked her lips. "She calls it the Ultimate Ava. Jeremiah said you want to speak to me?"

"Close the door, please."

"Sure. Is something wrong?"

"Yes. So many catastrophes, where do I begin? As of this moment, it's taken my crew two hours to light a scene we should have shot yesterday, I lost my leading man to a hypodermic needle, and, just now, I hear my leading lady is involved in a multi-million dollar lawsuit. Is this true?"

"Unfortunately. You just heard? It all went down a few weeks ago."

"I've been eating, sleeping, and breathing this film; I may as well live underneath a rock. How are you holding up?"

Callie shrugged. "Let's just say the negative press has upset my family more than me. My grandma called when she first heard it on TV, worried sick."

"I'm sorry to hear that. I was quite surprised, myself. I thought, 'What is this nonsense? Callie would not hurt a fly.'"

"I wouldn't go that far. I have been known to—"

Nanette held a hand up. "Listen to me, I am serious. I want you to know if there is anything I can do—money, whatever you need—it's yours. I like you, I trust you, you have my full support."

"Thank you, Nanette; you have no idea how much I appreciate that. This has been nothing but a big, expensive pain, but I'm honestly doing fine. I have a real rock 'em, sock 'em lawyer who's going to take her head off."

"That's good to hear. If he doesn't work out, let me know and I'll call my attorney. That girl, the one who is suing you, she is the most beastly thing." Nanette wrinkled her ski-jump nose. "I would never hire her for one of my movies. Tacky, tacky. Tres collant. I don't know what those Wilders are thinking, making her the lead. That's bound to be career suicide, but I digress." She took her glasses off and placed them in their case. "Callie, something is bothering me, something I know you can help me with. You see, it pains me when two people I care very much about are squabbling, pecking at each other like a pair of chickens. Life is too ridiculously short to hold a grudge and not sort out one's differences—even if that means putting pride off to the side."

"Oh," Callie said, "so Paul told you about our spat."

"He did. He is hurt."

"But, Nanette, from my point of view—"

"Blah! I am not reprimanding you. I am not a referee, I do not judge, I only want to bridge the gap. I'm asking you, please talk to him and sort this out and don't let something stupid get in the way of your relationship. You know how difficult it is to find someone in this industry that genuinely cares about your well-being, no? Paul genuinely cares about you, Callie—not just as a client, as a person, and that is rare. There, I've said my piece, that is all. The rest is up to you."

"I'll give it some thought," Callie said.

"Don't think too long about it. He is having lunch with Roger."

"Oh? I didn't know they're friends."

"Yes, I introduced the two of them and they're like brothers. The three of us have known each other for so long, we're like family. They're dropping by the set in—"

Bang, bang!

Nanette flung the door open. Paul and Roger Vernadeau were standing in the doorway.

38

"We were just talking about you both. Come in, come in." Nanette kissed each man on both cheeks. "Paul, you never change, you look the same as always."

Paul grinned. "You're being kind, Netty. You can see most of my scalp these days."

"My father went bald when he was twenty, the best man that ever lived, as far as I'm concerned," said Nanette. "Roger, meet our star."

"Ahhh, so this is mademoiselle Callie. My wife and I watched *Nympho Cheerleaders* at three in the morning, when we couldn't sleep. The movie, eh—not so great. But you— you were worth watching."

Roger's smile was large and welcoming; his eyes, framed by a heavy fringe of dark lashes, glowed with warmth. His voice was deep but soft, with a hint of an accent. "You'll have to pardon me if I'm not coherent. Just before I met Paul for lunch, I stepped off a plane from Hawaii. Now, that may sound well and good, but I was there scouting properties for my next film, in back-to-back meetings for three days straight. Nary a moment to myself, let alone any time to enjoy the scenery."

"Roger is producing a film on James Cook, the explorer. But for the next week, he's all mine," said Nanette. She squeezed his arm.

"Someone has to make sure we stay on schedule, darling. I just ran into the Grossmans and, two things."

"What now?" Nanette groaned.

"One, they want to know if we're all free tomorrow for dinner—they're very insistent, say they have a big surprise for us. And two, they want to know how you're planning on lighting the ballroom scene. They're worried it's going to be too dark."

Nanette threw her hands up. "What is wrong with these people? All they've done thus far is meddle, giving me their two cents on how to do this scene and how to play that scene. I ask you, who is the director? I am the director, and they need to be reminded of that."

Roger itched a graying sideburn. "They've sunk millions in this project, darling. They mean well."

"Just because they've invested in a film does not mean they know a single thing about film making, Roger. They're both astoundingly illiterate—especially that short little man. Bon Dieu! Ces deux-la sont sur mon dernier nerf..." Nanette's face was more lobsters-and-cream than peaches. Roger took her aside. They spoke in whirlwind French, leaving Paul and Callie to fend for themselves.

"Hi, Cal."

"How's it going, Paul."

Silence.

They both finally spoke, at the same, and their words tumbling together. Paul said, "You first."

"No, please, go ahead."

Paul cleared his throat. "Look, Callie, I think we make a great team. But if you don't think so, if you don't think I'm up to par, I can't do any more for you. I've dropped most of my clients to focus on you, your career. If you don't see it that way and my best isn't good enough, we need to cut ties—"

"Wait. Stop. You're right. You're absolutely right. It's all been a big giant cluster and I'm tired of it."

"I see."

"It's all been stressing me out, Paul. I hate being at odds, so, please, let's just put an end to it."

"I'm sorry you feel that way, Cal." Paul's eyes twitched and darted around the room. "I'm going to get going. I have some business to finish up at the office."

"Wait, I thought you wanted to talk?"

"What's there to talk about? You want to cut ties, we'll cut ties. There's nothing left to discuss, Callie."

"But, Paul—"

"Go find yourself a new manager."

"What? But that's not what I meant!"

Paul looked her squarely in the eye. "You just said you want to end it."

"Yeah, let's end this not-speaking-to-each-other bullshit, that's what I'm tired of. I didn't mean I want to end our relationship."

Paul breathed. "I misunderstood."

"Look, I was wrong and I'm sorry, Paul—I admit it. I didn't mean to come across as ungrateful and yes, I realize you've gone out of your way for me—with Jerry, with protecting me from the press, all sorts of things—and I truly appreciate that. I was really upset that day. I guess I just wanted to blame someone for that lawsuit and I wasn't thinking clearly."

"It's understandable," Paul said.

"I promise not to insult you that way again. Please, can we just go back to the way things were?"

"Absolutely. Man, I'll be more than happy to put this behind us. I'm not a fighter—I've never fought with any of my clients. In truth, maybe I overreacted a little. What I do know is, I've been a wreck these last few weeks, you little shit."

Callie hugged him. "I, uh...I'm sorry."

"I'm sorry, too. I guess we all need to have a tiff once in a while—when the tide settles, you can see the bottom much clearer. But from here on out, this is all water under the bridge. Deal?"

"Deal," Callie said.

Paul patted her on the back. "All a bunch of water under the bridge."

39

"Hey, darlin'. Am I waking you?"

Callie smiled and rolled over in bed. What time was it, anyway? 5:22 a.m. "Yeah, but no biggie. You in Scotland?"

"Not yet. We're really behind schedule, but I leave for Scotland tomorrow morning."

"But I thought you were coming home tomorrow."

"I would have been home tomorrow, darlin', if the weather had cooperated, but it's screwed everything up. Not much I can do about it."

"No, I know, I was looking forward to seeing you."

"I know, same here. But if Scotland is smooth sailin', I'll be back in L.A. in two weeks."

Callie exhaled. "But then I'll be in Detroit."

"Aw, damn it, that's right. Shoot."

"I feel like I haven't seen you in a year, Mitch."

"But the good thing is, it's not forever. We'll catch up soon, and when we do, we've got lots to fill each other in on. Lots of adventures and new people. Nice people, too."

Callie narrowed her eyes. "Oh? Who?"

"In general, I mean. The people have been real nice."

"I see. Who are you working with?"

"In terms of talent, a bunch of newbies, for the most part. Just about everyone's cool. Thomas Richie, this kid from Cincinnati—funny as hell. Everything he says is like a stand-up routine. He's got all of us on the floor most of the time. And Kennedy Bailon is somethin', too."

"Is Kennedy a boy or girl?"

"A girl. She plays a Maid Marian type with this tiny, petite build and you'd never think she could kick as much ass as she does. She's quite a pistol. Not just cute but genuinely tough."

Callie's cheeks flushed. "What do you mean by that? What, you like her or something?"

"Well, sure, I like her. I like working with her. As you know, when the other actors are good, it makes your own work that much better." Mitch laughed. "What's with the third degree? You sound jealous."

"Of course not, don't be silly. No girl intimidates me or makes me jealous." Hadn't he implied he found this Kennedy twat intriguing—or was it just her suspicious mind? Callie knew first-hand just how depraved film and television sets could be. The long hours, working in such tight quarters with fellow actors in often sexual situations...the whole environment was incestuous. After all, that's how she first hooked up with Bedroom Eyes—and Mitch himself.

"Good, because one of the things I like about you is how confident and secure you are with yourself. There's nothin' to be jealous over."

There's nothing to be jealous over because you're my girlfriend, Callie, and none of the others matter to me. That's what she wanted him to say. How much more did she have to try to pry it out of him? What was going on inside that brain of his? What was he really thinking and how did he feel about her? Callie wished he would say something definitive as to their relationship status. But she didn't want to ask. She didn't want to ask because she refused to be the vulnerable baby bird, anxious for a worm to drop in her beak. No, she wanted Mitch to say things on his own accord—provided, of course, he really meant it.

"What's new on your end?" he said.

"Let's see...my brain's a little foggy...well, Paul and I called a truce. I ran into him when—"

"Sorry, babe. Hold on a sec, 'kay?" He returned minutes later. "Sorry 'bout that. The AD was lookin' for me. You were saying you and Angers buried the hatchet?"

"Yeah, and I can't tell you how relieved I feel."

"I bet. Negativity zaps anyone's energy. Not good for the mind, spirit, none of it."

"That's for sure. It's not healthy to have all that negativity festering inside. I've had these knots in my stomach and I know it's been because of the tension between us. He's like a father to me and we've always had such a good rapport. I mean, I can tell Paul just about anything. So it really threw me for a loop when we had that fight and—hey, are you listening?"

"Cal, I'm sorry," Mitch said, "but we gotta continue this later. There's a problem on set and I gotta run."

"Okay, Mitch. Talk to you soon."

"Bye, missy."

"I love you—"

Click. He had already hung up. Callie drew her 1,000 thread count sheets over her face. "Missy"? What was she, his niece? Why couldn't he have referred to her as "honey" or "baby"? What was it with Mitch and his hot and cold routine? Just when she thought she had busted through his icy cool barrier for the last time, he dropped a load of icicles in between them. Not that she expected an "I love you" yet—she wasn't even sure she was in love with him— but a term of endearment, other than "babe," would have been nice. Great; woken from a deep slumber just to hear he's doing fabulous without me, thousands of miles away. Oh, the joy. She tried to fall back asleep but started thinking of all the bills that were due, particularly her largest tab: Earl, at $7,500 (a small cry from last month's $14,200). She sighed and climbed out of bed; it was only six o'clock. If she hurried, she could sneak in a workout before she was due on set. Tone those thighs and buns, make them their quarter-bouncing best. She wolfed down an English muffin and laced up her tennis shoes. The house phone rang before she could grab her keys. "Mitch?"

"Skank. It's me."

"Ty! Sorry about that. Mitch was supposed to call me back and I didn't look at the caller ID. How's Paris going?"

"Not good. Not good at all..."

"What's wrong?"

"I made a mistake."

"What happened, Ty? Talk to me."

Tyler could only answer in short, staccato breaths before breaking down in tears.

40

"Breathe slowly, Ty. Long, deep breaths," said Callie. Tyler steadied his breathing. "I'm alright. I lost it for a second, but I'm alright."

"What's happening? Is Paris not going well?"

"No, Paris has been fantastic. It's my situation with Timothy that's been awful. I can't deal with him anymore, Cal. I just can't deal. He's draining me and he's so mean and I'm miserable. And he's getting worse."

"How long have things been this way?" she asked.

"Too long. You remember when you were here and we had that spat?"

"Over the male model, right?"

"Exactly, jealous over the beefcake. I didn't realize it at the time, but this is an ongoing issue with him. He gets really mad when I work with hot guys and, mind you, I'm just doing my job—I'm not flirting or copping a feel or any of that. It's so frustrating because I'm not doing anything wrong to send him into a rage."

"Have you sat down and told him all this?"

"A million times, so many times my face is blue. And he says he's sorry and it won't happen again, yada, yada, yada, but then we go back through the whole cycle again. Well, last week, I was on a shoot with this actor, Luca Kanellis—"

"I've heard of him. The Greek actor, right?"

"Right. A real sweetheart and down-to-earth. So when Timothy heard I had worked with Luca, he got really paranoid and accused me of having a thing for him. For one, the guy's as straight as they come and two, even if he batted for my team, I wouldn't do anything about it. But for some reason, Timothy wouldn't let it drop and we got in an awful screaming match and he pushed me. Hard, too. I fell on the coffee table and broke it."

"Oh my God."

"And then today, he accused me of sending flirtatious messages to an old boyfriend on Facebook. Rande, remember him?"

"How could I forget? He was six feet of raw muscle."

"Tell me about it. A walking, talking He-Man. I sent him an e-mail that said, and this is verbatim, 'Rande, congrats on your new Versace campaign, looks great.' Timothy read it and got insanely pissed and threw a punch at me."

"Tyler, oh, no! Are you hurt?"

"Hurt? I look like Farrah Fawcett in *The Burning Bed*."

Callie gasped.

"Okay, that's a slight exaggeration," Tyler conceded. "But I could have looked like Farrah Fawcett in *The Burning Bed*. Another day with him and he probably would have Gabby Manx-ed my ass."

"You broke up with him, didn't you?"

"Of course I did. If that dumb goon thinks he can Ike me, he's got another think coming. I should have thrown him out last week, after he pushed me during an argument. I went to the drugstore to get some stuff for my swollen eye and told him when I returned, he'd better be gone, along with all his shit. Other than some clothes, he didn't have much. So, that's that."

Callie sighed. "Timothy seems like such a calm, nice guy. I never knew he had it in him."

Tyler sighed. "Funny how you think you know someone and then find out you never did. I really thought he was The One. In the beginning, anyway. Oh, well. It is what it is. I'm actually relieved I don't have to deal with his ball-and-chain ass anymore. He was too much, too draining. I can't change him, so I'm better off cutting my losses before he does some major damage and this bitch winds up six-feet-under. Besides, he wasn't very good in bed, anyway."

"I'm just glad you're okay."

Tyler downed a glass of water. "If there's one thing I learned from my mother, it's not to make the same mistakes she did. She put up with my dad's abuse for far too long. Ain't happening with me. Not only am I not stupid enough to put up with that, I'm too vain to deal with someone trying to rearrange my face for sport. Keep it moving, asshole, right on out the door. Next!"

"You're much too good of a person for that, Ty. Consider yourself fortunate to be rid of such a jerk."

"Thanks, skankazoid. I'm feeling better already." He blew his nose like a trombone. "On a positive note, work is going fabulously. Jean promoted me to Artistic Director already, can you believe it?"

"Of course I can. You always excel, Ty. Especially if it's beauty related."

"I drove my mom nuts when I'd rifle through her makeup as a kid, but look at me now—all that practice paid off. Hell, I loved makeup so much, I used to eat it. The shade 'Barbados Blue' was my favorite. Chowed it like candy. Oh, that's what I was going to tell you! Have you heard your girl, Candy, is getting married?"

"I have, actually," Callie said. "I ran into one of her friends a few weeks ago. How did you hear about it?"

"Because Troy is no bigger than my pee hole," Tyler jeered. "And because my mother and Candice have gone to the same hair salon for the past ten years. According to my mom—take this one with a fat grain of salt—she looks like a pre-Burton Liz, better than her *Coquette* days. A little on the plump side, but healthy."

Callie smiled. "She must still be sober, then. That's good news."

"Mom said, 'I don't know how she can lift her hand, her rock is so big.' If that fiancée knows what's good for him, he'll fly away. Not walk or run, mind you—fly, and in the fastest jet available."

"I say good for her," Callie said. "I may not want her in my life, but I'm glad she's happy."

Tyler snorted. "I'll tell you what's making her happy—the fiancée's bank account. That bitch isn't addicted to drugs, she's addicted to Benjamins. Oh, and remember that model, Arjana? She walked in on her fiancée in bed with another man. Lord, I have to tell you this story, it will make your head spin..."

Callie took a seat at the breakfast table—there was no way she was making it to the gym. She hadn't talked to Tyler in months; too much had happened in their lives to not take advantage of their in-tune schedules and catch up. Her glutes would have to wait.

41

"This don't taste right." Chuck Grossman held the glass up to the light and inspected his Sauvignon Blanc. He passed it to his wife. "Taste it, Vick, taste it. Don't taste no good to me."

Vicky stuck her pointy snout in the glass and sipped. "Tastes fine. What doesn't taste right about it?"

"I don't know, but it don't taste right. Usually I got no problem with Mastro's." Chuck turned to the waiter. "Benicio, dis is bad. Open a nudder bottle, will ya? See what you got laying around back dare."

Vicky rolled her eyes. "All of a sudden, after never drinking wine in his forty-nine years, Chuck's a connoisseur."

"Look, Vick, if I'm gonna shell out six bills per bottle, it better not taste like piss-stained carpet, you get me? I can't be serving dat to our lovely colleagues, here, 'specially da French ones. I'm liable to wind up under a guillotine." Chuck looked at his guests gathered round the table—Callie, Paul, and the Vernadeaus—and grinned. "You don't gotta be a wine connoisseur to know when sumptin stinks, am I right, folks?"

Roger leaned back in his chair. "I've always been partial to reds for precisely that reason. White is too bitter for my palate."

"Had I known dat, I'd have ordered a red, too. Where'd da waiter go? Hold on—"

"No, no, please. I'm fine." Roger pointed to his rocks glass. "Just Scotch tonight. No wine, not for me."

"Nan, you like red? I got no problem with dat."

Nanette gave Chuck a tight-lipped smile. "Just Perrier tonight."

"Suit yourself. Hey, since when did dis place stop playin' music? What happened to da piano player? I unnerstand da guy's gotta take a whiz at some point, but c'mon, it's been ten minutes already and no music." Chuck cranked his body around and scanned the restaurant.

From the beginning, Vicky and Chuck Grossman seemed like an unconventional couple. She came from Boca Raton stock; her grandfather made hundreds of millions off a patent on an aircraft module (the family piggy bank grew whenever and wherever a plane took off). Chuck had a far less glamorous background; a foster care Jersey kid, he built his fortune in the 90s as a massive distributor of pornography. But the pair had much in common—pack-a-day Marlboro habits, matching clothespin nose jobs, and they were both die-hard Humphrey Bogart fans. They first learned of *The Foreign Affair* after meeting Nanette's literary agent at a Beverly Hills fundraiser. With its Casablanca undercurrents, Nanette's screenplay was right up the Grossmans' alley, the perfect project for their production company.

Chuck tackled a shrimp cocktail. "Callie, you done sumptin differ'nt to yourself? Your skin, it's like buttah."

Everyone turned to stare at Callie and she blushed. "I don't know. Maybe it's this new at-home peel I've been using."

"And you've been staying out of the sun," Nanette winked.

"Dis girl, she gets prettier and prettier every time I see her. Matter of fact, she looks so good, it puts every udder actress at a disadvantage. Dare all gonna jump off a bridge when day see Callie onscreen. How come I look in da mirror every day and I only get uglier? Where's da fairness in dat?"

"It's all in the genes. My Grandma Esme has never had any surgery—she doesn't even use hair dye—and she looks half her age."

"She needs to bottle her secret and sell it to me. I got no good genes. By twenty, my ma looked like da Crypt Keeper. Nan, what's your secret to staying so daisy fresh?"

"Hollywood is enough to suck the youth out of anyone. We like to stay as far away from it as possible." Nanette patted Roger's hand and he smiled.

Callie sighed. Aloof as Mitch was on the phone, she couldn't help but wish he were at her side. Surely, he had a legitimate reason for coming off so detached—he was on set, for one, distracted with lots of people around. Plus, he wasn't a mushy kind of guy.

That was fine with her; she wasn't big on mushiness, either. Too much coochie-cooing was nauseating. And then, too, it was early in their relationship, and he liked taking things slower than she was used to. Just as well. The last thing she wanted was to come off as needy. Nothing good came out of acting desperate and overly available.

Remember, there's no big rush, she told herself. Just take it easy—

Bzzzzz.

Callie picked up her vibrating cell off the table. Mitch. Wanting her to know he's thinking about her. A smile stretched across her face.

"You look like a kid in a candy store," Paul whispered.

"It's my guy," she gushed. "We haven't had much of a chance to talk lately."

"That kid's really been on the go lately," Paul said. "He had a nice write-up in *The Hollywood Reporter*."

The piano player returned and banged out *Fly Me to the Moon*. Chuck clapped. "'Bout damned time. So, everyone, I'm glad we could find time to get togedder. At da rate we've been working, it ain't been easy. I got a surprise for all yous. A very special somebody is joining us tonight. Running a lil late, but should be here any minute."

Chuck leaned in on his elbows. "Guess who? Go on, take an off da wall guess."

"Judge Judy," Paul chirped.

"Tony Blair," said Roger.

"Nope and nope. He's male and dat's da only clue you're gonna get."

"Ron Jeremy," Callie said.

"Nope. He ain't old or fat or ugly. Guess again."

"Oh, for God's sake, Chuck." Vicky threw her head back. Her shoulder-duster earrings jounced in her frizzy brunette hair. "Nobody wants to play this game. Just tell them, already."

"Calm yourself, Vick. Some people—obviously not your-self—actually like surprises. I know I do. You people like surprises—am I wrong?"

Nanette coughed. "That depends what the surprise is in regards to. If I order a steak medium rare and it comes out burnt, that is obviously not pleasant."

"Nah, it ain't like dat, not at all." Chuck bit the tip off his pretzel bread. "Dis is definitely a good surprise, in regards to our movie. Trust me, you're all gonna love it. Matter of fact, I should prob'ly have Benicio pull a nice bottle of bub-bly. Oh, look—here's our mystery man now, comin' in." Chuck jumped to his feet. He was taller sitting down than standing up.

Callie stared at the approaching figure as though viewing a mirage and blinked. No, it couldn't be...surely, it could not be who she thought it was...

42

"Yo, Ev! Over here, buddy," Chuck yelled.

Bedroom Eyes himself, Evan Marquardt, strode over to the table, spruced and handsome as ever. Chuck slapped him on the back. "Look what da cat dragged in. Your ears ringing, bud? We was just talking 'bout choo."

Evan flashed his signature sexy grin. "I had a feeling you were. How's it going, Chuck? I love that suit, navy is definitely your color. Vicky, look at you! You should always wear your hair down, it frames that gorgeous face."

But wasn't this ass-kisser supposed to be in Japan? Callie turned her face away from the brown-nosing spectacle.

Vicky coiled her hair around a finger and stuck her cheek out for a peck. "My, for just stepping off a plane, Evan, you're looking mighty lovely yourself."

"Thank you. I may be unaware what time zone I'm in half the time, but I try to clean up well. Mr. Angers. It's been a while, hasn't it?" Evan shook Paul's hand and locked eyes with Callie. "Hello, Callie. How goes it?"

Callie pasted a smile on her face. "Just fine. And you?"

"Jet-lagged beyond belief, but other than that, fantastic."

"Nice," Chuck said. "You two already know each udder."

"Yes," Evan grinned. "Quite well, I'd say. Callie's one of my favorite people, as a matter of fact."

"Oh, dat's right—what am I saying? You two dated a coupla years ago. How could I have forgotten dat? Everyone, I know dis guy don't need no introduction, but allow me to present my guest of honor, Mr. Evan Marquardt. Evan, dis is Nanette, da director of dat film we was talking about and her hubby, Roger, who's co-producer. Please, Ev, have a seat. Yo, Benicio? My friend needs a drink. What'll you have, Ev?"

Evan collapsed in the chair. "You know, Chuck, I'm so jet lagged, I probably shouldn't. Okinawa to L.A. is no joke."

"What are you talking about? Even more reason why you need a drink—gotta unwind after such a long flight. Go on, order some'n, anything you want. You like Louis XIII? Benicio, get my friend a Louis XIII, straight-up."

Evan turned to Roger. "Monsieur, I have to tell you the last film you produced is my son's all-time favorite. He loves anything having to do with astronauts and outer space."

Roger smiled and the skin around his eyes rumpled. "Please, call me Roger. And thank you. It gives me great pleasure when I can bring joy to a young one's life. My wife and I have two boys of our own. They're grown now, so I can hardly call them boys anymore. How old is your son, Evan?"

"He's eight," said Evan. "But sometimes I feel like he's older than his old man—too clever for his own good."

"How has Riley been?" Callie said. She couldn't help having a soft spot for the kid.

"Fantastic, just fantastic, thanks. I took him on tour with me for much of last summer. It was a perfect time with school being out. Spain, Bali, the Greek Isles, you name it. He loved it. You would have loved the Greek Isles, Cal." Evan winked.

"I guess that would depend who I was with," said Callie. "Now, if I were with my boyfriend, that would be great. But I wouldn't want to go with anyone else and since he's in Ireland right now, it won't be happening anytime soon." She sipped her wine and stole a glance at Evan.

Evan grinned. "Boyfriend? That's great. Who's the lucky lad?"

"He's in the business. He's very sweet and trustworthy and very mature," she said.

"I'm happy for you. You deserve someone special."

"That I do," she said. *Why aren't you getting jealous, Bedroom Eyes, you freak?*

Chuck jumped in the lull. "So, onto da business at hand. A coupla days ago, I got a call from Ev's manager, Gary Benson. He heard about our lil situation regarding dat junkie, what's-his-face. I forgot da bastard's name already—"

"Pierre," said Vicky.

"Dat's right. Pierre. Gary heard about Pierre flunking outta our film and said he had just da guy for us—a certain talented, primo client of his. Well, I gotta tell ya, even doe Ev's a huge star and all, I was a lil hesitant. You know, sometimes singers who wanna be actors, it don't work out so good. But I says, 'what da hey, we don't got many prospects here on da horizon.' Dis role takes a special kinda someone and Nan, here, she's real particular about who should play Roland. To make a long story short, me and Ev and Vick Skyped while he was over in Japan and I'm now completely convinced he's da only man for da job."

Roger, hands clasped, leaned forward ever so slightly in his chair, but Nanette looked less than enthused. "How nice," she said. "But don't forget, we've been in talks with Clyde Kerbow's people, and we should know any minute if he's available. He's trying to rearrange his entire schedule for us."

"Wid all due respect, Nan, we don't exactly got time for some clown to get back to us. Besides, humor me—who da hell is Clyde Kerbow?" Chuck said.

"Isn't that the guy who swung by the set for lunch the other day?" Vicky took a large slurp of wine.

"Yes," Nanette said. "Roger and I have known Clyde for years. He's a classically trained actor with much substance and tremendous depth."

"He just finished a film with Vincent Cassel and already, it's getting rave reviews," Roger added.

"Well, I was none too impressed," said Vicky. "He seemed too sensitive. A big, wet blanket."

"Clyde was so exciting I can't even remember him," piped Chuck. "I don't care how many kudos he's gettin', he don't got shit on this man here. Ev's got more commercial appeal dan a bottle of Coca-Cola. You put his name on da marquee—Marquardt on da marquee, I like da sound of dat—and it's a done deal. Chicks will fly outta da woodwork."

"Chuck is being too kind," Evan said. "Madame, if I may say so, your screenplay is incredible. Pure genius. I read it within an hour and was blown away."

Nanette swirled her lemon wedge around in her water glass. "What exactly do you like about it?"

"Everyding," Chuck intercepted. "I faxed him da script, he loves it. And we already know dem two"—he flapped his hand at Callie and Evan—"got chemistry."

Nanette avoided eye contact with Chuck. "Roland is a complicated character, Evan. Very complex. He has a paradoxical personality—very warm and loving on one hand and yet he's a cold-blooded killer. What about him appeals to you?"

"He relates to da character, Nan—da good stuff, not da bad stuff. I found out a lot about Ev and his family, stuff dat truly surprised me dat I never knew before. Dis guy's deep, he's got a lotta soul to him."

Nanette shot daggers at Chuck but before she could raise her voice, Evan said, "Please, Chuck, allow me. Madame, vous etes Francois, non?"

Evan struck up a conversation with the Vernadeaus. The foreign syllables pinged and ponged off each of their tongues with such rapidity, Callie gave up trying to decipher any key words. Whatever Evan was saying to win Nanette over appeared to be working. She nodded and smiled, her blue eyes earnestly pinned to his.

"What da hell day talkin' 'bout?" mumbled Chuck.

"It's over your head, sweetheart," Vicky said and stared at Evan with googly eyes. Callie was sure she spotted a trickle of saliva spewing from the corner of the forty-five-year-old's mouth.

"How we doing, Cal?" Paul said with a nudge. He looked at her apologetically but she couldn't muster a response.

Why the hell did I mention anything to Gary at that Warner Bros. party? Gary would have eventually heard that a new leading man was needed, but still. Nothing like tying your own noose. Callie ground her stilettos into the hardwood floor. Damn it! There was no way she was going to be in a movie with Evan, that snake. That lying, disarming son-of-a-bitch! She wouldn't—couldn't- work with him. This wasn't part of the deal, part of her contract; when she signed on, she was told Pierre was co-starring.

Surely there had to be a way out. She'd have to sic Paul on it and have him find some wiggle room...

Benicio appeared, pen and pad-of-paper in hand. "And have we all decided what we'd like to order?"

"I'll tell ya, one ding, I'm so hungry, I could eat dis here table cloth. Benicio, why don't you gimme a New York, rare. Wid a side of your creamed corn. Love dat stuff. What's everyone else havin'?"

Evan said something in French to the Vernadeaus and they burst into laughter. The pit in Callie's stomach became deeper and she pushed her menu away. Her appetite had long since vanished.

43

"What do you mean there's no wiggle room?" Callie puffed.

"I mean exactly what I said—there's no wiggle room," Paul said. "There's no way for you to get out of doing this film. Not without a lawsuit on your hands, and I'm guessing you're none too interested in another one of those," Paul said.

Callie fell onto one of Paul's cushiony office chairs. "Oh, why not? Throw that in the pile."

"You don't have casting approval in your contract, so there's not much you can do, I'm afraid."

"I can't believe they want Evan! I just can't believe it. Of all the projects out there, he has to be interested in this one. He doesn't even have any acting experience, does he?"

"Not much, but Nanette is sold on him—and if she's sold on him, that's all that counts. He may not be as big of a star as he was two years ago, but he's still one hot ticket. Evan's already working on the soundtrack for the movie."

"The soundtrack? Don't they need to finish the movie before they can do all that?"

"The theme song, I mean," said Paul. "Nanette asked him to write a couple new songs."

"Great. Twenty-four hours haven't even passed and already it's an Evan Marquardt production. I feel so comforted knowing he's taking over the whole freaking movie. I hope they know, Paul, it's all just an act. Evan can charm the pants off anyone, but he's only interested in one thing, and that's himself."

"Well, he has something in common with the rest of Hollywood, then."

Callie rolled her eyes. "How can they afford him? He's gotta be super expensive, and aren't they over-budget?"

"He's taking a big pay cut. If the film does well, he'll receive a hefty percentage of the profits. You two don't have that many scenes together, either, if I remember the script correctly. What is it—five, six scenes?"

"Try nine," she bemoaned. "I already counted."

"Still, a relatively few number, considering you two are the leads. And your role is far bigger than his."

"But then there's promotion—the interviews and photo shoots. Ugh. The press will have quite the field day," muttered Callie. "Everyone knows he couldn't be faithful. How embarrassing."

Paul crossed his arms. "Wait a minute, young lady— you're the one who dumped him. If anything, he should be embarrassed. Watch playing the pity card—it's not attractive. Sympathy turns pathetic very quickly. The last thing the public needs is another Jennifer Aniston."

Callie sighed. "Point taken."

The phone rang and Paul picked up. "Hello? Sandy, how are you? Mmm-hmm. Mmm-hmm...Okay...You're talking about Steven's audition tomorrow, correct?...Mmm- hmm. Mmm-hmm...At two sharp, got it...Sure thing, I'll let him know the director will be sitting in on this one...Yes, he is always extremely professional...What's that?...Yes, Evan Marquardt is now on board...We are, yes—we're all incredibly excited...Oh, yeah, Callie's more than fine with it. She's able to separate her personal life from her professional one just fine...Yeah, I think they'll be dynamite together, too. Sandy, I'm with a client, how about if I call you back in five? Thanks, bye-bye."

"Sandy, as in the casting director, Sandy Gillick?" Callie said.

"Yep. Everyone's chomping at the bit to see you and Marquardt on screen together. Just look at it this way: the fact that people know you two have a past—that right there is golden. It's the curiosity factor and you can't pay for that kind of publicity. There are lots of positives in this, Callie, financially-speaking. It may not be the most comfortable situation for you, but it's only temporary, kid, so take a deep breath, suck it up, and you don't have to look at the guy again when all is said and done."

Paul was right, of course; he was always so logical and pragmatic and Callie appreciated how he put things in perspective. "You always keep my head screwed on straight, Paul."

"It's my job, young lady. Same thing I always say. Oh, *Movie Madness* wants you for a six-page layout."

Callie's ears perked. "The cover?"

"Absolutely. I told them we weren't interested, otherwise. The cover, guaranteed, along with an interview. They're thinking of a Vargas Girl theme. Most likely, it will be for their December issue. Probably in the next week or two."

Callie popped her knuckles. "Cool. Merry Christmas to me." "How's your Gabby foundation coming along?"

"It's coming. Slowly, but it's getting there. I'm thinking of kicking off the charity with a fall fashion show. Something fun and glamorous and my friend, Luci, knows a ton of people in that industry."

Paul tapped his pencil on his desk. "I like that. And doesn't she work for that entertainment show now? She could give you some stellar coverage."

"For sure. I was doing a little research on the net this morning. It's kind of overwhelming, all the preparation involved. I need to find a show producer, a backstage manager, sponsors, all sorts of things. I'm probably going to have to hire an assistant, but God knows that didn't exactly work out too well for me in the past." During her *Cheerleader Chronicles* days, she had hired a personal assistant twice, but because of one's chronic tardiness and the other's blabbing to the press, both employees had been canned in next to no time.

"That's an awful lot of responsibility to handle on your own," he said. "You're going to need help."

"But help is pricey, and I'm trying to cut back on expenses right now, otherwise I would have hired someone long before now."

"Well, whatever I can help you with, let me know."

"Thanks. Actually, I'm supposed to meet my friend, Luci, in a half hour, so I'll talk to her about my idea for a fashion show. She's finally picking up the rest of her stuff from my house." Callie failed to mention she was meeting Emily afterwards for lunch; better to keep certain things private.

"Scoot. Get out of here. Oh, and your call-time tomorrow got moved from 8 A.M. to 6 A.M."

"Aye-aye, captain. Catch you later."

44

"So..." Emily said.

"So," Callie repeated. She whisked a packet of sugar in her iced tea.

"So here we are. Sorry, I'm not usually tongue-tied." Emily buttoned her grass green cardigan. The hyperactive AC turned the Palm's usually cozy dining room into a meat locker.

"Neither am I. Usually you can't get me to shut up. I get it from Mom, I guess."

"Yeah, she does like to talk a lot." Emily planted a sprig of arugula in her upturned, rosebud mouth. Physically, she was as non-L.A. as Callie had seen in years; her face possessed trace amounts of pressed powder but was mostly bare and her hair hadn't seen a bottle of hair dye in ages, if ever. With her Keds and pedal pushers, Emily resembled a young, female version of Mr. Rogers.

"Have you decided when you're going to meet her?" said Callie.

Emily shook her head. "I'm not. I was going to but...I've given it a lot of thought and I don't feel the need anymore. I mean, I'm very grateful to Virginia for being so kind and open—she knows that, too—and I'd like to stay in touch, but it can only go so far. I already have a mom—a really good one."

Callie smiled; she didn't like anyone trespassing on her turf. "That makes sense. How does your mom feel about you delving in your past like this?"

"She's been the most supportive woman on the planet. I'm very lucky, very fortunate to have someone like her. She knows no one can replace her, so she doesn't feel threatened. But if I were in her shoes, I would feel threatened, I think, if my daughter came to me wanting to speak to her biological mother. I definitely wouldn't like it."

"I wouldn't, either. Do you want kids, Emily?"

Emily finished chewing and smiled. "Yes, I do. And soon. Once Wesley—that's my boyfriend—is a little more settled in his career, we plan on getting married and starting a family."

"What does he do?"

"He's a pediatrician, so, you see, we're practically mandated to have kids. It suits me just fine. I've always seen myself with four kids and two dogs."

"Four?"

"Definitely four, maybe more. I love children. What about you? Don't you want kids?"

"I don't see kids in my future," Callie said. "Nope, can't see that at all."

"Really, none? I've always wanted a big family. Maybe it was because I grew up without any brothers and sisters and always felt I missed out. I hadn't planned on starting so late, but what can you do? My mom got sick with breast cancer right around the time I was planning on going off to college. I was nineteen then. That delayed things quite a bit. I took care of her while my dad held down two jobs and she beat it. She's been officially free and clear for five years now."

"That's great news. How bad was it?"

"Stage III. She fought and pulled through like a champ."

Callie swirled a French fry in a pool of mayonnaise. "Has my mom—I mean, not just my mom but your mom, too—or our mom, whichever—"

"Callie," Emily said with a pat of the hand. "It's okay. You're not going to offend me by calling her your mother. Let's not get crazy."

Callie blushed. "I know, it's just a little weird still. The lingo and political correctness of it all."

Emily rolled her eyes—the same eye roll Callie practiced on an almost daily basis. "I hate being politically correct. Can't stand it, it's stupid and archaic. I'm sorry, you were saying?"

"Has Mom talked much about her cancer?"

"A little bit. Not much, but it sounds like she's kicking it right where it hurts."

"Definitely, she is. It seemed pretty grim in the beginning, but she's on the fast track back to health."

"Thank goodness. What little I know of Virginia, she seems like a very strong woman. That's something I picked up on right away."

"That's her, alright. She's been stubborn and strong my whole life. She's always had her own opinions about what I should be doing, how I should be leading my life and what I'm doing wrong. It used to really rub me the wrong way but we've both mellowed out a little. I still don't think she understands that just because I earn a living in a not-so-normal way, it doesn't make me a kook."

"No way, I'm sure she doesn't think you're a kook," said Emily. "She's never said anything close to that. Quite the opposite, actually; she told me she couldn't believe you made it but she sure is—"

Callie dropped her fork. "Made it? She said I made it?"

"Yes, made it—those exact words. The odds were stacked against you, but she's very proud of your accomplishments. And so am I. Who moves to Hollywood on a whim and gets to be a big-time actress? Nobody does that. I would give my left foot for your guts—gosh, for your whole life, what am I saying."

"Smoke and mirrors," muttered Callie.

"Take myself, for instance. During the time I was working on my bachelor's, I was a tutor. I haven't tutored since my father died—he left me a bit of money, so I've been solely focusing on getting my master's—but I enjoyed it at the time. It wasn't bad but it wasn't exciting, either—it was a job, the same task every day. Nothing remotely similar to what you deal with, what with all the glamorous costumes and celebrities. I can't even imagine how fun it must be for you to show up to work, if you can even call it work. Do you

252

just march to a movie set every day? How does that work, exactly?"

"No, not every day. I don't always have a TV show or film going on, that's what most people don't realize. And it's not a good feeling when I don't."

"But you've had a lot of steady work so you're obviously doing something right. And it must be so nice having your hair and makeup done all the time, right?"

Callie shrugged. "Honestly, the whole process is pretty boring. You should see how awful it is when a one-page scene turns into a ten hour catastrophe because of something technical, like a lighting problem or God-knows-what."

"I would love to see what that's like," Emily breathed. "Any time you feel like inviting me to the set, I'm yours. Just give me the word, I'll be your gofer, your guest, anything."

"It's not as exciting as you think. There's a lot of standing around."

"Then I'll be happy as a clam standing around holding your coffee or parasol, or whatever. Promise. I just want a glimpse of your world and see what it's like. That's it, just a little glimpse."

"K, I'll keep that in mind."

"But right now, there's something bugging me, something I want to ask you. There's just one thing I can't quite figure out."

"Okay, shoot."

Emily propped her elbows on the table. "How in the world do you stay so thin eating fries with mayonnaise? That's the most fattening thing out there and, look at you, you're to-die-for skinny! What's your secret?"

She liked Emily; it was difficult not to. The girl was unpretentious and smart and her naiveté, in a world of jaded Angelenos, was refreshing. Callie felt more like the worldly big sister than the younger shrimp and she liked that, too. A lot. This sister thing could wind up being kind of cool, she thought. Maybe.

45

"For ten years straight, I showed up on set—always on time, never late—spread my legs, made a shit-load of money, and now I have the luxury of chillin' on my fat stacks and enjoying myself," Eden Emerson proclaimed. "I just pick and choose the projects I wanna do and work when I feel like it. I live the kind of life most people only dream of and I feel an obligation to show people I'm more than just a fuck machine to jerk off to. I'm more than a sex icon. I'm much deeper than that—no pun intended, of course. I can sing—my first single's coming out later this year—and I run my own production company. I'm the top bitch, I run it like no one's business. And with all that, I find time to be a mommy to three Rottweilers and be a wife to Ray. See, no one gets that—I really am a real life fucking Donna Reed. And I make the most rockin' tuna noodle casserole you've ever tasted in your life. I'm a really, you know, diverse chick."

Eden adjusted herself in the director's chair. The 109 degree heat wasn't doing her makeup any favors; her gloss was in the midst of melting off her pillowy lower lip. Her pout was stuffed with so much filler, noted Callie, it was rigid as a duck's bill.

"I bet," Callie mumbled. She couldn't decide if Eden's lips looked more like a pair of mating slugs or a swollen labia. Given Eden's former profession, probably the latter.

Eden first started off as Elsa Morgenstern, an ordinary girl with above-average looks—by Austin, Texas standards, anyway. The dirty blonde had met her future manager and husband, Ray, while stripping at The Pink Monkey. For five straight months, Ray was her most ardent customer, stuffing bills in her G-string every Wednesday and Saturday night. His plans for Eden were far too grand for Austin to contain and he soon whisked her off to Los Angeles. "If you're gonna be an adult entertainer, you may as well do porn," he told her. "My buddy owns a huge distribution company and is quite the hook-up. You're gonna make a mint." Ray was right; by age twenty, Eden was the top adult performer and rolling in dough. Each new year saw a change in her appearance as much as her net worth; the teeth became whiter, the mouth poutier, the nose smaller, the jaw sharper, and the cheeks plumper (the press reported she even had a vaginoplasty but Eden denied it saying, "The only thing I've done down there is anal bleaching. But, let's face it, everyone does that").

"No one realizes how diverse I actually am," Eden said. "Or how much money I've made. I can buy and sell anyone's ass in two shakes of a lamb's tail, hands down. I made a killing and got out while I still got youth on my side. You know, Callie, you would be great in that industry."

Callie shooed a fly away. "Me? In porn?"

"Fuck yeah. You've got that whole girl-next-door-thing. Guys really bust a nut for that. It's not just the whole big boob blonde schtick, like me, you know."

"Good to know I have a back-up, in case my mainstream career doesn't go well."

"You gotta have options," Eden winked. "Hey, have you ever had Eggs Florentine?"

"No, what is it?"

"It's this dish my husband taught me," said Eden. "It's got spinach and hollandaise and is just hella dope. Florentine... what is that, Italian?"

Did this girl ever shut up? Callie needed to chill in her zone, the way she always did right before a scene. But Eden obviously had other ideas and Callie didn't want to be a snob. "I'm not sure. I've never been to Italy."

"Neither have I," Eden said. She unbuttoned her high-necked ruffled blouse and aired out her cleavage. "We've got such amazing Italian food and designers here in the U.S., I don't see the point. I got the sickest $8,000 Gucci python boots the other day. They're limited edition and so hard to come by, I can't believe I found a pair. You're telling me I'd be able to find those same boots over there? I don't think so. I mean, I love to travel, but I want to go to Milan, not Italy."

Callie gave Eden the side-eye. How this dense creature was supposed to be remotely convincing as a demure housewife was a mystery. Callie wondered what on earth Nanette had been thinking. Even though Eden was a friend of Chuck's and had just four lines, it wasn't like the normally meticulous Frenchwoman to overlook such a blatant miscasting. Strange.

Two dozen crew members bustled around the girls. "Has anyone seen Nanette?" said someone from the sound department. "Everyone's ready to block and get this scene up."

As if on cue, a rickety door slammed and Nanette appeared. Large, square-framed shades covered her face and her skin was paler than usual. The crew rushed to clear a path for her as she hulked on set. Her air was so heavy, so sour, Callie expected to see a black cape trailing her, à la Darth Vader.

"Who's that?" mumbled Eden.

"Nanette, the director," Callie said.

"Oh, really? Isn't she a little old to still be on her period? But, then, Chuck warned me she's a real pisser."

"Nanette's great, even though lately she's seemed a tad cranky."

Several yards off, Nanette stooped to inspect the old Buick parked in the driveway. "Jeremiah! Why is this car so clean?"

Jeremiah's flushed face went blank. "Gee, Nan, I think it was washed yesterday—"

"You think? If Jeanette has been busy trying to find out who killed her father, do you really think she would have time to wash her car? Continuity, Jeremiah. It's all about continuity, and my film must have it. Grab the set designer and tell him the car needs to be scruffed up, will you? His name escapes me at the moment..."

"Callum. Okay, boss, will do." Jeremiah ran off.

Eden whispered to Callie, "Cranky much? Maybe if she removed the baguette out of her twat she'd feel better."

Nanette swung around and faced the girls. Because of her dark lenses, Callie couldn't tell who she was staring at, herself or Eden. She marched over to the actresses with furious strides, grinding her Tod's deep in the soil. Callie pitied the blades of grass as they crunched under her feet.

46

"Mon Dieu! But what is this?" Nanette stood before Eden. "Excuse me, who are you?"

"Eden."

"Eden?"

"Yeah, Eden Emerson. You know, like the writer."

"No, no," Nanette said, "Who are you as in whom are you playing?"

"Mrs. Cartwright, the cop's wife. You know, the scene where Jeanette drives over to my house after she and Roland—"

"Yes, I realize what scene it is," Nanette said in a clipped tone. "I wrote it. But what I don't understand is why on God's green earth you are here. Where is Chuck?" She craned her neck and searched through the crowd of people. "Chuck! Chuck!"

Chuck ran over with a cell plugged to his ear. "Vick, I gotta call you back. What's da problem, Nan?"

"What happened to Melodie?" demanded Nanette.

"Oh, Melodie Scott? She dropped out 'cause of a scheduling conflict. 'Member? I told you 'bout it a few days ago. You said to find someone, so I hired my friend, Eden, here."

"What?! You hired this…this…thing without my permission?"

"Nan, it's a small part and ain't too difficult. Eden's up for it."

"Without my permission?" Nanette's delicate nostrils flared.

"Well, excuse me, Empress Josephine, but maybe you shoulda said sumptin before now. I showed you a picture of Eden. You knew who she was when you okayed her."

"Are you mad? It's a period piece, not the Folies Bergere. I would never in a million

years okay someone this cheap!"

"Well, you did, you just don't remember for some reason. And you don't gotta insult my friend, here, it ain't her fault. So what we gonna do now, huh? You got a better idea?"

"You in heels and a wig would be a better idea than this. Pour l'amour de Dieu! And another thing—" Nanette turned to Eden. "—the next time you're on set and see one of these chairs, here is a tip: it is intended for one person and one person only and that is the director."

"You know, lady, you're a real bitch," Eden snarled. A hush fell over the set.

Nanette took a step forward. "Mademoiselle, I'm sorry you were mistakenly told your services were needed—they are not, and it was an error on my colleague's part, one I will make sure never gets repeated. And if you weren't aware of this before, be aware now: this bitch standing before you is the boss around here. This is my set, my rules, and I call the shots. Understood? Now, before I get angry, move your putrid cunt off my chair and get the fuck off my set."

Callie sucked in her breath; had she heard that correctly? She knew Nanette had a temper but never would have guessed her tongue was so colorful.

"Your movies suck, anyway," hissed Eden before stomping off.

Chuck threw his hands in the air. "I don't believe dis shit. Unbelievable. Now we don't got no one for da part. How do you plan on solving dis?"

"Simple." Nanette manhandled her Smart Phone. "I'll call Roger and he'll send someone over. He always keeps dozens of actors on stand-by."

"Dat's gonna take awhile. Meanwhile, we're losing money."

Callie spoke up. "I have an idea."

"Not now, Callie, I got problems. I gotta get a broad over here ASAP for dis part. Udderwise, we'll lose da whole day and den some."

"I wasn't talking to you, Chuck; I was talking to Nanette. I have just the girl—my sister, Emily. She'd be totally believable as Mrs. Cartwright. She was helping me go over my sides earlier and knows all the lines. She's actually here right now."

"Huh? What do you mean?" Chuck squinted. "What, da whole family hangs wid you in case day need to make a special appearance or sumptin?"

"I invited her to the set," Callie said. "Last I checked, it's not a crime. I don't know where Em went, but she was here just a minute ago..."

"She went to get something to drink, Cal," said Jeremiah.

Nanette touched Callie's shoulders. "Callie, what an angel you are. I saw her earlier. She is perfect, real-looking and intelligent, unlike the other one. And she won't take long in the chair, either. Where is Miss D? Miss D, I want nothing but the bare necessities. A pale, matte lip. Unless a brothel or street-walking scene magically pops up in my screenplay, I want nothing remotely glossy on anyone's lips. And where is Stella? Stella, there you are. Don't make the hair quite so severe. I want it pulled back but not slicked back. Yes, Emily will do quite nicely."

"Is she union?" barked Chuck.

"Does it matter?" said Nanette. "If she isn't, Taft-Hartley her. We haven't time to nitpick over such things, Chuck. I need her in hair and makeup yesterday. And that takes care of that. Now, back to business." She turned to her crew to discuss a scene.

Chuck glared at the Frenchwoman. "Can you believe dis broad? What da fuck did I get myself into? Alright, I'm off to grab your sister. Un-fucking-real."

47

"I let down my guard and let you in and this is what I get? I trusted you," Callie sobbed as Evan touched her cheek. "Don't touch me! Don't you touch me. Keep away. I don't know you anymore. I don't suppose I ever did."

"Darling—"

"No, no, no! Don't you dare. There are no more darlings; it's too late for endearments. Good-bye."

"Please—"

Callie ran out and left Evan standing in the middle of the room with his head hung low.

"Cut!" La directeur tore off her headphones. "That was the best take thus far." She turned to her monitor. "Show me the playback."

Callie walked back into the room and wiped away the perspiration from her décolletage. Fuck, these lights are hot. The two-story house was stifling to begin with (the AC had to be cut for sound purposes) but coupled with the lighting equipment, it was a bona fide cremator. An assistant handed Evan and Callie their water bottles.

"You okay, Cal?" Evan said.

"Yeah, just spent." What an emotional roller coaster. Callie had always channeled her inner turmoil into acting—that was one of the many plusses of the craft—but this scene had been especially rough. Maybe because playing opposite Bedroom Eyes unearthed an array of emotions. Her whole body felt depleted, like a balloon out of air. The camera better be picking up every sliver of pain, she thought; otherwise, what was the point in reliving the blood, sweat, and tears?

"I have to hand it to you," said Evan, "I knew you were talented but I didn't know just how good of an actress you really are. I actually feel a little bad; my character is such a jerk, I almost feel the need to apologize."

"Don't," Callie said. "You know it's all just part of the job. Besides, why apologize for something you didn't do when you could apologize for something you actually did do? Kind of backwards, don't you think?"

Jeremiah clomped over. "Evan and Callie, you two are wrapped."

"Thanks, Jeremiah." Evan paused before saying in a hushed tone, "When are you going to forgive me and let the past go? What do I have to do, crawl on shards of glass, on hands and knees, and beg for my life?"

"That would be a start."

He smirked. "I've got a better idea; there's a thirty-year-old bottle of Scotch in my trailer. What do you say we knock back a few?"

"Aren't all your handlers and brown-nosers around? No, thanks."

"For your information, my assistant was the only one on set today and she left several takes ago. Come on, it's ridiculous how long it's been since we've caught up. And you look like you could really use a shot."

Callie felt like a discarded wet rag—sweaty, limp, and lonely. "Why not?"

Evan's trailer was just as loaded as Callie's, except he had a sixty-two inch flatscreen and Sub Zero appliances. Made sense; he was the bigger star, after all.

"Sorry about the mess." He cleared a pile of clothes off the couch and handed her a Baccarat glass.

"Yum," Callie said after a sip. The smoky-sweet liquid burned her pipes.

"Not too shabby, is it?" Evan plopped his feet on the coffee table.

"Mmm. Every day should end like this."

"I agree." He searched her eyes a moment before grinning. "Callie, Callie, Callie. What am I going to do with you?"

She arched a brow. "What do you mean?"

"The only way you'll talk to me is if I ply you full of a thousand dollar bottle of Scotch. A little pricey, don't you think?"

"You're getting off way too easy, Evan. Just think, it could have been a ten thousand dollar bottle. And I know you have it, too, because we've drunk it together."

Evan reached out to touch her knee. "God, I've missed you. You're gorgeous, talented, funny—you're perfect, really. Why aren't we still together?"

"Because I'm also smart," said Callie. "I don't believe in making the same mistake twice. And anyone who chooses to be with a low-rent like Stephanie Schueller doesn't deserve me."

"Aren't we spiteful tonight? You mean to tell me you haven't dated your share of tragedies?"

"Nope, I haven't. Not even close. She's just so....I mean, not to be rude, Evan, but what the hell were you thinking? And engaged?"

"She was fantastic, at first," sighed Evan. "Then she got a little too comfortable and in no time at all, she revealed herself to be the psychotic gold-digger everyone warned me about."

"I've got a theory on that. You can spot a gold digger based on their lips. Every girl in L.A. with inflated sausage lips is a bona fide gold-digger. Fair warning."

Evan laughed. "Really?"

"I swear," Callie said.

"I'll have to pay better attention then. To be honest, I've got a lot of empathy for the girl; her mother killed herself when Stephanie was fifteen and it really did a number on her."

Callie shrugged. "My dad died when I was five, but that doesn't give me a license to be an asshole. You don't see me throwing bullshit lawsuits at people."

Evan laughed again—she loved making him laugh—and moved closer. He placed her hands in his. "Listen, I know I fucked up. I knew it then but I'm really paying for it now. You may not believe me, but I swear I'm reformed."

"You're right, I don't believe you. In fact, I think you're full of shit."

"Christ, can't you ease up a little? I have my faults, but being full of shit is not one of them."

"Ha! Of course you're full of shit! Like every true blue player, you're full of shit. I just wish you had left me out of your little game and—oh, never mind. Whatever." She scooted further away and tipped her glass.

"Please, continue. You wish I had left you out—"

"Look, you're not a relationship kind of guy. Fine, I get that. I just wish you would have filled me in from the get go so we wouldn't be having this conversation."

"But I wanted to make it work with you, Cal, I really did. For the majority of our time together, I was on my best behavior."

"What?" Callie couldn't believe her ears. "If getting caught with two random sluts is your best behavior, what the hell is your worst?"

"I was an asshole. There, I said it. Yes, I was a giant, selfish asshole and I'm sorry. I'm imperfect—I made mistakes and will continue to make mistakes, but I've left those ways behind me."

Callie stared at his beautiful face; Miss D's team had done their best to scruff up his features, creating under eye circles and a scar above his lip, but it was impossible to erase his handsomeness. "Oh, you have?"

"One hundred percent. I'm a better man now."

He was pulling her in, she could feel it, suctioning her libido with every blink of his carnal eyes. *Don't let him suck you in*, she thought. "I have a hard time believing that."

"I swear I've changed. Give me another chance."

"I can't, Evan. I've changed, too. I've learned from my mistakes."

Evan freed her hands. "Fair enough. How's your family?"

Good. Better to stay on safe subjects. "Great, thanks. Grandma is fine—she still asks about you, actually."

"Tell her hello for me. I love that woman."

"I will. Lots of stuff has been going on lately, actually. I found out I have an older sister. I have to tell you about this..."

"Holy Christ," Evan said when she finished. "That's intense. Someone mentioned Emily the other day. Said she replaced some awful porn star at the last minute. One of Chuck's brilliant casting jobs. I thought surely they had their information wrong when I heard because I knew you didn't have any siblings."

"Truth really is stranger than fiction. Em was so excited, she hadn't even stepped foot on a set before. The first time she does, she gets asked to say a few lines. How cool is that? No audition, no screen test, nothing. They just threw her in on a whim and she aced it. Gotta love that. She did an awesome job, too."

"That's not surprising," Evan said. "I think acting must run in your blood. You can outact me any day of the week, I'll tell you that. So you two are bonding, is that it?"

"Yeah, I think we are. It's...I don't know, it's kind of cool. I feel like I have someone in my corner, on my team. We're not much alike, but I like her. I can't get too attached though, 'cause she's only here for a summer internship. I doubt I'll see her much in the future. Honestly, I think she would have been happier if you had done the scene with her instead of me, Evan. She's a big fan; she's even YouTubed all your foreign talk shows." The liquor slackened her muscles and she stretched her legs on the ottoman. "God, I was so pissed when I found out you were in this movie. It felt like a nightmare."

"It couldn't have seemed that bad, you're joking."

"No, I'm not. When I saw you stroll in to Mastro's, I was thoroughly shocked. Oh, and do you think you could have turned the charm on any higher? You schmoozed the Vernadeaus like a seasoned con man. I can see right through you, mister. You're not as sly you think. Of all the projects you have your pick of, you want this one. What's up with that?"

Evan circled his index finger around the rim of the glass. "I've always been ambitious, you know that. I want it all."

"Mmm, don't I know it."

"Come on, now—that's not what I mean. It's essential to be multi-faceted in this industry if you want any shot at longevity. I haven't done a film before, so it's the perfect vehicle for me. I can shed some of my pretty boy image and, with a little luck, gain a few accolades in the process."

Callie cocked her head. "Out of the hundreds of films in production this very second, you just happen to choose the one I'm in? Gee, what a coincidence."

"Okay, fine, it's true—while I love the script, it wasn't the first thing that attracted me. When Gary called and told me you were in a movie that had just lost their male lead, well...how could I resist? I'd be stupid to not be interested. You can't begrudge me wanting to get close to you. You're not the easiest person to get a hold of these days."

"You always have an agenda, Evan, I'll give you that." She rose. "I have to get going."

"Suit yourself. Let me walk you out. Callie..."

She turned around. "Yeah?"

"On my son's life, I swear I'm more than capable of being a one-woman man. Let me prove it to you. We were good together, you have to admit that. We really made a good couple, didn't we?"

"Evan, it doesn't matter anymore. I told you, I don't make the same mistake twice. What's done is done. And, anyway, I have other things going on."

"What, as in you're seeing someone? Really. Who is he?"

"What does it matter? There's never going to be a 'we' again." Callie opened the door and hopped down the steps. "Thanks for the Scotch."

48

Callie crossed her legs and sighed. She hated interviews. Written ones, not so much, but interviews on-camera—forget it. She always felt as though she were being interrogated, no matter how nice the reporter was, and with Bedroom Eyes sitting next to her, mic'd up and ready for his close-up, she was doubly nervous; they'd never been interviewed together and she dreaded the personal questions that would inevitably come up.

JuJu Phillips' pin thin lips gaped into a mile-long grin. "So, you two—tell me about where we are right now."

"It's an old automobile factory," Evan said. "It shut down years ago, but we're shooting a few scenes here for the next week or so. Rather dark and creepy, isn't it, JuJu?"

"I was just going to say how depressing it is," laughed JuJu. "Not exactly the glamour one would picture when making a movie."

"The producers wanted to film on the water in the Caribbean, but Callie and I decided that would be absolutely disgusting," Evan joked. "We told them, 'Look here, guys, if you make us go down to the bloody Caribbean, we're out of here. It's Detroit we want, take it or leave it."

"We had to put our foot down," Callie chimed in.

"I bet, I bet. You two are too funny. So, I just have to ask..." JuJu paused for dramatic effect.

Oh, boy, here it comes. No sooner had ten seconds passed and already the reporter was launching into something stupid, Callie could feel it.

"After being romantically linked in the past," continued JuJu, "what's it like working together on this movie?"

"Callie is one of the most professional people I've ever worked with," Evan said. "She's always prepared and has so many different ideas on how to handle a scene, I'm enjoying just watching her. In terms of acting experience, she's light years ahead of me, so I'm learning a thing or two, believe me. She's a generous girl, a generous friend."

"Rumor has it, you both were more than just friends." JuJu's smile grew.

"Rumor has it, indeed," he winked.

"Neither of you have spoken publicly about the nature of your relationship—or, for that matter, even acknowledged having been involved—so this is as good a time as any to come clean to all your fans, don't you think?"

"But then you'd grow bored with us," Evan said. "If we told you everything you wanted to hear, you'd all grow tired of us and we wouldn't be of much interest anymore, would we be?"

"Oh, I think there are plenty out there who will always find you interesting, Evan. I'm sure of that, I already know of one girl in particular..." JuJu bit her pencil and giggled.

Bitch, please. Callie squashed an eye roll. "Evan's right, we wouldn't want to bore you. All of the 'he said, she said, did they, didn't they'—it's kind of irrelevant."

"Is it safe to say it's easier for you to play onscreen lovers because of your past? Or does your past make it more difficult?" quizzed JuJu.

"No, you don't," laughed Evan. "JuJu, you bad girl, you. I'm not falling for that one."

JuJu kicked her pointed-toe pumps in the air and screeched. "You can't blame a girl for trying. Can you answer me this, Evan—are you single?"

"I am," he said.

JuJu gasped. "How is that possible? I can't imagine a guy such as yourself being single. No way, Jose. There's got to be a special someone, a gal who's recently caught your eye."

"Well, of course. I'm looking at her," Evan said.

Did he ever stop flirting? Callie watched the back-and-forth banter and inwardly groaned. As a bumble bee buzzed, so Evan Marquardt flirted; he couldn't help himself. "Actually, Evan has something to announce and he saved it just for you, JuJu," Callie said. She ignored Evan's blank stare.

"Ooh," JuJu panted. "Just for me?"

Callie nodded. "An exclusive scoop."

JuJu craned her body towards the cameraman. "You heard it here first, folks. I'm on the Detroit set of *The Foreign Affair* and only *Mission: Hollywood* has the lowdown on Evan Marquardt's big announcement. So, let's hear it. What've you got for me?"

"I don't remember having something to announce right at this moment, Cal," Evan said carefully.

"You remember," Callie winked. "You're such a joker. I forgot to mention that, JuJu. He's always trying to pull my leg."

"Is he? I love a man with a sense of humor. So what is it? What's this announcement, Evan?" JuJu inched forward in her chair.

Evan eyed his co-star warily. "I'll let Callie do the honors, since she knows so much about it."

Callie took a deep breath. "I've been looking for a way of honoring my friend, Gabby, ever since her death a few short years ago. She's been absolutely massacred in the press and the most vile things have been said about her—all lies I won't bother repeating. I've decided the best way of preserving her memory is through something positive that will go on with time and so I've created a nonprofit foundation in her name to aid in ending domestic violence."

"What a lovely way of honoring your friend," JuJu said. "Is there a gala in the works or what exactly are you planning?"

"I'm kicking off our very first fundraiser with a fashion show in Los Angeles on October 20th, Gabby's birthday. The clothing will be designed by up-and-coming L.A. designers and at the end of the show, everything will be auctioned off, with all proceeds going to charity. Mr. Marquardt has been kind enough to emcee the event."

"Oh, my," breathed JuJu. "Surely this is bound to be quite an evening, especially with your legion of fans, Evan. When did Callie first ask you to be involved in this?"

"Very recently," Evan said. "So recent, in fact, I just found out about it a few seconds before you did."

JuJu laughed. "What a joker you are. Well, I think that's a marvelous way of giving back. Just one more thing to love about you, Evan."

Callie yakked it up going for another five minutes before JuJu signed off. Evan yanked his microphone off and hustled Callie off to a deserted corner of the building. "What the hell was that all about?" he demanded.

"With a new charity, I can use all the help I can get," she said.

"But why involve me? I hate bloody curve balls, Callie."

"You owe me, Evan."

"Is that right? Owe you?"

"Yep. And I've decided this is the perfect way for you to repay me."

"It would have been nice to ask me first. Usually people ask for help instead of assuming it and putting the person on the spot, don't you think?"

Callie looked past his shoulder at JuJu's crew cleaning up. "I could have, yeah, but the idea just came to me. And it's a great idea, don't you think?"

Evan clenched his jaw. "Here's the small problem: what do I know about emceeing? Do I look like Ryan fucking Seacrest?"

"You say you want to do it all, Ev. Now's your chance," she said cheerfully.

"Yeah, well I would have appreciated a heads-up before being tricked into committing to something."

Callie crossed her arms. "I'm sure Tyler would have appreciated a heads-up before he walked in on your late-night session with those two girls, but he didn't get one, either."

"Goddamn it, Callie!" His voice echoed in the ramshackle building. A smattering of crew members strained their heads to see what the commotion was about. Evan lowered his tone. "I've had it with this guilt bullshit. I thought we buried the hatchet the other night. If I do this for you—"

"If you do this for me, Evan, I'll drop everything from the past and never mention it again. I swear. I'd really appreciate it if you'd be a part of this with me. Please." She fluttered her lashes.

He couldn't control the corners of his mouth from curling into a smile. "You little shit. If you weren't so adorable, I'd spank you. You just love dangling yourself in front of me like a carrot. Once a tease, always a tease."

"Isn't that what you like? The tease, the chase?" she whispered.

"And don't you know it. Alright, doll. I'm in. The cause is fantastic and I'm no good at refusing you."

"Thank you, thank you, Evan!"

"You can thank me later, and I can think of many creative ways of paying thanks, too. As of now, I have to get going. I have another interview to get to and my car will be here any minute."

"Where are you headed?" she asked.

"Homeward bound."

"Huh?"

"As in The Townsend, our home away from home. And after that, I'll probably raid the mini bar and pray I forget I'm in Detroit for the next month. What about you? Need a lift?"

"No, thanks, I rented a car. I'm going over to my mom's."

"You rented a car? Why in the world don't you just have a limo pick you up? The studio will pick up the tab, naturally."

"I know," she said. "They're the one footing the bill for my Jag rental. I like driving, it clears my head."

"Well, give your mum my best. Later, gorgeous."

49

Gong! Gong!

Where was that sound coming from and more importantly, why was there a cymbal in her room?

Gong! Gong!

Callie tore through her house in hopes of locating the gong. It must be coming from outside. She tripped over the garden hose as she raced across the patio. Still no gong. She ran along the edge of the swimming pool; nothing out of the ordinary. "Where the fuck is this motherfucking gong?" she shouted.

Gong! Gong!

She bolted upright in bed and exhaled; it was just a dream. No gong. But her iPhone was ringing its charger off on the nightstand. "Hello?" she said.

"Finally, she picks up!" Paul said.

"Good morning to you, too, Paul."

"Morning? It's almost afternoon, young lady. You were due on set hours ago and everyone's been trying to find you. Are you alright?"

"Yeah, I'm fine, why?"

"Because no one can find you and I've been worried sick. I talked to the staff of the Townsend and no one has seen you since early yesterday morning. Where the hell are you?"

"I spent the night at my mom's. I was exhausted and I guess I overslept." Callie touched her temples and winced. In a belated celebration of Virginia's cancer-free status, she had downed one highball too many. Why didn't Mom wake me up? Oh, that's right; she's at that stupid Women of Troy luncheon.

"You're about to spend tonight at the bottom of Lake Huron if Nanette doesn't see you on set, pronto."

"Shit. Apologize for me, okay? I'm on my way."

"You're probably going to want to smooth things over in person. Netty is a no-nonsense kind of woman, as I'm sure you've noticed. In her book, tardiness is nothing but self-indulgence."

Callie hooted. "Give me a break, Paul. When we first started filming, Evan threw a fit because my trailer was closer to the set than his. He demanded they move his exactly ten feet ahead of mine, remember? If that's not self-indulgence, I don't know what is."

"But did he hold up production? No. They smoothed his ruffled feathers and the issue was resolved. Now, I know you're not uppity like that and you're not a diva, and, quite frankly, I wouldn't want to work with you if you were, but, for God's sake, humor me and use a clock every once in a while."

"I told you, I'm on my way." She threw on a maxi dress and made it to the set in twenty minutes. Jeremiah informed her Nanette was in her trailer.

"And tread lightly," Jeremiah said. "Otherwise you're in store for one hell of a picnic."

Callie rapped once, twice, on the director's door. On the third round, Nanette finally answered. "I told you not to come back! I do not want to see you," she shouted from inside.

"Nanette, it's Callie."

Pause.

"Come in."

Callie found Nanette standing over the sink in her bathroom, patting concealer under her eyes. "What can I help you with, Callie? Now is not really the best time."

"I just wanted to apologize."

Nanette stopped primping. "For what?"

"For being late."

"Please, like I give a damn about that. I have more pressing things on my plate right now."

"I really didn't mean to be unprofessional and it won't happen again. It's just...well, it's a long story but—"

Nanette sliced her hand through the air. "Quiet! Please, I cannot bear any more babbling. The Grossmans are the ones upset. Talk to them, if you must. Me, I have better things to worry about. I can barely function and I don't give one donkey fuck about this goddamned movie! Why did I ever write this stupid thing? It will be the death of me. I am unravelling, I'm at my wit's end, do you hear me? And you think I care who is late and who is on time? I assure you, I do not! Do you hear me? I do not care! Ugh, mon dieu!" Nanette threw the pot of makeup in the sink. "What is the point of makeup? It does not cover shit."

Callie tip-toed to the door.

"Wait!" Nanette said. "Let me ask you something, Callie, and you better be frank with me."

"Okay." Callie swallowed hard and braced herself.

Nanette walked up to her and stood statue still. The blood vessels in her eyes surged as though hooked to an electric outlet while a large vein throbbed in her forehead. "How long have you known about my husband?"

Callie blinked. "I don't know what you mean."

"I asked you be frank with me, Callie. You must have known. Surely, you must have known. I've seen the pictures."

"Excuse me? I don't understand."

"Pictures of you and the whore. I've seen you two together, I know you know each other. Why haven't you told me? I've been good to you, Callie, why would you keep this from me? Since you are friends, surely you have known."

"Known what? Who are you talking about?"

"The whore! That demonic, anorexic slut friend of yours has been fucking my husband, goddamn it! Do not lie to my face and say you didn't know any of this."

Callie collapsed in the nearest chair. This was all just too much. "No offense, Nanette, but I'm really having a hell of a day and I'm a little lightheaded. And, frankly, I have no idea what you're talking about."

Nanette remained immobile. "Luciana Dickerson is your friend, is she not?"

"Yeah, she is, but why do you care?"

"Because that little cunt has been sleeping with my Roger. Has been for months. None of this rings a bell?"

50

Callie rubbed her head. "No, not one bit. I'm...well, I'm speechless. I didn't know any of this. Yes, I knew she was having an affair but she always referred to him as Mr. X. I had no clue who he was." *And she's my friend, so even if I had known she was fucking your husband I wouldn't have told you, you batshit crazy woman.*

Tears sprung from Nanette's eyes. "What am I going to do? He's leaving me, Callie, and whatever shall I do?"

"I'm so sorry, Nanette." What more could she say? "I've been cheated on before, too, and it's awful."

"No, no, it's not the cheating that bothers me; it's the humiliation. The last ten years...my God, we haven't had much of a marriage, I admit. For one, he is never home. And I have always been my own woman, I do my own thing. I have a female friend in Sweden I've been seeing for years. She's wonderful, makes me forget how obnoxious and stressful my life is..."

Callie was sidetracked by Nanette's lesbian confession but tried to focus on the real issue. "And what about Roger? Is this the first time this has happened?"

"Ha, please. Roger has been caught with his pants down more times than I can wag a stick at. He has always strayed, but I love him and none of these side things have mattered. Except this time. This time, it is different. He says he is in love with her and cannot bear to not be with her. When he first told me all this, I thought, 'let him have his fun and he'll come back to me the way he always has.' But this time is different. Oh, the humiliation...I cannot bear it..." She dropped her head in Callie's lap and her body heaved with sobs.

Callie's brain was spinning from the lowdown. Good Lord, how juicy—tragic, but downright juicy. "Well...maybe Roger will come to his senses."

"Blah! He should have come to his senses ages ago. If he leaves me, I don't know how I ever shall handle the publicity. I'll have to flee both America and France when he decides to give a statement."

"Maybe he won't give one."

"Of course he'll give a statement. He'll have to, if he wants to be seen in public with her. There will be much curiosity. He's public, I'm public, she's public. I'm so mortified, so embarrassed. I..." Nanette suddenly jolted and peeled herself off of Callie. She wiped her cheeks with the back of her hands. "Forgive me. I don't know what came over me." Her cell rang. "Yes? No, I don't need that many extras for the street scenes. Fifty, at most, but not one hundred. And make sure everyone goes through wardrobe, a quick once-over, at least. I'll be out as soon as I can, but I'm very ill at the moment. No, I don't need a doctor. I'm taking some Pepto Bismol and need to just lie down for a minute...Yes, I suppose it could be the heat, and I'm just dehydrated. I haven't even breaked for coffee or the bathroom in the last five hours I've been on this set, so I don't give a damn what Chuck thinks. If I need to take a moment, I shall, and I certainly don't need anyone's permission. And, yes, you can tell him I said that. Thank you, Jeremiah." Nanette hung up and avoided eye contact. "I'll see you later today, Callie. You have a few scenes coming up, no? You must get to hair and makeup, darling."

"Nanette, I feel awful about everything. If you need to talk—"

"Nonsense, I should not have said so much. Everything will be fine. Please, forget all my babble. Shoo, shoo now." Nanette steered her to the door and before Callie knew it, she was shoved back outside into the sticky Midwestern heat. She pulled her phone out of her purse and texted Luci:

The strangest thing just happened. Have to ask you something personal.

What?

Was Luci's immediate response.

Madame Vernadeau just broke down crying. Says her husband is leaving her and you're having his baby...

Callie waited for a reply but none came. Several minutes passed and Callie figured she had offended Luci. Oh, well. I'm the one who got dragged into this mess, Callie thought. She strode into Miss D and Stella's headquarters.

"Just the girl I want to see," said Miss D as Callie walked in. "Have a seat. Your skin's a mite sensitive today," said D. "Looks like a few breakouts, or are you allergic to something?"

Callie lifted her eyes to the ceiling while D began the ritual of spackling potions and powders on her skin. "No, just a breakout. My chin looks like something out of a horror film."

"Oh, come now," D said.

"I mean it," said Callie. "I've got a face only a pizza could love."

D's whole body shook as she chuckled. Long, flaming strands bobbed above her wide backside. "You are something. Stella, did you hear her?"

Stella was busy brushing out the pin curls of Lydia, a supporting actress. "That I did. Oh, the afflictions of the beautiful. Poor baby's got it rough."

"I'm serious," Callie insisted. "I've got the acne of a teenager. A troll. It's just the worst."

"I can't speak for anyone else, but I'd take a few minor blemishes over a double chin and a fat ass any day," laughed D.

"I'll co-sign on that," Stella said. She rubbed her dimply thigh. "Try waking up to this cottage cheese day in and day out. I'm tellin' ya, if you're what's called a troll, sign me up. I'll gladly switch with ya."

"You two are nuts," Callie mumbled. She pushed a tuft of hair behind her ears and caught Lydia's stare.

"Your earrings," Lydia gushed. "Oh. My. God. You can see those things from outer space. Are they real? How big are they?"

Callie touched her lobes and felt her diamond studs. She had forgotten she even had them in. "Yeah, about three carats each, I think."

Lydia bolted from the chair and studied the baubles at such close range her breath fogged the diamonds. "Ooh, I love, love, love! So sick. Oh, my God. How much did you pay? Like, fifty thousand?"

"I have no clue, they were a gift." It was a lie—she had purchased them herself the previous year—but she wanted to shut the girl up. What was it about L.A. broads and their tacky questions? Ugh!

"That kind of ice costs some serious cash," Lydia said. "If I had those, I swear, I wouldn't ever leave the house. I'd stare at those rocks all day long and just cum all over 'em."

Callie winced. What a low-rent.

"Lydia, honey, why don't you sit down?" Stella said. "I was told I only have a half hour to spend on you and that was up five minutes ago. Let me spray you and you'll be good to go."

Lydia plopped back down.

"Callie, soon as D's done, hop over in my chair. I'm sure what's-his-face will be back any second to see how long till camera ready and if he sees you haven't gone through hair yet, he'll really show his fangs."

"Who are you referring to?" said D.

"Chuck. That man is just clueless, he doesn't realize what happens before the camera rolls is just as important as the actual filming."

"Well, he should, for heaven's sake, considering his background is porn," D said. "Anything involving douches and enemas and grooming all body parts known to mankind can't be a speedy process, can it? You'd think he'd have some patience."

Stella let out a snort while she worked her rattail comb on Lydia. "My nephew is in porn—he's an actual performer—and I can tell you those people give a whole new meaning to the word preparation."

"I can only imagine." Miss D rubbed a petal stain on the center of Callie's lip. "Everyone's look today is very au natural, so Callie will be yours shortly, okay, Stell? I just have to give her a soft cheek and lip."

"Take your time, honey, take your time. They need Lydia before Callie, so we're fine. I'm just sick of having my ass chewed every day, telling me I'm taking too long, that's all I'm saying. That's my main gripe. Everyone's so stressed about running behind schedule, they barely let us do our jobs."

"But it's always like that, isn't it? Every movie I ever work on turns into crunch time," Miss D said.

Stella guffawed. "Not like this one. I could spend one minute on an actor or an hour and it's all the same—Chuck complains I take too long. Rides my butt like Zorro. Vicky, too. I know we're over-budget, but it's pretty bad when hair and makeup get dumped into one trailer. I was talking to Nanette yesterday and she said—"

Knock, knock.

"Delivery," said a deep voice from outside.

Stella opened the door to find a gigantic bushel of flowers. A man's head poked out from the blooms. She planted her hands on her hips and said with a smirk, "I'm going to take a wild gamble and say these aren't for me."

"If you're a Miss C. Lambert, then, yes, ma'am, these are for you," he said.

"Nope, I'm not, but I'll sure give them to her. Callie? You got a present, babe. About three dozen presents, looks to me. Have mercy, these are beauties." Stella handed the flowers to Callie.

Callie inhaled the floral aroma. Mmmmmm. Delicious. And Lilies of the Valley, too, her birth flower. How sweet. Must be from Mitch. But what was the occasion? Maybe he missed her and wanted her to know she was in his thoughts. It had been days—four, five, she lost track—since they had last Skyped. Different time zones and remote Irish castles equaled precious little time for chatter, let alone romance. But apparently he had found a way around the obstacles. He was coming around, after all. She opened the card.

Because I missed your birthday. Glad we're back in touch. ~E.M.

"Ooh, tell us, tell us: who's the admirer? Someone sexy?" Lydia panted. She was gobbling up every move Callie made with gaped eyes.

Callie gave a tight-lipped smile. "An old friend."

"Why don't any of my friends give me diamonds and flowers? All's I ever get is a box of turtles and gift certificates to Target. Callie, I so want your life," Lydia groaned.

The wail of a siren sounded in the distance. It grew louder and louder until it sounded as though it were smack dab in the middle of the room.

"What in the hell?..." Stella stepped outside and watched an ambulance pull up. Several EMT's jumped out and rushed past.

"What's going on out there, Stella?" D called out.

"I have no idea. Soon as I see someone..." She spotted Jimmy, the key grip, chatting with an underling. "Jimmy, what the hell's going on?"

Jimmy ripped the ball cap off his head and itched his scalp. "Man, it's bad, I can't even believe it. Real bad."

"What is?" Stella scratched her frizzy blonde head. "Spill it, none of us know anything."

"Jeremiah found Nanette unconscious a minute ago," said Jimmy. "Face-down on her bathroom floor. I don't know, man, she might be dead."

51

Callie stretched out on the pillow-top mattress. She picked her iPhone off the nightstand and dialed Paul's number. "Hey, Paul. I'm just relaxing at my hotel and was wondering if there's an update. How's Nanette doing? Have you heard anything?"

"I just got off the phone with Roger," Paul said. "Apparently, she swallowed a bunch of pills. Found in the nick of time, thankfully, but had it been a minute longer, she'd be six feet under. She'll be at the hospital for a week or more and she's not coming back to work until she's mentally safe and sound."

"How long is production shut down?"

"Sorry to burst your bubble, but it's not. They're flying in some Mickey Mouse director from Ontario tomorrow to finish what's left in Michigan. Chris something. Chris Kaczynski. You've only got another week or so left. Because of this new setback, maybe a little more."

She sighed. "I was hoping for a hiatus. I'm exhausted."

"Once you're back in L.A., maybe you'll get your hiatus. I'm sure there will be re-shoots of some sort, but at this point, no one knows what is what. It's just too early to tell. Too many variables."

"Chuck is such a control freak, I'm surprised he didn't insist on directing the rest of it," she said.

"Oh, he tried, from what I'm told, but was vetoed. He knows squat about directing, and with him at the helm... well, you can guess how that would turn out."

She scooched further down in the covers and wiggled her toes against the silken sheets. "Yeah, if that were to happen, I think we'd all commit suicide."

"Boy, oh, boy," muttered Paul. "I don't know about you, but I'm still in shock. I never knew this side of Nan, and I've known her for over twenty years. Never knew she had it in her. She's always been so proud, far too proud to stoop to something like this. Roger spilled it all, came clean about everything. Said he'd been having an affair—fell for some hot model and told Netty he was leaving her. Was brutally honest about it and she completely lost it. He feels so guilty, I almost feel sorry for him."

"Paul, I feel really guilty."

"You? Why would you feel guilty?"

"Nan told me all this when I went in to see her to apologize for being late. She wasn't herself—she was really erratic and upset, only I didn't know she was this upset."

"None of us did," Paul said.

"I had no idea she was suicidal. I never should have left her alone."

"Now, Cal, stop all this talk before you even start. The last thing you need to be doing is blaming yourself. No use feeling guilty, Netty's a big girl and there's no way

293

you could have known she was going to do something so stupid. The good news is she's getting cared for now by professionals—that's their job, that's what she needs. Roger's still by her side and who knows, maybe they'll even be able to patch this up. There's a lot of love between those two."

"I wonder where this leaves Luci."

"Who?"

"Luci, my friend, the one Roger's been cheating with."

"Oh, so that's your friend, Luci, the one you've spoken of," Paul mused. "Roger didn't mention her by name. Well, how do you like that? It's a parallel universe. Luci never confided in you?"

"She did, but she never went into much detail. She's kind of secretive, doesn't like telling me too much. I wonder how she'll get out of this one? She dates a married man whose wife tries to kill herself and meanwhile she's bearding for a big actor the public thinks she's having a fabulous romance with. If the press gets the full scoop, can you imagine? They'll burn her at the stake."

"Who's the actor she's bearding for?"

"Chad Blake-Shepard. I worked with him on *Cheerleader Chronicles*."

"Oh, that's right," Paul said with a hint of excitement. "Chad's been on one hell of a roll this year. People are calling him the new Robert Redford."

"Yeah, and he's had more beards this year alone than a team of Navy SEALs."

Paul chuckled. "Boy, and how. Nice guy, though, clean-cut and hardworking. Oh, man, what a mess."

"She's jerky," Callie said. "Luci will get fried in the press."

"I wouldn't worry about her too much. Their publicists will throw their heads together and put a cute spin on it. Business as usual. Reminds me of an Oscar Wilde quote: 'The only thing worse than being talked about is not being talked about at all.' I've always gotten a kick out of that line, and I've never quite bought it, but it's perfect for Hollywood, and for this particular case, too, I'm sure. You watch, in the end, this will all work in the film's favor. Scandal is the secret seasoning in any Hollywood recipe."

"I like that—the secret seasoning. Listen to you, Paul, getting all creative writer-ish."

"Ha, well, I'm not quitting my day job. Alright, it's almost midnight for you and I'm going to let you get your beauty sleep."

"Before you go, is my call time going to be later in the day tomorrow? I made plans to see my grandma in the morning."

"I'll have to get back with you on that. You may not even be needed on set, everything's still in such a tizzy. Tell me, how is Grandma Esme? I remember when she came to the *NCA!* premiere and—"

"Doll, have you seen my shaver? I saw it right here on my sink before you came over." Bedroom Eyes pushed the bathroom door open with nothing but a towel tied round his waist.

"Who's that?" Paul said. "That sounds like—"

"Nothing, it's just the TV," Callie said hurriedly. "Hold on, let me turn it down." She locked eyes with Evan and held her finger to her lips. "Sorry, you were saying, Paul?"

Paul droned on but Callie was scarcely listening. She was busy staring at the scrumptious man meat in front of her. She smiled as she watched Evan search the bathroom. He pulled his shaver out from underneath a pile of towels and mouthed, "Found it," before returning her grin.

How could she have said no to that? That face, that body... throw a heaping dose of charm on top, and anyone with a pulse would be done for. So she had gone back on her word. She had caved to his prowess. Big deal. Pride was overrated, anyway, and deep down she had known it was only a matter of time before she would experience a Bedroom Eyes relapse. Their chemistry was potent, still, and Callie was tired of feeling lonely and underappreciated. The day's manic events had shaken her up terribly. Mitch, as usual, wasn't available to talk. But Evan was close by and provided a welcome, eager ear. The talking gave way to massaging—massaging her shoulders, starting off. He had moved down to her breasts, then down her pants and before long, he was going down on her. The clothes couldn't come off fast enough. Her protests came in the form of moans and body spasms as she squeezed his head with her thighs. She shoved all guilty feelings to the back of her mind while she pushed Evan deep inside her. *Mmmm, I missed this*! Callie had said to herself. So big and hard and, fuck, does he ever smell good!

Guilt. Who needed it? Not Callie Lambert, no way. She could deal with that later—if at all—when her head cleared.

52

Callie dumped the contents of her suitcase out on her bedroom floor. Ahhhh. Home, sweet home. That was the thing about Los Angeles—it was the kind of place she just had to get out of every so often, but it was also the most wonderful place to come home to. She enjoyed the time spent with her family, but nothing beat being in her own house and stepping out to the dry heat and sunny skies—everything the Midwest didn't offer.

Ring!

Callie reached for her cell. "Hello?"

"Hi, Callie, it's Bethanny from Dr. Coop's office."

That's right. Her boob appointment was fast approaching. "Hi, Bethanny."

"I'm calling to remind you of your pre-op this Friday."

Wow, already? "I'll be there."

"Great. Now, remember, no Advil or Vitamin E from here on out until the doctor clears it. And try to eat lots of fresh pineapple, it really helps with the bruising. I'll have all the info for you to take home. And please, above everything, make sure to bring your remaining balance of $5,000, okay? We'll see you soon."

"Bethanny, quick question," said Callie. "I've had a head-ache ever since I boarded a plane this morning. What can I take for it?"

"Definitely nothing that contains ibuprofen," Bethanny said. "Tylenol should be fine, I would think. Tell you what, just to be on the safe side, let me ask the doctor and I'll buzz you back."

"Thanks." Callie looked down at her chest. My poor little boobies, she thought, about to be massacred. She squished them together and managed to procure a tiny amount of cleavage. They were a decent handful—depending, of course, on the size of the hands. And they were cute, too, youthful and firm. Oh, well; soon they'd be a whole lot firm-er. Puberty revisited, courtesy of Dr. Coop.

Her phone went off again and Callie picked up while star-ing at her nipples; she was trying to imagine a scar on her pink buds. "Hi, Bethanny."

"Since when did a Southern boy turn into a Bethanny?"

"Mitch!" She was thoroughly caught off guard. Their last conversation had been a week ago, a five-minute Skype convo, right before she was called to set. "Sorry, I thought you were a receptionist that was supposed to call me back."

"I've played a lot of different roles, but a receptionist—there's somethin' I haven't played yet. But there's a first for everything." His voice was toasty and Callie could tell by his tone that he was smiling.

"So how are you? When did you get back into town?"

"Yesterday. I tried callin' you first thing but your phone was off."

Callie swallowed. "Yeah, I was busy." *Busy banging Bedroom Eyes*, she added to herself, with a pang of remorse. "I just got back into town today myself."

"So you're at home?"

"Mmm-hmm."

"All by your lonesome?"

"Yep, just little ol' me."

"Well, I just happen to be about five minutes from your place. On my way back from an audition in the Valley. How would you like some company?"

"Sure. Come on over."

Oh, boy. It had been so long since they last saw one another; she wasn't even sure how she felt about him anymore. What with their wacky schedules and personality differences, they just couldn't mesh on a consistent basis. It was probably best they went their separate ways. Most likely, Mitch was meant to be a mini-chapter in her life, not a partner for the long haul. She cared deeply for him and he was enjoyable, of course, but that hot-cold attitude of his...how off-putting! Was he crazy about her or wasn't he? And if he was, why didn't he say so? Why must he leave her guessing his intentions at every turn? It was like trying to decipher Japanese. No one was worth that much work, she told herself. Simply put, they were built very differently. Oh, well—it didn't matter anymore. It was high time she moved on to someone who could match her emotional depth, and she'd tell him so when she saw him. Not in those words exactly, but something close. Better yet, maybe she should just tell him not to come over at all...

She dialed his number just as the intercom buzzed. Damn it. Too late. She bounced down the stairs and, on the monitor, watched him waltz up her driveway. Her heart squirmed; he certainly was handsome. She had missed him, undeniably, and he was a great guy...eighty percent of the time. But that pesky twenty was so annoying. She squared her shoulders and greeted him on the doorstep.

"Hi," she said with a stiff smile.

Mitch stood completely still. His eyes held sparks of yellow, little flames licking both irises.

"You okay?" she said. "You look kind of—"

Mitch lunged forward and gripped her waist. His lips swooped down on hers; he gnawed and sucked on her lips until they went numb. He led her inside the house and slammed the door shut. "I really, really missed this girl," he breathed in her ear. His hands wiggled up her maxi dress and rested on her cheeks. "You know how crazy I am for you, don't you?"

She stifled a giggle; his lower lip tickled her lobe. Before she could say anything, his mouth covered hers again. Knee-buckling tremors raced through her body and up to her head, making her vision blur. Every one of her muscles liquefied like a hot slab of caramel. She was toast, done for; a signed, sealed, and delivered pulsating mess. Her head spun but he didn't let her come up for air. No use fighting it....

Mitch abruptly pulled away. "There," he ordered, pointing her to the table in the foyer. It was the closest horizontal surface and he angled her body over it. The wooden legs squeaked with each of his thrusts. Callie moaned and gripped the edges of the surface until her knuckles turned white. Mitch was more determined than ever to pound any and all negativity out of her mind and she was powerless—happily so—to do anything but oblige.

53

"Tsk, tsk, tsk. What a skank. A giant, smelly skank."

"What, as if you've never slept with an old boyfriend?" Callie demanded.

"Nope. Once I'm finished with a man, that's it—I'm finished. Bye, out the door, don't want to see ya. Exes are exes for a reason."

"I don't know what came over me. I tried so hard for so long to push Evan away, Ty. I really wanted to resist him but—what's so funny?"

Tyler snorted in the receiver. "What is this 'try so hard' spiel? You and I both know your legs parted like the Red Sea. I can see it all unfold in front of me now...You tried so hard, puh-lease. You can't pull the wool over my eyes. He's been wooing you and you've never gotten him out of your system and that's all there is to it."

"Well, trust me, I've definitely gotten him out of my system now. I can say that without a shred of doubt." Callie used her free hand to spread the napkin on her lap. "I'm not exactly proud of myself, you know. Evan just caught me at a weak moment."

"Boy, he sure did. You gave him exactly what he wanted."

"Hey, what's with the guilt trip?" said Callie.

"No guilt trip. You know I love you like a used tampon. I'm just a little concerned, is all. It's not like you to do something like this."

"I know."

"It just goes to show you the hold Evan still has on you. That boy is no good. You know it, I know it, and he knows it. He's a tumor, and the sooner you chop him off, the better."

She nursed her iced latte. "It definitely wasn't my finest moment. Trust me, I feel like the worst girlfriend in the world."

"I've got news for you, there are a lot of girls out there doing much worse. Just yesterday I found out our marketing director has been cheating on her husband with five different men. Bitch is busier than the Grand Canyon."

"Well, I don't grade my faults on a curve, so it's irrelevant. Honestly, in my mind, I had already broken up with Mitch and I was planning on telling him so when I got back. I was sure everything was over between us. But ever since he came over, I've had a change of heart..."

"You mean after he banged you in the foyer?" Tyler snickered. "His penis pulverized you. It's called being dick whipped."

"No, no, it's not just the sex. We're on the same wave length now, ever since we've been back in L.A. Like all that time apart made things perfect between us."

"No such thing as perfect. Unless you're talking about a Ryan Reynolds lookalike—with Tom Ford's wardrobe and Bill Gates' wallet—who sports a ten inch pink penis. God himself couldn't cook a man like that up."

"I'm serious, Ty. We're back on track. He's so much more...I don't know...open, I guess is the word. It's not crazy bells and whistles like it was with Evan—mostly we just make dinner at home and watch movies—but I love it. It feels natural. I'm really happy with him and he's so good to me. That's why I feel so guilty. Guilt is awful, the worst feeling."

"Forgive yourself, girl, you're only human. If you can make something good out of something bad, your mistakes aren't in vain. The only wise advice Timothy ever came up with."

Callie sighed. "True. I'm going to chalk up this whole Bedroom Eyes incident to a temporary loss of sanity. He waved his magic wand and cast a spell on me but I've come back to my senses."

"He sure did wave that wand," Tyler chuckled. "Look, you're a big girl and you can put your big girl panties on all by yourself. I just want you to put clean ones on, that's all."

"Great analogy, Ty. Thanks."

"You know what I mean. I don't want to see you hurt again and I'd like to think you're making healthy decisions and not letting no-goods like Evan drag you down. Lord, listen to me. When did I start sounding so old and matronly? Ugh. Must be my L.A. withdrawals. I've got to mosey my ass back to La La Land, and soon. Just a quick visit, a week is all I ask. I miss my L.A. crew, my In N Out, my WeHo bars...If I have to look at one more crepe, I'm going to jump in the Seine. I'm an American, damn it, and I miss home."

"When do you think you'll be back?"

"Who knows. We're sponsoring a red carpet shindig in Beverly Hills next month but I doubt I'll be going."

"My Gabby fashion show is on the 20th and I need a couple makeup artists. You, of course, will be head of that department."

"At least I'll be getting head one way. Honestly, I'd say there's a one percent chance of me being there, so you better count me out. I'll round up some friends for you, though. Top makeup artists, too, none of those sad rejects."

"Awesome, I'll owe you big time. You know, I really miss you, Ty. All of California does, for that matter."

Tyler groaned. "All I ever do anymore is work. Don't get me wrong, Paris is fabulous, but a lot has gone on in my life lately and I just want a minute to slow down and breathe and—"

"Ty, I'm sorry, but my lunch guest just arrived. Can we talk later?"

"Lunch guest?" he said. "Why you getting all bougie and sly on me? Who's there with you?"

"You remember Luci, the supermodel? We're having lunch at The Ivy."

"Luciana, the one from Paris?"

"That's the one."

"Supermodel," scoffed Tyler. "Lord, the only thing super about her is when she leaves. Her absence makes every-thing super. I can't believe I'm being dumped for that."

Callie rolled her eyes. "Dumped? Come on, really?"

"If you hear of a lonely gay boy falling to his death off the Eiffel Tower, you'll know why. Because his best friend ignored him on account of a towering, bitchy twig."

"Umm, who's the bitchy one here, Ty?"

"Whatever. Call me later, whore bag."

54

allie hugged Luciana before looking her up and down. "You look fab."

"You must be joking," Luci said. "My allergies are acting up. I look like I have Pink Eye. Thanks for meeting me on such short notice."

"My pleasure. It's been a while since we've caught up."

"And lots to catch up on," added Luci with a smirk.

"I know. Where do we start?"

"With some caffeine." Luci signaled the waitress. "May I have a cappuccino, please? A double. Thank you. So, business first. What's the latest with the Gabrielle foundation? The show is only a month away."

"The venue's all set, the invitations and press release have gone out, and the catering is taken care of. Paul found a fantastic event coordinator who's taking a major pay cut because all she really wants is the publicity, and she's killing it. But even still, so much needs to get done. What have you got?"

"Five models are confirmed so far," said Luci. "Four local girls and one from New York who just happens to be in town."

"And one from Canada," Callie winked. "Or Paris, how-ever you want to look at it."

Luci hurried on, scrolling down her iPhone. "I haven't heard back from the others yet. I'm working on a few more, it shouldn't be difficult. The hardest part is their availabil-ity, but with most people, they'll jump through hoops if, one, there's guaranteed mega media coverage and two, they know it's important to me. I have tons of friends in this industry, thank goodness. The one thing I learned from my father in business is how important networking is. My good friend, Drummond, is a fantastic hair stylist and owns his own salon, about three blocks down. His staff is on board. But I haven't worked on makeup yet."

"Tyler has that part covered," Callie said.

"How is Tyler? It's been a while. I like him, he's very funny."

"He's a character all right. He's doing well, still working for Jean Girard. Luci, thank you so much for helping out with this."

"I'm glad I can be a part of something so positive and, anyway, it hasn't been as much work as you'd think. It's been easy, really, a small way I can pay tribute to a girl who was so nice. Too nice, compared to someone like me." Luciana picked at the blue packets of sweetener in front of her. She was even more put together than usual; the camel sheath was both effortless and effortful and her always-vibrant skin was extra lucent. And that hair...Callie wondered exactly how much time went into conditioning it. It was so lustrous, each strand looked to have its own lighting crew.

"Alright, I guess that's my cue." Callie leaned forward. "So, spill it. I want to know the drama straight from the horse's mouth, because I've heard lots of crazy things and I don't know what's true and what isn't."

The waiter deposited her cappuccino. Luci stared at the foam a good moment before speaking. "Your text the other day caught me off guard."

"I shouldn't have asked," Callie said. "It's none of my business, except all of a sudden Nanette chose to involve me and I couldn't help but be curious."

"I can't blame you. It's true, everything you've heard, Callie. It's all true."

"Luci, can I ask, why Roger?"

"A better question is, why Luciana? Why did he have to fall for me? He's the married one, after all."

"What I'm trying to figure out is, if Nan knew you two had been having an affair for a while, why all of a sudden did she try to take her own life? Maybe I'm off here, but it seems like if she was going to snap, she would have sooner."

"I think I know what made her snap." Luci took a sip from her mug.

Callie cocked her head. "If you expect me to guess what that could be, we could be here awhile."

Luci sighed. "I spoke to her before she tried to kill herself."

"You spoke to her?"

"Yes, I called her. Right around two o'clock. I remember the time because E! was running a special on the twenty hottest Canadians and I came in at number two. I couldn't believe I was behind Pam Anderson—like anyone thinks she's hot anymore." Luci blew a strand of hair out of her face.

"What did you two talk about?"

Luci hesitated. "I was upset Roger still hadn't left her. He told me they were going to split months ago, and it never happened. Even after he confessed to Nanette about us, he still hadn't moved out. It was just excuse after excuse, delaying and procrastinating. Nanette wasn't happy about the situation, but she wasn't going to kick him out, and I was fed up with the whole clusterfuck. So I called to speak to her myself. I wanted to give her a piece of my mind."

"So did you?"

"You bet I did. In fact, I told her too much, I think. But I didn't expect her to go all psycho—I hadn't planned on that part. But, anyway, she did, and I kind of blame myself."

"What did you say?"

"I told her the truth. That I'm tired of being the other woman and she needs to stop caring what other people think and just let Roger go. I said, 'His heart doesn't belong to you anymore.'"

Callie frowned. "And then she tried to kill herself?"

"Yes. After I informed her I'm four months pregnant with his baby." Luci turned to their waiter at an adjacent table and pointed to her empty mug. "Excuse me, sir, can I bother you for another, please?"

55

allie closed her slack jaw. "You are? Four?"

"Well, almost," Luci said. "At the end of the month. That's why I didn't say anything when you mentioned me in your show. I'll be there with *Hollywood Hotspot*, of course, but I can't exactly walk down a runway with a basketball for a stomach."

"Does Roger know?"

Luci let out a cackle. "Oh, yes. He knows. That's why I was so upset he kept putting me off. Like, hello, I'm not exactly getting any less pregnant here, you son-of-a-bitch. Either tell your wife or I will."

"I can't believe you called Nanette."

"A lot of good it did me in the end," Luci said. "It completely backfired."

"What did she say, exactly?"

"Other than my uterus should be gutted?"

Callie wrinkled her nose. "She said that?"

"Did she ever. She screamed so loudly, I had to put the phone on the floor, and even then, she sounded like she was on speaker. I said, 'Stop beating a dead horse, he's not in love with you anymore.' The whole thing bit me in the ass. He's home with her now in France, as we speak, helping her recover."

"That's what I heard, that they were back in France," Callie added.

"Yeah. How do you like that? I let the cat out of the bag, trying to move things along, and I'm getting screwed royally for it. God, the nerve of that man." Luci narrowed her eyes into slits. "After all the lies, all the promises—making me sneak around like a criminal and jump through hoops, like a deranged circus freak—now he's decided he wants to stay with his bats-in-the-belfry wife."

"And she's actually taken him back?" Callie said. "No offense, but if my husband got another woman pregnant, I couldn't take him back. No way."

Luci snorted. "That's how insane this bitch is—she still wants him, after all he put her through. Not that he ever officially left her, but still. Her ego is insufferable. She'd rather have died than lose him to another woman. Even though I don't think she really wanted to die—she just wanted his undivided attention. And it worked. Well, good for her. Words cannot describe the crazy oozing from that brain of hers. They deserve each other."

"So what's your plan now?" Callie said. "How are you going to handle all this?"

"What choice do I have? I can't exactly publicly shame him, otherwise I'll look like a home wrecker from hell. One thing is certain, I don't want one red cent from the son-of-a-bitch. He doesn't exist, as far as I'm concerned. My baby and I will do just fine without him. So, that leaves me no choice but to focus on the original plan: bettering my career. I'm going to make lemonade out of this mess, if it kills everyone involved. Nanette included. Maybe she allows a man to make a fool of her but Luciana Dickerson most definitely does not."

A table full of women erupted in laughter. The skinny jeans-clad trio all sported sky-high cleavage their stretchy tops could not contain.

Luci made a sour face and whispered, "Anything more than a handful is completely tacky."

Callie almost spilled her plan for a fuller chest but, given Luciana's anti-big boob stance, decided not to. "What do your parents have to say about everything?"

"My parents have as much say in my life as that busboy over there. Remember when we first met and you told me to ignore those who bring me down? I should have done that a long time ago. Honestly, right now, all I care to do is focus on what's for lunch. I'm craving a great big cheeseburger...perfect, here comes our waiter."

With each bite of her calorie-rich meal, Luciana's spirits seemed to lift.

"Spectacular," she breathed after the last bite. "Although I ate more onion rings than I should have."

"If you can't splurge while you're pregnant, when can you?" said Callie.

Luciana sighed. "You're so lucky you're thin. I used to be that thin—thinner, even. I've gained ten pounds already.

It's so very depressing." She threw her napkin on the table and pushed her Bulgari shades up on her nose. "Shall we?"

They made their way to the valet stand and were greeted by a smattering of paparazzi.

"Well, well. Hey, there, Luci and Callie! Over here, girls, over here." A dumpy woman in Birkenstocks snapped the girls' picture. "Whatcha two lovely ladies up to on this fine Indian summer day?"

Luci smiled and said, "Oh, you know, just catching up. You'll be sure to make it to the Gabby Manx: Strut to End Domestic Violence fundraiser next month, won't you, Linda?"

Linda aimed her camera at Luci's face. "You betcha. Marked it on my calendar soon as I seen the press release." Snap. "Callie, you gonna have Luci walk your runway?"

Callie hadn't planned on small talk. Shit. What am I supposed to say? "I'd love to have Luci in my show. But only if she wants to. It's totally up to her."

"We want to see you strut your stuff one more time, Luci," said a male pap loitering on the sidewalk. "One more time, bring that Dickerson drama."

"Not this time around, Bart," Luci said. "But Callie has a terrific lineup of models and I'll be there with *Hollywood Hotspot* covering all the action."

Bart snapped a few photos and said, "You're not gonna be in the show, Luci? What gives?"

"I'm in no shape for it." Luci patted her midsection. "Chad and I are expecting our first child."

The swarm of paps rushed closer just as Luci's Bentley pulled up. "But you're so tiny! When are you due?"

"Congrats, Luciana! Boy or girl?"

"Callie, do you plan on babysitting?"

Luci waved as she ducked in the driver's seat with Callie in shotgun. "See you all at the show."

Callie smirked. "Well, that's one way of making an announcement."

"Just in time to make it on the evening news, right before the weekend lull. I'm a little disappointed, actually. There are usually a lot more paparazzi..." Luci pulled away from the curb. "Chad and I renegotiated for nine more months. Gary Benson made me an offer I couldn't turn down."

Callie shot her a questioning glance. "I figured you would have had enough of those two a while ago."

"Between the homo's diva antics and Gary's sliminess, I've barely managed to stomach them," Luci said. "Having to fake public appearances is so obnoxious but Chad's on the up and up; his going rate is now seven million a film. At last, everything is paying off."

"He's giving you a big payout, you mean?" Callie asked.

"Along with other perks, like this beauty." Luci rubbed the steering wheel's lustrous wood. "But I was actually referring to my career spike. Film offers have been pouring in. He scored a supporting role for me in a Jean Dujardin film as well as a Russell Brand comedy."

"That's fantastic, Luci, but what about the belly situation?"

"I've lined all the films up for next spring. I'll have my body back by then." Luci hung a left on Melrose. "This is just the kind of press Chad wants and he's kissing the ground I walk on. Voila! The perfect family unit, baked fresh in Hollywood. We already have the first baby pics sold to *Celeb Secrets*, too, so all in all, I'd say this little guy—or girl—has made a nice return. Too bad twins don't run in my family, otherwise the pay day would be even better."

Callie shook her head. "It's all too much for me, Luci. I couldn't do it. Way too complicated."

"Believe me, if I had known Roger would go crawling back to that loony tune, I would have had an abortion. Would have made things much more simple and my waist line would have thanked me." Luci sighed. "But sometimes life throws a wrench in one's plans."

Callie felt nauseated by the conversation. She couldn't imagine living a life built on so much drama, so many false-hoods. The very thought was migraine-inducing.

"So, are you up for a little shopping?" Luci chirped. "I spotted the most gorgeous Venetian chandelier by Alberta Ferretti the other day..."

Callie was relieved for the change of subject. "Sounds great."

56

Callie unbuttoned her shirt and slipped her arms through the paper gown. *This is the ugliest outfit. Paper. Why paper? It won't even close all the way. Isn't there a little tie somewhere?* She tugged on the edges and tried to cover her exposed chest but the frock kept popping open.

"Callie? How you doing in there?" said the nurse on the opposite side of the curtain.

"Pretty good, Janice."

"You about ready?"

Callie pushed open the curtain. "I guess so."

"Having trouble with your gown? Here, let's get this tied..." Janice cinched the two small strings on the gown.

Why couldn't I find those? Callie thought. "Thanks."

"And don't forget to put on your booties and your cap. We don't want any contamination in the operating room. You can just slide them over your sneakers. Give me your hand, I'll help you. Now, step your left foot in this one...and now the other...there we go."

Callie looked in the mirror; with her blue booties, cap, and gown, she resembled a newborn. All that was missing was a bottle. "Janice, can I have some water?"

"Nope, can't give you any, sweetie. Afterwards, you can have as much liquid as you want but absolutely no liquids before, lest you vomit and choke while you're under. Anesthesiologist's orders. Okay, follow me, please…"

Janice led Callie to the operating bed. "Go ahead and make yourself comfy and Walter will be in shortly to hook up your IV."

Callie shivered, even under the blanket. Why did these facilities have to be so cold? Like they were storing a corpse instead of operating on a live human. Her nipples grew hard and poked through the blanket. Poor things. In just a few short minutes, they'd be sliced up. She placed her digits on them and gave them a pat. Where was Walter? *I could use a sedative. No need to be nervous,* she told herself. It was an easy peasy operation. Standard. In and out. Dr. Coop could probably perform the surgery blindfolded. And Mitch was there, waiting nearby to pick her up right where he dropped her off. She'd see him in just a few hours. He was the only person she had confided in—not even Tyler knew she'd soon have a new set of breasts. She was tired of hearing everyone's opinions, so why bother saying anything in the first place? Waste of her time.

Walter breezed into the room. "Hello, young lady. So you're scheduled for some new additions in about—oh, twenty minutes or so, is that right? How are you feeling?"

"A little nervous," she said.

"Don't be. I'll give you a little something to help with the nerves. In the meantime, just think of all the fun you'll have

318

shopping for new clothes. My sister had the exact same procedure performed this summer. Says she wishes she would have done it sooner, that the small amount of pain she felt was worth it because it gave her an excuse to buy a whole new wardrobe. She only went up about a cup, but that was enough to warrant new tops and bikinis and such. Don't you just love any excuse for a shopping spree? I sure do."

Callie had a mental image of all her La Perla and Agent Provocateur falling in the toilet and grimaced. "Hopefully I won't have to throw out everything..."

"So, I see you're on Wellbutrin, is that correct?" Walter referred to a chart.

"Yeah, and I took an Ambien last night."

"Mmm-hmm, mmm-hmm." Walter scribbled in his chart. "Anything else?"

"I don't think so."

"Nothing to eat or drink last night or this morning?"

"Nope. But I took a tiny sip of water when I brushed my teeth earlier."

"Mmm-hmm, mmm-hmmm, got it. As long as it was just a small sip, that shouldn't be a problem..." More scribbling. His immaculately buffed fingernails scraped against the paper. "Okay, well, I'm going to start you off with a mild sedative intravenously. You're going to feel very relaxed, like you're on the Mediterranean enjoying a fabulous vacation. Only thing missing will be a piña colada." Walter's pale, thin face stretched into a smile. He held Callie's arm and tapped a vein.

"Am I going to get a chance to talk to Dr. Coop one last time?" she said.

"You will, indeed. I just ran into the doctor around the corner, washing his hands. He'll be here momentarily. Okay, slight prick, now...just picture all those spectacular new clothes you'll be wearing in St. Bart's and take a deep breath..."

Callie was smacked with a flashback of Luciana frolicking on the beach; no one could say she wasn't all woman and 100% sexy, with her slinky limbs and skimpy breasts...The big picture was suddenly so clear and terror filled Callie's heart. What am I doing here? I don't need big boobs to feel hot. Who wants to look like every other tramp here?

The sedative started to take effect just as she yanked the tube out of her arm. Walter's eyes swelled to the diameter of a hubcap. "Walter, I can't do this."

Walter clasped a hand to his chest. "What on earth do you mean? The doctor will be in shortly—"

"I can't go through with it. I'll tell Dr. Coop myself. But I can't do this, it would be a mistake."

"I don't understand. What do you mean, 'mistake'? You've already paid!"

"Better now than after my boobs get hacked. It's not all about the money, you know. Who was I kidding? I'm just not a fake boob kind of girl. And the thought of starting over with a whole new wardrobe...I mean, in bras alone, I have, probably, five grand. I don't know what I was thinking but thanks for helping me see everything clearly." Callie swung her feet to the floor.

"Umm....well, okay, if you say so..."

"I'm going to go change and call my ride. Nice meeting you, Walter." Walter continued staring at Callie as she stumbled out of the OR.

57

Mitch couldn't stop laughing as he sped along the 405. "You really are somethin' else. I can't believe you just up and bolted, like a flea on a dog. I can only imagine the look on everyone's faces in there. Must be thinkin' you're certifiably nuts."

"Maybe I am," Callie said defiantly. "Better to be nuts and scarless than hacked up and sane."

"You've always got a point of view, I'll give ya that. You gonna take that hat off or are you keepin' it on as a momento?"

She had rushed out of the facility so quickly, she had forgotten to take her surgical cap off. "I'm glad you find me so amusing. Just be careful not to run us off the road, okay?"

"I'll have you know my drivin' skills are supreme. Don't you worry your pretty little head about that. You gotta admit, this is all kinda sporadic and goofy, right?"

"Goofy, maybe, but I don't think I was ever totally sold on implants to begin with. Which goes to show you how stupid I am to have taken things this far. You sure you don't want to dump me right here and now?"

"I can deal with goofy," Mitch grinned.

"This is the dumbest thing I've ever done. What a big waste of money. I've always been insecure about my chest and I kept trying to convince myself I needed this. But when it all came down to the wire..."

"You just couldn't do it," Mitch said quietly.

"No, I couldn't."

"Well, you know what? I'm glad. I've never been a big fan of standard equipment, anyway. That's what I call implants—standard equipment, 'cause in L.A., a real set of tits is about as rare as Halley's Comet. But it's your body, and who am I to tell you not to do somethin'? I support you regardless."

"Thanks, baby." She rested her hand over his. "God, I'm such a fool wasting money like this."

"Look at it as just a drop in the bucket, darlin', and don't beat yourself up about it." Mitch turned up the radio. "*Strangers in the Night.* One of my favorites."

She looked over at Mitch humming and felt a wave a gratitude; he had a way of soothing her and making her believe everything would be fine again. But something rubbed her the wrong way, a feeling in the back of her noggin she just couldn't shake.

I don't deserve him. He's so kind and supportive, and how do I thank him? By boinking Bedroom Eyes. What a lowlife you are, Callie. You've had a great guy in front of you all along but you were too blind and silly to see it...

"Cal." Mitch interrupted her thoughts. "You hungry? You gotta be. It's been awhile since you've had any chow. Why don't I pull into Burger King next exit. I could eat a little somethin' myself."

"Great, thanks." *I should just come clean and be done with it. I hate lying and I hate lies. I've never been a liar. How did I turn into one all of a sudden overnight? Wait, that's not true; just because I'm not telling him all my deep, dark secrets doesn't mean I'm lying. Not all secrets are lies—and everyone has their secrets.*

"What'll you have?" Mitch pulled into the drive-thru.

"I'll take a number one." *No, it doesn't make me a liar, but it does mean I'm a cheater, and I've always hated cheaters. I was cheated on, damn it, and now I'm no better than Evan! How ironic....*

"And to drink?" said Mitch.

"Iced tea, please." *Damn Luciana! If it weren't for her inviting me to that stupid Warner Bros. party, Evan never would have heard about the movie and I never would have seen his face and therefore I never would have been tempted. Well, if you're smart, you'll keep your lips zipped, girl. No harm done if no one knows—*

"Cal, I'm talkin' to you."

Callie started. "Sorry, what?"

"You alright? You look scared."

"I'm fine," she smiled. "What were you saying?"

"You want any sugar or lemon for your tea?"

"Equal is fine." *No one knows what I've been going through. How could they? I've kept all my problems—everything—bottled up inside. I can't keep it bottled up much longer, though. I feel sick from it all. I just want to be true to myself...This whole day so far has been crazy, why not just finish it off....*

"You know, I was thinkin'," Mitch said. "How about a little getaway? There's this resort in Puerto Vallarta I've been checkin' out online. A buddy of mine recommended it and it's just your style, right on the ocean and it's got this totally sexy vibe. Since you won't be recoverin' from any surgery now, why don't we go?"

"Umm—"

"Next week, I was thinkin'. Just four or five days. I'm still a little jealous your ex-boyfriend got to see more of you than I have in the past month. I gotta make sure his memory is permanently erased." Mitch winked.

Callie sighed. That settled it. "Mitch, I need to tell you something."

"What's up, darlin'?"

"I have to come clean about something that's been weighing on me. And it's not something I'm proud of. You'll probably hate me."

"Oh, come on, now. It can't be that bad."

"It is."

"Okay, then. Shoot."

"When you asked me how everything went in Michigan—you know, when we first saw each other and were catching up—I lied. I said everything was great. Remember?"

Mitch nodded. "Right."

"But the truth is, it wasn't great. It is now, but it wasn't. I, umm...I was actually planning on breaking up with you. I had already broken up with you in my head, but I hadn't gotten a chance to actually tell you because we were hardly able to communicate."

Mitch pulled forward in line. "I'm missin' somethin', I guess. Why had you broken up with me? I never knew there was a problem."

"This isn't an excuse, but I was sick of feeling alone in this relationship. It was headed nowhere—it felt like it at the time, anyway. You only let me get this close before pushing me away. You never once called me your girlfriend or told me you missed me or—"

"That's baloney and you know it, Callie. I've told you plenty of times I miss you and care about you."

She shook her head vehemently. "No, you didn't. For a while there, you did not. And it left me completely confused about where we stood as a couple."

"I guess your speed is different than mine. Me, I don't see what the big hurry is. Relationships are supposed to grow, they don't just happen overnight, right? I don't know about you, but my trip made me realize how special you are to me. And I think I've shown that to you. I'm more open than I was in the very beginning."

"Yeah, you have been. And I agree, since we've been back in L.A., things have been amazing. Which is why I feel like such an ass saying this, but—"

"Let's forget about past problems between us. All water under the bridge." He touched her leg.

"Please, just let me get through this, Mitch. I just want to get this off my chest and then if you want to forgive me afterwards, that's up to you. And I really, really hope you can forgive me but I don't want it hanging on my conscience anymore."

Mitch cocked an eyebrow. "You gonna spit it out or are we gonna play guessin' games all the way home?"

"I slept with my ex."

"Your ex?" Mitch said in a controlled tone. "Marquardt? You slept with Evan Marquardt?"

"Yes."

"I don't get it. What the...how did....why would you do that?" His voice grew louder.

"I don't know, I was just lonely and confused, I guess. I regret it, Mitch, every bit of it. If I could go back and undo everything—"

"I thought you broke up with that bastard a long time ago? You told me you hated him and all cheaters in general, or some such bullshit."

Callie choked back tears. "I know...I made a mistake."

"How many times? Once? Or did you try to make an Olympic sport of it and really go for the gold?" Two veins in his forehead swelled. "Well? Answer me."

She dropped her chin. "Twice."

The drive-thru attendant held a bag of food out of the take-out window. "Here you go, sir. You have yourself a wonderful day."

58

The breeze on the rooftop of the SLS Hotel swirled Callie's hair like a chestnut brown tornado. Finally, her locks had grown back to the length she was partial to—past her shoulders with subtle layering. Her gold bangles clanked as she adjusted the hem of her skirt to reveal more leg.

"That's beautiful," said Karina. She twisted the lens of her camera, baring her teeth in concentration. "This is going to be perfect." Toni Rae Tindal was in charge of shooting *L.A. Pop*'s annual issue of "The Twenty Most Tantalizing Angelenos." Callie clocked in at #11. Not the top ten spot she had hoped for, but not exactly the bottom of the pile, either. Toni Rae was a 51-year-old, one-time middle school history teacher with a buoyant, graying mop and a fondness for anything left-wing. Nothing made her happier than to discuss her political views, and as often as possible. But not today. Today, she was quiet and all business, and Callie was grateful for the peaceful set and small crew of seven.

"You always this mellow?" Toni Rae said.

"Mellow is better than my flip side, trust me." Callie just couldn't get into the shoot. Her movements were mechanical and lethargic. Her mind lay elsewhere—with Mitch—and she just couldn't care less about the superficial task at hand. "I haven't had any caffeine today."

"You want me to fix you some coffee, Cal?" shouted Paul several yards away.

"Yeah, thanks, Paul." She pivoted to the left and stared into the camera. Snap, snap.

"Luckily, mellow is the look we're going for with this," said Toni Rae. "Nice and easy and not trying too hard. Okay, next outfit, please."

Two dress changes later and it was a wrap.

"I called down to the valet," Paul said. He handed Callie her purse and jacket. "The car's waiting up front."

"Good, I'm not in the mood to wait around," said Callie as they headed to the elevator.

"I can relate. If I have one pet peeve—other than tardiness—it's waiting for my car. Don't know why, but that's something that really puts a crease in my britches. Toni got some good stuff. That last round was the best of the bunch. It's interesting watching you morph into these different characters. You're truly a chameleon. Some actors, whether it's a Western or SciFi, only play one character. Take Ashton Kutcher; always the same stupid buffoon in every movie. Then at the other end of the spectrum is someone like Sharon Stone who, every time, gives you hard-boiled crazy. But you've got a versatility that sets you apart. Even in still photographs, it's very apparent. That's what this business takes, all right. And you're not even listening. Don't mind me, I'm just having a conversation with myself."

"Huh?"

"Exactly. Okay, young lady, want to talk about it?"

"About what?" she said.

"About what's going on. Sorry if I'm prying, but there's a big, black cloud hanging over you and I'm not sure what to make of it. Something clearly is bothering you."

Callie exhaled loudly. "Mitch and I broke up."

"Oh, I'm sorry," he said. "A mutual kind of thing or—"

"Yeah, it was mutual. I'm just...I'm too busy for a boyfriend right now, that's what it is. I really, really care about him but I just don't have the time. Or the energy." Big lie, but big whoop.

If I wanted the world to know about my colossal fuck up, she thought, *I would have held a press conference.* Her iPhone beeped. It was a text from Emily, wanting to know if she felt like dinner in the next few days. Callie shoved the phone back in her purse.

"It's unfortunate," added Paul, "but sometimes it's best this way. You know, it could be better in the long run—"

"Paul, no offense, but I don't really want to talk about it, okay? I'll be fine, don't worry." As awful as she felt about falling prey to Bedroom Eyes, as many tears as she had shed—mentally lynching herself over and over for hurting Mitch—having held it all in felt ten times worse. She didn't regret coming clean, not even after Mitch dumped her. At a drive-thru, no less. No thinking it over, no time apart; he was done, he said. Finished with her. The car ride home was a long and silent one. She may have been boyfriend-less and depressed, but she was comforted that at least her conscience was finally clear.

"Got it. Switching gears, *Helena Magazine* wants to interview you for a piece on what women really want for Valentine's Day. Just a fun, fluff piece. This week, preferably."

"Valentine's Day? Already?" Just what she wanted to think about. Love. Or her lack of it.

"They're always running ahead, as you know. I'm still working on getting a cover shoot out of them, so it's good business to be a part of it."

They retrieved the car from the valet and headed up La Cienega. Callie startled Paul by slapping her car seat. "I almost forgot," she said. "I have to pick up my dress for tonight. It's at the tailor's on La Jolla. You know, I'm not feeling very social. I really don't even want to go to that thing tonight..."

Paul shot her a thunderous look. "I suggest you try your hardest to get social. Suck it up. If someone were paying me fifty grand to hang out at a nightclub for a couple hours, you bet your bottom dollar I'd be turning handstands and backflips all night if they told me to."

"I'm just saying I'm not in the mood, Paul. Of course I'm not going to cancel."

"Good. Because, don't forget, you're scheduled at that other club in New York this weekend, so consider this a warm-up."

(The pending Schueller trial had Callie freaked for cash. At the end of each day, as she lay her head on her pillow, all she could picture was The Trailer Lady dipping her acrylic-tipped fingers in the Lambert piggy bank, stealing her blind. To help ease her mind and generate extra income, Paul had lined up a few media appearances. Callie was even fine with starring in a fitness infomercial for Jim Holmes' Home Gym—she didn't mind pumping a little iron on camera for two hundred grand—but Paul had put his foot down. "No way. An appearance at a nightclub will be forgotten, but film lasts forever. You can't endorse everything, Cal, otherwise, you'll be like that Desperate Housewife. The short one, I forget her name. She shows up to the opening of a toilet bowl, and you're too precious to go that route.")

"I know. But I do need that dress, Paul, so if you wouldn't mind—"

"I can swing by the cleaners. Traffic's not too bad." An orange Ferrari cut Paul off and he slammed on the breaks. "Goddamn idiot," he muttered.

"Crap," she groaned. "I just remembered I have to pick up my meds. I'm completely out. It's at CVS, up a few blocks."

Paul held up his watch. "I'm cutting it close to my meeting as it is. You know, it would be wise to consider an assistant at this point. Sounds like you could really use some help."

Callie bit her tongue; she was in no mood to be lectured, even if he did have a point.

"But since it's so close," he continued, "I may as well."

"Thank you, Paul. I'm not trying to drive you nuts, I promise."

"You sure about that?" Paul grinned. "I got a call from Netty today. Sounds healthy as a horse. Everything is smooth sailing with Roger and she'll be in town in November for re-shoots. She wanted me to remind you to stay out of the sun."

"I know, I know. How could I forget, it's written in my contract." Callie knew she had dodged a bullet with the surgery-that-never-was. With Nanette's hawk-eyes, there was no way she could have successfully concealed the implants, even with multiple sports bras or loose clothing. The fast cash from the nightclub gigs helped soothe the sting of losing ten large to Dr. Coop, so Callie figured it all turned out for the best.

She grabbed her iPhone to check her messages and re-read Emily's text. Hmmm....Paul had plans for the evening and her only confirmed guest was her sometime-makeup artist and friend, Dehx. Decisions, decisions....Callie texted back:

I'm playing host tonight at this Hollywood club, Cobalt. Care to be my guest?

59

"Cal-lie! Cal-lie!"

   "Callie, can I get a pic with you?"

   "We love you, Callie!"

"Can I have your autograph?"

"My brother wants to marry you! Look, he made a video proposal!"

Callie walked past the fans along the velvet rope outside Club Cobalt. She had spent the last twenty minutes posing for paps on the red carpet but was forbidden, per contract, from speaking to the general public. If anyone hoped for an autograph or one-on-one time with her, they needed to be a paying customer inside the club, so said the owner, Firouz Zamani. No Cobalt, no Callie.

"Miss Lambert, hello. I'm Ani, the manager. If you'll follow me, please, I'll escort you to your table." The decked-in-black Ani swished through the huge, double glass doors and up to an elevated area occupied by a jumbo bouncer. Glossy, dark leather seats circled a table decorated with buckets of ice and loads of mixers. "Deanna will be takingcare of you and your friends this evening—she's our best girl. She'll bring whatever you like—Cristal, Dom, Karlsson's Gold—"

"How about Five O'Clock. Any of that laying around?" asked Callie. Ani grimaced. "We don't carry that brand."

Dehx burst out laughing and Callie said, "I'm just kidding, Ani."

"Of course. Deanna will be right over." Ani scurried off.

"This is incredible," said Emily with wide eyes. She slid into the seat and peeled off her cardigan. "Look, we can see the entire dance floor from here. If I had known it was such a fancy place, I would have dressed up more."

Callie eyed Emily's ensemble; *aye, aye, aye,* she thought. The flouncy dress and Mary Janes had to go, as did the mousy hair color. An entire makeover was in order, and badly. Very badly.

"I'm off to the ladies' room," Dehx announced.

"She seems nice," said Emily. "She's a makeup artist, I think she said?"

"Yeah, she's the best," Callie said. "She started off doing theatre makeup on Broadway, so she really knows how to make everything last. We should have Dehx do your make-up sometime." *And teach you a thing or two about doing your face.*

"I'd love that," smiled Emily. "Thanks so much for inviting me tonight, Callie. This is so nice of you. You've got some life, I must admit. I mean, I knew it was different than mine, but it's not just a little different—it's worlds-apart different. A different hemisphere. It's weird, sometimes I feel like you're the older one, instead of the other way around."

Callie looked up at the waitress standing in front of her and asked, "Em, what would you like to drink?"

"Oh, I don't really drink... I guess I'll have a little sip of whatever you're having. I'm more of a plain fruit juice kind of girl."

"How about some fermented fruit juice?"

Callie wiggled her eyebrows and turned to Deanna. "We'll have a bottle of champagne, please. The best you have." She smoothed her black leather sheath and took a seat.

"That dress is incredible," Emily breathed. "It complements you so well."

"Thanks."

"It reminds me of something Wesley bought for my last birthday—mine is much cheaper, I'm sure, but the color and cut is similar."

Callie couldn't picture Emily wearing anything body-conscious, let alone an outfit with a nod to S&M. She had a nice figure—small waist, slender limbs, graceful neck—she just needed to show it off a little more. "We should go shopping. I'd love to pick some things out for you, Em."

"Yeah? I know my wardrobe's a little sad, but remember, I live in Ohio. Not exactly the capital of style. Wesley always liked me to show off my legs."

"You must be excited to go back home and see him."

Emily frowned. "No, we broke up."

"You broke up?" Callie said.

"Several weeks ago. We just weren't on the same page. I thought we were...he'd led me to believe we were."

"What happened?"

"He had this giant epiphany when I came out for my internship and decided he's not ready to start a family any time soon—if at all. Those were the words he used, oh so matter-of-factly, too. 'If at all.' Everything we talked about, all the plans for the future—it's like he just tossed them out the window."

"Men," Callie grumbled.

"They're awful, aren't they? I'm sorry, but my ovaries aren't getting any younger. I want to be a mom. I want to settle down, and soon. You know, I think it was mostly his parents doing and he used the kid angle as an excuse. It's because I'm not Jewish. They've always had a problem with me."

"Well, you don't seem too upset about it, all considering."

Emily shrugged. "I was, but the initial shock has worn off. So the guy doesn't want a shiksa; what am I going to do about it? It's pretty simple, I don't want to compromise myself, and I don't want him to compromise himself, either."

"Hmm," Callie said contemplatively. "Good point."

"I'm glad he told me before I bothered moving in with him. We hadn't been as close right before I came out to L.A., so deep down, I knew something was off. Say, how is Virginia doing? It's been awhile since we've spoken."

"She's great. Strong and healthy."

"How did her part in the film go?"

Callie smiled at the memory. "She had a blast! She kept asking Chris, the sub-director, 'are you sure you don't want me to say my line again?' All she wanted was to stay on set all day. I think Mom missed her calling."

"Here we are," Deanna said. She held a giant tray of libations.

"Hey, Cal." Dehx tossed her leather jacket in the booth. "You'll never guess who I just ran into. And I literally mean ran into, because she plowed right into me, totally wasted out of her mind."

Callie shrugged. "Who?"

Dehx smirked. "S—"

"Well, well! Look who we have here. The lady of the evening!" Firouz rushed over, camera crew in tow, and pressed her hand to his lips. His charcoal suit was, as usual, expertly tailored to accommodate his big belly. Chunky diamond cufflinks dangled from his sleeves.

"Hi, Firouz," Callie said. She dreamt of running in the opposite direction; his breath reeked of garlic and cognac.

"Are you enjoying yourself? You have everything you need?" he said.

"Yes, thanks."

Firouz leaned in closer, away from the cameras. "If you need any—shall we say—party favors, you have only to ask."

"Oh, no, I'm fine." She held her breath.

"You have only to ask, remember that. Firouz is at your disposal." He beamed while patting his lapels.

The DJ's microphone screeched overhead; he lowered the music long enough to say, "We have a very special guest tonight, ladies and gentlemen. Where else but at Club Cobalt can you party with one of Hollywood's hottest stars? Give it up for the one, the only, the gorgeous Miss Callie Lambert!"

A spotlight swung on Callie and the crowd below erupted in cheers. She waved and smiled like a seasoned pageant princess but she couldn't make out a thing; the light was too ferocious and she squinted from its glare. A Pitbull remix boomed from the speakers. Flashes and bottles popped in unison. Firouz clapped his hands and smiled so broadly, Callie could count the number of fillings in his mouth. Finally, the spotlight disappeared and she turned her back to the crowd.

"Okay, Callie, in about, ohhh—" Firouz raised his twinkly Rolex. "—thirty minutes' time, I'm going to send some special guests up here for a little meet-and-greet. Some pictures, some autographs, a little chit-chat..."

"Sounds good," Callie smiled.

Firouz cracked his knuckles. "Good, good, good. Enjoy yourself. Have anything you want—and I do mean anything. See you shortly."

Callie drained her drink. Better to be buzzed and have the time go by quicker. Where was her posse? Dehx was busy dancing, flipping her hair around while bouncing in her knee-high boots. *That's nice*, Callie thought; *at least someone was enjoying herself*. But what about Emily? She didn't see her anywhere. She felt responsible for her older sister's well-being; Em was out of her element and probably uncomfortable. She was more innocent—delicate—and they just weren't cut from the same rugged cloth.

"Don't you know who I am? I'm a fucking star!" The voice was loud enough to rise above the music. Emily was by the stairs, blocking Stephanie Schueller. The Trailer Lady was in fine form. Squeezed into a micro-mini, she flailed her arms around, yelling, oblivious that one of her extensions had come loose; the long blonde chunk trailed down her back. Oh, yes; the Empress of Elegance, the Grande Dame of Sophistication, had arrived.

"You gotta know who I am. I'm Stephanie Shueller! I'm on a hit show and I make more in one day on set than you make in a whole fuckin' year! I wanna see Callie. We go way back and I wanna say hi and get our picture taken. The bouncer guy already told me I can, so what's it to you? Nice fuckin' shoes, by the way."

Emily's face turned crimson, but she ignored the insult. "Where is security? Security, please!" Her eyes bore into Stephanie's. "I don't care who you are or who you think you are, you aren't invited."

"And just who the fuck are you?" Stephanie waved her drink in front of Emily's face. Rum and Coke sloshed on the carpet.

"I'm the one who doesn't allow degenerate tramps past this point. Now leave before I have you thrown out!" The bouncer appeared and Emily turned to him. "Did you tell this thing she could be up here?"

"Sure didn't," he said. "I was just talking to the boss, never seen this lady before. Ma'am, this is a restricted area. You're going to have to leave if you're not a VIP—"

"She's not a VIP," Emily said. "She's not on Callie's list at all."

"But I just wanna say hi," Stephanie wailed. "I wanna tell her that, even though I'm suing her for, like, a billion dollars, it's nothing personal and she's still cool."

The guard crossed his thick arms. "Ma'am—"

"Look, mister." Stephanie swayed in her platforms. "I'm a hot, rich, super successful actress and everyone wants me in their corner, okay? I'm a way bigger star than Callie! Where is she, anyway? Hey, Callie!"

"Ma'am, out. Let's go."

"And by the way," Emily yelled to Stephanie, "next time you venture out of your cave, you may want to think twice about dressing like a two-bit crack whore. Since you're so famous and all."

Stephanie hissed as the bouncer escorted her down the stairs.

Callie chuckled at Emily's voracity. What a bulldog! She was impressed. And mistaken. Maybe their fabrication really was similar, after all.

Emily approached Callie. "Just to let you know, I'm not usually like that. She's just so crass and drunk and I know how much you dislike her."

"Actually, Em, that was kind of cool. I just didn't know you were so feisty."

"I'm extra feisty tonight," Emily said. She slumped into the booth. "I guess it's because I'm so frustrated about the whole job situation. Or the lack thereof."

"What do you mean? You have a job waiting for you when you get back, I thought?"

"I did, until they decided to lay off a bunch of people, including myself. All the schooling I've had, including a minor in business management, and I have a better shot working at Subway. It's so frustrating. Obviously, since you witnessed me acting like a maniac."

"Trust me, Em, you haven't been in L.A. long enough if you think that was acting like a maniac." It was perfect; Callie needed help, and from someone she could trust. "What would you say if I asked you to work for me?"

"What do you mean, like an assistant type of thing?"

"Kind of, yeah. Not really an assistant in the typical sense. I'm just so busy, I could really use some help, especially with running my new foundation. And with your business training, I know you could give me pointers."

Emily stroked the ends of her ponytail. "But I don't have a place to live. I've been staying with one of my professor's friends, but that was only because of the internship and that's now over."

"Live with me. My place is huge. Half of the U.S. Army could move in and I'd never even know it."

"I would be imposing. I'm sure you and your boyfriend want—"

"I don't have a boyfriend anymore," Callie said. "See? We're in the same boat. Look, if you don't like it and can't stand me by the end of the month, go back home. But I could really use your help, and plus, I trust you. I don't trust many people.

"I can start you off at four grand a month, which I know isn't that much, but since you don't have to worry about rent, it's more like six. And I'll have to check with my friend, Tyler, but I'm sure he wouldn't mind if you used his car, since he's in Europe. C'mon, it could be fun. Who knows, we could make a great team. What do you think?"

Emily grinned. "I think I've got nothing to lose. You've got yourself a deal."

60

The private dressing area at Vibiana was packed with hairspray fumes and half-naked models. Tyler may not have been available to work his makeup magic, but he had procured a group who was more than up for the task. Drummond's team twirled brushes and irons through the girls' hair, and with their glistening cheekbones and featherweight curls, the models appeared ethereal, exactly the look Callie was aiming for. But at the moment, she was in a panic and unable to appreciate anyone's artistry. "Has anyone seen Evan?" she said. "He was supposed to be here an hour ago. This is crazy! He's MC'ing this thing. Where is he?"

"He's here, Cal. I saw him just a minute ago. Settle down, everything's in place." Emily was the picture of poise in a DVF wrap dress. Her hair was now a pale blonde bob—Callie insisted on a full makeover, complete with a new wardrobe—and the shades of peach and bronze on her features complemented her fair complexion.

"I sure hope he remembers everything like we rehearsed," Callie said.

"He's an entertainer Cal; this is a piece of cake for him. He only has to say a few names and make small talk when the models come down the runway. If I can get a part in a movie with no experience, how hard can this be for a guy who performs for millions of people?"

"You're right, it's cake."

"I bet you're just nervous about your speech." Callie itched the back of her neck. "Just a little."

"Here. These notes should help." Emily produced a stack of index cards from her purse. "I made them this morning. Jotted down all your bullet points. And if for some reason you freeze and can't speak, just wave one of these cards and that will cue the music to start up. I've already alerted the sound coordinator. I know you'll be fantastic, but, you know—just in case."

Callie smiled. Emily had been helping her prepare for the fashion show less than a month, but she was a natural at organization. And she looked fabulous to boot, a sophisticated, California golden girl.

"There you are." Lisa, the event coordinator, waddled over, panting. Her forehead was perspiring and, mixed with her thick layer of pancake, the sweat beads were opaque and greasy. "I've got some guy out front who doesn't have a ticket and isn't press but says he's got to see you. Says you're expecting him."

"What's his name?" Callie said.

"Oh, God....What the hell name did he give?" Lisa clamped her hands to her cheeks. The tips of her fingers turned beige from her foundation. "You know, I'm really losing it because do you know I can't remember? But he's cute. Real cute."

"Blondish hair, about five ten-ish?" said Callie.

"Yep, that's about right."

Mitch. Callie stood straighter and, inadvertently, arched her back. "I'll go grab him. Thanks, Lisa."

"You got it. Oh, and your parents just arrived with Mr. Angers. I asked them if they want to come backstage but they said they don't want to bother you and they'll meet you at Spago afterwards."

"Thanks, Lisa. Can you make sure someone keeps an eye on them? Make sure they get anything they need." Callie turned to Emily. "Did I mention we're all having dinner tonight? Tony, Mom, myself, and you, too, if you like. You're welcome to join."

Emily weighed Callie's words before saying, "Last night was a lot to take in for me. No offense, but I think I'll sit this one out." The DiPrizios had flown in the previous evening. Callie and Tony went out for pizza and left Virginia and Emily alone at the house. For the first time as grown women, mother and daughter, had been face-to- face.

"No offense taken," Callie said. She still wasn't entirely comfortable with her familial situation and she didn't inquire about the details of Emily and her mother's meeting; she had no desire in knowing what was said and how many tears were shed. It was still too....awkward. If only Grandma Esme had agreed to come, she would have made everything more enjoyable. ("Honey, I'm so proud of you, but I can't cancel my bridge plans," Esme told her. "The girls will be so disappointed and I won't be able to find someone to sub for me so late in the game. But I'll be watching for you on the news, dear, you better believe it.")

Lisa cleared her throat. "I don't mean to interrupt, but I need to know how we're looking on time."

"The girls are almost ready to go," said Emily. "One of the designers is mending a blouse that ripped, but other than that—"

"I ask because people are getting anxious out there and we're running behind. Callie, will you be ready to start in ten?"

"Definitely."

"Okay, everybody! Boys and girls, please listen up!" The models and stylists focused on Lisa. "I've got a packed house out there and they're hungry for some fashion! I need you all suited up and ready to prance down that runway in five. You got that? Five minutes to show time. Thank you, that's all, I'm leaving you alone. And now, I have got to do something about this air conditioner. With all the bodies in here, it's a good seventy-five degrees and would you look at me? I'm about to sail away in sweat." Lisa straightened the hem of her skirt suit and took off.

Callie handed the cue cards back to Emily. "Can you hold onto these? I'll be right back." She made her way up front, past the throngs of people, including Luciana. Resplendent in a blush satin gown, she was positioned next to the catwalk, interviewing various celebrities. Callie waved before feeling a tap on her arm.

"Hey there, gorgeous." Bedroom Eyes. It was the first time they had spoken since their rendezvous in Michigan. A bodyguard stood next to him along with a curvaceous young redhead.

"Hello, yourself," Callie said coolly.

"I swear, Callie, you're getting hotter every time I see you. Isn't she gorgeous, Jacinda?" Evan wound his arm around the redhead's waist.

"Beautiful," agreed the girl.

"Callie, my friend, Jacinda here, is a big fan of yours. She's seen every episode of *The Cheerleader Chronicles*."

"Only the ones you're in," said Jacinda to Callie. "Before they ruined the show with that blonde."

Callie smiled. "That's sweet, thank you. Evan, show time's in a few minutes, okay?"

"I'm ready, doll. Based on the turnout alone, it's already a major success."

"Yeah, well, we'll see," Callie muttered. "If you'll excuse me, I have to go meet someone."

"Oh, and Callie..." Evan's eyes glinted. "I was thinking, if you're free later, we should get together at my place. An intimate party, just the three of us. Could be fun."

Jacinda focused her heavy-lidded gaze on Callie. "Could be a lot of fun. I'm a big giver."

"Good for you." Callie glared at Evan. "Leopards sure don't change their spots, do they, Ev? Good luck out there." With a toss of her head, Callie sailed past the amorous duo and out the door. She scanned the mob out front—pedestrians, mostly, trying to talk their way past security—for that handsome, much-missed face. But no sign of Mitch. Where was he? Did he leave already?

"Skank!" Tyler, his hair freshly bleached, emerged from the crowd dragging a gigantic suitcase. "Surprise! Bet you didn't think I was going to make it, but look, here I am. You look disappointed. Aren't you happy to see me?"

61

Callie did her best to recover from the surprise of Tyler—a blonde Tyler, at that. They embraced and she said, "Of course I'm happy to see you. What's with the hair?"

"Don't you like it?" He patted his spikes. "I was in the mood for something different and did it myself a few days ago. By the way, there's this contraption called a phone and the skank I know used to use one. I've been trying to get ahold of you since I got off the plane."

"Sorry, I've been so busy, I haven't even looked at my phone, Ty. So how did you manage this? Come on, follow me. We're almost ready to start. We can dump your luggage off backstage." She led Tyler inside the building.

"One of my co-workers became violently ill with food poisoning. She couldn't make the flight for the Beverly Hills shindig tomorrow, so Jean sent me instead. But barely. I had to beg and plead like a helpless little nelly but it worked. It won't be a long visit—I'll only be here three days, then I'm off to Michigan to see my Mom for two before I'm back in Europe—but a short visit is better than none at all. Heavens to Betsey, it's good to be back in the good ol' U.S. of A."

Tyler sucked in his breath as he took in the spectacularly remodeled archways and Art Deco fixtures. "Will you look at this place? When you first told me it was downtown, I was expecting some Armageddon kind of dump. But this... this isn't exactly slumming it."

"Not a bad spot, huh?"

"I'll say. Well done, skankazoid. A good amount of media here, too."

"And the red carpet was packed earlier. Lots of celebs showed up. Now if we can just raise a small slice of the net worth in this room, I'll be thrilled."

"Exactly. Let's hope the clothes are fabulous. I can't wait to see what these designers came up with. Stick some queens with a needle and thread and stand back, bitches."

"There are only a handful of queens, Ty. The rest are girls."

He giggled. "Same thing, isn't it? I don't care if my mother's blind aunt stitched some scraps together; I'll take fashion any way I can get it. You'd think I'd be burnt out, what with Paris and all, but I never get enough. Oh, look, there's your mom and step-dad. Ooh, she's gorgeous in red. Definitely her color." He flapped his hands over his head to get the DiPrizios attention. "Hi, guys! They can't see me. I'll go over in a minute. Oh, and at which table am I supposed to be sitting?"

"Anywhere you like. I'm so excited you're here, Ty. This is really special. I'm surrounded by everyone I care about." *Well, not quite everyone, but almost.*

"Hey, it's not every day you pull something like this out of your hat. And, lookie, over there—there's that crazy limey, charming a big group of women. Big surprise. Every one of them looks like they got beat by a stick named Ugly. Nothing new on that front, I see. So, how exactly is this going to work—you both are hosting this together, like a Sonny and Cher thing, or what's the deal?"

"Nooooo. I'm just going to say a few words and hand it over to him. He'll be his smooth, snake-like self and he definitely knows how to work a crowd. In fact, I think most of the people just came to see him, but, then, that's the only reason I wanted him involved in the first place."

"Of course, because you're one crafty cookie. But don't sell yourself short, either. You've got more drawing power than you think."

"I just want to get it over with, Ty. I'm nervous."

"Please. You're going to knock 'em dead like always."

Emily waltzed up behind them. "Cal, Lisa's trying to find you. She wants to know if you're all set."

"I am, yeah. Can I have my cue cards? Let's get this show on the road."

"And here's your mic, too," said Emily. "Make sure you flip the switch before you say anything."

"Thanks. Oh, Emily, I'd like you to meet my best friend, Tyler. He just flew in from Paris. Ty, this is Emily."

Tyler shook her hand and grinned. "Well, finally. I've heard so much about you. Wow, you two don't look alike at all."

Emily blushed. "Nice to meet you, too."

"Don't mind Tyler," Callie said. "He's always incredibly blunt."

"The only way to be," he quipped.

"I like straight-forward people," said Emily. "Maybe not the most subtle, but honest, at least."

"There you go," said Tyler. "I'm as subtle as a typhoon. But you get used to it. Alright, I'm off to find a seat. Emily, I'm sure we'll be seeing more of each other later on and as for you..." He kissed Callie on the cheek. "Go break a leg and kick some ass."

The lights dimmed and Callie took to the runway. An overhead light beamed as she reached the end of the catwalk and a hush fell over the crowd. A battalion of faces, most of them unfamiliar, stretched before her. All eyes and cameras were on her. She owned the floor. Taking a deep breath, she said, "Good evening and welcome to the first annual Gabby Manx: Strut to End Domestic Violence. Thank you for supporting this issue that is very close to my heart." *So many people out there. Don't screw this up.* Was that a snicker from someone? Were they making fun of her? Did she sound stupid? She hadn't done public speaking before. Alone, in front of so many strangers, she felt naked. All that was missing was a guillotine; she was sure the audience wanted her head to roll. Her underarms were a cavern of moisture. *Thank God my dress is sleeveless.* She glanced at her notes but her damp palms had smeared the ink. Her tongue was like lead, unable to form words. Plop. A drop of perspiration splat on her shoe. She was officially a pile of wet cement.

62

How did that next part go? God, help me get through this alive and I'll never ask for anything else. I swear I'll never cheat again as long as I live or even curse. An elderly woman in the front row began hacking. She covered her mouth with her gnarled hands and did her best to stifle a coughing attack. *That's right! That's the next part.* "A few short years ago, when I filmed *Nympho Cheerleaders Attack!,* I had no idea such a silly, ridiculous movie would change the course of so many lives, my own included. It was during this time that I was introduced to a young woman on the set and we clicked right away. She was kind, loyal, and humorous—the three top qualities in a friend. She told me she wanted to leave the entertainment industry and move back to the East Coast to start a new life, one more simple, though not nearly as glamorous. She wanted to open a bed and breakfast, marry, and have her own family. Her name was Gabrielle Manx."

A smattering of applause. *Good, good, this is good.* She forged on. "Gabby never got the chance because her life was cut short by domestic violence. I've never spoken out about her death because I haven't wanted to be a part of anything salacious or negative or crude. I didn't—and still don't—want to dwell on the horrific. But what I do want is to turn her tragedy into something triumphant, to give her a voice, give her justice, and honor her in a way that impacts the well-being of others. We cannot sit back and watch one more person suffer from this epidemic. I will not allow anyone, whether it's a loved one or stranger, to go through what Gabby did." Callie's eyes met Tyler's; he wiped a tear from his eye. "With your help tonight, and with the help of some amazing designers who have donated their talent and time, we can do just that. Please join me in making this night a success—for Gabby, and for so many others who can't speak for themselves." A roar of applause filled her eardrums and she struggled to speak above the noise. "So, without further ado, I present to you a man who needs no introduction, your MC for the evening, Mr. Evan Marquardt." She exhaled and took a step back.

Fuck! How did I remember all that?

Bedroom Eyes joined her onstage; suddenly she was opposed to relinquishing her domain. The acclamation, the whistles and cheers from the audience….she could get used to public speaking. She handed the microphone off and Evan kissed her on the cheek.

"How about another round of applause for this wonderful woman?" he said.

What a bullshitter. Callie dabbed her sweaty brow. Narciso Rodriguez was sticking to her trunk like a post-coital condom, but she didn't care; this was her moment and she wanted to savor it. She took a bow amidst the flashes of cameras.

"You were amazing!" Emily greeted her off the runway. "I don't know why you were so nervous. You've obviously made speeches before."

"No, I haven't." Callie threw her wet index cards in the trash. "Monologues, yes, speeches—not on your life."

"You sure had me fooled. Oh, good, the music's starting."

The models filed past, one after glamorous one. Evan described each ensemble's attributes and the amazons lined up together on stage afterwards. "Opening bid on this chiffon number designed by Gwendolyn Singer starts at $500," Evan said. A flurry of paddles later and Callie was ecstatic to see the gown at $3,500. "Might I remind you we are looking at bona fide couture, folks, and made-in-the-U.S.A., at that. Completely hand-beaded. At least, that's what my notes say. Personally, I think it's all velcroed or glued because the time and effort involved would be enough to keep me on tour all year round..." Evan inspected the model's dress and looked back at the audience, his face awash in mock-shock. "What do you know, it really is completely hand-beaded. I'm just kidding, of course. Gwendolyn, you sly little minx, I see you glaring at me. She's wondering whether she wants to kill me now or later. After the show, love, after the show." The audience laughed and Evan pointed to the back of the room. "This reminds me of a Valentino worn by Salma Hayek recently, but only about, oh, $30,000 less. Thank you to the gentleman in the blue suit, we're now at

$4,000. Just to let you know ahead of time, sir, this beautiful blonde, here, is not—I repeat not—included."

Callie rubbed her hands together and whispered, "Twenty-nine more outfits to go. This is even better than I hoped."

Several yards off, she spotted her mother making her way to the bathroom. After a dozen steps, Virginia seized the back of a chair. Tony rushed to his wife's side but by the time he reached her, she had collapsed, convulsing, on the floor.

63

Callie kicked off her pebbled leather pumps and collapsed in bed. She was fried, emptied, physically and emotionally spent. She had exhausted herself at the hospital for the last four hours. She clutched a pillow to her chest but it was sterile and cold. She wanted Mitch. She missed him and needed to hear his reassuring voice telling her everything would be okay. But when she dialed his number, he didn't pick up. Not on the second ring, nor on the third. *God, he's going to think I'm some psychotic freak. You're going to make an even bigger fool of yourself than you've already done.* She nixed dialing a fourth time. He hadn't returned any of her phone calls in the last weeks; why would tonight be any different?

A knock at her door. Emily waited in the hallway. "Hey, Em."

Emily gave a small smile. "So how is she? I tried calling you earlier. Paul and Ty, too."

"Yeah, I know," Callie said weakly. "Thanks, I just haven't felt like talking. And I'm too exhausted to talk much now. How did the fundraiser go?"

"Really, really well. Things were a little tense after the paramedics came and went, but Evan loosened the crowd up and everything went off without a hitch. We raised almost $60,000. Lisa kept saying she couldn't believe how high people went with their bids but I wasn't surprised at all. People automatically want to help out when it's for a good cause."

Callie smiled. "That makes me feel good. And it's only the beginning."

"Exactly. Tyler went to bed an hour ago, but we stayed up talking for a while. He said the audience loved your speech and there's already lots of interest in volunteering. He's a really nice guy, I like him."

"Ty's a good egg."

"Well, I'll let you get some sleep. If you want to talk, don't worry about waking me. I'm a light sleeper."

"Makes two of us. I'll probably have to take an Ambien."

Emily snapped her fingers. "Oh, before I forget, Paul told me your interview tomorrow at The Polo Lounge is—"

"Cancel it."

"Okay. Do you want me to reschedule or...?"

Callie shook her head. "I honestly don't care. Tell them I'm sick. And I'm taking the rest of the week off, so can you clear my schedule? I can't remember what's lined up, but I won't be able to make any of it."

"Sure, I'll take care of it. The new script is ready, too, so I'll pick it up tomorrow. I'm sure you'll want to go over it ASAP."

"What new script?"

"*The Foreign Affair*. Reshoots start in two weeks, remember?"

"Oh, right." Callie massaged her puffy eyes; her bags felt more like a three piece luggage set. "I'm just run down, I guess."

"Go get some sleep and recharge. You've been through a lot today."

"That's an understatement. Night, Em." Callie peeled her clothes off and got back in bed. Her makeup smeared the sheets but for the first time in a long time, she didn't care. She stared at the ceiling and drifted back to the conversation earlier at the hospital.

"She's frail, much frailer, perhaps, than you realize. We did an MRI and found metastases to the brain."

"How 'bout English?" Tony barked.

"Meaning, the lung cancer has migrated to her brain. We found several tumors."

"But she's been cleared," Callie said.

Tony nodded. "That's right. She can't have cancer, doc. Ginnie's oncologist says she's clean as a whistle."

"It's possible for metastases to occur even when a patient has gone into remission," said the doctor. "Loss of balance, vision changes, confusion, severe headaches, seizures—what Virginia had earlier—these are not uncommon."

"Come to think of it, last few days she's complained of headaches," Tony said quietly, as if to himself. "So what's this mean, doc? Operate and start chemo again?"

"Unfortunately, it's not as simple as that, Mr. DiPrizio. You see, her lung cancer has returned. I realize this is news no family ever wants to hear, but recurrence happens more often than not."

"No..." Callie murmured.

"I don't believe an operation would be beneficial," he continued. "It's not just a question of removing one or two tumors—there are more than that. Radiotherapy is the best option, in my opinion. Of course, you'll want to go over all options with your oncologist—"

"But she can be cured," Callie said. She crossed her arms and waited for a reply. "Right?"

The doctor sighed. "There is always hope. But you must realize any time cancer has spread to the brain, the situation is grave."

There was no way around it; Callie was gutted.

"Come on now, kiddo," Virginia told Callie later that night. She wore a brave smile in her hospital bed. "Wipe that frown off your face. You know I hate anyone feeling sorry for me." Virginia pursed her lips and patted Callie's hand. "Tony's staying with me overnight. They just want to monitor me and make sure I'm good for the night. Get your rest. You're not doing anyone any favors by staying at the hospital. I'm fine, I can tell you that. It's a set-back, sure, but I'll lick it. Again. I'll just start over, simple as that. I'll go back home and start from square one and that will be the end of it. Honestly, go home and I'll see you tomorrow." She pursed her lips and patted Callie's arm. But she couldn't block the pain in her eyes. Virginia was breaking inside, Callie could feel it.

Appearing blemished, even to family, had never been her mother's style; she had presented a front of indestructibility and picture-perfectness her entire adult life. As far as Callie was concerned, vulnerability didn't make one less valiant—the opposite, in fact—but Virginia apparently felt otherwise.

Callie squeezed her eyes shut and willed her mind to go blank. She wanted only to sleep. Bottomless, heavenly sleep.

64

STEPHANIE'S SAD SPIRAL trumpeted the headline from the latest *Got It!*. A disheveled Schueller, snapped as she exited Cobalt, shadowed the article. Callie thumbed through it while reclining in her dressing room.

*Friends of **The Cheerleader Chronicles** star are worried about her. "She parties hard, real hard," says a source close to the television show. "She stumbles in hours late—half the time she doesn't show up at all—and she's still drunk from the night before. Or worse. There are whispers she's strung out on something harder than booze, like meth or coke. She looks rough, too, far older than someone in her late 20s. It's all the lighting crew can do to try to make her look decent. Needless to say, the Wilders are furious with her antics and now they're slipping in the ratings, too. They regret hiring her. She is one hard-to-handle broad."*

Callie chuckled. *Good,* she thought. *Let them sweat.* The Wilders deserved the headache after dumping her for Stephanie, that plasticized strumpet. It was only a matter of time before The Trailer Lady showed everyone her true colors. If there was a God, the ratings would continue to plummet. She threw the magazine on the floor. She was pissed. In a foul mood. Had been ever since her mother's news. Someone upstairs was playing a cruel joke on her family, she just knew it. And there she was, trapped on *The Foreign Affair* set with reshoots. Acting and movies were so inconsequential in such a grave time, she didn't want to be bothered with it. But, there she was, at a soundstage in Burbank, as she had been for the last three weeks.

A knock on her dressing room. "Callie? They're ready for you."

"Be right out." She made her way to the soundstage. Thanks to the dozens of people and hot lights, it was more sauna than set.

"Bon apres-midi!" said Nanette. She gave Callie a kiss on either cheek. "How are you today, my dear? There's been a small change in plans. Before we reshoot Scene 13, we need to redo part of 40. They both take place in Jeanette's bedroom, so it is convenient for all." The bright lips and flushed cheeks photoshopped five years off her age, easily. She was a different woman from the one of three months prior; no longer gaunt with a hair-trigger temper, she seemed relaxed and exuberant. Callie was happy Nan's private life was going well but wished she wasn't such a fusspot; the Frenchwoman's perfectionism was taking up too much of Callie's life. She wished the film would wrap and everyone would call it a day already.

"What do you mean, 'change'? What's changed?" Callie asked.

"In 40, after Roland leaves, after they make love, Jeanette is in bed. Chris, that incompetent nincompoop who dares to call himself a director, had you wear a nightgown, for some reason."

"Right," Callie said.

"That makes zero sense. Why would you be wearing any clothes after the throes of passion? I need to reshoot it with you naked and then we'll move on to Scene 55."

"Excuse me?" Callie said.

"You can have the covers covering part of you, of course, but this has got to be believable. So you need to be naked under the covers." Nanette swooped over to the rickety bed and flung herself on it. "I want you to be just like this, on your side. I'll see just a bit of shoulder and a tiny bit of torso."

"Um, yeah, and some side boob."

"Very, very little. Maybe one square inch of the side of your breast. Even Chuck agrees with me on this and you know how we disagree on everything."

"Chuck is a porn peddler, so I'm sure he agrees on anything involving nudity," Callie snorted.

"It has nothing to do with nudity, Callie. This is about the integrity of my picture. Continuity and common sense; all my films have it and *The Foreign Affair* is no exception. So it is a little skin. Who cares, so what?"

"So what? Who cares? I care, that's who!"

Nanette gave a small laugh. "I see. Now you are playing the saint. After the parts you've taken on, all of a sudden you are a puritan."

The crew quieted down. Everyone stood still, watching. Reese, the man in charge of lighting, spoke up. "Callie, I'm going to light you in a way where you'll be mostly in shadow, and—"

"Thank you, Reese, but I am handling this," said Nanette. "What is this puritanical side of you Americans? You want to play the slut, then you want to be the nun. Slut, nun, slut, nun. Which is it?"

"Is there something you're trying to say, Nanette?" Callie cocked a hand on her hip. "Maybe you should just spit it out."

Nanette threw her hands up. "You always play a slut! Obviously, it comes very easy for you. I booked you because you are so talented at playing a multi-faceted slut. In everything else, you are more than happy to toss your clothes off. Any excuse to show yourself, you do it. And yet now...now you protest at showing a smidgeon of skin for a true work of art?"

"Maybe you didn't get the memo, but I don't do nudity anymore. Taking my clothes off isn't in my contract," said Callie.

Nanette stomped her Chanel ballet flat hard on the floor. "This is ludicrous! I have had far too many catastrophes strike me this year to let a ten-second scene get in my way. Maybe you are confusing this with that pornographic crap

366

in your past. Do not! You have done nothing but junk. You hear me? Junk! Finally, thanks to me, you get handed a masterpiece and suddenly, you are too good for it? Have you lost your mind?"

Callie rested her hands on her hips. "Ohhhhh, I see. So you think you're doing me a favor, is that it? That I should bow down because you took pity on little ol' me? That I somehow owe you, the great Nanette Vernadeau, her Serene Royal Hagness?" Her voice boomed louder and louder.

"How dare you," Nanette seethed. "And how ungrateful you are. This is not some silly, monkey spank magazine or jiggly TV series. Or have you forgotten, since that's all you are used to?"

Callie stood with her nose an inch away from the director's. "As I told you, this is not in my contract. Sorry, Nanette, but I think you forgot to take your meds. Maybe I should get Luciana to remind you."

"You stupid little pig! Get off my set!"

But Callie had already stomped off, leaving a dumbfounded crew in her wake. "Go to hell, you nuclear bitch!" she screamed over her shoulder. So much for the new and improved Nanette, Callie thought as she raced to the safety of her dressing room. Ugh, that woman was just too much! She picked up her phone; it blinked with a voicemail alert, but she first wanted to talk with Paul.

"Aye, aye, aye," Paul moaned after Callie explained the situation. "When egos collide."

"We all know she's a little crazy, but she's never made it personal before. She's a slave driver, a postmenopausal Nazi," Callie spat. "I'm through feeling sorry for her. She's an asshole. And by the way, all these reshoots that were supposed to be minor, aren't so minor."

"It's minor in the sense that it's local, and they're small bits of scenes."

"More like a trillion bits." She tore the bobby pins out of her hair and gave her head a shake. "Evan and I shot a scene yesterday that should have taken an hour but wound up taking ten." *And it's not exactly easy acting next to my former boyfriend who fucked up my life*, she almost added. She found Evan to be the definition of grotesque, the epitome of sleaze; he was the reason she was no longer with Mitch, and she was reminded of her mistake each and every time he came near her. Evan symbolized her failure as a girlfriend and she despised him for it.

"She hates the footage Chris directed," Paul said. "The studio is bending over backwards to insure she doesn't have another breakdown."

"They better realize they're gonna have another problem when their female lead has a breakdown," Callie bitched.

"You're not having a breakdown. Stop being so dramatic."

"Paul, do you realize what's going on in my life right now? My mother is battling for her life a second time around as we speak and you expect me to give a flying fuck about a stupid movie? What's wrong with you people? Jesus Christ!"

A long pause on Paul's end. "I know you're under a lot of stress right now, Cal. I feel horrible about it, too, and I've told you so. But if there's anyone who can handle it, it's you. You're not built like the rest of 'em; you're tougher. You've got an inner core of teflon and you always pull through, especially under pressure. You're *this* close to being done with the whole ordeal and then you can move on."

"Will I ever," she grumbled.

"Let's just get through this last leg, and in one piece. Netty won't be happy until everything's as she envisioned. That's just the way she is. It's always been that way with her in business."

"I've got news for you—a crocodile Birkin crammed with Harry Winston himself wouldn't make her happy. I'll walk, Paul. I have no problem walking right off this set because no one talks to me like that."

"Hey, I'm on your side. I want to get through this as smoothly and diplomatically as possible. Tell you what, I'm coming by. Stay where you are, I'm going to get everything straightened out. Give me thirty."

"Okay," she muttered. Paul had made a good point; she did get through everything, somehow. She was tougher than she gave herself credit for and had battled a hell of a lot more obnoxious things in life than an off-her-rocker, scorned director. And, anyhow, dealing with yet another Hollywood egomaniac was par for the course. Predictable and boring, like knowing the end of a crappy novel after the very first chapter. Working with someone who didn't have a swollen ego would be alarming, Callie reasoned—creepy, even. She flopped on the sofa and played her voicemail.

"Cal Cat, it's Tony. It's about six o'clock here. Things aren't lookin' good. I, uh, I think it's a good idea if you... well, I think you better come home, Cal. It's not goin' too good. Your mother needs you."

65

allie knelt next to her mother's bed and stroked her face. Virginia's breathing was strained and irregular. The layers of blankets dwarfed her shrunken, pallid body, and she drifted in and out of consciousness. Callie marveled how things took such a gigantic turn for the worse in a span of four months. Cancer spreading to the brain almost never meant a positive outcome, but she was shocked by how quickly her mother's health deteriorated. The day after Tony's call, she arrived in Michigan. For the first few weeks, Virginia was coherent—exhausted and frail, but relatively coherent. Radiation therapy had only succeeded in making her sick with a severe skin rash; it hadn't shrunk her tumors any. By Christmas, a seizure left her partially paralyzed and bedridden. Callie flew in a specialist from Germany, a recommendation of Paul's—a former actress/client of his claimed the German guru cured her aunt's cancer, and Callie was desperate to try anything, costs aside. But nothing worked, and all Virginia wanted was to live the rest of her life in peace, in the comfort of her own home.

"No more hospitals," she said in a small, affected voice. "Just give me my family. My family and my home." By the time February rolled around, she was a one-hundred-pound wisp of a woman, incapacitated, intertwined with a feeding tube. Callie didn't allow herself to dwell on the negative; she was too busy spending her days (and many sleepless nights) tending to her mother—reading to her, rubbing her feet, helping the nurse bathe her, and relieving a shell-shocked Tony of household chores. It was like she was sixteen again, living with her parents, only the circumstances were twisted.

"Mom, can you hear me?" Callie said. She talked to her as she always had; she told her about the fight with Nanette and how nervous she was about her upcoming defamation trial. And about how sorry she was that she chased Mitch away. "I miss him so much, Mom. I know I screwed up. I've always been impatient and I expect everything to happen on my time table. And then when it doesn't, I ruin a good thing. Maybe I'm just scared of falling in love again. I push them away before they beat me to the punch. You'd be so ashamed of me. Honestly, I'm ashamed of myself, and I'm glad I never told you about what I did. Ack, what a mess I am. I've tried getting a hold of him but he won't return any of my calls. Can't say I blame him. My friend, Luci—you'd love her because she's so pretty and glamorous—she told me he's dating some Spanish model friend of hers. Isabel, her name is. How predictable is that? A Spanish model named Isabel. I guess she looks just like me, only taller. Live and learn, right? My charity is going well. We've been getting a lot of donations and I'm so, so proud of it, Mom.

It's been a lot of work, way more than I bargained for, but it's absolutely been worth it. It's, hands down, the best thing I've ever done. Emily's doing a great job helping me. We're planning on doing another fundraiser later this year, only it will be even bigger and better. She's so good with that kind of stuff; she has much more of a business mind than I do. I've always been better at creative things. I can't concentrate where numbers are concerned. She's flying in this evening, so I'll be sure you look your best. I bet you never thought we'd all be under one roof, did you? Let alone in the same movie together. How weird is that? Definitely one for the record books—mother and her two daughters in the same movie. Your footage came out so well, Mom, you look ultra-glam. You would definitely approve. I can't wait for the premiere so you can see it. It's been pretty stressful, but I think it's going to turn out all right. The thing you'll really like is there's hardly any nudity. Complete opposite of my earlier days. Mmmm, smell those? All those pretty flowers? Grandma Esme brought them, plus that little teddy bear over there. It looks just like that bear you got me for my eighth birthday. Rex, was his name. Remember him? Grandma's the sweetest. I know you haven't always gotten along, but she loves you, Mom. We all love you..."

Virginia died early the next morning. Her funeral fell on Valentine's Day.

66

Callie perched over the six-foot hole in the ground. The wind was bitter as the pastor recited a chapter from her mother's favorite scripture and her cheeks and nose burned from the chill. What stung most was the inexpressible void in her heart—a fierce, arctic twinge. Her soul, the core of her being, was far more ravaged than her frostbitten extremities. She felt directionless, marooned at sea with neither paddle nor compass. Was this all really happening? Maybe this was just another one of those dreams that turned out to be nonsense. She'd snap out of her slumber and there would be her mother—alive, healthy and smiling. She'd give anything—her career, her sanity, her right arm—for her mom to be next to her, in the flesh. They could bicker over who was the superior driver or who scrambled better eggs and which crappy chain restaurant had the best mozzarella cheese sticks, as they used to.

"Cal, do you want to sit?" Emily whispered.

Callie looked down at the folding chairs next to the casket, most of them occupied by the older guests, and nodded. She thought she would have been fine to stand, but she felt woozy. Emily must have seen the pallor on her face.

She took a seat in the metal chair; it was as cold and un-comfortable as block ice. Grandma Esme, seated in head to toe black wool, squeezed her hand.

"For dust thou art," said the reverend, "and unto dust shalt thou return."

Callie barely heard any of the reverend's speech, and, in an instant, it was over. Time to say good-bye.

"I just can't believe it..." Tony murmured, dazed, to him-self. "...Can't believe it." His face was puffy as a soufflé, his bloodshot eyes remote. He stared at the casket for several moments before draping it with flowers.

Callie surveyed her father's headstone to the left of the freshly dug plot. She recalled a line from an old movie: *Only after the death of both parents does one truly become an adult.* Tears threatened to spill down her cheeks but the air froze them in their ducts. She blinked long and hard and willed the strength to stand. As she bent down to kiss her mother's coffin, she was sure, in that instant, there wasn't a girl in the world as lonesome as she.

67

"It's been two weeks now and still no word from you," Paul said in a voicemail.

"When we spoke at the Mercy dinner, you promised you'd call me soon and let me know how you're doing. Look, I have no idea where you are. Are you in L.A. or still in Michigan? When you get a second, I have some business I need to discuss with you. Important business. At least let me know you're okay. I'm worried about you, young lady."

Callie texted,

Back in Cali. Taking a long break.

It would suit her just fine if she never read another script again for as long as she lived. For easy, extra money, she could always make a guest appearance at a nightclub and she had enough money to last several years—live well, too. That is, unless she got socked with a ten million dollar judgment. As if she didn't have enough to worry about, dealing with the aftermath of her mother's death—a massive lawsuit awaited her around the corner.

"Fuck me," she growled. The silence of the house was deafening. Emily had left for Dallas that morning for a job interview. Callie just couldn't justify keeping her on payroll, what with all her down time over the last four months—and there would be even less for her to do in the future, since Callie wasn't planning on resuming work any time soon. Em was brilliant at promoting the Gabby foundation and keeping it organized, but it wasn't keeping her as busy as she'd like. Flat-out, she was antsy, and Callie couldn't blame her. Their mother's abrupt departure had thrown a monkey wrench in everything.

She rolled over in bed, her primary dwelling of choice for the last two weeks, and looked at the clock. Three o'clock. In the afternoon. A commercial clamored from the TV:

We traveled to India to bring this enchanting blend of eucalyptus and lemongrass. Ask everyone who's anyone what their favorite brand of luxury air freshener is and, undoubtedly, their answer will be, Tarasha.

"Bullshit," Callie snarled and turned the set off. It was as good a time as any to get out of bed. She hadn't done a thing all day except make a few trips to the bathroom. No food, even. She just couldn't muster up an appetite, even though she could feel her hipbones protruding from her sweatpants. It didn't take much for her already-thin frame to drop weight. Her mother wouldn't be very proud of her, she knew. Virginia had always despised laziness. But Callie didn't have the strength to go about day-to-day tasks.

The last few weeks had been nothing but a whirlwind and, for her own sanity, she had to lay low. Regroup. The wake, the funeral, shaking all the hands of people her mother had known, nodding her head and smiling. "Thank you for coming," Callie had said, or "My mother spoke very highly of you, too," or "No, it sure isn't. Life isn't fair, you're right," all while staying poised and impenetrable, as her mother would have liked. And in between her duties as a daughter, she had to process her own grief. Dr. Freisch did not help. Her grandmother, despite her plethora of wisdom, could not help. Tony was so beside himself with grief, he couldn't provide any comfort or insight—not that they had ever been close, anyway. Tyler hadn't been able to make the funeral, but he had sent a lovely and monstrous bouquet of flowers. There weren't any other people Callie cared to so much as talk to. She went downstairs and rummaged through the pantry. Ah, chocolate. When in doubt, turn to chocolate. Her phone buzzed.

"Cal-lie, Earl Barletta, here."

She groaned. "Hi, Earl. I mailed you your check yesterday—"

"I'm not calling about that. How would you like some good news? No, no—great news. I have some mighty fine information to relay. You ready? Sitting down?"

I'm going into menopause waiting, asshole. "Uh, yeah."

"She dropped the case."

"Who?"

"Schueller. She dropped the case."

"What?"

"I told you the news is great." Earl's tone was decidedly kicky; he enunciated each syllable even more than usual. "She caved. I figured she would, if she had one single brain molecule."

"But that's just the thing—she doesn't, so why would she drop the case?"

"I'd love to think my abilities as an attorney shook her and her shit-for-brains lawyer to their core. To begin with, I never thought she had much of a case; there was a battalion of evidence that proved she started misrepresenting you in the press way before you ever made that comment to the reporter. Her position was weak from the very beginning and it was logical of her to dump the case."

"Yes, but Stephanie isn't smart or logical, so—"

"Then let's chalk it up to dumb luck. Feels like a sack of potatoes has been lifted off your shoulders, doesn't it?"

"Yeah, I'm...just...wow. I'm speechless."

"In my line of work, this type of thing doesn't happen too often, so soak it up, kick back, and toast your good fortune with a libation. Better yet, have two—one for me. I'd join you, but I have a gallery opening to attend with the Missus."

"I can't thank you enough. Seriously, Earl, thank you, thank you, thank you."

"I didn't get a chance to do much of anything, but you're quite welcome."

"Oh, by the way..." She mulled over her thoughts before diving in. "It's been a while since I've spoken with your nephew. How is he?"

"Mitch? He's well as can be. Not that I see much of him these days. He's in New Zealand, last I heard."

"Oh? New Zealand?"

"That's right, filming some action movie for the next three months. He's always zipping around the globe. I can't keep track of him most of the time."

"Oh. Good for him." She gave a short laugh. "I only thought of him because of the TV show he and Schueller and I did, that's all. Jogged my memory. Anyway..."

"Well then, on that note—not that I mean to cut this short—but I have a tux laid out for me and it will take all the butter in my refrigerator to slide into this thing. Remember to stay away from carbs when you get to be my age. Now, go celebrate, while the day is still young. For your sake, I hope we don't have the pleasure of meeting again. For my sake, I hope to see lots of you in the near and distant future. Toodle-loo, Miss Lam-bert."

Callie let out the longest, loudest exhale of her life. Maybe this was the start—and a damned good one—of a reversal of fortune. About time.

68

ichaela Dickerson Shepard blinked her dark, long-lashed eyes; she was the mirror image of her mother, down to the downy, inky hair on her head. She gnawed on her chubby fingers and giggled.

"She's the best baby," Luciana raved. "Aren't you? Aren't you the best little baby? My little Pisces princess." Michaela giggled as her mother held her up in the air. Callie had to agree; she was never the type to coo over infants, but Michaela, in her pink designer cashmere, was cherubic perfection.

"She's adorable, Luci." Callie decided to join Luci and her mini-me at the park, but only after she was promised no paparazzi would be in tow. ("I'm in no shape for pictures, Luci. I'd love to meet the baby but promise you won't turn this into a photo op."

"Done," Luci said. "No paps, unless they're there for someone else, of course. I need to be outdoors. It's the most gorgeous spring day, and days like this that make me miss Paris.")

"I'm just thankful she looks nothing like Roger," Luci smiled. "In fact, if anything, Michaela looks a little like Chad, as little sense as that makes. Look at that smile."

"And look at the size of her mom." Callie inspected Luci's petite waist. "Are you sure you were ever pregnant?"

"I was all belly," Luci said proudly. "Twenty-five pounds, but I've since lost half of it. And just in the nick of time, too, for my film coming up."

"What does *Hollywood Hotspot* think about you venturing out on them?"

"Didn't I tell you? I quit. They still haven't found my replacement yet, either, which I'm kind of tickled over. They begged me to come back after the birth, but it's just not my forte. Been there, did that. This girl has left the building."

"Hey, when you're ready to move on, you're ready to move on. I know the feeling. Like when I posed for *Coquette*. It was fine then, but I'm not going back."

"Exactly. You grow, you change...at least, you're supposed to. There are plenty of people whose gears remain in neutral their whole lives. Bimbos or drunks or plain old scumbags. Oh! I nearly forgot. Have you heard the latest regarding my favorite scumbag?"

"Who would that be?" said Callie.

Luci placed Michaela in her stroller. "Gary Benson. He was arrested for consorting with a minor."

"Seriously?"

Luci smirked. "Mmm-hmm. Just last night. Busted with a seventeen year old at a hotel."

"How did they catch him?"

"A little birdie could have tipped the cops off or maybe his dirty ways finally caught up with him. Gary's been a pervert for some time, so it's hard to know for sure." She winked and took a sip of bottled water.

Callie giggled. "Luci, you're bad."

"Chad's got about fifty managers circling him right now, ready to swoop down like buzzards. How's it going with Nanette, speaking of buzzards? You survived her lunacy?"

Callie stretched her limbs in the sun. "Barely. Thanks to you, I think her head is permanently warped. After all her shenanigans, all the reshoots—guess what? The movie's been shelved. Indefinitely."

"What?" Luci gasped.

"Yep. It's collecting dust as we speak."

"How disappointing. Why?"

"Because it's one hot mess. It was supposed to be some fabulous epic and ended up sloppier than Michaela's diaper."

Luciana laughed. "I've seen some of the footage and I didn't think it was that bad."

The new mother had never been an ebullient type, and Callie hadn't recalled ever seeing her so light-hearted. Even Luci's eyes looked different; they were warmer, more relaxed, with sparks of bronze and gold. Motherhood clearly agreed with her.

"How did you see the footage?"

"Roger showed it to me a while back. You were great. You know who else was good? Your sister. She has a certain air about her—poise and grace, especially in person. When I met her at your fashion show, I immediately pictured her as an entertainment reporter or TV host."

Callie clucked her tongue. "No way. Emily's too smart for showbiz. She's been in Dallas the last few days for a job interview in Human Resources. One of her best friends lives there and I think she's ready to ditch L.A. in favor of normal people."

"Normal is subjective, but good for her. Personally, I think she has a future in television and she'd be a perfect fit for *Hollywood Hotspot*. She's a young Diane Sawy— "

"Miriam, go grab him!" yelled a bleached blonde from a nearby bench. "Quick, grab Louie! I'm not running in these Louboutins, there's no way in hell." A middle-aged Latina raced across the lawn and nabbed the toddler. She plopped him down next to his mother. "We're going back to the Aston Martin if you don't behave, Louie," said the blonde. "You act up every time Mommy drives you in Mr. Martin. Miriam says when she takes you in the Mercedes Mommy bought her you're an angel. If you run away one more time..."

Luci groaned. "I plan on raising my daughter far away from here. As much as possible, we're going to be back in Paris. I refuse to let Michaela morph into one of these Hollywood brats, even though my parents are intent on making her one. They came to visit when she was first born and brought enough toys to fill the Pentagon. I swear, I never had half as many toys growing up. They're more in love with Michaela than they ever were with me. That suits me just fine. One can't get spoiled on too much love, and at least they approve of something about my life."

"Did they stay with you while they were in town?" Callie asked.

Luciana's eyes bulged. "Goodness, no. My mother only stays where there's an in-room masseuse and dermatologist on standby. I suppose I have a better appreciation of her, in spite of all her idiosyncrasies, now that I'm a mother. It's the perfect role for me, definitely the greatest role I'll ever play." She beamed while tickling Michaela's blanketed feet.

Callie watched the fashionable duo and sighed to herself. *I had a mom not long ago, too.....Stop, it Callie. Just stop it. You're not going down that road.* Her mental state had improved since receiving Earl's bombshell news three day prior, and she wanted to continue with the upswing. Yesterday, she had even met up with Dehx and Tessa for drinks and started the morning off with a lengthy jog, her first run of the year. She refused to topple back in a funk. That was all there was to it. Only losers throw pity parties. Enough Romper Room, anyway; she'd promised Emily she'd cook dinner for her and she still had to make a Bristol Farm's run. Luciana interrupted her thoughts.

"Callie?" Luci said. "I have a question to ask you. And I want you to be completely honest with me."

"Okay. I'll try."

Luci smoothed her long, silky hair and took a breath. "One of the reasons I've become more comfortable with myself—like standing up to my parents, for instance—is, frankly, because of you. You've made me realize a lot of things about myself, among them that I don't need anyone else's approval to be happy. It's not necessary that I please everyone, but it's integral that I please myself. It may sound like a simple thing, but it's something I've kind of....struggled with, shall we say. I have many, many acquaintances, but few people I can really count on to tell me the truth. You've always told me the truth, and, with that said, I'd like you to be Michaela's godmother."

"Godmother?"

Luci nodded. "I can't think of another female I'd trust my daughter to."

"No one's ever asked me something this heavy before. I'm kind of speechless..."

"Speechless as in a yes or a no?"

Callie smiled. "Definitely a yes. I'm flattered and very, very honored."

"Oh, good. For a second there, I was worried you'd turn me down."

"When's the baptism?"

"Probably June, as soon as I'm done with my film. Dominic's going to be Godfather."

"Talk about the world's best-dressed baby," Callie said. "Michaela's going to knock fashion, as we know it, out of the park."

"Is she ever. Her wardrobe is already as expansive as mine. We're talking major clothes. Dominic surprised me with about one year's worth of onesies and these adorable dresses he designed. It's amazing, the detail he put in these tiny outfits. He's coming over for dinner tonight, so

I'm going to dress her in one of his baby couture creations. Join us."

"I'd love to, Luci, but—"

"My chef, Pasquale, is preparing braised salmon. You don't want to miss it."

"Sorry, but I have to; I'm cooking for Em. I still have to run to the grocery store, too, so I should get going. How about a rain check next week?"

"That should work. Hopefully by then, I'll have dropped another three to four pounds, too." Luciana patted her twenty-four inch waist.

Nine grocery bags and a trunk of road rage later, Callie turned onto Lookout Mountain. Her BMW's headlights cut through the dusk as she bore down on her driveway. Up ahead, parked outside her gate, was a car. The lights were off and the interior was dark, as though someone anticipated her arrival. Callie's heart rate soared. Who was waiting for her and what did they want? "Maybe it's a stalker," she said under her breath. She grabbed her phone and unlocked the keypad. And then, she made out the rest of the picture: leaning against the bumper, arms insolently crossed, wearing a paltry trace of a smirk...

69

as Mitch. She parked and got out of her car. "Hey."

"Hey, there," Mitch said with a smile. "Hope I'm not disturbin' you."

She itched the back of her neck. "No, I was just getting home to make, umm, dinner for Emily and, uh...Mitch, what are you doing here?"

"I wanted to talk to you. That okay?"

"Sure. I'm just a little taken aback, that's all. I didn't exactly expect you. Your uncle said you were in New Zealand."

Mitch took a step forward. "Yeah, I haven't spoken with Unc in a while. He doesn't know it got pushed back to the fall. And I may drop out altogether. I got offered to play a lawyer in a Daniel Day-Lewis flick and I've never played a suit before. Shoots the same time and I can't do both. I wanna round out my resume. Keep it diverse."

"Mitch, I'm confused. I've been leaving you messages for months now, ever since...well, the last one was in December. And then, out of the blue, you decide to show up on my doorstep?"

"I just came from Herb's and ran into Vicky Grossman," Mitch said. "She was meeting with him about casting an actress he reps for her new film. I remembered you mentioning her and we got to talkin' and your name came up. She told me how great you are and what a nice job you did under—what was the phrase she used—under trying circumstances, she said. And she also mentioned your mother. It was the first I heard of it, Cal, otherwise I would have gotten a hold of you sooner. I am so sorry about your loss and I wanted to tell you so in person."

"Thank you, Mitch, I appreciate that. The Grossmans sent the nicest floral arrangement. So thoughtful of them."

"How are you holdin' up?"

"I'm doing better. It's been a lot to take in, but I'm better." A man walking his Cocker Spaniels on the sidewalk craned his neck, trying his mightiest to hear their conversation. Callie scowled and said to Mitch, "Do you want to come inside?"

"Lead the way."

The gate opened and they drove through. Mitch helped carry in her groceries, despite her protests. "How did you know I'd be home tonight?" she said.

"Well, tonight's Monday and you always loved watchin' *Home Away From Home* Mondays at eight," he said. "So I took a gamble."

"And what if I didn't show up? How long were you going to wait?"

"I was gonna give it a good hour. I'm a patient guy. Waiting doesn't bother me like it does some people. But some of us have no patience at all."

Callie slammed a package of butter on the counter top. "If you stopped by to criticize me or remind me of my mistakes, you should probably—"

"Sssh, take it easy, girl, take it easy." Mitch touched her forearm. "I was makin' a joke. Kind of."

"Humph," she grunted and slung a jug of milk in the fridge. "So how's that model, Isabel, doing?"

"She's good, thanks for askin'."

"My friend, Luci, knows her. Said Isabel used to be some Saudi prince's paid piece for years."

"You're kiddin'."

"Yeah, Luci said her reputation precedes her. She's the village bicycle. For the right price, of course, like any true whore."

"I've never paid for it from her or anyone else, so I can't say for certain."

"Well, I can say for certain that it's definitely not a rumor, it's a fact. Just so you know." She stuck a pint of ice cream in the freezer.

"Well, what I do know is she's got the longest legs I've ever seen. Not sticks, either. Real nice, tanned stems with these shapely, toned calves—"

"You know what, Mitch?" Callie spun around to face him. "I've had a really rough couple of months and the last thing I feel like hearing is how hot my ex-boyfriend's new flavor of the month is. So, if you please, either stay on neutral subjects or leave. I'm not joking."

He took her hands and placed them around his waist. "Relax. You're such a firecracker. Take a chill pill or somethin'."

It struck Callie that she hadn't taken Sister Xani in a while—four months or more. She had been so preoccupied with other goings on, it hadn't even occurred to her. She tried to ply his arms off her body. "Just what do you think you're doing?"

"I'm holdin' you, unless they're callin' it somethin' else these days," he grinned.

"I'm serious. This isn't a good idea. I'm not getting involved with someone who's taken. I'm not interested in that. Let me go, Mitch, I'm serious. I'm done with sneaky people, and that includes myself. Sneaky sucks, and I want no part of it."

"I'm not bein' sneaky. And I'm not taken, either."

"What are you talking about? You just got done saying you're with Isabel!"

"No, I didn't. You asked how she was and I told you. But the truth is, I haven't seen Isabel since New Year's. I broke things off. I'm not datin' her. I'm not datin' anyone."

Callie stared into his eyes and blinked. "You're not?"

"Nope."

"Oh. Why did you guys break up?"

He gripped her shoulders tightly. "Because I got tired of comparing her to you. She can't come close—no one can.

You're unlike anyone I know and I want the real deal, not some substandard substitute."

"Really?" she breathed.

"You bet. And, besides, you're right; I found out she was a leased piece and it really turned me off, so I let her go." They laughed and he pulled her closer. "I miss you like hell. I want my girl back. Flaws and mistakes and all."

"Oh, Mitch," she sniffled. "I'm sorry I screwed up. I screwed up big time and, on my mother's grave, I will never do that again. Please believe me. I hate cheating. I hate the way it makes me feel. I hate how—"

He kissed her deeply. After coming up for air, he wiped a tear from her cheek and said, "Callie, I love you."

The phone rang but they paid no attention to the high-pierced jangle.

"You what?" she gasped.

"I love you, and I should have told you so a while ago. It takes me a while to warm up, but that's the way I've always been. I've got my pride and all that and sometimes, I just come off wrong."

"You mean like standing me up on our first date because you were too embarrassed to tell me you were sick?" she said with wide-eyed innocence.

Mitch rolled his eyes. "I did not stand you up—I called and left a message, but, yeah, somethin' like that. Don't ever mistake that or anything else for not caring about you. I know I'm a pain in the ass. But I'll overlook your faults if you overlook mine."

Callie ran her fingers through Mitch's hair. "I love you, too. And, honestly, even though I hurt you, I'm glad I came clean."

"I respect you more for it," he said. "Shows character. I actually trust you more now because of it, strange as that sounds. But I'm still gonna kick Marquardt's ass when I finally see him."

"He's not worth it. Trust me, I've wanted nothing but to redo everything and be back with you, Mitch. Let's start over. Please, that's all I want."

"You got it, darlin'. Now, give this Hick Prick another kiss and we'll have ourselves a deal."

The answering machine buzzed. "Greetings, Amelia Earhart, remember me? This is your manager," said Paul. "I can't reach you on your cell so I thought I'd try your house. It was worth a shot, anyway. Listen, I've been wanting to talk to you about a call I got from the Wilders. Schueller's done. They fired her. She's at some rehab in Utah. To make a long story short, they wish they never let you go. Look, I know you have some ill will, but they really want you back. They're offering $400,000 an episode with a three year contract. We'll counter, of course, but either way, you'll be one of the highest paid actresses on TV. But that's not even the half of it. The senior VP of Jean Girard just called me. They want you to be the new face of the entire line. Lipstick, hair care, nail polish, you name it. A two million dollar contract. Are you listening to me, young lady? Two million, I said! Looks like your buddy, Tyler, had a little influence.

Look, I know you've been through a lot, but I'm begging you—on bended knee I'm begging you— do us both a favor and give me a call, okay?"Mitch peeled his lips away from Callie's. "Jesus, babe. Congratulations! Better call him back before those assholes change their minds."

"Nah." Callie leaned in close, until she was nose-to-nose with her cowboy. "I've got more important things to do. Let 'em wait."

About the Author

The chronicles of Callie Lambert are loosely based on author Shamron Moore's real life experiences as an actress and model. Shamron left her home state of Michigan to pursue the excitement of Los Angeles. She has appeared in numerous commercials, television shows and feature films. FHM named her one of the 100 Sexiest Women in the World. Nowadays, she prefers to focus on writing, one of her lifelong passions. Beyond Hollywood Strip is her second novel.

www.ingramcontent.com/pod-product-compliance
Lightning Source LLC
Chambersburg PA
CBHW061536170626
46811CB00001B/2